Als

Rattle-Day Snakes

BRIAN JORGENSEN

Second Edition

Special thanks to Ron Freeman for his help in reviewing, editing, and making valuable insights toward the completion of this work.

"The greatest deception men suffer is from their own opinions"—Leonardo da Vinci

"Just because something isn't a lie does not mean that it isn't deceptive. A liar knows that he is a liar, but one who speaks mere portions of truth in order to deceive is a craftsman of destruction"—Criss Jami

"Man is not what he thinks he is, he is what he hides"—André Malraux

CHAPTER ONE

BETTING ON THE HOUSE

"One day, perhaps today, things are going to backfire on that judge," the doughy one murmured snidely. He craned his neck and glowered because neither of his fellow law graduates immediately responded. "Hey! I'm talking here. I want to up my wager."

Again no response.

From his spot in the center of a marbled hallway, he stuffed his hands in his pockets and paced, imagining his young bride's protests if he lost. For the moment, he ignored his associates. The three had labeled one another in a way reflected in how they handled these betting situations. The demure one, the diminutive one, who stood occupied at the window and consumed with the psychology of things, carried the label of Hercule Poirot. The rotund one, wishing to up the wager, went by Charles Emerson Winchester the III. He was snooty, balding, and threw around polysyllabic insults as if chicken feed. The one with his nose practically glued to the side light at the courtroom door reveled in his Matlock title. With wavy hair and a penchant for theatrical courtroom prowess, he always feigned a southern accent, thinking it masked his intellect.

"You can't up your wager now," Matlock grumbled without looking. "My wife would have a cow if she knew the kind of risk I was taking on today's bet."

Poirot kept an eye on the crowd out front for seconds before turning and pushing his big round, telescopic-like glasses up his sweaty nose. "Crowds getting out of hand. If the judge doesn't give them what they want, who knows."

He felt Charles step up behind him and look over his head. "Yes, yes. You see why I want to change my wager. She'll take that into account and falter."

They stayed quiet for a moment, observing. "What an oppressively hot Philadelphia August day," Charles murmured. "Feels like they turned the air conditioner off in here. I believe that will affect her sentencing decision as well."

4

The computer inside Poirot's head had already calculated that aggravating factor. He seemed unfazed. The crowd on the left demanded leniency, and the crowd on the right—death. A small contingency of Philadelphia police officers, for the moment, had the ruckus crowds separated. Morning shadows had now melted away and forced a gaggle of news media to cluster into the shade of a nearby ash tree. As if that would protect them once the sentence came down. You could sense the din of a riot about to erupt, but you could sense the tension. Someone in the back would shout, causing a wave to roll through the crowd. It would then leap the line of officers and roll through the opposing crowd until the sloshing ripple died halfway back.

Poirot spun on a heel and crossed over next to Matlock. An obese, frumpy, graying defense attorney stood arguing some supposed mitigating factor, which elicited a purposeful look out of Judge Meghan Jacklyn Bailey. "It's all about the psychology," Poirot purred. "It's always about psychology." He paused briefly to gauge the shaved and scarred thirty-something Perv and Perp, sitting up front in his bright orange prison jumpsuit. With a jaw that queerly jutted out, the man had a lizard-like head. "Of course," Poirot added, "you have to reason in the effects extenuating factors have. But not even that sometimes can alter the deep-rooted motivations and flaws in psychology. For instance, look at Judge Bailey. The middle-aged Honorable Meghan Bailey. Look at how attractive she is. Attractive and yet untouched. At least that's the rumors."

"Umm boy," Matlock drawled. "A little makeup and she'd be a looker. I love that copper/ginger hair of hers. The way it frames her face in parenthetical mystery. Sure, her nose is a bit narrow and long for my taste. But damn… those are captivating eyes. What is that color? Bluish-green? And those full lips. Hot damn!"

"I wish just for once she'd smile," Charles sadly said. "Has anyone ever seen her smile? I haven't. Never. A dried-up, unloved soul. Of her own making no doubt. And I don't know what you're talking about. I see skepticism in those eyes of hers. It's like she's sending you to the electric chair with those alone. If she's as bitter as you claim, her decision, on any given day, all depends on her mood, right? She gets twisted by her temper and laying a piece of meat on the scales evades her. No scientific precision when she tries to dissect the complications of case law."

"Perhaps mitigating factors," Poirot said. He turned and looked at Charles. "You still think she'll let him off, so to speak?"

"I'm wondering if I've miscalculated."

"And you still think she'll drop the death penalty on his head?" he turned and asked Matlock.

"Not sure. Now you've got me doubting too."

"What are you worried about?" Charles said. "You wouldn't let me up the ante. You're not going to lose that much."

"And I've got a kid and wife to support. She isn't out there earning big bucks like your ball and chain... who keeps a short leash on your allowance, by the way."

Charles mildly chuckled, somewhat embarrassed at the truth. He instantly looked for a way to divert. The way he always did. "At least I'm not like Hercule here. I don't go home and peruse pornographic sites like our solitary little friend. He has no other choice. He can't help himself. Not a woman in the world would have him."

"Knock it off, Charles!" Matlock grunted. "Do you always have to insult him like that? You know very well he cares little if nothing for trash like that. Two weeks? Isn't it two weeks before you take the bar, Poirot? He's studying every night all night. Right, Poirot?"

Poirot didn't even grant a look of gratitude to his advocate. "What is interesting here," Poirot then said, "is that this hearing is taking unusually long. Have you ever seen a sentencing hearing drag on like this? If she were to sentence him to death, I think she would have cut it off already. Who knows what the defense is doing? Regardless, I believe she would see mitigating issues where none exist. Merely due to her motivations and flaws."

"Would you care to expound on that?" Charles countered.

"We have to ask ourselves... what drives that woman? I believe she feels she has to repay societal debts even where no debts exist. I think she has a moral streak, simply hoping for a better world. True, she reveals one thing in what she says and does, but she has a moral backbone. She is usually polite and respectful. You can always depend on her."

6

"And I heard she suffers from hybristophilia," Charles grumbled. "Paraphilia if you would."

"What?" Matlock snorted.

"Exactly," Charles looked down his nose. "She's sexually attracted to people who commit crimes. The worse, the better. That's why she goes easy on them. That's why she let this perv off the first time around. You know that about this case, don't you? A year ago the same guy stood in the same place and she turned him loose. Set him free. Next thing you know, he's out there perving-it up with the first innocent kid he can find. He killed three of them before they could get their claws into him again. Yup. A self-destructive force if allowed. What else would you expect from someone attracted to dangerous things?"

"And perhaps that will have an aggravating influence here," Matlock said. "That's why she'll give him death this time around. Not because of the perp, but because of her deep-seated guilt for allowing it to happen at all. Right, Poirot?"

Poirot pensively stroked his jaw and looked into the courtroom. "She attempts to intimidate, covering up her terror of offending people. That's another consideration. This is taking a very long time. I'm sure she wants to get it right. Or she's conflicted."

"Hah!" Charles hooted. "Even the great Poirot is muddled by this one. And where uncertainty rules, markets win. He thinks she's going to go easy on him and I'm taking your money. I'm sure of it."

They were so consumed with their little pow-wow that they failed to notice the sound of heavy footfalls clomping in their direction. They didn't realize an officer stood behind them until they got a hint of his overwhelming cologne.

"Huh!" Charles gulped when he turned to see the large, swarthy-looking Officer Greco. An officer they already knew. By name sure, but mostly by looks. The one Matlock called the Russian tank driver. The one that Charles said belonged on the radio and nowhere else. The one that always looked oddly resplendent in uniform and always gruff in his mannerisms.

"I thought I told you boys you can't come around here and keep gamblin' the way you do. You tick people off and Judge Bailey doesn't like it."

"It's a small game of chance!" Matlock rifled back at him. "Nothing wrong with that. No harm in that… at all!"

Officer Greco scowled at them. He cinched down on Charles' shoulder with his right hand and likewise to Matlock with his left. He gritted his teeth, scowling. For a full minute, he stood as if corralling that smart-aleck little one in the middle. And then the man grinned wide, showing off a shiny gold tooth center right. He suddenly laughed. "Hah!" he laughed loud. "You three are pathetic. Should see the looks on your faces. You go in front of a judge looking like that and the opposing attorneys will shred you alive."

"Unhand me, damned Yankee," Matlock saw right through the officer's game, sounding as much like Foghorn Leghorn as he could.

"Hah, Hah!" Officer Greco bellowed in response. "Good. That was dang good. I wouldn't be loitering here much longer though. I think she's about to wind it up. I didn't come out here to hassle you boys, mind you. Just thought you'd like the warning."

Those words caused Matlock to spiral and look in. The crowd was on their feet and moving for the door. "It's over? The sentence… what was the sentence?" he excitedly asked. "What was it? What happened?"

Officer Greco said nothing. Next, he tugged them hard, getting away from the crowd that suddenly burst through the door. He pulled them some distance down the hallway. "Sorry, boys. Just lookin' after your welfare."

"Death? Did she sentence him to death? What happened?" Charles snapped.

Officer Greco gave him a snide simper, mildly shrugging his shoulders. "Beats me. I was just killin' time. Just bidin' my time 'til I had to pass on the bad news."

"So, it was the death penalty!" Charles declared. "Dang! I lost. I knew it, I knew it, I knew it!"

Officer Greco reached and tenderly patted Charles on the cheek. "Like I said… I don't know what that news was. I've got bad news for Judge Bailey. I'm on bereavement duty." He cocked his neck and seemed to morph in front of their eyes. One second jovial, the next a sad pout drew the man's jowls down. His eyes softened as well. "I hate bringin' chaos to an orderly situation. But hey… they say I'm good at it. Keep your noses clean, I've got to go hunt the judge down."

That left the three in a sort of stupor. They didn't move all the time, watching Officer Greco stroll down the hallway. He paused to insert a key in a door and then disappeared without acknowledging them.

The first hint Officer Greco received of the sentencing was the look on the face of Judge Bailey's clerk, Erica Dennis, a young—mid-twenties—svelte girl who now stood, leaning at the judge's chamber door. Despite elegance, she couldn't mask the weight seemingly bearing down on her. She noticed the officer but seemed determined to protect the judge from everything and everyone. Officer Greco halted a few steps short. Not out of deference, but to get into the proper state of mind. A second later, the two seemed locked in mental combat. The elegant one—the one with darkly exotic, almond-shaped eyes and shiny auburn hair. And the other one with a pitted, rugged face. One with long black eyelashes which enhanced the exquisite pallor of her cheeks. And the other with black sockets, screwed in deep. One with soft lips, scarlet and inviting. The other stood working his lips until they appeared white with anger. Officer Greco sighed, the anticlimactic effect creating a sinking feeling. "Is the Judge in there?" he sympathetically asked.

"She's exhausted. What do you want?"

"It's bad news. I'm sorry. I have bad news. Could I have a private moment please?"

Erica looked in and got a morose look on her face. She said nothing. Officer Greco stepped up and peered. Judge Bailey sat behind her desk, her head back and her fingers nailed into her hair. "Ahem!" he cleared his throat.

"I heard you," Judge Bailey said. "What is it? What bad news?" She scrubbed her face mildly before rocking forward and locking her fingers together. A subconscious defensive measure the officer had seen many times. Direct is always best, flashed through his mind as he stepped forward and sat opposite her. Creating the best caring look he could muster he sincerely touched a hand to the desk and said,

"I am so sorry, Judge Bailey. They found your sister dead this morning."

Officer Greco was used to limited responses. Shock and disbelief. Outbursts of sudden grief. Taking out their anguish on him in a fit of anger. Complete and utter denial. He wasn't sure what he was getting out of Judge Bailey. Her expression didn't change for several seconds. And then it was as if someone was typing out the words on a manual typewriter. Little by little words formed as she came to realize what he had said.

"My sister? You're kidding. I thought she was long dead before now. What? Where? Homeless? Streets of New York City? Los Angeles perhaps?"

"Huh...?" Officer Greco hemmed before pulling a note out of his pocket. "No, Kermit Falls, New York. Tompkins County. Finger Lakes area. Near Ithaca."

"You're kidding."

"No, I'm serious. Got the call from Sheriff Hackett. Dean Hackett. Here's his phone number if you need to call." He slid the note over. The judge studied it for a few seconds.

"What... in a ditch?"

"Eh—no Ma'am. A neighbor checked in on her. In her home."

"Her home? She owned a home?"

"Perhaps you should call the sheriff."

As Judge Bailey fished her smartphone out of her top desk drawer she mumbled, "Dead. Hah. I can't believe it. I haven't seen her since..."

She paused and stared past Officer Greco. Erica's look of concern and sympathy caused the judge to cover her mouth. Seconds later, the slow, deliberate voice of Sheriff Dean Hackett answered. "Hackett here. How can I help you?"

"Sheriff... this is Judge Meghan Bailey. I'm calling from Philadelphia. I understand you have information regarding my sister."

"Yes, Ma'am. I'm very sorry. She was a sweet gal. We're all shocked over this."

"Wait a minute. Are you sure we're talking about my sister? Dana Bailey. She'd be... forty-five years old."

"I'm sure of it. She knew who you were."

"And she owned a home?"

"Of course."

There was a long pause. "I'm stunned. I haven't seen or talked to my sister since the day I graduated from high school. That would be…"

"Twenty-seven years," the sheriff slowly said.

"Uh—I don't know what to say."

"I understand. I can give you the funeral director's name and number. He had to transport her body to the medical examiner. That's common in an unattended death. You can be comforted in knowing there were no signs of a forced entry or any trauma. She simply slumped over at her desk and was gone. A neighbor found her after he didn't see her out on her usual morning walk."

"Feh…" Judge Bailey exhaled. "Sorry. I'm a bit flummoxed. This was the last thing I expected to hear."

"Should we expect you here then? Arrangements will need attending to?"

"Uh… I guess I have no choice. Yes, I'll come. Give me that name and her address. I'll come as soon as I can get away."

Judge Bailey sent a message to Erica as she jotted down names, numbers, and addresses. Erica stepped toward her when the judge laid her phone down. "You want me to come with you?" Erica said sadly. "Do you want me to drive? I'll drive if you want."

"No, I'd better drive. I don't even know if they have electricity where we're headed."

CHAPTER TWO

ICK

A dim yellow porch light cast long shadows at the home located at 775 Penny Lane. Gravel crunched as the judge's year-old deep-blue Volvo rolled to a stop. Penny Lane had no curb, gutter, or sidewalk. 775 sat on the outskirts of town where, for all the judge could tell, merely three houses sat. Dana's home stood on the south side of the lane. A similarly modest home sat directly across the road, where light from a kitchen window felt eerie. Another ranch-style home sat well past a pasture where horses docilely stood, their heads low and uninterested. And the single reason you knew that was because off in the distance, beyond a thick, defensive-line stand of woods, bright lights from either a baseball diamond or soccer field back-lit this corner of darkness. At the ten P.M. hour, it was so dark it felt cold. Especially to Erica Dennis. She rubbed her arms, shivering.

"So… this is the place, huh?" Erica said softly. "I like the oval window in the front door. I like the chiffon-yellow color of the clapboards."

"I guess so. That's the right number. Sheriff said he put a key in the frog's mouth. Do you see a frog? He said there was a big clay frog on the porch."

"All I see are those tall irises. It feels old-fashioned."

"What else would you expect for such an out-of-place town?"

"Yeah… I guess. I think it's kind of cute. I liked that lime-stone courthouse in the center of town. That grocery store with an awning stretched over the sidewalk and the malt shop made it feel Norman-Rockwell rich. So…" she doubtfully looked at Judge Bailey, "do we go in?"

"I guess. I hope she has beds. I hope she has an air conditioner."

"We saw those cabins when we came off the interstate. We could go back there."

"No. Let's go check it out," Judge Bailey nervously said. "I'm just not sure what to expect."

Moments later, Erica fished a key out of a giant frog's mouth and smiled with surprise. They warily entered a second later and didn't move once Erica flipped on a light switch. Three lamps came on. "Holy!" Judge Bailey gasped. "Holy cripes!"

"Not what you expected?"

"Not at all. Unbelievable."

The front room sat stretched to the seams with overburdened bookshelves. Knick-knacks personalized a knowledge of the world and traveling. One bookshelf looked ready to collapse upon a corner desk. A large fig tree sat in the far corner and a sill aglaonema, reddish in color, sat nearby. And though cluttered, there was an orderliness—as if river stones in a chimney. Situated on the opposite bookshelf, a bold French script stood out, framed in black. The Glory of God is Intelligence. Enlightenment should be the pursuit of every human mind, it read.

Judge Bailey now stood there speechless. Erica crossed the room and started perusing the titles. The judge stepped to the desk where a desk calendar sat filled with doodles, notes, and chicken scratching. "Can we touch stuff?" Erica asked. That brought the judge around. She gave Erica a surreptitious glance before spotting a small photo framed in gold. No response, she crossed past Erica and seemed instantly caught up in a time machine. She took the photo, turned her back to Erica, and shuffled in her pacing.

"I can't believe this," Judge Bailey said, vexed. "I just can't believe it."

"What's in the picture?"

"Dana and me. Just before her graduation. She was a year older." She stayed quiet for a minute as if the long melancholy cry from a train whistle held her memory. Oddly, her lost look seemed locked to certain demands of justice. "I can't believe I hated her so much. I have always thought it was right there under the surface. I'm kind of shocked that it's not there all of a sudden."

"Hated?"

"You know how girls are. I hated her and for some reason have held to that thought. Now, I feel vacant. I felt picked on. I felt ignored. It was like she and her friends got giddy at excluding me. She had all the

13

friends. I had almost none. She always brought strangers home like they were lost puppies. She had the attention. Always. She was capricious— like a whimsical fairy who you couldn't hold down. The day after she graduated she left with friends to explore the world. They were going to go pick pineapples in Hawaii to earn money. She came back the day I graduated and I never saw her again. Mom and Dad thought she ended up in a commune or a hippie farm. I had no idea she ever did anything. I wonder what she did to survive."

"I think she maybe did something involving rare books."

"Huh?" the judge grunted and turned to look. Erica held a small, hard-covered book in one hand, her smartphone in the other. "I just looked this up. Close to thirty-five bucks for this tiny thing. Ever heard of N.C. Hanks. Up From the Hills. I've never heard of that title. Nor any of these books on the shelves. Wait… maybe I shouldn't be touching things." She quickly stuffed the book back in its place.

"I wouldn't worry. I'm sure we're okay. Sheriff said the only prints on the door knob belonged to Dana and the neighbor." The judge returned to the desk. The two went quiet as if lost in the coolness of the uninterested. But that was far from the reality. The two soon became engrossed in what they were finding. Erica was the first to speak again. "Religious books. She's got a ton of religious books. Was she religious?"

"I don't know," the judge responded absently.

"Bible, Quran, Epic of Erra, Tale of Aqhat, Torah… She's even got a Book of Mormon here. Do you think she met Joseph Smith? Didn't he find his gold plates around here somewhere?"

The judge ignored her.

A moment later, Erica read from an underlined text, "For ye shall never taste of death; but ye shall live to behold all the doings of the Father… What do you think that means?"

When the judge didn't answer Erica turned. The judge's face looked carved out of wood. "Problem?" Erica asked.

The Judge raised both a note and her brows sardonically. "You're kidding. That's the same thing I was reading." She then flashed the note as if flea-infested. "It was under the calendar. Exact phrase. You've got your phone. Look this up… I'm not sure how to pronounce it. It might be Spanish… El Ateneo… Grand Splendid."

Erica made a quick search. "El Ateneo Grand Splendid was a historic, palatial theater, now one of the world's most beautiful bookstores. It's in Buenos Aires, Argentina."

"Serious?"

"Serious."

"Look up the name Antione Banda. Tie it to Buenos Aires or the bookstore."

A second later. "Antione Banda. Facebook, Instagram, and LinkedIn. Graduate student in economics. Likes soccer… no surprise there. No references to El Ateneo. That doesn't mean anything."

"How old does he look?"

"Early twenties."

"Doubt it's the same guy."

"What else is in the note?"

"Just a reference. That text, his name, the bookstore, and a string of numbers. A long string of numbers. 5065134943600085353270. Would that be an ISBN? Those numbers are long, aren't they?"

"Must be a book. Maybe she was trying to buy a book from him." Erica paused and studied her screen for a second. "Says here Buenos Aires is a novel oasis. Bookshop capital of the world. That would make sense if she's a book trader, right?"

"I guess," the judge sounded reticent, ramming the note into her pocket. Impetuously, the judge then sighed. "I need air. It's stuffier than a tomb in here." An air conditioning unit in the front window drew her over. Erica then heard the judge crisply gasp but didn't turn. An envelope protruding from between the Bible and the Quran interested her. She merely flicked and it tumbled out as if weighted. "Ick!" she gulped a breath later. "Gross!"

"My exact sentiments," the judge's disdain sounded nasally. The two turned to look at one another, wondering if they were referencing the same thing. Erica stood pointing at the floor where two fangs, close to three inches long had fallen out. The judge stepped over. Erica crouched and pulled the accompanying note out. Back off, Bitch, it read. Stay out of my business, Red.

They frantically looked at one another. "You think that's bad, look at this." The judge grabbed Erica by the arm and pulled her over to the front door. She turned the lights off. Across the road, standing at a kitchen window the most grotesque figure either of them had ever seen, seemed to be looking for constellations. His face was disfigured with lumps and bumps and huge liver lips. He stood shirtless. The same horrid malady seemed to cover his whole body. "Ick!" Erica whispered. "That is disgusting. Is that a man?"

"Oh, dear God," the judge breathed a second later. "We have another problem here."

"What?" Erica was panicky.

"See that. Over there. Coming around the house. Can't you see that shadow? Broad shoulders, narrow hips. He's got a gun in his hand."

No hesitation whatsoever. Erica turned away and pounded out 911 on her phone. The judge didn't move. While Erica kept the muffled tones of a panicked call quiet, the judge watched. The figure snuck up to the front corner of the neighbor's house, peered briefly, and then rapidly tiptoed right under where that monster stood staring. The judge had seriously expected the gunman to stop under the window and shoot the creature. Instead, he dashed by and soon stopped at a railed fence. He now looked like an impaled scarecrow. Judge Bailey couldn't help but see the irony in the way Dana's front wire fence with its drooping top rails seemed to smile in the hopes of justice. None came. The figure, a second later, bounded over the pasture fence and then raced like a madman to such a degree that the horses in the pasture separated and ran like prey hunted by a lion. He crossed the pasture, bounded over the far fence, and instantly car lights popped on. "He's escaping. What did he do? Did he kill someone? O, my God," she whispered when seconds later a minivan tore by, racing for downtown Kermit Falls.

Erica grabbed Judge Bailey's arm the instant she gripped the doorknob. "You're not going out there, are you?"

The judge knitted her brows together, the most serious look overtaking her face. "I can't let a criminal get away."

"But the police are coming. They said they were coming."

"You stay here. If you feel safe go out there after they come. I'm following that guy."

Judge Bailey yanked on the door. The door banged against Erica's toes, rattling the window. Judge Bailey quickly scampered for her car. She left a cloud of dust as she spun around and tore away in pursuit.

In close to three-quarters of a mile Penny Lane took a snaking turn before changing into Delaware Ave. Three blocks later Delaware Ave. crossed directly in front of McKinney Funeral Home. The judge was fully aware when she sped by, having made note earlier, but felt as if death tendrils reached through her as a block later, she hung a sharp right onto Main Street and almost missed seeing the same minivan parked, lights still on, situated kitty-corner from where she leaned hard. Twice she cranked her neck, unsure that was it or not. And then there was no question about it. That was it. She didn't think she'd catch it. Didn't think fate would that easily surrender. It terrified her. So much so that she drifted down a sleepy, empty Main Street for two blocks before cranking the wheel and slowly returning.

There the van sat parked in front of what looked like a once thriving gas station and where the garage door had a slit of light, razor-sharp against the blackness. Drifting by, the judge pulled off in front of a tidy bungalow where window beds seemed overweighed with hearty red geraniums.

It felt like the first salvo in a foreign war when the judge crawled out, her heart pounding in her chest. Watching over her shoulder, she crept back to the garage. One thing she was grateful for. She didn't have to round the building. A greasy, filthy window sat propped open where she sidled up. First, she listened and peeked once. There she saw two men and a half disassembled 60's era red Corvette.

"I can't handle it. Somedays I just can't handle it," one of the men raised his voice, the harsh sound of hard metal banging against flimsy steel, echoing a breath later. This felt like needles in her skin. To the point that she couldn't help but look. A somewhat beefy man in coveralls with a bald head and blonde handlebar mustache stood behind a metal bench, intensity on his face. His mustache was waxed to the point, looking as if daggers slicing through his lip and protruding in opposite directions. He shook his head, his eyes darting about, as bright and sharp as a hawk's.

"What do you want me to do? What do you want out of me?" he begged.

"I don't know. How do I get rid of this demon? This haunting demon that constantly harasses me? Just once I wish it would leave me alone."

The man who spoke had his back to the judge. He was dressed in slacks, a crisp white shirt with his sleeves rolled up just below his elbows, and wore what looked like a suede vest. He grabbed his pistol and slammed it down on the bench again before clutching his head in his hands and visibly shaking. "I'm exhausted and it still comes for me. It constantly demands my time. Can't it see I don't want it? Can't it see I'm not handling this well? I don't want this. Please… I wish it would leave me alone."

"Where now?" the bald one asked. "How soon?"

"Soon. Very soon. Freeville. I know it's in Freeville. Someone is about to die in Freeville and there is nothing I can do about it."

It shocked the judge when the bald man merely looked on with empathy. Incoherent thought seemed to flow out the window and overwhelm the judge. The only clear thought she could muster was racing back to where she knew for certain an officer already was or soon would be. She covered her mouth, sighing convulsively. She would have turned and run, but one last thing was haunting her. His face. She had to see his face. Ducking past the window, she tiptoed on her low pumps, rounding the garage, and then eased up to the crack in the door. She couldn't believe how much she could see through such a narrow gap. But there he stiffly stood. All six foot one, two, or three of him. 210, 220, 230 pounds. No. Not 230. He's not that big. And no mistaking that face again. He was ruggedly handsome. Grisly and devilishly handsome. Unshaven, but ruggedly handsome, the neatness of his trimmed brown hair was an antithetical punctuation mark to what stood there. She memorized for just a second more. Just one second more and then she was gone, even if it meant returning and confronting that hideous Ick fellow if need be.

CHAPTER THREE

UNHAPPY HOUR

Judge Bailey found Erica and an officer standing in the middle of the road, a nearby sheriff's pickup truck with its lights flashing when she sped to a stop. Erica stood waving an airy hand and excitedly talking. Judge Bailey merely raced up, braked, and rolled down her window. "You can't waste your time here," she barked in a deprecating tone. "You have a murderer on the loose with plans to kill someone in Freeville. Where is Freeville, for Pete's sake?"

"I'm sorry. What did you say, Ma'am?" a young officer stepped towards her.

Judge Bailey quickly jumped out. She pointed. "I saw them. I heard them plotting," she bleated like a sheep. "I followed that van into town. A garage. He stopped at a garage. He was plotting with some big bald fellow. Hurry! He's going to kill someone."

Instead of jumping into his pickup and peeling away, the officer got on the radio and took what felt like an inordinately lengthy time. Judge Bailey paced in place and then snapped at Erica impetuously, "Name? What's his name?"

"Sorry. Whose name?" Erica sounded like a well-trained servant. Even had the expressionless, disapproving face of such a being.

"I want his name. The deputy. He's taking too long. When things go south I want to know who to pin against the wall and fry. What a jackanapes!"

"He's doing something," Erica sounded ready to cry.

"Not enough. Name, name. Do you know his name?"

"Uh... uh... Todd... Deputy Todd Shay."

Judge Bailey rushed and banged a hand against the pickup door. "Ma'am. Please," the deputy calmly responded. "Someone is responding. They are responding right now! I'm not the only officer

19

around here. Trust me. Someone is on it. Now, if you'll just give me a minute, we'll finish up here."

"Finishing up here has everything to do with what's going on there."

"Not quite. You don't have the full picture."

That was like a sudden slap in the face. The judge flinched. "Judge Bailey. Meghan," Erica sympathetically said. "Step back here. I don't want you in trouble. That's the last thing you need. You're a judge. Handle it like a judge."

A wave of embarrassment washed over Judge Bailey. Methodically, patronizingly, she studied both Erica and the officer for just a second before understanding how out of control she'd acted. No apology, she merely turned her head away and joined Erica. Moments later, the officer stepped over and folded his arms. "They've got that issue under control. We appreciate your help, Ma'am. Now... as far as things are concerned here..." he paused, looking around. "It's an ongoing issue."

"Are you talking about that creature? Tha-tha-that monster inside that house. Ick!" the judge groused.

A quick look over his shoulder before the officer cocked his neck like a curious dog. "You know his name? I mean... that's not his name, but that's what everyone calls him. Even he calls himself that."

Both Erica and the judge squinted at one another with confusion. "We didn't know his name," Erica said. "He was... ugly. Didn't know what else to call him."

"Ick and his mother Velma Barlow. Let me explain. Ick Barlow has had neurofibromatosis all his life. That's what causes all that deformity in him. It's rare. He gets harassed. Kids are constantly out here harassing the poor folks. People are terrified of them. It's a game. It's a challenge. They come and see who can push the envelope the furthest without getting caught."

"You mean..." the judge said and covered her mouth. "Never mind."

"Do you have any other issues or concerns? I think I know which group of trouble-makers were out here... and if I time it right, I'll find them sneaking into the hollow down at Creamery Springs. That's way off down there in the trees. I'll give them a warning and that will keep them away for a good long time. Any other questions?"

"Do you know who that was? I mean in the minivan. He had a gun. Was he a part of that? He wasn't any high school kid pranking a neighbor. Have you had a rash of murders in the area?"

"Ma'am, I can't even tell you the last time there was a murder around here. And that's under control. That's all I can tell you. Anything else? I've got to hurry."

The judge made a squirrel-like sound. By that Erica knew of the embarrassment the judge felt. "No. Thank you, Officer," Erica said and took hold of the judge's arm. Flashing lights off, the officer backed away, spun around, and drove toward the thicket to the east.

"Well…" Erica sighed. "That was exciting."

Judge Bailey stood there staring at a kitchen window where grotesqueness peeked and disappeared several times.

"What do you want to do?" Erica asked.

"I guess we should find out if we each have a bed in there. We're to be at the funeral home by nine in the morning. I doubt I'm going to sleep at all."

It surprised Judge Meghan Bailey to awake to the aroma of coffee percolating. From her perspective she still lay there, her mind racing and wishing to fall asleep. She knew she'd checked the time at 2:30 in the blessed A.M. and now the shock of opening her eyes to a room growing with morning light felt insulting. She reached for her watch the instant a light rap came to the door. "Eight! It's eight o'clock," the judge scolded herself. "Just a minute. Give me a minute."

"Just wanted to see if you were awake. I was afraid you'd miss your appointment. I have coffee ready," Erica said from behind a closed door.

"I'll be there in a minute." The judge sat up and looked around the tiny room. It felt like something their grandmother would have put together. A tied rug, a patched quilt, dolls arranged in a rocking chair, old-time photos of dream homes. She scooted out of bed and tiptoed across the room to turn off the air conditioning unit. She thought of showering but opted for a spit bath. Ten minutes later, dressed in

21

yesterday's teal-colored pantsuit, she found Erica at the kitchen table, just then turning the page on an old text. She did pause to note that Erica had changed out of a dress to skinny jeans and a flowery blouse.

"I forgot to bring my bag in. Could you be an angel and fetch it for me?" the judge murmured.

"No problem." Erica stood, still reading as if the words on the page had a chain around her neck. "She was deep. If she read this stuff, she was deep. Very sophisticated authors. Dostoevsky would be light reading."

"I don't remember that about her," Judge Bailey said in a derogatory tone. "As you said before, might be a trader. Just because you trade doesn't mean you read."

Erica lightly shrugged and smiled. "I guess. I'll be right back."

Less than a minute later, Erica appeared without a suitcase and yet with a look of intense distress. "Flat! All your tires are flat."

The Judge had the coffee pitcher in hand. No words. A look of shock. She placed the pitcher down and rushed by Erica in disbelief. Seconds later, they stood shoulder to shoulder on the porch. "The filthy little skunks! The filthy little skunks!" Hotter. Louder. "I'll wring their necks!" Caustically.

Erica already had her phone in hand. "Call the cops again?"

The judge didn't respond. She skipped off the porch and seconds later worked her fingers into her hair as she rounded the car in disbelief. She kicked the front passenger's tire. "Damn them. Damn them all to hell!"

What startled Erica was that the judge didn't hesitate. Didn't say another thing. She simply spun and began marching toward town. At the moment, Erica wasn't quite certain what to do. First, she turned to the door, then back to the car. The judge didn't have any of her personal effects with her. What horror that thought brought. But then… "Shoot!" Erica hissed, turning and rushing back in, turning everything off. If the car key hadn't been sitting on the front desk she wouldn't have stopped at the car to get the judge's handbag out of the trunk. A breath later she was half trotting, trying to catch up.

Close to a half mile later Erica caught up and already knew by how white the judge's lips were to keep her mouth shut. Fifteen minutes later they marched right by the funeral home and minutes after that they stood on the corner of Main and Delaware. "Over there. They were right over there. How brash can people be? I hope they caught them and they're behind bars."

Judge Bailey puffed a minute as if uncertain of what to do next. It gave Erica time to soak in how lovely and peaceful the hamlet of Kermit Falls, New York felt. Especially on a pleasant August morning. Birds were cheerfully singing from every direction. Kids were on their bicycles and skateboards. It seemed to have a surrendering effect on the judge. She sharply sighed, spun around, and casually returned to the funeral home. "We're early," she said, checking her watch. "I'd rather get this over with anyway. I've been dreading this. Ugh…" she grunted. "I've got so much to do. I'll have to figure out estate matters and then put the place up for sale. Who knows how long that will take?" Another sigh, this time almost smiling at Erica. "At least I can get this out of the way. I feel like that will break the dam. From there, it's all easy— comparatively speaking."

Erica returned a sincere smile and led the way up to the funeral home door. It was a stately, red-brick home half covered with ivy and neatly framed by trim ornate topiaries. A bed of red roses lined a front terrace where a multi-paned window glistened in the sun. A chime called for an attendant the instant they walked in. The dark teal Berber carpet felt steady under her feet. And then it happened. Almost instantly. It felt as if her heart leaped out of her chest the moment the same man from the night before walked through double doors.

How obtuse! He warmly smiled. He was still unshaven. "Morning," he said, sounding very Cosmopolitan. And duplicitous. "Dana's sister I presume? My name is Roger "Kip" McKinney. I'm the funeral director."

The only sign Erica got that something was wrong was when Judge Bailey dug her nails into her arm. "I need your phone, Erica," she whispered. "And a restroom." She glared at McKinney. "Where's your restroom?"

Erica could tell the calm was forced. Still, she saw no point in fishing for the judge's phone and handed hers over.

The heathen, the Judge scrunched her shoulders, thinking.

McKinney stepped and gestured to the far side of the entry "Ladies is on your right."

23

Seconds later, the judge's hands were shaking when she curled her toes, pressing her back to the restroom door and frantically dialing.

"911. What's your emergency?"

Judge Bailey cupped a hand. "I have to keep my voice down. He's here. I'm at the mortuary. Oh, gosh… you don't know what I'm talking about. I followed a man last night who talked about killing someone. He's here. He's the mortician. I need an officer here right now. Please. Hurry."

"A moment. I'm going to put you through to an officer."

The line went dead for a moment. Seconds later, a hefty push came to the door, rocking the judge with a bolt of fear. The door partly opened as the judge's toes stuttered across tiny black and white tiles. She nearly dropped the phone. Someone kept pushing. Judge Bailey partly lost her balance, reaching out for the wall. Another weighty push and there was no stopping that force. The judge slid up against the wall as the door pushed her aside like a plow truck rocking over a curb.

"My word. What is wrong with you?" a gravelly woman's voice said.

Judge Bailey stood shocked to suddenly find a female officer standing there, a rather annoyed look on her face. The Kevlar jacket under her uniform heaved with her heavy breathing. "Was that you on the phone? You dialed 911?"

"You sure got here fast. My God. I didn't know you could respond that fast. The killer. The mortician is the killer. I know. I heard it all. Last night."

"I'm Deputy Cheryl Dawkins. Come with me, Ma'am. We know all about the mortician and his alleged killings."

"What?!"

"You'll find this hard to believe."

Judge Bailey couldn't form a sensible thought. The officer stepped back and motioned with her hand. Judge Bailey eased forward, still seeing Erica standing next to the mortician and nervously shaking her head. She had a clumsy look. The officer waited. Judge Bailey edged out and stopped before entering what was a small chapel. "Continue," the officer encouraged. Judge Bailey didn't move until the deputy took her by the arm and led her through the chapel. They passed through a sheer curtain before stopping inside a small viewing room. Just then a large officer stepped through a sliding door and halted. He had a pair of bloodied latex gloves on. "Sheriff Hackett," the deputy said. "I think this is Judge Meghan Bailey. I think she's ready for you. Shall I bring the others?"

"No..."

Judge Bailey instantly recognized the sheriff's deliberate baritone voice. His body type fit. Large, barrel-chested man. Bushy eyebrows, crew cut, and red cheeks.

"Would you like to sit?" he asked the Judge.

Judge Bailey stood there suddenly aware of the presence of a dead body. Lying on a gurney across the room, it sat under two dark lamps. A neat burgundy spread covered it up to the chin. Velvety mauve chairs lined the room. The sheriff pushed the sliding door closed with an elbow and then sat.

"Come over here and sit down. I'll explain. We have several issues to talk about."

"Is that my sister? Is that Dana over there?"

The sheriff glanced. "Oh. No. That is Mrs. Latham. Victoria Latham. I'll explain that as well. Well... I'll explain that first."

He waited. Judge Bailey gave the female deputy an unwanted look and cautiously crossed the room. Eyes wide, she stared at the body, easing down unto the edge of a chair two away from the sheriff. He didn't say anything until eye contact. "Roger McKinney is a very special kind of man. What you heard last night was not what you think it was. He has this..." the sheriff paused and waved his hand, searching for words, "connection. A kind of gift. A sixth sense. It causes him terrible anxiety. He gets a sense of when people are going to die. Even to the point of knowing where. He doesn't know who. Just where. We've been dealing with him and that issue for several years now. That woman over there is ninety-one years old. She died of old age... heart failure. He knew it was happening, he just didn't know who. You followed him to the garage. That's his compadre... Tony "Nuts" Ford. They call each other, compadre. He goes there to vent when the feeling comes."

"But he was at the neighbor's. Dana's neighbor. He had a gun."

"Yes, yes… we know. Let me backtrack. Roger had just returned from retrieving your sister's body from the Medical Examiner's Office. He would have normally gone right to work. Instead, Velma Barlow called. Roger is a neighbor to the Barlow's. Was to your sister as well. Well, whenever he responds we have no complaints. We appreciate it. We don't have time to run down there every time some snot-nosed kids decide to harass those folks. You understand about the Barlow's?"

"Oh, my word," the judge exhaled, slumping back. "This has been about the worst night of my life. Why didn't that deputy explain that last night?"

"He was busy, we were busy… I guess he should have done better. Sorry about that."

"Hooo…" the judge exhaled, her head now resting on the chair's back.

"Well… don't get too comfortable. I have more. Roger called us here this morning because of some strange findings."

Judge Bailey still sat there relaxed. "Findings? What findings?"

"He thinks your sister was murdered. Something very strange going on here. I've been in there looking at things. I think he might be right."

Suspicion as wide as galaxies kept the judge unmoved. "Go on."

"Roger brought a death certificate back, indicating the cause of death as massive cerebral hemorrhage due to an aneurysm."

"Well… then that's what she died of, right?"

"Not from what I'm seeing in there. It would be obvious. A burst vessel and bleeding would show up. I've been in there and there is no sign of that at all."

"That can't be possible. The coroner couldn't make that kind of mistake."

"Well… I need to talk with him. I've called. The Medical Examiner will be out here post haste. He needs to look into this. The thing is… Roger also pointed out… oh… I'm not sure of the terminology."

"Blood clot near where the descending aorta bifurcates. Into the common and then right and left iliac. Near the belly button. Fourth lumber. Only on the backside. Along the spine." Roger "Kip" McKinney poked his head through the curtain and said.

What irritated the judge the most was how much this McKinney fellow didn't fit, how he wasn't the image she expected for an undertaker. He was supposed to be old, pale, and gaunt. He was supposed to be dour and hauntingly boorish. Erica followed him in as he crossed the room and crouched in front of the judge. "Sorry about last night," he sounded sincere.

Judge Bailey didn't like that. Feigned. Fake!

"Sorry about your sister as well. Either someone messed up at the M.E. or…"

"Or what?"

"Well… we've never seen anything like this before," the sheriff said. "I don't know how they could mess this up."

Years behind the bench suddenly triggered a thought in Judge Bailey's mind. "It's a crime scene. We shouldn't have stayed there. Erica… go back. Keep an eye on Dana's house."

"We'll take care of that," the sheriff said. "I'll be sending Officer Dawkins promptly."

"My tires. Someone flattened all my tires last night. Who would do that?"

The sheriff raised his brows. "Not sure. Todd never did track those kids down. Perhaps they circled back and took it out on you."

"Nevertheless… there's a crime scene. Erica. Go back. Just watch things 'til I get there. I'm going to need help with my car."

"I can help with that," Roger McKinney said. "I'll call Tony. He'll do anything for me."

"I guess that ties up what we can handle here for now. Wish the M.E. would show up soon." the sheriff said, standing. "And don't send your clerk running back to the house. It's unnecessary."

Erica exchanged a look with Judge Bailey. Instantly, the judge knew Erica didn't want to go. The judge patted the seat next to her and Erica sat.

27

"One problem," Roger added, looking at Sheriff Hackett. "I'm still scheduled to fly out tomorrow. John Jenkins out of Ithaca will handle arrangements for Mrs. Latham. He always covers when I go out of town. There's nothing I can do with this sudden investigation." He looked at Judge Bailey. "But we can discuss your needs and take care of whatever arrangements you wish."

"Where to this time?" the sheriff asked.

The Judge heard the words, but it didn't fully register until Roger was up and moving away. "South America. I fly to Buenos Aires, Argentina. I'll then return on a dime."

CHAPTER FOUR

STEPPING ON ALL THE TOES

Sheriff Dean Hackett followed on Kip's heels. Judge Bailey's mind was searching for a fitting reply but words were like chalk dust on the floor, piled up below the blackboard. "Judge?" Erica nudged and whispered. "You hear that?"

"Yes, I heard that."

"What do we do?"

"I'm not sure. I have to think a minute."

"Do we tell them about the bookstore? Maybe there's ties… some criminal tie or something."

Judge Bailey quickly searched her pocket, ensuring the note remained. She left it concealed. "No. I don't want to tell them about that."

"What about the other note… and the fangs?"

Judge Bailey gave Erica a gloomy glance and mildly shrugged. "What did you do with it?"

"I didn't touch the fangs. I left the envelope on top of the books."

"Then they'll find it. Or we'll tell them. If anyone is suspect, that's the party. What was the name?"

"Red. Just Red."

"I don't feel comfortable with these people. I don't trust them. I think that the undertaker is trying to act smarter than he is. The way he tossed out the word bifurcate. He's not that smart. And then that story about a sixth sense. Hogwash! Do they think they can pull my leg like that? I'll turn the tables on them. Good grief. What nonsense."

"Sixth sense? What do you mean?"

Judge Bailey measured Erica briefly. "Nothing. Never mind. Bunch of hicks is all."

"So… what do you want to do?"

The judge sat quietly for a minute. "Why would he go to South America?"

"Do we dare ask?"

"I think I'm going to go. I'm going to make an excuse and go with him."

"Why make an excuse? There was nothing implicating about that note. Tell them about it and since he's going, you would like to tag along. So you can meet this Banda fellow to find out what Dana's connection was. Are you sure you feel safe traveling with him? You don't know what you're getting into."

"I'll get insurance then. Call Franklin. Find out who the state attorney general is. Find out who the district attorney or prosecutor is around here. Then contact them and tell them of my plans. Don't say anything about us being suspicious of these two. But I'll make sure these people know that others are fully aware of what I'm doing."

Erica stepped aside and made the call to Franklin Cobb, the Pennsylvania State Attorney General. A dear friend.

How often light shines in the darkness and the darkness recognizes it not? Sixth sense, my foot. That was the thought in Judge Bailey's mind as she glanced over at dead Mrs. Latham. Her impulse was to step over and inspect the body, looking for gunshot wounds. Instead, she became lost in thought. It's all about justice, drummed inside her brain.

Everything is about justice. No better world without justice. And then a sudden change of thought. She wondered why such an unfeeling empty void for Dana. She'd heard of it. When someone in a family disappears, a painful void is normally left until resolution. She was feeling a good deal of that—resolution. Perhaps, I've come to terms. Am I that cold and unfeeling? Was the hatred that deep? She recalled how her parents had both died five and six years back now and how they mourned until their dying day.

Judge Bailey considered what a private person she was. How she hated divulging feelings. As if that was a weakness. She was well aware of her hubris. Of her intellect. Instead, she considered her peaceable instinct. How she hated confrontation and conflict. Didn't want to, nor could she even begin to consider, at all, that there might be some deep-rooted alternative motive in her wanting to tag along. Not in the least. No hint at all of a self-destructive inkling buried hidden, though sweetly nourished. She sat in a stupor a moment later when Erica sat down next to her.

"I talked to Franklin. He'll make the contacts. I've got phone numbers if you'd like to call."

No smile, but Judge Bailey did pat Erica on the arm. "Thank you. Now… where did those knuckleheads go? Leave us abandoned like this. That was kind of rude wasn't it?"

Erica inhaled but said nothing. The judge stood and went looking. She found them in a front office just as the sheriff was hanging up a landline. "They're not far out. If it's all right, I'll wait right here."

"Please do."

Roger McKinney had a thick folder in hand. He politely raised his brows. "We should sit down and discuss your desires." He nodded to Judge Bailey. "I have a more comfortable sitting area inside the chapel. Unless you have questions."

"I do," she responded sharply, her judgmental self-coming out.

McKinney gave her a patient look.

It surprised Erica when the judge flashed the note at him. "Why are you going to South America? Why Bueno's Aires?"

McKinney got an almost guilty look on his face. He exchanged a look with the sheriff. The sheriff hemmed a second before clearing his throat. "I don't think he can divulge."

"Clarify," the judge demanded. "It wouldn't have anything to do with my sister's death, would it? Who's this Banda fellow? What does this note mean?"

Sheriff Hackett reached for it and Judge Bailey pulled back. "Just so you know, I've been in contact with Attorneys Soto, Lowe, and Cobb. They'll be tracking my every movement."

The sheriff sneered at her before snatching the note. He paused a moment. "An-tea-own-ee Banda. Never heard of him."

"Book store in Buenos Aires. Is that where you're going?" Judge Bailey said hotly. She had seen the look McKinney now formed a million times before.

He was feigning innocence like a two-bit thief. "I have no idea who Antione Banda is," he pronounced it like a native speaker. "Why? What does that have to do with Dana?"

"What does this saying mean?" the sheriff interjected. "Never taste of death…"

"I assume Mr. Voodoo here would know. Doesn't he have some sort of gift?"

Roger reached for the note. He read it. "That's Dana's business. I have no idea. And she talked a lot about her business."

"And what was that?"

"Wild, eclectic interests are about the best way to describe it. She dealt with her books but worked at odds and ends. She even helped out here. The bar ecosystem was something totally out of her realm, but she even worked there. The scoundrel echelons. Or cheaters. Or drifters without ambition. Those were her words, describing the place. But she waited tables occasionally. She liked meeting people. She was friendly. Accepted everybody."

"Bar? What bar?"

"Harbor Light Tavern," the sheriff added. "North end of town. Ben Sanders is the proprietor."

"Here? She worked here. Why here?"

McKinney shrugged. "She said it reminded her of her favorite movie. She helped with hair, nails, and makeup. Never took a dime. By the way... I'll cover any costs. No matter what you choose to do, I'll cover the cost."

That left the judge defenseless for a moment. She could sense Erica edging closer. She cocked her neck to look. "What?"

"My Girl. Her favorite movie was My Girl. That's kind of sweet. I like that movie too."

"Umph!" Judge Bailey grunted. "Who's Red? That's what you need to look into."

"Red? What do you mean, Red?" the sheriff asked. "What does she mean, Red?"

"You mean Red the Loon?" McKinney got a twisted look. "The supposed CIA agent? Is that who you mean?"

"Tell him, Erica."

"We found an envelope. It had fangs in it." She got a grotesque expression. "Long fangs. And a threatening note. Told her to back off or else."

Roger McKinney began chuckling mildly. "I could see her doing that. Didn't know she knew him, but I could see that happening. She was a protective little thing."

"Who is this Red," Sheriff Hackett now demanded.

"Frankly, I have never met him," Roger said. "Sure... I've had lots of contact. I simply think it's an insane asylum patient who picked me out of a hat. At first, I would get calls. Said the President was sending him on a secret mission to Costa Rica. If my body shows up, you'll know I failed. That kind of stuff. He would send a letter two or three times a year, detailing this strange clandestine world that made little sense. Told a good story sometimes, but he had to be insane."

"Then where'd he get those fangs? Why send them to Dana?"

"I assume he offended her. He then lashed out when she barked at him. I guess she took a call. He was probably just playing the role."

32

"I'd like to see this note and fangs," the sheriff lowered his voice, authoritatively.

"They're back at the house," Erica said. "I touched them. I didn't know they might be evidence. The fangs fell on the floor. I put the envelope back on the shelf."

"What's more important, is this trip to Buenos Aires," Judge Bailey spat. "How do I get on that flight? I want to watch every move you make."

"You suspect me. Fine," Roger said lightly. "Private strip this side of Ithaca. We leave at eight o'clock sharp in the morning. Private plane so you don't have to buy a ticket. Hope you have your passport."

"Don't get the wrong impression," the sheriff said as if consoling a child. "He can probably tell you whatever you want to know once you get on the plane. He's promised confidentiality otherwise."

"I suppose we don't have to do anything about Dana then until you're finished with your investigation. I'm just going to cremate her. Don't need to do anything else. Just cremate her," the judge said coldly.

"That's fine," Roger said. "There are many people around here that would feel cheated without some kind of service, but that can be done without your involvement. Won't be a problem at all. Would you like to view her body before cremation? I'd recommend you do."

Judge Bailey looked at him as if he were trying to plant a seed of guilt. Sure, it sounded sentimental and idealistic. Not her preference, of course. It triggered another thought. "No. I don't want to see her. Tell me…" she started just as the entry chimes sounded. Two sour-looking men stepped in and instantly produced a response out of the sheriff. He kind of jumped and scooted.

"Dr. Gray. Glad you're here," the sheriff sounded even.

"Where's the body?" the single exchange before the sheriff escorted the two away.

Judge Bailey filled the space vacated by the sheriff as if a tactical defense-attorney display. "Tell me… I guess you might know just as well as the sheriff. Who else around here would kill somebody like this?"

"That thought has already crossed my mind. Can't think of a soul or a reason why someone would do this. Sure… we have our usual cast of oddballs like any other town does. But to do…" he shook his head. "Small gage needle in the lower back. No evidence of even a prick. Substantial bruising internally. Biological specimens will reveal something. I'm sure toxicology tests were ordered. That would be run-of-the-mill. I…"

"Can I interrupt you?"

"Go ahead."

"I don't like you. I don't trust you. I think you're pretentious. I think you're pretending to be something you're not." The judge paused and Erica looked at her starkly, blown over by this odd militant side of her. "I'm going to have you investigated." She paused to gauge his reaction.

He seemed amused by her words. Like he had an unprepossessing face full of false benevolence. "Do whatever you want. I'm not going to stop you," he finally sounded like he was getting hot under the collar.

A breath later, Dr. Gray, a middle-aged man, not very fit, with a trim salt and pepper beard led his companion and the sheriff right up to the doorway. "Judge Meghan Bailey?" the doctor said.

"What?"

"I'm sorry for all of this. From what we've determined, someone hacked our computer system. Mr. McKinney showed up right after the change of staff and they wouldn't have known. They printed out a death certificate as they thought correct. It should have read, pending. My apologies. Can I answer any questions for you?"

The judge strangely looked at Roger McKinney, as if pleading for help.

"Should be six weeks or so, right?" Roger said. "Before tests are complete?"

"That's correct," Gray added.

"So, she was killed," the judge said lowly. "Someone killed her?"

"Can't say anything right now. Her death is suspicious. Very strange."

"So, I just have to wait."

"You can go on with whatever plans you had. Service, burial, whatever."

"Cremate?"

"Yes. We already have what we need. Finding out who's behind the hack though is a different matter." He pulled his wallet out and gave her his card. "Any questions you have, feel free. Looks like the good sheriff here has got his hands full with this one. I'll offer what I can. I hope for the best."

With no questions asked and nothing seemingly left to say, Dr. Gray spun on a heel, snagged hold of the sheriff, and stepped out of earshot.

"I'm hungry," the judge said abruptly. She had a vacant look.

"You'll need a car," Roger said. He fished a key out of his pocket. "Take the white van in the back. You probably passed Twyla MacDonald's roadside inn—her Siesta Retreat—when you came off the interstate. Bill's Diner is right next door. That's about the only place to get food right now."

Judge Bailey looked at Erica warily. "Let's get out of here," she said. "I've had enough for now."

She snagged the key and spun away. Before she got out the front door, she heard Roger McKinney's last words, which felt tactless. "If you run into Twyla, don't take offense. She's all sass and flavor with no shame."

CHAPTER FIVE

TWYLA STIRS THE POT

They would have completely missed Bill's Diner if not for the large red orb atop a tall post. Situated way back near the right angle of Twyla's L-shaped Siesta Retreat and partly behind the bright red, blue, and yellow colors of a next-door Sunoco gas station it was practically hidden. Mostly because of all the pickup trucks parked like wolves devouring a carcass.

Judge Bailey stayed quiet until the van's front tires dropped off a crumbly edge of bitumen where a cotton field of discarded Morley cigarette butts lay scattered. "We may not have the right calling card to get in here," the judge said.

"You think it's private?" Erica elevated her voice.

"No. Probably need a wad of chewing tobacco in our lips."

Erica raised her perfect brows, amused with the judge's humor. Rare, almost singular wisecrack. She had to look away and soon wondered why only every other window along the backside of Twyla's retreat had air conditioning units. It caught her off guard when the judge quickly crawled out. She didn't catch up until the judge stood holding the glass door wide. The place was packed. Side booths, a half dozen tables, and a line of plumber cracks along the bar. A thousand eyes suddenly seemed captivated. Some sat erect briefly and some merely looked with their heads still low.

"Stack of jacks!" broke the tension. The waitress who had barked out the order snapped her fingers and pointed. The judge beelined it. Erica danced across the black and white tiles like she feared breaking her grandmother's back.

"Mornin' ladies," the tawny, aging waitress said. "Want menus?"

Judge Bailey paused and looked around the room. Erica couldn't help but smile. Their waitress, Ruth stitched across her left breast, looked like the spitting image of Madeline Kahn—from Young Frankenstein. Except her stack of tawny hair, which nearly matched the color of her dress, was a short stack under a net and not streaked.

"We'll take menus," Judge Bailey said and slid into the booth.

"Hope they're not ancient in their menu," Erica said, once the waitress was out of earshot. "We'll walk out of here on the verge of a heart attack."

Then suddenly, you couldn't ignore the distraction. "I'm tellin' ya, Bill..." a high-pitched nasally voice cut the air like molten lava kissing the ocean. "He has a connection to the devil. I swear... I know he's got a connection with the devil."

A breath later, a large fellow with a large gut spun around close to their booth and cleaned a spatula off on his greasy apron. His white T-shirt looked fresh and unmarred. A large Roman nose jutted out boldly and was an affront to the man's deep, dark eyes.

"Look, Twyla… I told ya 'bout comin' over here durin' the mornin' rush. I don't got time for this."

"The feller's too damned slick. Smart ass, he is. I told ya what happened when my old man croaked, didn't I? Ya know all about that don'tcha? Same thing all over again. 'Cept he's got half the rest the world involved. Sent Ick over there, he did. Ya knew 'bout that, didn't ya?"

"Look, Twyla… I've told me a zillion times. Don't go on about that now. I've heard it. Just go home and leave me alone. Come back later. I'll listen to ya then, but not now."

The man stomped off and Twyla, dressed in a ratty pink house coat and with equally ratty yellow hair in curls, stepped sideways and scratched her rump. Thirty packs a day yellow. Dirty pink slippers half-flopping off fit the image. As did her milky white and muscular calves. Bowling pin calves. Crepey and sagging skin on her bare arms felt an affront. She glanced at the two and looked away. A deep crease between and across the top of her nose ached with separation anxiety.

"I like her," Judge Bailey muttered. "I like her a lot." She snapped her fingers. "Excuse me. Ma'am."

Twyla ignored her. The waitress delivered their menus, merely flashing by with a pitcher of steaming coffee, leaving its aroma thick.

"Ma'am!"

Twyla honed in on them and stepped over, still scratching. "You think you're all so damned smart, don'tcha?"

"Ma'am?"

"Eh… what do you know? You strangers?"

"Sort of. What were you talking about? Was that Bill?"

"Hah! What does that matter to ya? You special or somethin'?"

"Perhaps you would explain. I'd like to know what you were just talking about."

"Eh… nobody knows what they're talkin' 'bout. Neither did them doctors nor Chris when it all went down. He showed 'em, though. Hah! Talk about outsmartin' the smarts. Outlived every damned pre-dic-tion! Said he was a lucky son-of-a-bitch to be alive after two years. That's what they said. What do you 'spect out of a rough, tough, scrappy fighter thrown into the ring with that shitty cancer? It didn't have a chance. Not against him. Yup… he outwitted, outplayed, and outlasted that sucker for near seven more years. And then the damnedest thing. We stood around scratchin' our asses with a finger and with our mouths agape tryin' to make sense of it when he drove his old Chev off the Davenport Bridge. He was like Beelzebub at the helm from the day he was born, but held 'er steady in all that time. And it was fluff that reached out and cold-cocked him dead. They call that finishin' up the diploma. You inherit a wagon full of redneck stepchildren and wonder why the good Lord didn't plan things out better. You live like a cowboy, find an old lady with little tits, and evade natural disasters and calcium-impacted thinkers. And what does it getcha? Same ol' thing. Nuttin'. Ya still end up dead. Ya just as well turn up the country music, dance around in your holy underwear, and not worry about who's gettin' a peek of yer ass. Because it don't matter in the end anyways. Not gonna matter now either. Mark my words. Not gonna matter."

"What are you talking about? I don't mean your husband. Before that."

"Oh… that pretty little thing. Bet he was parked out there hidin' in the shadows. Bet he was droolin' over that one. Had that sicky little Ick pretend to sneak in there and find her. Them two are in cahoots. They just like to have things molderin' in the ground."

"You're talking about the mortician, right? McKinney?"

Twyla laughed out loud. "Who else would I be talkin' 'bout? Who else was already loadin' his stretcher before the old man launched off the bridge? He knew. Says he knows stuff like that. My ass. I think he talked Chris into it, I do." She roiled Judge Bailey with a pugnacious pucker of the lips. A right fine pickle pucker of the lips.

"Have you had breakfast? Would you like to sit with us? I'll buy you breakfast."

"Hah! I eat my breakfast before the birds wake up." She looked around. "Wouldn't mind a cup of that coffee. Ruth is always temptin' with that stuff. Damn good stuff."

38

Judge Bailey scooted over and patted the seat. Twyla plopped in. The judge handed her menu to Erica. "Order two of whatever you want when she comes. I'm getting acquainted with my new friend."

And Twyla did most of the talking. About that old man of hers, Chris. That ornery, loud-mouthed, cigar-suckin' twit. According to Twyla anyway. Went on about his boom-boom powder (whatever that was). Which came out about the same time as a bowl of oatmeal and a cup of yogurt. Went on about his affinity with dirt and grease and old pickup trucks just so you had somethin' to bust your knuckles on. Went on about his guns and blowin' ducks out of the air. Went on and on and then when she started in about his sexual preferences Judge Bailey grabbed her by the arm.

"The girl that died... you knew her? Dana Bailey?"

Twyla looked at her crossed-eyed. "You foolin'? Course I know'd her. Everyone know'd her. Purdy little thing."

"My sister. She was my sister."

Double cross-eyed, lifted lip into a scowl. "Oh... you poor thang. You poor little thang. Why didn't you say somethin' before now? You're here for the funeral."

"Yes, yes... we're making plans. What can you tell me about the mortician? Do you know any dark secrets about him? Something specific."

"Of course."

"What?"

Twyla got a lost look, puckering her lips and then exhaling. She fluttered her lips in horse-lip fashion. Another deep inhale and she covered her mouth, working her brain cells about as hard as humanly possible. Another exhale.

"Well...?"

"He's a computer geek."

"McKinney? Right?"

"No. Ick. Ick is a computer geek. Who knows what kind of weirdo stuff that freak looks at? You ever met Ick? He's like that with that undertaker." She crossed her fingers. "Real friendly those two. Most folks want to bite the freak's head off, but he friendlies up real cozy-like. He probably conjures things up too. You know… decides when somebody's gonna die." Twyla looked off as if caught up in a youthful moment of infatuation. "He's a looker, he is. Damn good lookin', he is. Probably got my go-out date scribbled down in a book somewhere. Most likely wants to see me naked."

Erica giggled. Judge Bailey looked annoyed.

"How often do people die around here? How about murders?"

"Murders?" a finger to her lips, exclamation point-style. "Uh… uh… my old man. I think McKinney had somethin' to do with my old man dyin'. Had to because he knew."

"How about anyone else?"

Twyla shrugged. "I'm not the obituary lady. Not sure."

"A lot of people dying though, right?"

"They need to do a better job with that cemetery." She pointed west. "Right up there through the trees. What a mess that is. They need to cut the grass more often."

Erica finished her oatmeal and the judge began to dabble a spoon in an empty cup of coffee.

Nothing else said, Twyla jumped to her feet and hurried out. Erica leaned and watched until she was well out the door. "Coo-coo," she uttered. "That woman is coo-coo."

"I'm not so sure. She may have been reliving a moment of grief. We'll reserve a room with her and come back later. We'll let her think. She might have more to say."

Erica stared at her as if part of an outbreak of insanity. "In the meantime?"

"You schedule an appointment with Attorney Lowe. For tomorrow. The day of grace is well in the past, as far as I'm concerned. While I risk my neck, doing who knows what, I want you to meet him and twist his arm. Get him to investigate these people… if he already hasn't or isn't. Insist on the FBI taking over. Get a profiler involved. We're looking at a possible professional hit here. Who knows what that means?"

"We didn't gain much out of this little chat, did we?"

40

"Are you kidding? Computer geek. Hack! I think we're well on our way down a rat hole here. It's just how deep and convoluted it is."

CHAPTER SIX

FLYING GILDEROY

True to her character she wasn't chatty. Judge Bailey couldn't even muster a kind morning gesture. A quick-moving cold front had crossed through overnight, bringing a shower, crisp air, freshness, and an ethereal mist everywhere. It would be some time before morning's rays would burn it off. Until then, ghostly figures played games with the judge's mind. In her mind's eye, cows were knights on mighty steeds, fence posts skinny ghosts, and crooked, half-fallen trees, dragons. Riding in the passenger's seat, she rested the back of her fingers on her lips and gazed off, working her thoughts like a cement mixer. Her travel attire was a Silk & Salt Staycation sweat set in pink. Erica wore a navy blue skirt above the knee and a light blue blouse.

"That was easy enough," Erica uttered.

The judge quizzically glanced and said nothing.

"The airstrip. It's right over there."

"Hm…"

They turned right moments later. Erica reached over with a mere pleading look. Nothing. Still nothing. Less than a minute later, a fellow in a dark jacket and looking make-believe playboy met them at the gate and kept his distance even when Erica lowered her window.

"Bailey party? Judge Bailey?"

"That's correct," the judge raised her voice.

"I'll need to see ID. Anything will do."

The judge dug through the handbag in her lap and produced her passport.

41

"Excellent." He punched the code for the gate and pointed. "Straight between the hangers. Hang a left and take the tarmac down to the Pilatus PC-24. I'll wait here so you don't get locked in."

"I don't know what that means," Erica sounded empty.

"Sleek little blue and white number. It's the only thing with color. Have a nice flight."

Before she made the turn, passing the hangers, Erica touched the judge's arm. "You're in a bad mood. Is that phone call still bothering you?"

"I have no problem with the phone call. The FBI should call. It was their attitude. The accusatory attitude." She glared at Erica. "Like I did it. Like I'm responsible somehow. I swear she didn't believe a word I was saying."

"At least they're letting you go. I mean… they could have prevented that, right?"

"No!" The judge snapped. "I didn't see a computer. Did you see a computer? They wanted to know about her laptop and phone. I didn't see anything like that."

"But you did tell them about the geekish neighbor. Wasn't that enough? If anyone took them, he did, right?"

"Not good enough for them. It chaps my hide."

It's good to experience the world from the other side of the fence, Erica was thinking when they approached the plane, its engines whining in warmup. Sun reflecting off the windshield prevented them from seeing who sat at the controls until they swept around the nose and stopped. "You've got to be kidding," Judge Bailey snarled.

"That's the guy who brought your car back with four new tires. What's going on here?" Erica added.

"Not him. Is he now trying to suggest he's our pilot?"

"The undertaker. That's the undertaker in there with him. He's shaved. I didn't recognize him." Erica noted the change in the judge's face. "You don't have to go. You realize you don't have to go."

"What kind of a game is he playing?"

"I guess he could be a pilot, right? No reason he couldn't be a pilot."

"Everything about this is bothering me. I think they're trying to get under my skin. I wonder if this is the treatment Dana got."

"They are playing mind games, aren't they? First, they yank your chain. Next, he offers to pay for his services and then the bald one won't take any money for new tires. I think they're trying to get into your head—cause confusion. Or just act superior. More benevolent."

"Makes me trust them even less."

"What are you going to do? We can just drive out of here."

Judge Bailey thought for just a moment before climbing out. A moment after she did, a dark minivan whipped around the tail of the plane and stopped angularly from where they sat. A casually dressed man and woman climbed out, followed by a young man who instantly removed several pieces of aluminum luggage. As he began carrying them on board, Erica climbed out. In time to overhear the man and woman exchange a few words.

"I couldn't get my hands on any Demadex, but the Furosemide will most likely be sufficient," the slightly pudgy fellow said. He was lightly bearded and leathery-looking. The woman was slender, blonde, and had worry lines that prematurely aged her.

"I'm worried about more than fluid retention. Pulmonary edema, hyperkalemia… I'm aware those have been issues so far. I'm not sure of the care. We'll have to assess on the fly. Let's get on board and inspect before we get off the ground."

Judge Bailey and Erica flashed a look of concern. Erica rounded the hood and kept her voice low. "That was medical talk."

"Right. Or it's some kind of funeral director's convention."

"Or body harvesting. You've heard of that, haven't you? What if they're harvesting body parts? You may not come back. You may end up in several different people… all over the world."

It startled but didn't surprise Erica when the judge walked over and climbed on board. Erica merely stepped far enough to look in. A curtain was pulled behind the second row of seats, which muffled their voices.

"Get my bag. I'm going with them."

"You sure?"

"I'm sure. You've got your appointment scheduled, don't you?"

"Yes."

"Just worry about that. I can handle this. I'll see you when I get back."

"It's now three days, right? They said three days?"

"At least. He said three or four. Possibly five. I've got to do this."

"You're not worried?"

"Not so much. Now, I'm more worried about this Banda guy." She pulled the note from her pocket.

Minutes later, Erica sat parked a short distance away watching the plane taxi toward the north end of the airfield. It didn't take long. Not long at all. A roar of the engines and the speedy glistening number swept by and quickly lifted off into what felt like a steep climb into oblivion.

They hadn't leveled off for five minutes before Tony "Nuts" Ford stepped out of the cabin and gave everyone a friendly salute. "Ladies and gentlemen, I always feel closer to Jesus way up here in the air. Don't ya love it?"

"Amen," the other two passengers responded.

Judge Bailey had made a note of keeping her nose practically pressed to the window, ignoring them up to that point. It alarmed her when Nuts leaned in and almost, brushing the tip of his stiff mustache across her cheek, growled in her ear. "Écoute, ma chérie. Vous êtes jolie et chic, mais vous trompez de route. [Listen up, my dear. You are pretty and chic, but you're walking down the wrong road.] By the way... No better enemy than those falsely accused. You've probably seen that in your work. Don't be a pathologic, venom-spewing troll. It will strike back, the language of creative destruction eating you alive if you're not careful."

The words gurgling out of him felt just as described. Didn't understand the French. If she hadn't felt so intimidated and without a dozen court officers to back her up she couldn't bark at him. Instead, she bit her tongue. He leaned back and she caustically glared at him.

44

"I know you don't like him. I know you don't trust him, but I think it's high time someone bent your crooked nose back into place."

Judge Bailey sat there fuming, her lips already white and her cheeks persimmon, going on crimson red. "First of all..." he sat opposite her, dropped an armrest, and rotated in his chair, facing her. He crossed his legs. "I'd give my life for that man, any day, any time. He's done more good than General Mills has Cheerios. No fanfare. No want of recognition. No recompense. Just a right-down good guy. Just so you know, this is a flight of mercy. We're flying to pick up a critically ill missionary. The reason no one dared share a word is because her pappy is a U.S. senator and he didn't want anyone to know he turned to charity for help. Arrogant bastard. Swore us to secrecy. What do you think of that?"

Judge Bailey didn't want to believe him. She looked over her shoulder to find sympathetic eyes staring back. "I'm Doctor April Parker," the woman said. "Attending nurse, Jesse Cole is right behind you. We didn't know we were going to have a passenger. We've flown with Kip several times. He's a great pilot. This new plane of his gets us back and forth much faster."

Judge Bailey glowered at Nuts. "You're telling me this is his plane? Hah! That's a lie if I've ever heard a lie."

"Hah-hah-hah..." Nuts threw his head back, laughing. "Why is that so unbelievable?"

"I know morticians charge a lot, but not enough to buy a plane like this. That's outrageous."

"You're only seeing a tiny corner of the picture here, lady. You get too nasty and I might punch you in the nose." He smacked his fist into his palm.

"Here now, Nuts," the doctor said, reaching over and patting his arm. "Don't lose your temper."

Nuts smiled at her. "I'm just showin' off. Want her to know I mean business." He then rapped his knuckles on his head. "I've got her under control. Doing much better now. I don't go off the handle like I used to. See I rapped on that titanium plate of mine and I didn't blow up. I used to blow it, even if you touched that spot."

"PTSD," the doctor said calmly. "Iraq."

45

"Whew, whew, whew…" Nuts whirled his finger, blowing. "Took my Apache down. Beat the living hell out of me. Tracey and the kids used to run like hell when I went on a rant. Until Kip came along. Gave me a job, and gave me purpose. Saved my life and most likely my family's too. Who knows?"

The judge glanced at the doctor, merely for a confirming nod. She accommodated. "You're telling me he bought you a garage?"

"No. He owns that. I do all the work though. Usually fabricating or souping up. And if there's no work… I spend a lot of time with his horses. He breeds and trains. He spends a lot of time with those horses too. Soothes his soul. Mine as well."

"You're making him out to be an angel. That's hard to believe."

"Dana didn't see it that way. She lusted over him for a while— wanted him to be one of those pirate types. Or a vampire. Werewolf would have worked too. You know what I'm talking about, don't you?"

Judge Bailey lowered her chin and indifferently blinked. She rested her eyes on his hands, which he nervously rubbed. Was that a subconscious tell? she wondered.

"Do you know what I'm saying?" he asked again.

The judge shook her head.

"You know… there are those people drawn to high-status sorts. Rich, powerful people who they envision as a sort of vampire. They think, as an attractive woman, they can tame them. She soon learned she got that wrong. Didn't need to tame anyone and he was no vampire."

"Morticians don't make that kind of money. I'm not stupid."

"Didn't make his money that way. He gives away more than he makes there."

"Go on."

"He was a multi-millionaire before he graduated from high school."

"A techie?"

"Stock market. He had a knack. Bright as a whip. Ten years as a Navy pilot, a few years of aimless wandering, and now this. Aside from occasionally reading some writer named Vincent Wampler, he's normal.

Just like a lot of other families. He's a widower. A drunk driver killed his parents a few years back. He's got a school teacher brother named Adam who, despite their differences, would like to have a relationship, but his sister-in-law, Helen reacts like a fat moth hitting a windshield at eighty miles per hour. Smear the juices all over the windshield and she's so green with envy and jealousy there is no way to reconcile."

"A man like that doesn't choose to be a mortician."

"He didn't make the choice. It chose him."

"Bah!" the judge grunted and looked away.

"He's invited you to sit up front if you want. Great view from up there."

"No. Here is fine." Smug tone.

"Fine," he slapped his knees. "It's a long flight. Two thousand mile hops. Unless the unexpected comes along, we first touchdown in Punta Cana, Dominican Republic. Manaus, Brazil, then Asuncion, Paraguay. Finally, Buenos Aires. Anywhere along the way, you can take a front-row seat."

The judge hated him. Hated that he sounded so believable. Hated that it made perfect sense. Hated that a tear came to her eye as she looked away and stared out the window.

CHAPTER SEVEN

A LOWE CONSULTATION

With time to kill Erica drove the streets, amused by the many venerable, old, gray stone, and yet stable churches. On just about every other corner. Like providence snatched them from the English countryside and chose this as a repository. Trees and all. It was at the side of one such church where she parked and then casually walked, worried that an early arrival for her ten o'clock appointment would work against her. The architecture felt old, yet refreshed in the red-brick and granite courthouse where the District Attorney's office resided.

Security required she sign in before passing through a detector and then showing her ID again to an officer at a counter. "Second floor," the black woman refused eye contact. "There's a row of chairs in the hallway. Take a seat and wait until you're summoned."

"Thank you," Erica spryly responded, clutched her phone a little tighter, and chose marble stairs simply for the echoing effect—something authoritative about that echoing effect.

She didn't realize D.A. Lowe's first name was Prince until she saw the gold lettering on a smoky glass door. It seemed anecdotal to the common man's feeling of the space. Drawn Venetian blinds in a row of windows proudly stated these people preferred privacy.

Inside the office, a sour, gray-haired secretary focused on a computer screen, more out of fear than deference. Prince Lowe, his silk mauve tie loose and sleeves rolled up, stood studying the stack of subpoenas she'd just handed him.

Prince Lowe was a somewhat good-looking man but had a lonely face. A face intense, full of false compassion in his brow and insipidly cruel wide, judgmental eyes. Good eyes for looking down a nose, squared off at the tip. A feature that always caused him to subconsciously touch his nose when hoping to impress. Blonde hair combed sideways tended to fall across his forehead when he tucked his chin to read. He brushed his bangs aside just before tossing the pages back onto his secretary's desk. "One more subpoena," his voice was suave. "There was a delivery man. Was it FedEx? I think it was FedEx. Didn't I read or hear he witnessed the crime? I want him subpoenaed as well."

"Yes, sir," sounded the contrite. Lowe glanced over her head. Not in a domineering act, but because he detected Erica nervously bouncing a foot as she waited. Prince Lowe rounded his secretary's desk, wedged the blinds with his fingers, and stared. He couldn't stop from smiling. He lingered, thoroughly enjoying those long silky legs until it suddenly occurred to him. He brusquely turned.

"I had an appointment? Didn't I have an appointment this morning? What time was that?"

"In ten minutes."

"And when were you going to remind me of that?"

"It seems you are aware." The secretary made eye contact. "You scold me when I remind you. Have we now changed the rules?"

Prince Lowe stood there divided for a moment, part of him shameless, the other begging conflict. Shameless won out. He rounded the desk, paused, considered for just a moment, and then deposited one hand in his pocket, merely for the effect. He then casually opened the door. "Morning. Are you my appointment?"

Erica jumped up and extended her hand. "Judge Meghan Bailey. I'm her clerk, Erica Dennis."

Prince Lowe lowered his chin, smiled, and made the obligatory touch to the nose before removing his hand from his pocket and then taking hers the way Judge Bailey envisioned an undertaker doing it. Deceitfully. "Come in!"

"Thank you."

Passing by the secretary, he droned, "Hold all my calls. I think we owe Ms. Dennis legal deference, don't we?"

His office door sat wide open. Hand extended, he almost bowed, granting her entry. His office was just what she expected. A desk is buried in legal folders as well. The boxes stacked around the room presented the exact image of a man who liked the perception of overburden. He closed the door behind them and then hurried around his desk. With a smile on his face, he wheeled his plush, comfy chair around and situated it opposite something that looked like it belonged in a Soviet-Era interrogation room. "Sorry," he weakly said. "That's makeshift for now. Take mine. Please."

Erica sat with propriety. Lowe sat, crossed a leg, and pressed his fingers into a steeple. "How are you today?" he inquired.

"I'm fine. I'm sure you know why I'm here."

"Uh... you see how busy I am. Remind me."

"Judge Bailey. Her sister Dana died... well, now they suspect murder. Kermit Falls."

"Oh, yes!" he struck his fist resolutely on the desk's edge. "Outrageous! It's all suddenly coming to me." A sheepish duck of the chin. "With all due respect... it's just... no offense intended here... but... but to be frank, you're a tremendous distraction. I hope you take that as a compliment. I'm not trying to be chauvinistic. You just… you got this intrepid old heart of mine fluttering. I couldn't hold a train of thought."

Erica didn't blush. She boorishly sighed, however, and leaned slightly forward. "We have concerns."

"Let me think. Don't we have the FBI involved now? I got wind of this in between some rather terse words with some knot-headed defense attorney."

"That's right."

"So, what exactly do you want out of me? Law enforcement usually brings me evidence to charge."

"You have the authority to investigate persons."

"True. We usually don't have time for that."

"Are you acquainted with any strange happenings in and around Kermit Falls?"

Lowe paused, lowering his chin further. "Some. Let me explain. I was appointed to this position a few weeks ago. My elected predecessor, Cary Burk died tragically. Terrible car crash. She didn't take very good care of herself, but I believe bad health would have been a better way to die. Shame. Nevertheless, I'm coming in mid-stream with a mountain of work I'm trying to navigate. But…" an exclamation point with his finger. "I am aware."

"Are you telling me this is a waste of your time?"

"Not at all. We should professionally accommodate one another, shouldn't we?"

"Of course. And I appreciate that. Can you share with me what you know or suspect?"

"Now…" he hesitated. Eyes darting, he began tracing his finger along the edge of the desk. He sighed twice before exhaling sharply. "You're not an investigating official here. I have to be careful."

"Judge Bailey doesn't trust these people. From Sheriff Hackett to the undertaker, Roger McKinney. Do you realize he claims to have some special connection to the dead? Has a sixth sense, they say. Knows when

50

someone is going to die. Doesn't that sound crazy to you? Some fear he has a hand in people dying and merely feigns this weird gift."

Lowe briefly made penetrating eye contact. "Sandy!" he barked. "Come in here a minute!"

Almost instantly his secretary appeared. "Yes, sir."

"Check on something for me. Find out if the rate of death in and around Kermit Falls is unusually high. The Health Department should have that kind of data. Look for anomalies... is the rate of accidental death high? Things like that. Also..." he barked when she turned away. "Who took care of Cary Burk when she died? Didn't she live out of town somewhere? If he was involved in that, it won't look good, will it?"

Erica thought for a moment. "So, have you heard of this before? You've heard these rumors?"

He tried a sympathetic tone. "This is a morbid matter. I don't have bumper sticker morals. I don't use bumper sticker words. I'm no politician at heart. But I do believe we need to respond to these things as if we were."

Erica wasn't sure what that meant. She cocked her neck as if encouraging further explanation.

"Look," he stood and started walking for the door. "I hate the saying, justice for thee and mercy for me. We like an even-handed approach, but this may require a little bit of out-of-balance justice. I promise we'll get right on top of this and do everything we can. We'll work hand in hand with the FBI. I assure you." He paused at the door and waited for her. She delayed briefly.

He's in over his head, she thought. He just slapped a bumper sticker across my butt, he did. She thought to sit tight and press him further. A glance at the look on his face and she knew that wouldn't be happening—no point in trying to suck blood out of a turnip. Erica stood and politely smiled before walking out. He snagged two cards from Sandy's desk and seductively slipped them into her hand. "Write down your number on one of them. I'll need a way to contact you." He stepped, opened the door, and raised his eyebrows—like he was hinting at something erotic.

She hesitated before quickly jotting her number down. She handed the card to Sandy.

"Contact me any time," he smiled and almost pushed her out the door. Erica paused a moment, considering the closed door and feeling like she hadn't accomplished a thing. Ten seconds later, he heard the echo of her heels clacking down the stairway. He peeked after opening the door. He then darted down the hallway and paused where a window looked down. He didn't move. Not until he watched her walk to her car and then after the Volvo disappeared among the trees.

CHAPTER EIGHT

NIBBLING THE BAIT

Intricately knitted webs of wretched and gloomy emotion drug the morning out and left Judge Bailey feeling weary and longing for rest. It felt like an eternity and the ocean an endless slate of grayish-blue misery. When widely dispersed and fluffy white clouds seemed to slowly rise to their level it rocked Judge Bailey out of her stupor. It suddenly dawned on her she didn't know the day nor the hour. Thus far she had refused the niceties. She saw no reason to get to know these people and didn't want to break the ice now by asking. A few breaths later that slate of dull color evinced character flaws. White blemishes appeared seconds before the waters turned turquoise and then the abrupt world of land. A beach with dispersed homes and what Judge Bailey assumed was a jungle. Until they began to glide in for an almost imperceptible landing—now trees didn't look so tall.

Still her zipped-up self, she held her neck craned while they, raced, slowing. They taxied and came to a stop. Either Kip or Nuts opened the door and let a wave of warm sultry air wash in. The intensity and thickness of the humidity nearly sucked the air out of her lungs. She didn't look until someone touched her knee. There Roger "Kip" McKinney stood politely smiling. "Good time to stretch your legs. We'll refuel and get a bite to eat." He checked his watch. "Ten minutes faster than planned. Same time zone if you're interested. Next stop we'll lose an hour. Twenty minutes before noon now." He waited for a response.

She attempted to convey intense feelings. Perhaps a frozen ball of ice, a strange mixture of intelligence, thought, and madness. It flew over his head as he ducked out, soon followed by the doctor and nurse. Judge Bailey didn't move. The group congregated at the bottom of the stairs and planned briefly. One thing now bothered the judge that she hadn't particularly paid attention to. Both Nuts and Kip were dressed like they belonged in an episode of Magnum P.I. Kip in a bright red Hawaiian shirt and Nuts in a tight dark T-shirt. The longer they stood there and the longer she stared, the more she realized a certain crumpling in her emotions. Because she knew exactly how they looked, but couldn't conjure a single thought of how Dana might look, standing there with them. It unsettled her to the point that she swiveled her neck, and snapped the vision out of her mind, now looking out a starboard-side window. She figured a VIP terminal, framed in palm trees. A moment later, after she witnessed Nuts hold the door for them to enter the terminal, another wave of emotion relaxed her. "Finally," she uttered, feeling relief in isolation.

Freed and alone she tried to stand, but quickly realized she couldn't move. At first, she thought they somehow drugged her. Until she understood that the pressure around her waist was a seat belt. She couldn't even remember fastening it. She almost stumbled getting onto her feet. And then she had to hold on, edging her way back to peek through the curtain. Medical equipment and a narrow patient bed. "Damn," she sounded disappointed. "They just might be what they claim. Flying medical mercenaries." She heard a refueling vehicle pull up. "No. Everyone I know is full of snakes."

While they took care of business, she paced. Six steps forward, about-face, and back. Three times in an interior of eggshell and lush taupe leather before she stepped into the cockpit. Everything was so clean and new and fresh. Ultra-modern displays and Gameboy-like controls felt like barbs on her brain.

A softening. "Why do I want these people to be criminals?" she said, lifting a latch on a door. It opened up into a tiny lavatory. The idea that they too were human seemed a small dose of Valium. She'd used the bathroom and paced but a moment longer before she realized they were returning. For the moment, she wouldn't accept the cracking of her hostile crust. She locked herself back into her seat, crossed her legs, and returned to the realm of stubbornness.

She did acknowledge when the smiling doctor first climbed onboard. The doctor handed her a brown paper bag. "I didn't know what you like so I got you fried fish and tostones. Those are smashed and fried plantains. There's also a dish of braised chicken. Delicious. Whatever you don't want, Jesse will vacuum it down. I also got you mild lemonade. Not too sweet, not too sour."

The judge hesitated, made eye contact, and gave her a truncated, "'cue," as thank you.

Judge Bailey still retained all the barriers. Rounded edges, but still there. From Punta Cana to a just as steamy and miserably hot Manaus, Brazil. She gave them the same treatment there with little variation in the meal. It was after takeoff—somewhere after the five o'clock hour when Nuts appeared and pounded his chest. He nodded. "I'm officially surrendering my seat up front. Need a nap before I take over on the red eye. Feel free, chère Madame." A wink and he disappeared.

What stunned Judge Bailey more than anything was how eager she now felt. No melting, well... not so much. A flipped switch and the impression was the same after sentencing a man to life. She couldn't stand another second in anyone else's presence. A breath later she was on her feet. She didn't go straight for the co-pilot's seat, but halted and strained, looking out the windshield. No wide expanse of Amazon jungle. No carpet of endless green. Instead, a blanket of clouds stretched in every direction. No response at all out of Kip. Which felt welcome at the moment. Like in the courtroom, the judge turned, recognizing the relief of separation. The disconnecting from one world and the crossing to another. At the moment, she couldn't fully frame it. Nevertheless, she inched forward. When Kip glanced up she made sure to evade eye contact. "Do I have to guard against touching things? I don't know if I can get into that seat without knocking us off course or something."

"Step over the console. Don't worry about stepping on the seat. Then just slide in."

A few seconds later, Judge Bailey sat there like an embalmed civil-war era corpse, stiff in a closet. Kip pounded his chest. "Belt."

She strapped in. "What day is it?" she uttered.

"Thursday."

And then nothing. No words. No breathing. No looking beyond dead ahead. Until she couldn't take it anymore. With a heavy sigh, the dam merely cracked. "What? No chewing out?" she asked, a quiver in her voice.

Kip glanced casually. "What do you mean? Why would I chew you out?"

She glared at him for a minute. A kind look came in response. Damn him. Whether it was his disarming nature or the comfortable feeling she couldn't tell. Suddenly, the monsters inside of her felt shattered. Suddenly, fragmenting apart in a thousand different directions. And then a sudden gushing that shocked and alarmed even cold, impersonal Lady Justice herself. Tears burst forth as her face fell into her cupped hands, the flood of sad emotion a confusing tidal wave, a near-hammer blow to the emotional control she'd always had. Sobs poured out of her. Sobs, and sobs, and sobs. No cheap, insincere words of comfort out of him. He simply sat there and let her go. On and on.

She felt a poke in her arm. She knew she ought to react with venom. Instead, she barely looked. He was offering her a box of tissue. Not until she blew her nose several times did she regain a level of control. Deep sighs and then silence until her breathing eased into several liberating sighs. She glanced, expecting to see either a condemning stare or a brisk look of satisfaction. Instead, he appeared the perfect image of a Navy pilot, totally calm, ready to engage an enemy.

"You cannot believe…" she had to catch her breath several times. "You cannot believe the feeling when I walked into that home and saw all those books. I would have never in a million years, imagined Dana having books like that. I think she read one book growing up. Suddenly, I was seeing something reflected that was so much me and that I had… I can't even describe it. Here I had a sister… never once did we try to find one another. We probably had so much in common. I didn't know her feelings. She didn't know mine. I couldn't believe it. She had a meaningful life. She had friends… purpose. I don't know how I smothered the feelings of guilt surging up. I'm sorry. You probably think I'm an idiot. You probably think I'm the coldest, most bitter woman alive. I didn't even…" she choked and faltered. "I didn't even want to see her. I have no idea what she looks like now. What is wrong with me? All of a sudden it all comes pouring out of me. I didn't realize I had so many deep and powerful feelings." She glanced, expecting words.

Nothing. Until he glanced around several times. He then looked her in the eye. "We all have different and unique ways in which we handle our grief." He checked the panel before looking her in the eye again.

"Look in the mirror. She looks a lot like you. She was pretty. It's easy to tell you're sisters."

"Why didn't you say something? You should have said something to me."

"I've learned it is far better to listen. You work things out far better and far sooner if left to your instincts."

"Oh... I can't believe this." She blew her nose again. "I've never experienced anything like this in all my life. You think I'm a boob?"

"I think you're human."

"Probably better you than that gorilla of yours. He's rude. You know how rude he is?"

"Don't misjudge. He deals with his issues in his way."

Judge Bailey felt minuscule compared to this man. How emotionally stable he seemed. How in control and savvy. "He still needs a lesson or two. I thought he was going to beat me up."

"Hah-hah... Tony? No. I don't think you need me trying to explain him."

"Meaning?"

"Some people lose faith in God because they're dissatisfied with who they are and the frailties that manipulate them. With Tony... he identifies physical maladies with his stature as a man. It's too deep and complex to explain here. I don't even know if I can. Sometimes a mind extends beyond your brain and head. One moment he's settled, saying something like... pushing a Jacuzzi button in Paris makes everything okay. I keep telling him to go. Even offer to pay. The idea somehow terrifies him. He feels safe as long as I'm within a stroll. Then he rattles off lines in French. Not because of French, mind you. He does it, simply because it makes him feel smart. To cast a spell in words, so to speak. He has a level of insecurity. He feels inferior. That helps him feel on par."

She thought for a moment. "He doesn't have to feel like that."

"I know. He's working through it. But he isn't the issue here. You know that, don't you?"

She thought for another moment. "Yes. But I'd rather talk about anything else. Ask me about the cosmos, but don't ask me about what I don't want to talk about. I have to work it out myself, right?"

Kip smiled. "We'll arrive in Asuncion in about three and a half hours. Nuts will take us the last leg. We'll be in Buenos Aires between midnight and one our time. Two to three A.M. their time. Sorry about the views. It's usually a lot better than this. Who knows... clouds may break up before dark. Sometime before then, we really ought to consider the question."

"What question?"

"Who killed Dana... and why?"

CHAPTER NINE

NIBBLING THE BAIT FROM THE UNDERSIDE

"Sometimes, she's no better than a bucket of spit," Bill had told Erica about Twyla when he delivered her evening meal—vegetarian burger, no bun, smothered in mushroom gravy, house salad, the vegetable of choice.

"Not that I dislike her," Erica had responded regarding Twyla. "But..."

"No need to explain, Missy. Glad to deliver. She usually doesn't show up around dinner time. Somethin''s got her spirits runnin' on overdrive. Good thing ya saw her comin' over. To tell ya the truth, I was glad ya called, wonderin' if I would deliver. Didn't mind escapin' from her myself."

That occurred thirty-five minutes ago now and dinner is already a memory. Erica stood at the far corner of Twyla's Siesta Retreat, eyeing Bill's Diner and wondering if she had to run or not. What she wanted, needed now more than anything was time to herself in an evening walk. And an enticing trail this side of the highway felt the best option. This little enclave of Kermit Falls sat isolated among the trees and about a mile and a half from the nearest home. Sun about to fall below the treetops was making her uncomfortable and that was the impetus that sent her scooting across the wide stretch of bitumen that granted entry to the gas station and Bill's.

Shadows swallowed her before she disappeared between a stand of willows and she didn't slow to a walk for another twenty yards. Then she paused to look around. Suddenly, that fast, the only hint of civilization was the lone silhouette of a power pole that reached above the trees, a sacrificial image if she'd considered it.

The trail twisted, dipped, and rose following the contour of a small trickling ditch. Until it climbed up close to the road surface and to where a thick stand of hickory trees felt like Eden. An abrupt turn and trail's end. At least for this side of the road. No problem spotting the trail, climbing through the trees opposite. A delay for a puttering pickup truck to pass and she darted over.

The air felt cool and invigorating. Stones, black dirt, old-growth forest. All of it felt revolutionary in American history. Even when she rounded the first large pine tree she came to and was suddenly welcomed back to the here and now. On two counts. She happened onto Kermit Falls Cemetery just as her phone rang. She touched her back pocket, her heart leaping in her chest, thinking it was bad news regarding Judge Bailey. With that thought, she didn't even consider checking the number.

"Yes," she evenly answered.

"Ms. Dennis. Prince here. Did I catch you at a bad time?"

It took her a moment to place the name and face. "Oh… Attorney Lowe. What can I do for you?"

"I have news that may interest you. We've been doing some digging." Erica began to stroll. "First of all, is your line secure?"

"Ah… uh… I guess. Why wouldn't it be secure?"

"Have you ever been hacked? I don't want anyone getting wind of what I'm about to tell you. Anyone there close enough to eavesdrop?"

"I highly doubt that."

"Just where are you?"

"Out for a walk. In the forest I guess. There was a trail."

"Okay. I think we're safe." That locked Erica in her tracks. She simply listened.

"I always wondered about the bizarre way in which Attorney Cary Burk died. I don't know why no one ever looked into this. Did you know Burk and McKinney butted heads over a piece of property?"

"No. What happened?"

"I won't get into the property issue here. And although your mortician there didn't get directly involved with her burial or anything, he was involved with just about everything else surrounding it."

"What do you mean?"

"You don't know the story, do you?"

"Of course not."

"So, Burk is driving home late one night when she abruptly comes across a body lying in the roadway. She swerves to avoid it and wraps her front bumper around a tree with such violent force that it slices her face in half."

"And how does that involve McKinney?"

"The guy in the road... he'd spent a good amount of time with McKinney earlier that day. At a funeral. Friends said McKinney pulled him aside and talked for the longest of times. Later that night, the guy ends up in a rather opportune place... a camping spot McKinney tells him about... and who knows how, but the guy ends up on the road just before Burk gets there."

"Are you suggesting McKinney planted him there, knowing Burk would come along? Any extenuating circumstances?"

"Well... the guy was drunk out of his gourd. At least two vehicles ran over the poor sucker as best as they could tell. He lay there dead as a doornail. Bait possibly."

"Oh, my gosh."

"So, McKinney ends up burying that guy and nobody asks a question about how McKinney drove him there and made sure he had all the alcohol a kid could ever dream of. If that were the end of it... who knows?"

"That's not the end of it?"

"There's some kind of an old hermit lady that lives down there. Have you seen the vacated plants north of town?"

"Heavens no. What about them?"

"Old textile and shoe factories. There's an old homestead back in the woods by there. I have it on good word, McKinney frequents the old woman in there regularly. Name of Mavis West. She has no problem housing an oddball or two. Eldred Simms and Hank Wallis. Ex-cons. One of their prison buddies shows up there one day… say… what was it… six months ago. McKinney was already on his way and the guy was already swinging from the rafters. Or so he claims. He gets there before any law enforcement knows about it. Figure that."

A sickening swirl churned in Erica's gut.

The line went quiet for a moment. "Erica? You still there?"

"Yes. I'm listening."

"You sound troubled. Are you okay?"

"It's just…"

"What?"

"Judge Bailey is with him right now. They're flying to South America. Private jet. Oh, my gosh. What has she done?"

"South America? Why South America?"

"I have no idea. I don't know." Lowe couldn't see the way Erica now reacted. She paced in a circle, her fingers splayed in the air before raking them through her hair.

"Out of the blue?" Prince sounded punched in the gut. "They just fly away with no reason?"

"Well… yes and no. There was a name. We found a note and a name. We gave it to the FBI. Banda. Ant… something Banda. A book store. The judge insisted on going because of that. Her sister had the name and other stuff. The note said something about never tasting death or nonsense like that." The panic in her voice sounded like a distant howl.

"Where exactly?"

"Buenos Aires. I can't remember the name of the bookstore. El something Grand Splendid."

"Maybe I should make a call or two."

"Yes, yes… whatever you have to do."

"I wish that were the end of it."

"There's more?"

"Did you know his wife and two daughters died suspiciously? About three years ago. I think we may need to open another investigation. You were wise to come to me."

The lump in Erica's throat robbed her of saying what she felt.

"Erica?"

"I… uh..." she struggled. "I'm here. It's just… I'm having trouble with this."

"I'm so sorry. I wish I were there with you. I shouldn't have called and dumped all this on you over the phone. Is there anything I can do?"

"I don't think so. I'm just so terrified. I feel helpless."

"Was there a time and date scheduled for their return?"

"I'm not sure of that either."

"Listen… it's only about a thirty to forty-minute drive. Why don't I come and check on you? We'll make sure you're in a safe place and there isn't any chance of trouble. Would that be okay with you?"

"Yes. Please. That would be fine. I've got a room at the Siesta Retreat. It's off the interstate."

"Erica?"

"Yes."

"Don't fret. Stay calm. One other thing."

"What?"

"I'm not sure of McKinney's relationship with law enforcement there. I'd use caution before turning to them. At least for now. I believe he may have a lot of suspicious connections."

"I understand. Thank you. Thank you, very much."

"Okay. I'll see you soon. Bye."

"Bye."

Erica couldn't help but spin around and take in what there was of the cemetery. She now stood in the old section. As old as the revolution. Easy to tell because of the tilting, barely legible soft-stone grave markers. And the uneven ground—washboard uneven. It was starting to feel eerie. Starting to feel like Roger McKinney. That's why it was so weird what she then did. Instead of spinning on a heel and running, she wanted to explore. For justice's sake. To balance the scales. At least begin the action. She walked out of the old section and crossed a snaking gravel road before cutting through a still old, but newer section. In five minutes she'd found the section where fresh mounds held precious packages of rotting flesh. Minutes later it was an easy spot. A giant India Red marker with McKinney elegantly etched. She rounded it to find smaller markers indicating who and when.

"Kallie… beloved wife and mother," she read out loud. "Kami…" she said and calculated from the dates. "Sixteen… she was sixteen. Katie was fourteen. They all died on the same date. God help me," she whispered with a determined tone. She then clutched her phone to her breast and denied Kip McKinney any future mercy on the spot.

Twyla stood at the front counter, sipping her special nighttime medicine—rum hot toddy—all ready for bed when a darkened-out Audi A4 raced in and braked hard outside her cabin office. A man looking urbane and city-slick stepped out, looked around, and loosened a button on his crisp white shirt. He closed the door with smug confidence. He spotted her, walked to the door, and instantly found it was locked. "Hey! Woman… a little help here," his voice was shrill and plaintive.

Twyla was in no hurry. A scratch of the rump and another sip of her medicine. He stood impatiently rattling the door before she ambled over. "What?" she barked.

He chuckled, disbelievingly. "You're kidding. Aren't you going to help a customer?"

"You ain't the kind to stay here. Slicker place down the interstate."

"I'm not here for a room. I'm looking for a guest. A friend of mine." He looked around, unable to spot the Volvo.

That caused her to open the door and poke her nose out. Instantly, she grimaced as if the man road-kill carrion. "Lordy boy… what'schoo doused in? You got a fartin' problem or somethin'? Pheeewie. Gag a maggot."

Partly amused, partly bemused, he looked aside. "Erica Dennis. I'm looking for Erica Dennis."

It was as if he'd poked her in the eye with a stick. She jerked back and scowled. "Says who? Who's a lookin'?"

He pulled a card out. "Prince Lowe. I'm from the District Attorney's Office. I have a meeting arranged. Erica is expecting me. Which room?"

"Oooo…" sounded deflated. "Legal stuff, huh? I guess that's okay. Those ladies… the one's a judge."

"Yes. I know. Which cabin?"

"Right yonder there. Number 2."

A glance. "Thank you, Ma'am," and he spun away.

In his walk over he licked his fingers and tried washing off a good dose of his cologne. A lamp behind a drawn curtain invited the mood for love. A quick look around, an ear pressed to the door, curious about tastes in TV, and then a soft rap when he heard nothing.

"Who is it?" sounded as if her voice whispering pillow talk in his ear.

"Prince. Just checking in on you."

The door cracked as wide as the lock chain would allow. She peered with one eye. He had his hand covering his mouth and nose. "I feel better now. You didn't need to come. I don't think I'm in any danger. The judge is a different matter. I realize that. I'm sorry you had to come all this way."

63

He rotated his hand up slightly. "It was no problem. I'm happy to serve. Are you sure you don't want to talk about it? I'm a good listener."

"Did you get hold of someone in Argentina? Who would you call?"

"I didn't call Argentina. I contacted the State Department. Just gave them a heads-up. Someone will be on top of them before they touch down."

Erica sighed heavily. "I hope that's where they went."

"They have to file a flight plan."

"Are you sure? I thought that was just recommended."

"Um…" he went blank for a second. "I'm not a pilot. I guess I'm not sure. Listen… is there anything I can do? Do you need anything at all? I'm genuinely concerned."

Erica showed a slight crack in the chink. "Uh… I can't think of anything. Well… actually… one thing that's bothering me."

"Yes."

"You said suspicious circumstances. You know… regarding McKinney's wife and kids. I found their graves. I know where they're buried. It made me sick to my stomach. If it was suspicious, why wasn't anything done?"

Prince hemmed and glanced aside. He suddenly seemed sentimental and idealistic. Not his preference. A bit appealing to Erica, however. "Could I come in? This is kind of silly, us talking like this through a crack in the door. I mean… we're allies. Aren't we? On the same side of justice?"

"Sorry. I guess I'm overly guarded at the moment."

"I won't take long. I'll explain what I can and get on my way. Just long enough to settle your nerves or answer your questions."

Erica let him in. She was dressed in a white sweat suit. Instantly, she retreated to the far side of a double bed and sat where she'd left her phone. Though he smelled ready to kill on a night club level he acted the perfect gentleman. He peeked out and then left the door ajar before standing at ease where he stood. "Hm… not what I expected," he said.

"Sorry."

"The room. I met the attendant. I thought this would be a dump or something."

"Hah…" a slight guffaw. "I know what you mean. What was it… lots of sass and flavor, but no shame? It's a cozy little room, neat and clean, and no hint of cigarette smoke. That surprised me. I feel like she carted me off to Canada. At least that's the feel."

He approvingly nodded, the simper on his face comfortable, no longer guarding his insecurity. "So… you want to know circumstances. The fact is, the man is a vile malignant growth. McKinney was out of town. He flies a lot. The alleged story is that he was trying to contact the wife and couldn't raise a peep out of her. Calls his buddy Tony Ford who stops to check in. Finds the girls dead in their beds and the wife at the bottom of the basement stairs with a screwdriver in hand. Carbon Monoxide poisoning. The suspicion was… she figured it out and was headed to the basement to try and do something about it. At the time they figured the blow to her head was from a tumble down the stairs. You know… overcome with fumes or something. That seemed to settle the matter. Now, and this may have something to do with what happened to Cary Burk."

"Your predecessor?"

"That's right. If I'd have been here sooner, I could have been on top of it. I found notes in a folder she'd been compiling. Someone had recently contacted her. Said she needed to be savvy and check up on that Kip fellow. Said he and his wife were having all kinds of tiffs. I didn't have a clue what that meant until you came along, raising red flags. I didn't know who Kip was. I checked it out. At the time of the deaths, he was a mere forty-minute flight away. It could have been staged. Someone had tampered with the furnace. Perhaps he rigged it, knowing what it would do. Or he had time to come back and bash her in the head. McKinney and his buddy Tony Ford both suggested… what was the wife's name? Uh…"

"Kallie. Her name was Kallie."

"That's right." He snapped his fingers. "They suggested she would have tried to fix it herself. Sheriff bought it hook, line, and sinker. Burk didn't. At least not after more info rolled in. Do you see why I suddenly need to open a new investigation? It's good you came to me."

Erica didn't say a thing. She sat there with a hand over her mouth, growing pale in the face. Silence lingered for a full thirty seconds. Prince took a step forward. "Listen. I'm merely concerned, but are you sure you feel safe? If not..." he pulled a pistol from behind. "I can leave this with you. It's 9 mm. It's mine."

Erica got an alarmed look. "Isn't that illegal? I thought New York State didn't allow anyone to lend a gun."

"This is a unique situation, wouldn't you say? The only person you'd be in trouble with is me."

"Uhh..." Erica stood and vigorously shook her head. "No. I couldn't. I just couldn't."

"Hey. No problem." He held a hand up. "Merely concerned." He stuffed the pistol back into his belt. "Sorry. I didn't mean to alarm you. I'm trying to emphasize the danger you could be in."

"I understand the danger. It's not me. It's Judge Bailey, right? She's the one to worry about right now."

"Yes. I know. Look... I've embarrassed myself. I've put you in an awkward position. I should go. I don't know what I was thinking. I just don't want to see anything terrible happen to you."

"Thank you. I appreciate your concern. I'll be careful. Thanks for coming. I'll contact you if I have to."

It felt like she was pushing him out the door. He stepped out and paused before closing the door. "Listen... I can't just leave here without saying something more. I uh... I think you're wonderful. You're bright. You're very beautiful. I've been thinking about you ever since I met you. I don't know... I know this might be the most awkward and terrible time. I'm not asking you out right now, but... when this settles... would you consider going out to dinner with me? Something to consider later. Don't make a decision now."

Erica could tell his insecurity. Could read his concern. To be frank, she found it kind of cute. "Yes."

"Yes, you'll go out with me?"

"Yes, I'll consider it. I can't indulge in something like that right now. Not while Judge Bailey is in the circumstance she is in. Understand?"

66

"Of course. That's why I didn't want to put you on the spot now. I'll go. Lock this door and don't fret too much. I feel confident, we'll get to the bottom of things." He stared for a second, winked, and was gone.

Erica rushed to the window, cracked the curtain, and watched. Like a schoolboy he skipped along, clapping his hands in front and then behind, as if the most fortunate one. A warming smile and Erica turned away, wishing the judge felt a fraction of the elation she now felt at that moment.

CHAPTER TEN

YOU SNOOZE, YOU LOSE

The effect was narcotic. Malignancy dulled to the point of complete emotional surrender. Overwhelming. Judge Bailey barely fought the power, pulling her down a swirling drain into the abyss of dark, deep sleep. Somewhere over the Paraná River, the snaking border to Brazil and Paraguay. Over two hours ago.

And now this. Two-twenty-five Ante Meridian and a sudden rattling, jarring her awake into a realm that made little sense. Broken lights flashed by as the Pilatus jostled with the touching down of the nose. It gave her a start. She jumped, reaching out as if bracing for a fall. "Landing?" she groggily muttered. "We're landing."

She fully expected to see a man totally in control when she glanced over. Instead, Tony "Nuts" Ford sat there, leaning forward, an electrical gleam in his eye. He licked his lips. "Made it. Another controlled crash landing and no damage. Crazy, huh?" He glanced over at the Judge and grinned. "Moustamin doux," [Sweet muffin] he added, licking his lips.

The judge wasn't amused. She sat up and looked around. "Buenos Aires?"

"Aeroparque Internacional Jorge Newbery. Bienvenidas, bienvenu, welcome, welcome. Take your choice."

"Oh..." she sighed.

Nothing else was said until they taxied to a stop near a brightly lit hanger. It was Dr. Parker who stepped in and touched her on the shoulder. "Have you ever been to Buenos Aires?"

"No."

"Beautiful city. You'll stay with me. We're in the same hotel as the fellows. Different rooms of course. About a mile away. The taxi will be here soon. The hospital is situated across the street from our hotel. If it's okay Jess, you and I will make a quick stop. I want to check on my patient. I want a preliminary assessment. I'll be able to determine how quickly we can turn around and head back."

"Fine," Judge Bailey said hesitantly. Her thoughts instantly turned to a bookstore. What a waste it would be to come this far and fail in that. She wished no ill will on anyone. Still… she almost smiled, looking up at the doctor.

By the time she crawled out of her seat, her luggage sat waiting. The air was cool. 40 degrees F. perhaps. She now felt a bit insecure, unable to spot Roger "Kip" McKinney anywhere. A gull-wing door stood wide open aft of the wing's edge and this side of an engine. She knew something was going on inside there, but reserved the right of refusal. A breath later a small black taxi with a yellow top raced around the hanger and stopped near the nose. Dr. Parker and Jesse Cole burped out of the jet a moment after and seemed in a hurry. The rush of it caught Judge Bailey in its eddy and pulled her along. One last look over her shoulder and the fear now was that a consuming medical affair would pull Kip from her and leave her aimless and somehow mute in a foreign land.

Buenos Aires was not what she expected. Streets lined with modern buildings ten to fifteen stories tall, intermixed with trees of every kind, and old structures not only gave it a cosmopolitan, but culturally rich milieu. The compacted nature of it certainly gave it a Goliath-an feel. This was the oversized head of a beast and she knew it. In no time they wheeled into a secluded hospital compound and swept up to an entry. "This may be quick. This may take half an hour at the most," Dr. Parker said once she stepped out, looking back in. "You can join us or wait. The driver will remain here."

Conventionally, Judge Bailey felt the need to know. Was there truly a confirming patient here or not? No words, she merely climbed out and then had to hurry to catch up. It was as if they were waiting. A nurse came around a corner, met them, and then without breaking stride escorted them to a second-level ICU where dim lights seemed to cast the shadow of death upon a twenty-year-old sandy-headed girl. To Judge Bailey, the girl looked comatose. Dr. Parker approached, laid a hand on the girl's forehead, and leaned over. "Elisa... I'm Dr. April Parker. We're going to be looking after you. If you can hear me, we're going to get you home."

She then stepped away. "Jess, monitor her vitals for a moment. I'll check the charts."

Dr. Parker stepped out and Jesse occupied himself with the monitors.

"Elisa?" Judge Bailey asked. "Elisa who?"

"Barton. Senator Jack Barton."

"Um..." Judge Bailey nodded knowingly and pursed her lips.

Some fifteen minutes later they had crossed the street and entered a parking garage to what felt four or five stars. Judge Bailey felt slightly sick to her stomach, having imagined these people as some sort of malevolent monsters. It kept her zipped up. They had a seventh-floor room on a fifteen-story building. Dr. Parker went straight for the bathroom and Judge Bailey to the balcony. Consumed briefly with a city far larger than what she had imagined, and then a guilt-ridden surge held her for a moment. That she didn't feel the compassion she ought to for a poor sick girl, right down there... right over there in that tree-enclosed enclave of a hospital enhanced the chill. By the time Judge Bailey turned and stepped back inside Dr. Parker was already in bed and turned away on her side. As quietly as she could, the judge undressed, turned out the light, and crawled into bed.

Her mind felt like it was running, bulldozing heavy mountainous thoughts. A state of mind, which she supposed, would keep her awake. It seemed minutes, but five hours later she awoke, feeling as if she'd never fallen asleep. Eight-thirty sunlight pouring through the sliding glass doors had stealthily broken in and robbed her as well. Intuitively, she sat up and looked for Dr. Parker. Covers thrown aside and no sign of her. Judge Bailey bounced out of bed and went straight to the bathroom. "She's gone. Didn't hear a sound."

She leaned against the sink, staring in the mirror, a fog causing her to feel as if wandering lost in the dimly lit stairway of life. "What's become of me?" she asked. "What's wrong with you, Meghan? Have you become that tainted? Consider the crowd you run with, I suppose." She then considered her suspicions. Her disdain for McKinney. "I guess I needed to focus my grief on something. A moment of psychosis, I guess. Or the revenge of a lonely woman. Or you're well on your way to becoming a professional agitator." That thought brought a shiver. "Or I'm like a cloudy cataract, unable to see clearly, and they're becoming my conscience." She shivered again. She found a full-length terry cloth robe folded neatly on a credenza behind her. She threw it on simply because she didn't like the company any longer. Her single avenue of escape was out onto the balcony.

Instantly, the loud din and stench of city traffic. Or an odd combination of it. Diesel fumes. The aroma of coffee. An odd chemical taste. Like burning rubber. A weird peanut odor. Every sense awakened. Senses she didn't even know she had. She had no interest in looking down and studying a hospital face she only knew in the dark.

"Hey!" a jovial call halted her. "Jackie! What's up, Dear Lady? Or do you prefer Megs? Bonjour!"

It shocked her, but it didn't surprise her to turn and see Tony "Nuts" Ford sitting on the adjacent balcony, leaning back in a chair, his feet propped up on the railing and toasting her with a cup of coffee, or coco, or tea. Perhaps rum. "Which do you prefer? Jackie?"

She glared at him. Hair stood up on her skin.

"Saw it on your luggage. You don't want to go by the cold title of judge all the time, do you? How do you expect to make friends… cher ami."

She was in no mood. Instinct was to curtly jerk her robe in protest and march away. But then Roger "Kip" McKinney appeared, stepping forward. He smiled. "Morning. Buenos Aires takes time to get used to. You'll never forget these smells."

She felt suddenly torn over which part of her she wanted to use, dealing with such a morning. McKinney didn't give her a chance to decide. He stepped to the edge of the separating railings, which one could cover in one giant step, and nodded. "I checked out the bookstore. It's about a mile and a half that way." He nodded east. "Open's in about a half an hour. I just got a call from Dr. Parker. Plans are to fly out at four or five tomorrow morning. We've got time."

It felt like he'd rammed a javelin right between her ribs. It jolted her. "Now! Go now?!"

"No. I figured an hour or more. Whenever you're ready. After breakfast. Whatever?"

"Okay," she started and stopped nervously. "Breakfast?"

"We ordered up," Nuts sounded like a barking dog. "You can go down if you want."

"I'll uh... I'll knock on your door when I'm ready."

At ten minutes after ten Roger McKinney opened his door to find a wary-looking Judge Bailey hidden behind a pair of dark glasses and under an apricot-colored baseball cap. She stood more concerned with activity in a hallway and failed to respond to his mild chuckle. She glanced at him twice before she realized how flippant his smirk was. Her snarky cock of the neck was hard for him to read. "We're not going undercover," he wiggled his fingers. "No need for the getup."

"Says you. You're not the one... I might be... I look like my sister, don't I? These people might not take too kindly... they might think..."

"Relax. No need to explain. Besides... I don't think you're look-a-likes. Sisters, yes. Twins, no."

She stood there wondering whether that was an insult or not when Roger stepped out, took her by the elbow, and escorted her to a brass elevator door. Moments later, a taxi sat parked and waiting under the front portico. The judge slid across the back seat and Roger followed her in. "Librería El Ateneo. No tome una ruta directa. No queremos que nadie nos siga. Esté atento, ¿quiere?" Roger "Kip" McKinney rattled off the words as if a native speaker. The driver gave him a lengthy stare in the mirror and then swept out into bustling traffic as if it were an emergency.

With the judge's suspicious veneer sanded off, she didn't suspect a thing.

They changed lanes several times before hanging a sharp left. Two left turns later and a right and the judge excitedly sat up and looked out the back window. "What are we doing? I know I'm not a native, but this

71

is strange. Are we driving in circles? I thought the bookstore was east. We've gone west, east, and now south. What's he doing?"

"He wants you to feel safe. I told him to take an indirect route. Make sure no one follows."

The judge's heart skipped a beat. She gave him a long stare before sitting back. Looking out a side window now, a sudden thought accompanied an unfamiliar feeling. He said Dana thought she could tame him. He said she viewed him as dangerous. A pirate, a predator to conquer. The judge never saw herself as that kind of woman, but couldn't deny the sudden attraction. Deliberately washing herself in a bath of nonchalance, she seemed indifferent when they pulled up to a busy curb. He climbed out and held the door before paying the man.

Foot traffic was already heavy and the modest flow into the bookstore pulled the two as if a literary vibe. And although the façade reverenced the building's genetic theatrical roots, first impressions were nothing more than a run-of-the-mill bookstore. Kip led her straight to a counter where a pretty, though sad-looking girl was just about to finish up with a customer. The judge removed her note and nudged Kip. "You'll need this. Give her this."

Kip gave her a look of disbelief. "Isn't that evidence? You took evidence. You should know better."

"You tell me, relax. You relax. That's a copy. The sheriff has the original," she chided sarcastically.

A moment later, he leaned an elbow, "Perdona, ¿este nombre significa algo para usted? Quizás puedas buscar ese número de referencia. Nos gustaría información sobre ese libro."

Judge Bailey appeared as if a bodyguard, surveying a crowd as Kip inquired. She didn't see the girl's suspicious and strained look as he passed the note over. No words, she picked up a phone, turned away, and covered the mouthpiece. A second later, it sounded as if bullets thudding against a cement wall before a man suddenly emerged from a side hallway, an agonized look on his face. He was middle-aged and looked like a hard-core book critic. With the same agonized look he met up with the girl, studied the note, every other breath looking over her shoulder and eyeing them. He finally approached and now looked like the falsely accused, pleading his case to the judge.

"Americans?" he asked.

"That's right," Kip answered.

"Who are you? What do you want with this man? How do you know him? Where did you get this name and reference?"

"My sister," the judge sounded bold and insolent. "Is there a problem?"

"Uh…" he stared at the note. "You don't know him?"

"Never met him," Kip said. "This woman here… her sister died. This note was found in her home. We're here to inquire as to what that means."

The girl hotly poked the man in the shoulder. He turned and they briefly and lowly argued a moment. She looked defiant. He looked in need of an enema. He finally shoved her mildly and then turned, giving the note back. "This way," he grumbled, spun on a heel, and walked as if on hot coals—straight to a double escalator where gilded columns stood proud. Kip and the judge quickly followed but trailed far enough that the man seemed to have disappeared. The judge gasped at what greeted them as they rose through what felt like the central oval propylaeum. There they rose into what had once been a grand theater turned bookstore. Three levels of gilded and brightly lit balconies swept around to the stage where a bright red velvet curtain hung parted. "Have you ever…" the judge mulled in disbelief. "They must love their bookstores."

"And books. Where'd he go?" Kip muttered and then instantly spotted him. The man stood half-cowering behind a bookshelf, which sat below the balcony. A nudge and Kip casually walked over. The man seemed in a panic as at first he merely gestured with his eyes. Kip looked at the ceiling.

"Don't tell him I told you," the man said. "Straight up. You'll find him at a table. Second balcony level." That said, he spun and disappeared into another expanse of bookstore.

"Wait here," Kip said.

Judge Bailey stood aghast as he rounded the central oval bookshelf simply to look. The long gray hair of a gray man appeared below a brass railing. Kip met up with the judge, took her by the arm, and led her to a broad carpeted stairwell that seemed to have absorbed and silenced voices just yesterday. Emerging on the second level, Kip held his arm out impeding the judge. "You always assess your target," he whispered. "Give me a minute."

The aging man sat alone at a small round table with an empty chair opposite him. A book lay open before him, a cup of coffee or tea at the ready. His fingers were long and heavily be-ringed. A white, long-sleeved shirt made a scratchy sound when he methodically and didactically turned a page. And despite looking as if he'd never known manual labor, and as if he needed a good dose of penicillin, his long sallow face gave him the air of an apex predator. And while Kip assessed, Judge Bailey felt a pronounced sacrosanct feeling of justice wailing up inside of her. She knew she could never contain that. Not in the face of a man possibly stained by the blood of her sister. No matter the estrangement. Kip thought she clung to his arm out of fear. A need for strength perhaps. Instead, she pushed his arm aside and stormed straight at the man. "Killer!" she uncontrollably cracked. "Are you the killer?"

Kip had lunged but had missed her. A breath later, he stood behind her, holding her by the arms and watching a man unfazed. The man calmly glanced at Judge Bailey. The same at Kip. He sipped as if they weren't there.

"Answer me!"

"Calm down!" Kip coolly pressed his lips to her ear. "Just calm down. Let me handle this. Your emotions have you going down a road you're going to regret."

"I believe you have mistaken me for someone else," the man said in perfect English. His words were clear and courteous, yet completely autocratic. He gesticulated a greeting, pointing at the chair opposite.

"No, thank you!" Judge Bailey curtly barked.

"Yes! Sit!" Kip hissed in her ear. He manhandled her and sat her down. Twice she tried to escape and twice he held her down.

"Perhaps we should introduce and explain ourselves," Kip offered. He had the note. He passed it over. The man studied it briefly.

"The book is not for sale. You're wasting your time."

"You know my sister? You know Dana Bailey? She's dead. Did she die because of that?" Judge Bailey demanded.

74

"I don't know why she would die because of that."

"Did you know her?" Kip asked.

"I've never heard of, nor ever met anyone named Dana Bailey. Perhaps she inquired elsewhere. The book is not for sale."

"What book? What's the name of the book?"

"If you don't know… you will never know. I tell you and I cause myself problems. Maybe I would end up dead like your sister."

"What does that saying have to do with it?" Kip asked. "You know… never taste of death."

"I don't know. Can't you see you're disturbing me? Respect would dictate a more civil approach."

"My apologies," Kip said. "Meghan…" he hesitated and leaned over. "Do you go by Meghan or Jacklyn? Regardless…" he nodded at the man. "The judge is very emotional right now. Perhaps a clause or allowance should be made for her, considering her recent loss."

The man gracefully nodded an odd twinkle in his eye over how unfamiliar the two were.

"You are Antione Banda then?" Kip asked. "That is you?"

He again gracefully nodded. "Could I offer you coffee? Tea perhaps? I prefer coco."

"No, thank you," Judge Bailey wasn't quite as brisk.

"There is nothing we can do here," Kip then said. "We're sorry for bothering you."

"My condolences," Antione Banda bowed.

"No. Just like that? We can't leave just like that," Judge Bailey sounded lost. "But… but…"

"But what are we going to do? This man doesn't know your sister. If she was trying to buy a book, it was not for sale. Consider other avenues. You're thinking this was the only possible lead. Judge?"

"Oh…" the judge moaned, collapsing her forehead into her hand. "What am I thinking? I'm sorry. I'm just so emotional over this." She paused and pleadingly looked at the man. "Forgive me."

Again, a mere gracious nod. He returned to his drink as if the two weren't present. A moment later, Kip had Judge Bailey by the arm, leading her down the stairs. Before they hit the last, Antione Banda picked up his phone. A simple text: Apricot baseball cap.

CHAPTER ELEVEN

AMBUSCADE PARADE

A mile and a half away, in a nondescript small warehouse, this side the Jorge Newbery airport, the air felt tense and the mood a reflection of the dimly lit space. Two men. Dark complexion. Dark clothes. Bearded. Extreme.

Smoke wafted from where the slighter of the two sat at a bench, penetratingly concentrating as he soldered the last wire connection. It was a homemade detonator. The second crouched at the side of a motorcycle, rubbing out the last bubbles to the opaque film he'd just applied to the gas tank. A regular practice and yet he took pride in his work. At that moment a message came over the smartphone just out of reach. Instantly, the one next to the motorcycle looked and stood. The one at the bench reached for the phone. He studied the message briefly and then flashed it at the other. They dropped everything they were doing. They donned black leather jackets and black helmets. While the slighter one stowed an Uzi inside his jacket, the other threw a leg over the motorcycle and revved it to life. A moment later, the two were onboard, the image of a black panther racing for its prey, awaiting them in the heart of the city.

Judge Bailey didn't say a word until they stepped out the front door. "I'm so embarrassed. I couldn't help it. It suddenly came over me and... I never imagined me doing something like that."

Kip inhaled deeply and sighed sharply. "I say we walk. A walk would do us good. I want to expend enough energy so I can fall asleep early. I'll need rest before our early morning flight. We'll need to be up and moving by three. I hope Dr. Parker and Jesse sneak some rest in too. I know what it's like to do several all-nighters in a row."

Talk of a vampire, the judge thought. Maybe he is a vampire. She then studied his calm and pensive face for a moment. No. This is a decent man. She felt a surge of attraction but wasn't sure which personality appealed to her more.

"We won't take the roundabout way we did getting here," Kip added. "I don't see the point. You fine with that?"

No answer, Judge Bailey set off, her eye focused on a row of red awnings stretching out from a pizzeria on the near corner. Neither noticed the shabbily dressed beggar just then milling about tables near the curb. Worse than a beggar no doubt. Homeless. Vermin, searching for a morsel. A crumb. That morning's breakfast. Perhaps a dropped coin or two would mollify him. Kip noticed him when he stayed crouched but rose slightly. The judge didn't notice until he inched between the tables as if a cat heightened at the prospects of a meal. Instinctively, she slowed a bit, situating Kip as a shield.

"Por favor. Un gesto amable para un hombre hambriento," he said when they were still a first-down marker out. He had his filthy hand at the ready. His peppery hair was mussed and matted. His ratty brown jacket and trousers appeared heavy with filth. Like worn motorcycle leathers, hanging stiffly. His boots looked two sizes too big and nicked from a trash bin. The whiskers on his chin appeared as if scraggily remnants from poor nutrition. "Por favor," he coaxed, politely cocking his neck. "Amigo."

Kip had a hand in his pocket, fishing for whatever was there.

"Don't," Judge Bailey snapped. "Don't encourage him. Hunger is a good incentive for change. You're compounding his problem."

He ignored her, depositing all that he had found as they walked by. A block away, assassins tore around a corner and spotted the bookstore. You could hear the growly braaaap of a motorcycle engine echoing among the buildings. At the time, a passing bus impeded their view of Kip and Judge Bailey. The braaaap slowed to a potato-like putter. An occasional rev meant nothing to all but the driver. The assassins couldn't see the exchange suddenly going on between Kip, the judge, and the beggar.

"De vo-man…" the beggar hissed. "Vye she no like me? She like me to die?"

"Hey," Kip spun. "Mind your manners. I gave you everything I had. Leave her alone."

They stood in a brief standoff. Long enough for the bus to pass and long enough for two assassins to drift by. They briefly spotted the judge and her cap. Then—opportune... or not. A second bus abruptly blocked them.

Kip again spun away, prepared to leave the man to his grumblings. Call it fortune. Call it misfortune. Call it the expected fate of the condemned. The instant Judge Bailey turned to follow Kip, the beggar lunged, snatched her cap, and set off running like a gazelle, bounding and dodging foot traffic as if fire hydrants. Kip took off chasing, and the judge intuitively followed but a few steps. A second later, the beggar slid to a stop, and donned the cap, gloating. And the timing couldn't have been better. From a certain point of view. Assassins had made a turn and were now burping back at an indecisive pace. Darting between traffic didn't help. But everyone within blocks around knew exactly when they spotted that hat.

Brrrrrp! Rang out. Brrrrp! Rang out again, storefront windows shattering.

Military instincts sent Kip dodging behind a newsstand. Judge Bailey nearly jumped out of her skin, cringing and then dropping to the ground. Oddly, there was a sudden moment of eerie silence before— braaaaap! The escape of a fleeing motorcycle sounded as much like Uzi bullets as an engine at its limits. Braaaap—braaaap—braaaap resonated and quickly faded within what felt like a heartbeat. Seconds later, Judge Bailey sat there less interested in whether a dead beggar lay bleeding to death or not. She felt more concerned that she was about to get stampeded by a sudden fleeing mob. She rolled, bumping chairs aside, and finally ended up under a table. Next, she sat there stunned at how quickly Kip reached for her.

"Quick! We've got to get out of here! Move! Now!" Kip blurted.

"But... but..."

"No buts... we've got to go. Get out of there," he tugged on her arm. She dug her toes in.

"No! We've got to..."

"No, we don't! Last thing we need is to get tied up in the middle of this. I've got a patient to worry about. I don't need this. Besides…" he paused and looked around. A second shooter wasn't out of the question. No more argument. No more hesitating. Kip reached in, took her by both arms, and yanked her out like she was a bale of dry straw. Her toes barely touched down as he nearly carried her, tugging her by the hand, racing diagonally, dodging through halted traffic, through an intersection, and north for an entire block. Judge Bailey looked as if a rider bouncing off the back of a horse and then snagging its tail the way he carted her around a corner. Lungs and thighs already burning, she gasped as Kip pulled and then tucked her into a shop alcove. He held her back, looking out and assessing their predicament. Some pedestrians were still fleeing the area, and others rushing to the scene. He didn't realize the judge's state of mind until he felt her sobbing against his shoulder. He turned. She smothered her face against his chest.

"It's okay. We'll be okay," he tried to soothe. She sobbed for a moment. "Why are they doing this? That was meant for me. Wasn't that meant for me?"

Kip rubbed her shoulder. "I don't know. I highly doubt it. Why would you be a target?"

"I don't know. Something to do with Dana. What on earth did she get herself into?"

"I don't know, but we need to keep moving. We need to get off the street. We'll work our way back."

"I can't run anymore. I don't run. My legs are on fire."

"You can walk, can't you? I'll carry you if I have to."

That seemed too much. Judge Bailey pushed away and stumbled forward like she knew where she was going. Thirty minutes later, they quietly and pensively rode an elevator to the seventh level. She refused her door and clung to him as they walked in to find Tony "Nuts" Ford in a bad mood. He had company. Across the room, situated smugly, the young fellow in an expensive suit sat back with a leg crossed. "Finally!" Nuts barked. He glared briefly at Kip before shooting a look of contempt at the man. "You sit there and keep your mouth shut," Nuts pointed at the man.

"Hey…" the fellow gestured, throwing his hands in the air.

79

"What gives?" Kip sidled up to Nuts, eyeing the fellow.

"We've got a winner here. You just saved his life. I was about to toss him off the balcony onto his head. What an irritating brat."

"Who? Who is this?" Kip whispered.

Nuts was even quieter. "Moron from the U.S. Embassy. He claims he's here to help arrange the preparation and disposition of our recently departed. The wife and kids are dead he says. Let me tell ya… he's dumber than swamp mud. Couldn't tie his laces if they were Velcro. Uncle Gordon runs the embassy. Shows you what you get when you mix crony nepotism and the gene pool. He's been trying to console me for the last ten minutes. He doesn't have the slightest clue."

"What did you tell him?"

"I keep telling him to call Senator Barton's office. His daughter ain't dead. He won't even call over to the hospital to find out. I don't know how to talk sense to him. And where he gets the idea of wife and kids blows my mind."

"Name?"

"I don't remember. Hell… I don't care."

Kip passed Judge Bailey off to Nuts and approached the fellow like he would a horse with ill-respect. "Name's Roger McKinney," he extended his hand. "I think you're misinformed. We have no dead here. We're transporting a patient back to the States tomorrow. All the paperwork was in order. Elisa Barton. Senator Jack Barton's daughter."

"Hey…" the dull-looking fellow jumped to his feet. "I'm just following orders. Said to get over there and help with the arrangements."

"What's your name?"

"Bob Phillips."

"And your uncle is Gordon Phillips?"

"Spot on."

"Well… go back and tell Uncle Gordon to let the dead bury the dead. We're all alive." He then turned and snapped his fingers. "Nuts. Get Dr. Parker on the phone. Make sure we're on solid ground."

"Uncle Gordy is out of town," Bob muttered under his breath. "I'm not a kid."

Nuts gave the fellow a caustic glare before turning away and making the call. Bob became nervous as Kip stood there inspecting him mildly.

A few seconds later. "No problems," Nuts grunted. "Still on track to fly out early. Says Elisa is actually in good spirits."

"See… no problems here," Kip said. "Why don't you get on your way? You're wasting your time here."

"Hey… don't shoot the delivery boy. That's all I can say. Hope ya have a nice flight."

Like a wet puppy, the fellow sidled out of the room sheepishly.

"That was weird," Nuts said after the fellow closed the door.

Kip rubbed his jaw, thinking.

At this point, Judge Bailey scooted over to the bed, a handout, like she was ready to faint. A deep breath and she sort of floated away as she slowly fell back.

CHAPTER TWELVE

BREAKING RANKS

At precisely four-o-five in the blasphemous A.M. Judge Bailey stood watching as they hefted a stretcher through the gull-wing door of the Pilatus. Someone had cracked a joke to either lighten the mood, or they already were in a good mood. There was a wave of light laughter that poured out of the door. Either way, it felt the trigger for Judge Bailey. With no invite, she climbed aboard and went straight for the co-pilot's seat. At first, it was mesmerizing, with all the colorful screens and buttons. And then it seemed terrifying, imagining the mind that had to know what it all meant. A breath later she quaked in her skin.

"Ho…" Kip McKinney hooted upon finding her there. "You flying us out of here?"

81

"I thought it would be okay. You let me ride up here coming down."

"No problem. I'd rather have Nuts up here while we go through the pre-flight checklist."

"Oh... should I move?"

"No. It will be alright. This thing is designed for a single pilot. He comes along for several reasons. Especially on long flights. No way on earth I'd fly this far without him."

Judge Bailey seemed intrigued by the early hour and the steady activity of an airport. She pressed the back of her fingers to her lips and watched as several different vehicles sped about. "Jacklyn," she said.

"Sorry."

"Jacklyn. You can call me Jacklyn. You asked yesterday. I just thought you should know."

Kip smiled. "Good morning, Jacklyn. I was getting tired of that judge stuff. So stuffy and impersonal."

The urge was to explain herself. How few friends she had. How her work occupied nearly every thought. How... and then it didn't seem right. None of that would matter to him. Or he'd accept it in his usually charming way. A few minutes later. "You must find this enthralling," she said. "I can't even tell what a single one of these buttons means."

"Hah-hah... that would take a while."

"You find it exciting though, right?"

He paused a moment. She could see the magic in his face. "On the flight deck... that's where it's exciting. One last check to make sure the ejection seat is armed and your blood starts pumping. Might just be a day ULT... unit level training sortie. Doesn't matter. The plane captain releases you. Chalks and chains are removed and you start rolling when your director tells you to pull forward. The faster he waves his arms the faster you go. PC gives you the thumbs down, telling you to stop and I would settle into a calm frame of mind that's hard to describe."

"What if he never gives you the thumbs down?"

"You get a thumbs down. They've got a million things to orchestrate. You drop your hook so they can inspect it. The last thing you want is to come back without a functioning hook. The director comes back, thumbs up, thumbs down, overall thumbs up and you're looking good. Closed fist keeps you pat."

"Zoom, you're off?"

"Hardly. You watch your yellow shirt... your director. He'll maneuver, calculating where he wants to direct you. Gives you the brakes release signal and he pulls you forward."

"Waving of the hands?"

"Yes, by waving of the hands. Before you move make sure you have wing clearance and then pull forward. He'll direct you right or left depending on whether you're starting port or starboard and then he points to another director and you focus on her or him. If another pilot is primed and ready, the jet blast deflector will be up. If it is, he'll usually direct you right up there close. I always preferred Catapult Three. Good and centered."

Jacklyn didn't remove her eyes.

"You get a bit of a bumpy ride crossing over the arresting gear and then it's usually a short wait. All depends. Might have a plane prepped and ready to go on catapult four. Lots of variables. Nevertheless, the adrenaline builds as you flip the wing fold switch and watch your wing tips lower, spreading into place. You're good to go. I flew the EA dash 18G Growler. I could tell you all about the JBD... that's jet blast deflector, but I don't think that would help. You wait. If JDB is up, your plane bounces around in the turbulence when the plane ahead of you goes mill or max power. A moment later he roars away. Almost instantly the JBD lowers, a mist of steam wafting across the deck, making you think heaven just gobbled your buddy up."

He paused, a dreamy look causing him to bite his lip.

"Colored shirts scurry. In no time they have you positioned properly. A green shirt—holdback operator—hooks up the holdback fitting to the nose gear and cleat. That puts the plane into tension. Launch bar over and into the shuttle. All that. You'd think that would be the moment of intense buildup, waiting on that catapult. Mentally, I'm already over the water. Wipeout signal, run-up signal. Check with the shooter. He points down range. Bam! Here we go."

"Zoom."

"Roar. Next thing you know, after getting hammered back into your seat by this immense, incredible power, the world goes still and it's suddenly all in your hand."

"Incredible."

"Insane. You take care of the sortie. Next thing you know the dream is coming to an end and you've got to circle this bug and somehow land on it. If the seas are choppy the deck will pitch. One second it looks like a nice-sized hot dog bun. No problem. Other times it appears as thin as a dime. Sooner or later you've got to use your best judgement. How it happens… beats me. Somehow I honed in and put her down. I remember less about that than anything. No buildup. Bam you're down."

"Miss it? This must be dull, flying this."

"No." He smiled, patting the dash. This suits me just fine. Better than fine actually. Wouldn't go back. Loved it, but wouldn't go back. Age has an effect."

"Hey… lover boy," Tony "Nuts" Ford poked his head in and nudged Kip in the shoulder. "All set back here. Whenever you're ready." He sort of sneered at Jacklyn and, unnoticed, returned to buckle in. The only thoughts going through Jacklyn's mind… she hoped the flight home would take far longer than the flight coming down.

5400 miles away, Erica Dennis couldn't take it anymore. "Augh!" she grunted, throwing the sheets aside. She sat up, dropped her feet off the side of the bed, and rested her elbows on her knees and her head in her hands. "This is worse than a kidney stone," she grumbled. A breath later she stumbled for the bathroom. She didn't want to look in the mirror. Didn't want to squint and didn't want to know how misery looked at this ungodly hour. A shot of water and she punched out the light with a stiff finger. Straight for the small window on the back. A quick scan. Night lights at the gas station. Black as coal at Bill's Diner. Across to the front window where she knelt in case some peeper sat parked out there somewhere. A part in the curtains and the only life came from Twyla's green, red, and white neon retreat sign. It had a little red cabin and green pine trees. Flickering pine trees.

Next, her last option. The one she hated and didn't want to, but just had to do. A gigantic undertaking in her mind. Back to the nightstand. Plopping down, her hands were already shaking when she picked up her phone. It felt like her eyeballs quivered, hoping to see and not see a new message. It took several blinks before she finally realized no new messages. She opened the last.

"Erica…" she read out loud. "Prince here. Just wanted to touch base one last time. I will contact the State Department tonight. I'll instruct them to contact me about statuses. Keep your spirits up. No matter what happens, I'll call you tomorrow. I like this quote whenever the world seems darkest. 'The wound is the place where the light enters you.'- Rumi."

She dwelt on it for a minute. She turned the phone over and sat it down. Flopping back onto her pillow, she laid her forearm across her forehead. "If Meghan ends up dead, it will be the end of me. I couldn't live with that. The stupid nut. Why would she do something so stupid?" A deep sigh and she winked a fresh round of tears. "This is such a waste of time. I'll never sleep again in my life if this doesn't come to an end soon." Another deep sigh and she clenched her toes, thinking she could expend enough energy to knock her out.

Five hours later, as the clock ticked exactly to the eight o'clock hour, she climbed out of bed and shimmied into a fresh pair of skinny jeans before pulling a white sweat top over her head. Dressy sandal flats on and she paused at the door as if expecting the knock that abruptly came. The instinct was to ask. Instead, she tugged the door open. There Twyla stood, dressed up, probably elegantly in her book, cheap redneck flare by Erica's account. Erica had to cover her mouth to stop the guffaw. She held it all in.

"Mornin' Darlin'," Twyla batted her lashes. She had a pair of leopard-spotted slippers on, fishnet stockings, and a red dress with big white buttons and fringe across the breasts. A western cut and, thank God, not too short nor plunging at the neck. The way her hair twirled around her head, it appeared as if a hat in and of itself. "Uh…" she sounded nosey Nellie curious, poking her head in and looking. "That feller was a smeller. He didn't sneak around back and spend the night, did he? I'm chargin' ya cut rate. Wouldn't be fair if ya shack'em up in here, ya know."

Erica smiled. "Sorry. He just stopped by to discuss a legal matter. Here and gone."

"Ugh!" Twyla sounded disappointed. Sounded like a good hefty catch of gossip just got off the hook. "Well…" she closed one eye.

"Treat ya to breakfast then. When's your friend comin' back? You didn't specify how many days ya want the place."

"I'll be staying until I hear from her. She had to fly to South America."

"Yeah... with that cowboy. Him and his loony bird sidekick. Gone wraslin' up a who-knows-what. Don't trust those two. Ya know, I don't trust those two." She pressed a finger to the side of her nose, somehow taking on the image of Mrs. Hubbard from Murder on the Orient Express. "Oh! Yes! Somethin' wrong 'bout those two. Talkin' to the dead, those two. My ass." She scratched. "I'd bet my grits they séance'd themselves into a hunch-a-bunch a nonsense. Had themselves a vision. Who knows what... that younger crowd? I'm not stupid. They smoke and chew all kinds of stuff. Mushrooms maybe. And the pills! You heard 'bout all the weird kind of pills out there nowadays. Lordy! Shouldn't be a bit surprised with those two. Stab 'em and slab 'em. Heard that's their motto. Yup. Scared ta death a those two. Scared up to my Billy bones, I am."

"Mrs. MacDonald... Twyla!" Erica halted her with a politely curt snap. Also grabbing her by the arm. "Please! I'm worried enough. The more you go on, the sicker I feel. Do you have to do that?"

Twyla looked shocked. Never had anyone responded like that when she had something juicy to tell. She closed one eye and studied Erica briefly. "Breakfast then? We'll mosey over to Bills. You must get sick a lockin' yerself up in this room the way you do. Granted... I know I make 'em cozy. But... ya need some air, girl."

"Oh... okay. But I need a minute. I need to make a phone call. I can't go anywhere unless I make a phone call."

Twyla looked like she just got a big kiss on the lips from her favorite—George Clooney. "Whoopee," she blurted. "You make your call. I'll shuffle on over. See ya soon, Girlie. Don't dawdle long." She reached and patted Erica on the rump before hurrying away.

A second later, Erica dialed Prince Lowe, more out of desperation than anything else.

"Is this call really necessary," Lowe answered. "I'm due in court and I don't have much time."

"Prince. I'm sorry. Erica Dennis here. I need to know. Have you heard anything? I'm worried sick."

You could hear the change in his demeanor. "Erica. Sorry, I was brusque. I'm under pressure. I called. I called the State Department. I didn't get a very clear response. I know they sent someone, but they seem confused over what happened. Listen… I'm driving… I'm going to be late. I'll figure something out. I've got some appointments and I can be there later today. It might be eight o'clock or so, but I'll come."

"I need to know if she's alright. That's all I need to know. Don't worry about the details or this or that. Just find out if she's okay. Can you do that?"

"Guaranteed. Try to stay calm. Rest assured someone is working on this."

"Yes. I know. Thank you. Sorry to bother you."

"No bother at all. I'll talk to you soon," he said and hung up.

She stared at her phone for a minute and then exhaled. "Oh, Twyla," she groaned. "I hope you find something else to talk about. I need to keep my mind off of things. Lord help me," she said and locked her door.

Breakfast took two hours. And it wasn't because Twyla was lonely. Every person that walked in, she pulled into whatever the conversation, which thankfully, revolved around mosquito abatement, the price of eggs, and bad haircuts down there at Sylvia's Clips and Curls. Sympathetic looks from Bill helped, but it all finally ended. Later, lunch was light. A walk in the afternoon. No dinner. When her phone rang just after seven P.M. she was sure it was Prince Lowe. Didn't even look at the ID. "Prince!"

"Prince? No. Erica… it's Meghan. How are you?"

"Oh, my God. Meghan! I've been worried sick. Where are you? Are you okay?"

"Fine. Just fine. You sound awful."

"I am awful. Well… I have been. I'm suddenly feeling better. What happened? Where are you?"

"We're currently at Ronald Reagan International in DC. We're passing our kidney transplant patient off to another medical crew. She's going to Georgetown. Should be home in under an hour. You'll come to meet me, won't you?"

"Oh, my word of course. Are you sure you're safe?"

"Of course. Why wouldn't I be?"

"These people aren't what you think they are. I've learned some terrible things. He killed his wife. He killed his daughters."

"What?!"

"Yes. The McKinney guy. They're investigating him here. They've just opened a new investigation. They got new information. This is all unraveling. I thought for sure I'd never see you again."

"I don't believe you. I can't believe you. You wouldn't believe what I've just been through, but there is no way on earth this man is a killer. He couldn't be."

"I think that's part of his lure. He's got a lot of people deceived. Don't say anything. Just get home as soon as you can. Don't lead on that you know. I'll fill you in when you get back. I'll leave now. I can't stand to just sit here another second. Please, be careful."

There was a short pause before Meghan haltingly said, "Bye," and hung up. The second she did she looked at Kip and Nuts and how they were kindly granting well wishes to Elisa Barton. Just as they were loading her into the back of an ambulance.

Erica instantly dialed Prince Lowe and got the answering message. "Prince," she rattled. "Sorry. Something has come up. I can't meet you tonight. Don't come. I'll call you as soon as I can. It might be later tonight. I'm not sure. Thanks. Bye?"

CHAPTER THIRTEEN

Dance of the Dead

Stunning golden rays from a setting sun cut through the treetops and warmed Erica Dennis' back as she stood there waiting for the plane to appear. Arms folded, she nervously paced left a few steps, and then back. Third spin on her heel she spotted the landing light just before the Pilatus turned slightly, suddenly becoming a reflector in the sky. Moments later, the sleek little wonder glided in faster than she expected and touched down, bringing a crashing wave of relief. Suddenly, she couldn't move, anxious on one hand, elated on the other. This was exactly where the attendant told her to wait and it was the ideal spot to keep her distance and yet see with perfect clarity, two dark-spectacled devils as they brought the plane to a stop. She refused to look at them. Even after Tony "Nuts" Ford lowered the stairs and then stepped aside, granting Meghan deference.

Erica held her emotions knit as Meghan disembarked. Instantly, Meghan spotted her and rushed to meet her. They embraced. "Thank you, God," Erica whispered. "Thank you, God in heaven."

"Me too."

Erica pushed her away, searching her eyes. Searching for a confirming word of how awful these men were. "They threatened our lives. I can't believe it. I'm sure he's behind Dana's death. I just have no idea how they're going to handle it," Judge Meghan said.

"Then why are you flying with them? I don't get it. You could have fled. They contacted the State Department to come to your aid."

Meghan's face turned into a cheeky pout of confusion. "Are we talking about the same thing?"

"Of course. I don't know why they don't have someone here to arrest them."

"You're talking about Kip and Nuts?"

"Of course. What are you talking about?"

89

"Banda. We met that Banda fellow in a bookstore in Buenos Aires. Next thing we knew, someone tried to gun us down on the street. I don't know if I'd be alive if it wasn't for Roger."

"What?" Erica's voice elevated.

"Yes."

"But... but... this isn't making sense." She shut up when she noticed Nuts crossing over with Meghan's suitcase.

"Ladies," he muttered going by. He now stood next to the Volvo giving them a get-with-it look. "Been a long day. Who's got the keys to this thing?"

Erica didn't realize she did for a few unbearable seconds. As if prodded by a shock she suddenly flinched and fished the key out of her pocket, simultaneously popping the trunk. He stowed the suitcase, closed the lid, and winked going by. "Thank you, Nuts," Meghan said. "Enjoyed all your stories."

Erica glared at her in disbelief. "Drive," Meghan said and crawled into the passenger's seat. Erica still had an incredulous look on her face as she began to pull away. "I don't know what's been going on around here, but I think I've just met some of the most decent, remarkable people I've ever met. Did you know that was a medical-mercy flight? We retrieved Senator Jack Barton's daughter. Elisa. Failing kidneys. She might be under the knife by now. Transplant. All on his dime. He pays for all of it. Well... not the operation. Everything else though. Kip's a very amazing man."

"What? I can't believe I'm hearing this."

"I couldn't believe it either. He is different than I had imagined. I've never seen strength like that."

"He's a killer. They're investigating him."

They exchanged a juxtaposed look. Erica then went on and told her how she'd met with DA Prince Lowe. How they suspect McKinney is somehow involved in DA Burk's death. How he's suspected of a strange relationship with one, Mavis West. And how, worst of all, they're looking into new leads regarding the death of his wife and daughters. Those words caught Judge Bailey like a knife to the heart. Finally, she produced the kind of look Erica wanted.

"I'm serious. I saw their gravestones. Kallie, Katie, and Kami. All died on the same day. Carbon monoxide poisoning. They suspect he tampered with the furnace and ran off on one of those flights of his. They were having trouble. Who knows how he kept it a secret, but Prince says DA Burk was compiling a folder and evidence when she then up and died suspiciously."

No words. Judge Bailey sat there shaking her head.

"You don't believe me?"

"I don't. I don't think there is any way on earth."

Erica got a part black, part chagrined look on her face. "You like him. You have feelings for him. That's what's wrong. You're not thinking straight."

"Oh… don't be silly. I have new eyes, however. I see things perfectly well. Whatever they believe, there is an explanation. I'm sure of it."

"We'll see. We need to meet with the DA. FBI is now investigating too. You're a judge. Wait until you see the evidence. Please don't fall for his cunning. They say psychopaths are experts at deception. They manipulate on the pro tour and then strike once their victim is most vulnerable."

"I think I understand where you're coming from, but I'm sure you're wrong," Meghan calmly and patiently said. "The concern here, is Antione Banda. What do we know about this Red fellow? Those are the concerns. It's my sister who's dead and they're most likely the ones responsible. And why on earth would they try to cover it up the way they did? And please recognize these people probably haven't dealt with a crime scene like this before. I grant them leeway."

"Well… that may be true, but it's more complicated. Who knows if McKinney played a role or not? For me… I think he did. I know he did. Something tells me you're wrong."

Judge Bailey stayed quiet, watching Erica for some time. "This is what we'll do. I want you to get to know him better. We'll walk in there tomorrow, make ourselves a nuisance if we must. I doubt that will be necessary. He'll take no offense and let us observe whatever we please. I'm confident in that."

"Really? That's what you want to do?"

"Absolutely."

Erica hesitated briefly. "Under one condition."

"Name it."

"Talk to Prince Lowe first. Hear what he has to say and then decide."

"Fine." Meghan pulled out her phone. "Number."

Judge Bailey learned absolutely nothing from Prince Lowe that she didn't already know in the time it took to drive the rest of the way to Kermit Falls. She was just hanging up when the old factories on the edge of town came into view. "Do me a favor," Meghan said. "Drive by Dana's house. I want to see if police tape is still up."

"You want back in the house?"

"Eventually. I'm in no rush. I just don't feel like going back to Twyla and her cozy little rooms."

"Aren't you tired? Don't you want to go to sleep?"

"I feel oddly refreshed. I slept on the plane. It's a long way."

"We might be here a lot longer than expected, won't we?"

"I'm afraid so. I told them I wouldn't be back for three weeks. I had it coming. So did you. What else am I going to do?"

"I can think of better things than this," Erica sounded distressed.

"I know. I just hope we're here long enough to sort things out."

Those were their last words before they slowly crept up on Dana's home. Erica locked on to the police tape and how it gently fluttered in the evening air. She expected to note the judge morosely staring as well. Instead, she sat there staring off where horses grazed and a modest ranch house sat secluded among a few giant oak trees. Erica pulled in front of a rutted drive and stopped, hoping to break Meghan's gape. A breath later, and it seemed to have the intended effect. The judge opened her door and dropped a foot out. "I never noticed that."

"What?"

"She has a little garage. She has a car. No police tape. I guess we can look."

"Maybe it blew away. Wouldn't they cordon off everything?"

"Or they're finished up out there. We'll just peek. We won't touch anything. I want to know what she drove."

"Ugh!" Erica grunted with frustration when Meghan crawled out and walked like she'd abandoned all sense. A moment later, Erica stood there more interested in knowing if that Ick creature had an eye pegged to them and conniving some weird ritual for their deaths. That lasted but a few breaths.

"Erica! Come over here. Look at this."

"Ugh! She's gone nuts. She'll get herself kicked off the bench acting like this." A quick look around, checking for surveillance, and then Erica trotted, hoping to end this nonsense.

"Look at that. A cute little yellow Bug. A VW Bug. I like it. I like her more all the time."

"This is crazy, Meghan. Let's not stand here. You've seen it. Let's go."

"Oh, be patient. I'm not hurting anything."

"How do you know there's no evidence in here?"

"Hm…" Meghan mulled. "Right. I'm just so anxious to learn more. Everything I see I connect. Do you know what the separation and now getting to know her is like?"

"Of course not. Let's go."

Meghan complied. Not in the way Erica hoped, but she did move. Right past the Volvo and down the road. Erica couldn't believe it. Meghan was marching across the road as if headed straight for Roger McKinney's home.

"She's gone nuts. She has gone nuts." And then sense must have knocked her in the head. At least from Erica's perspective. The judge angled straight for the white vinyl fence where two monster black willow trees stood. There she stopped, put one foot on the bottom rail and elbows on the top. This is where Erica caught up. "Now what?"

"I just wanted to see. Those horses are beautiful. What kind of horses are those?"

"How would I know? This is about as close as I've ever been to a horse."

The two stayed quiet, the disappearing light of day masking the variety of glistening coats. It took less than a minute before a buckskin and red roan began ambling their way over. Erica stood ten feet back when they nudged up near Meghan. "You sure that's safe?" Erica groused. "They're huge." Meghan simply froze, waiting to see what the horses would do. A good sniff is all she got. Big beautiful brown eyes begged her before she dared gently stroke a cheek with the back of her fingers. The closest Erica got was out of reach of a curious nose. There they stayed. Connecting. Gaining confidence. Erica, certain Meghan stood there staging this until that sponge, Kip came home, held her distance. It got dark. Almost too dark to see before Meghan merely turned away and strolled for the car.

Best to keep your mouth shut, Erica already knew. And so, in silence, they turned around and headed into town. It was just after making the S-turn when headlights swept off of Main and came toward them. The offering on the plate seemed too good. Too perfect. The timing was ideal when the lights swept into the funeral home's drive and drove into the back lot. Erica instantly pulled to the curb and stopped. A quick doleful exchange before Erica grabbed Meghan's arm. "That's him. I don't know what he's doing, but I'm sure it's probably not right. I'm going to see what he's doing."

"Erica?" an alarmed tone in Meghan's voice. "Don't be foolish. It's his business. I don't see any problem here."

"Well… maybe you don't, but I do. I've heard enough. Where there's smoke, there's fire. That's always the case. I'm going over there."

Before Meghan could get another word out, Erica jumped out and ran for the shadows. A breath later, Meghan piled out thinking she could catch her. Younger legs and nimble toes had Erica out of sight before Meghan got halfway up the drive. In the back, she found what looked foreign even though familiar with the lot. A covered ramp. A short set of stairs. Two broad doorways lit up by a cloudy sconce.

Legs still ached from the prior day's escape as she climbed the stairs. The first door had the warning: Authorized personnel only. The second door stood closed, but ajar. Judge Meghan crouched, wedged a finger in, and leaned. She could see a sliver of light cutting Erica's face in half where she lay on the floor, the slice coming from a slightly cracked prep-room door. "Psst," Judge Meghan hissed a stern look on her face, motioning.

A mere defiant shake of the head out of Erica.

Judge Meghan looked left, looked right, and hated what she was doing. Staying crouched, she pushed her way in, eased the door closed, and soon knelt, straddling over the top of Erica. She pressed her lips to Erica's ear. "Please. Let's get out of here. Don't do this."

Another defiant snap of the neck. Judge Meghan peeked into the prep room. There Roger stood with his back to them, just then donning a white lab coat. He was humming. She didn't want to but saw no choice. She edged the door slightly. Curiosity now had the best of her. White cupboards, white cabinets, a big white cast iron embalming table. A stretcher with a maroon cover. An aluminum dressing table, a sink, and an embalming machine. And Roger McKinney now standing over the stretcher, gingerly unzipping the cover. He paused, rested a latex-gloved hand, and looked down on his victim.

"Sarah, Sarah, Sarah," he dolefully said. "Why are you doing this to me? Always when I feel beat. Always when I need rest. Can't the dead leave me alone just once? Sarah… you hearing this?" He paused. "One last dance. Jan said you were upset because you didn't get one last dance. Sorry about that. I ought to show up one day. I'd like to see what one of those rest-home dances looks like. But…" he sighed, "can't help when you suddenly get sick, can you? Oh, well. I'll play you some music anyway."

He stepped to the counter and seconds later Bob Segar's soulful voice seemed perfectly apropos. If you were in the mood for "Night Moves."

Stepping back he unzipped the cover all the way and positioned the stretcher next to the table before tenderly moving the frail little white-haired thing over. She wore a pink nightgown. The first sign of humanity—for Erica—was when he sort of sashayed moving the stretcher out of the way. Next, was when he placed a towel over Sarah's body before slipping her nightgown off. Couldn't see a thing when he then blocked the view. There were a couple of popping sounds before he spoke again. "You look about right. We'll put a little more fullness in your cheeks as we go."

By the time he rounded to the head of the table a new song played— Bob Seger and "Still The Same." Roger turned a faucet on and water began to flow from a hose attached to the table. A breath later, he wetted her hair before applying a good dose of shampoo. This song appealed to him. Not only did he begin to sing, but he began to sway from side to side. Seconds later, he was fully into, two-stepping and jigging, singing at the top of his lungs. Shampoo flowed like a slow white waterfall as he stepped around, took Sarah by the hand, and ducked under, pirouetting.

"Oh, God," Erica then whispered. "I can't watch this anymore."

She pushed back, pushing Judge Meghan off of her. Eyes full of tears, she covered her mouth to keep the sob in. Judge Meghan took her by the arm and pulled. Seconds later, the two crept out and closed the door silently. "Now do you believe me?" Judge Meghan asked.

Erica needed a moment to compose herself. "He's sure got a nice butt, doesn't he?" she whispered lightly. A cathartic muffled laugh and Erica had Judge Meghan by the hand, leading her back for the car. Now, that is when the trouble started. A wholly different and unexpected night dance. They turned the corner and merely one step into the dark. A head-on collision with a solid, barrel-chested man not only sent Erica tumbling backward but left Judge Meghan wishing she owned and carried a gun.

CHAPTER FOURTEEN

DEAD ENDS AND NEW ENDS

No sooner did Judge Meghan crouch to Erica's aid and a second man appeared, the silhouette of a pistol gripped in his right hand and appearing just as nasty and frightening as bullets shattering Buenos Aires peace. She wanted to scream, but couldn't because of what felt like 15 tons of jet sitting on her chest. A breath later devilish noises emanated from the two. A low grumbling. A steamroller, crushing-skulls kind of sound. Skulls full of all the meats and juices sound. Incoherent grumblings about the fastest route to hell are what she thought she was hearing. Until Erica's clear voice somehow disconnected the horror. "Yes, yes," she said. "It's Judge Bailey. Don't shoot us!"

Next thing Judge Bailey knew, one of the shadows stepped into the light and leaned down, taking her by the arm. She was still too frightened to resist. "Ma'am," she finally recognized his voice as human. "Judge... you shouldn't be here. You're interfering with our work."

"Huh?"

"Judge..." the man flashed his FBI ID and badge. "Names Agent Reed. Eddie Reed. We'd like to get you out of here. You're interfering with a surveillance operation. Do you mind?"

It took a moment for the words to register. The moment they did, her heart sank, not wanting them to be true. "He's innocent," she vacantly said. "He's innocent."

"Ma'am. Please."

She took his hand and stood up. The two agents put their heads together briefly. "Could we go somewhere and talk? We've got ears and eyes on this. We just don't want you interfering."

"We've got a hotel room," Erica sounded oddly justified.

"Yes, we know. Could we follow you there and discuss things? We've been wanting to talk to you for a couple of days now."

The judge's walk to her Volvo felt the Green Mile trudge.

Agent Eddie Reed sounded Brooklyn-bred. Shorter, street tuff, a nose bent sideways. Short dark hair. Agent Shaun Duggan felt homespun. A big man with sandy red hair and solid jowls. He had a twinkle in his eye and a boyish grin. The accent sounded like Carolina Coast. "Judge," Agent Duggan drawled, the moment they walked into the room. "You're a hard one to track down. You've had your phone off."

"She's been to South America," Erica sounded a bit infantile. A bit accusatory.

"So?" Judge Meghan glared at her.

97

"Well… shall we sit and get comfortable? This will take a little while," Duggan scraped a hand through his hair.

"We're not under investigation. What do you want?" The Judge said.

"Of course, you're not. We're investigating your sister's death. And a few other annoying things."

"Oh… right."

"If it involves Kip… well, she's rather protective of him," Erica said. "Don't drop it on her like a wrecking ball."

The agents exchanged a deadpan look. Agent Reed pulled two chairs over. The two agents stood there, waiting for the ladies to sit. They both plopped onto the nearest bed.

"First of all," Duggan began, leaning on his knees, "anything you can tell us about your sister?"

"We've been estranged ever since high school. I didn't even know she was alive. It's a shame because I think we would have got along brilliantly."

"I'm sorry. This trip…"

"Yes, yes… this trip. Someone tried to kill us. You have no investigative authority overseas. I don't even know if that matters to you."

"We heard about things. Didn't know you were a target. What happened?"

Judge Bailey stared at Erica. "Antione Banda. I don't know what my sister's connection was, but he's behind it. All of it. He has to be. We went down there, inquiring about a book, and the next thing you know bullets are flying everywhere."

"And what did the authorities down there say about that?"

A guilty look was shared with Erica. "Well… we didn't talk to authorities. Kip… Roger knew we couldn't get involved. We were right there but didn't see enough to identify anything. We had to get Senator Burton's daughter back. Kidney transplant. He flies for a medical charity or something. Check with Georgetown."

"Look… to be honest. There is little we can do about that. Argentine Federal Police have jurisdiction. Unless they invite us."

"Well… that's who killed my sister. Has to be."

"Over a book?"

"Didn't you get the note? There was a note with his name and number. Didn't you get that?"

"Yes. We have it."

"What about the fangs?" Erica said. "Did he send those?"

"We have no idea. Had the lab check them out. Fangs came from a Gaboon Viper. You find them in the sub-Saharan savannas and rainforests of Africa. Analysis of the envelope indicated an African origin as well. The stamp on it is Costa Rican. Somebody is well traveled."

"You're investigating Roger McKinney then, aren't you?" Erica said. "He flies a lot."

Agent Duggan leaned back in his chair and looked at Agent Reed. Reed sat up straighter. "Someone loves fishing with red herrings. We've dealt with him many times. We're just appeasing the man for now."

"What? What do you mean?"

"You're familiar with Prince Lowe, aren't you? The DA?"

"Of course. Are you investigating for him?"

"The man abuses his position. He's annoyingly dull. Something comes along and he uses… or maybe better said, fabricates suggests, or manipulates facts all in an attempt to win favor. Has he made a pass or anything?"

Erica now went flush. She didn't say a word.

"We've heard it all and know what he's been feeding you."

"I talked to him too. I didn't believe him," Judge Bailey said. "Are those lies?"

"Well… not exactly. There's some truth. Attorney tactics. You know all about attorney tactics."

"Care to divulge," the judge said.

"Cary Burk… hah. That's a stretch, trying to peg that to Roger McKinney. She was as drunk as the guy on the road. She was one of the ones that ran over him before wrapping her bumper around a tree."

"McKinney wasn't fighting with her over a piece of property?"

"She had a real estate developer friend who was bent out of shape because McKinney wouldn't sell a piece of land. No exchange between the two. The developer was trying to see if she could muscle him some way, somehow."

"Mavis West?"

"Uh… that's a stretch too. Checked this out long ago. Mavis West is a sort of hermit. I wouldn't go out there for a visit. You'll want a checkup with a Vet when you're done. She's an old coot who likes to house the unwashed. Walk into her place, which is a shabby two-story, rotting asphalt-single dump that seems grown out of an X-Files episode, and you find yourself scratching for fleas."

Duggan chuckled. "Everything in her front room is covered in sheets. There is a narrow path from the front door to the back. Burns a coal stove so just imagine. Wears black plastic cowboy boots and clomps around. Wears a flowery, threadbare house coat too, where, if the light is just right you get a peep show. Deflated boobs and all. She'll offer you a V-8 with either Vodka or wine. She talks about creamed peas and pees of cream. In the back, she's got four twin beds scrunched together. Brown stains on the sheets… I can only imagine. They dug a hole into the ceiling above the beds. A while back one of their ex-con buddies shows up… what was his name…? Winslow. It was Winslow. Don't know if you've ever heard of this or not. Some pervs like to wrap a rope around their necks and pleasure themselves right up to the point of going unconscious. That's what happened. Accidental suicide. McKinney had nothing to do with it. He shows up about once a month because Mavis won't leave the house and is trying to, ten bucks at a time, pay for her bedmate's funerals."

Erica didn't dare ask about McKinney's wife and daughters. Judge Meghan hinted. "The carbon monoxide poisoning?"

"I don't know why Lowe even suggests it. I'm not even going to go there. Roger was hundreds of miles away and had witnesses. They had recently moved into this older home. Before they could install

100

detectors the furnace went caput and you know the tragedy. Ma'am... whatever Lowe has told you, was at most a ploy to hook and reel you in. Sorry about that. If you'd been around long enough, we could have discussed this."

"I was here," Erica defended herself.

"Yeah... well... we like going to primary sources first," Reed interjected.

"But you're still surveilling him?"

"More out of appeasement," Duggan said. "We knew about your flight. Just wanted to listen in... you know... just in case there was some kind of exchange."

"There won't be," Judge Bailey firmly said. "So... we have two leads."

"Well..." Duggan again drawled. "Not that simple. Agent Reed has another theory."

"Do tell."

"Considering your position, Judge... we think there may be a strong possibility of someone trying to exact revenge on you."

"I doubt that. Do you have any idea who hacked into the Coroner's computer? Why would they do that? Those who stand in front of me couldn't do that? Most of them don't have the IQ to count on their fingers. Why wouldn't that involve international players, considering what we know?"

"Kid in a basement. Dad, uncle, brother unjustly sentenced... at least in their minds and who knows how they think."

"Can't you track them down?" Erica asked.

"Of course. You have to understand; however, at least according to the coroner, no valuable information was stolen. A single document manipulated that would have come to their immediate attention right away was obtuse. An astute mortician helped, but by nature, it's a lower priority."

"I'd say my sister's killer is not a low priority."

"I understand," Agent Duggan sighed. "I'm not trying to sound insensitive. But the victim here is the coroner. Rest assured, we're working on it, but even at that, I'm certain someone willing to kill in this manner has put up many barriers. Most likely hired it out, or… if they're savvy like most hackers are, they use various proxies, layering their identity, hiding behind multiple IP addresses. It could take a long time. Relatively speaking."

"One thing I'd like to know," Judge Bailey stood and paced briefly. "What is that book? The one Antione Banda refuses to sell."

"If you're referencing the note with his name on it," Agent Reed said. "We can't tell that that number identifies with any book. It's no ISBN. We've checked it as a phone number and it's not a phone number. Could be a code or reference. Who knows? Coordinates? Too many numbers for coordinates. We're considering every option. If you're thinking that line or phrase is significant, it's just a line of scripture. You can get that book for free. Stop any Latter-day Saint missionary on the street and they'll give it to you."

"Of course," Duggan added. "There may be a connection to that phrase, number and Banda. It will take time to put that together."

"Now…" Agent Reed said. "We don't want you to think we're ignoring these issues by suggesting your sister's death has some tie to your work. After all, dealing in rare books… or art for that matter, is a scheme used by many nefarious parties in laundering money. I'm not suggesting your sister was involved in criminal activity. We'll consider that, however. You understand we have to pursue that as well."

"I understand," Judge Bailey carelessly shook her head even though it felt like a bank-shot insult.

"So…" Duggan drawled. "Any ideas? Any suggestions of who might like to take out a little revenge on you, Judge?"

"Huh! Just about everybody," Erica said. "Who wouldn't? Just about all of them claim innocence."

"I'll have to think about that," Judge Bailey said. "There's nothing on the top of my mind."

"We're already considering certain individuals. We're not willing to pinpoint anyone in particular. We'd like to consult with you if you come up with anything," Duggan said while retrieving a card from his pocket. They stood. "Any questions?"

Judge Bailey took his card and studied it for a minute. "Not that I can think of."

Agent Reed extended his hand. "And harassing or investigating that mortician... leave that to us. Not your job. You'll only get in the way."

"How soon can I get back into Dana's home? I'd like to stay there instead of here. I'm hoping to get better acquainted with my sister."

The agents exchanged a look. "I think we've got what we need. We'll take the tape down in the morning. It really would have helped if there had been a phone, computer, or something. We took everything else we felt necessary. You understand that, don't you?"

Judge Bailey nodded. A few pleasantries and Agent Duggan paused before closing the door. "What's the deal with this Twyla lady? Have you had much exchange with her?"

"Like's to gossip," Erica said. "She loves the attention. Sure... the bats are out of the belfry, but for the most part, she's harmless. A lot a sass, flavor, and with no shame." She sheepishly grinned, knowing exactly where that line came from.

Judge Bailey stepped to the window to watch them pull away. "They've got their hands full. I don't envy them."

For Erica, one thought and one thought only now stirred her like a boar, rutting in the mud. A man that she saw as something less than a polyester blend. A man with make-believe morality. A man she planned to ambush at the first opportune moment. Like first thing Monday morning.

CHAPTER FIFTEEN

MAKING NICE

A distant church bell rang on an early overcast Sunday morning, a signal they'd walked into a world foreign if not forgotten. Erica Dennis sat up in bed, scrolling through her phone when Judge Meghan stepped away from the window. "Are you afraid of Twyla or is there something else bothering you?" Erica asked.

Judge Meghan checked her watch. "Do you think they'd have that tape off by now? It's almost eight o'clock."

"How would I know? I doubt it. I'm sure they sleep in on some days. I'm surprised you're not in bed. Aren't you exhausted from all the excitement and traveling? I would be."

"You are in bed. I'm resting by surrogate."

"Yeah... but I'm wide awake," she uttered, the brewing anger against Prince Lowe still feeling like a toxic dose of adrenaline. She noticed how stoic Meghan stood there. But then that was Judge Bailey in her mind. Stoic in the face of insult, criticism, and threat. She didn't know whether to envy her or think her foolish. Certain human frailties give you power... and innovative creativity. It pleased Erica to have a level of darkness. At least for now.

"I'm hungry. Are you hungry?" Meghan asked.

"Starving. Shall we order in? Bill's a decent guy. He delivers. He's especially accommodating when he knows Twyla has subjected you to her complaining."

"I can't get that tune out of my head?"

"Which one?"

"You know... from last night."

"I know. But which one? "Night Moves" or "Still the Same?" Erica had a grin. "' Still the Same'—the one when he was dancing kept going through my head in the night. His swaying butt was the first thing I saw when I closed my eyes."

"Hm..." Meghan sort of laughed. "Me too. Except I liked the first song."

Erica merely smiled. Judge Bailey somehow felt a little worried about it. "Call Bill. You decide on breakfast. I hardly know myself anymore. Don't even know what I want to eat."

Thirty minutes later a knock came to the door. Meghan opened it to find Bill in an incognito sort of stance. Because of the way he leaned against the wall, glancing time and again toward the office. "She said to surprise you. Hope you like it. I'll change it out if you want."

The rich aroma of hot coffee was all Judge Bailey needed. A kind simper, forty dollars in cash and she took the sack. "It will be fine."

Both were shocked to enjoy a breakfast of chicken fried steak, two eggs sunny side up, grapefruit, and coffee. By nine-thirty goodbyes to Twyla and off, whether police tape down or not. And what a relief to find Dana's cute little place vacant of tape and feeling welcoming. The sickening feeling was to walk in to find every single one of Dana's books gone. It was expected, but still disappointing. "Shoot," Judge Meghan moped. Erica followed on her elbow as she paraded from room to room, taking her time, looking in every drawer and cupboard. By noon, Judge Meghan plopped down in a cushioned Chase Lounger on the screened-in back porch. A long sigh and almost instantly she floated off into deep, restful sleep.

"Good," Erica uttered. "You need the sleep."

Judge Meghan had seemed to settle, finally finding a place that suited her as safe. Erica found a light alpaca-designed blanket, tenderly laid it atop the judge, and felt pulled out onto the front porch. She stood there, looking at Dana's leaning RFD box, wondering if that's how they had found it days before, and then felt obliged to rectify the matter. Like so many country mailboxes, its post sat in an old rusty milk can, a misplaced wedge the cause for its crippled appearance. She had it repaired and standing erect moments later and, frankly, feeling quite good about a kind deed when the aluminum screen door across the way slapped shut. Whether the creature saw her or not, she didn't know. But that fast, it felt as if some weird circus had crept in and the night-show a feigned memory. Ick stood there for a moment, adjusting a big straw hat atop his head. Dressed cowboy for a rodeo, except in sneakers, the fellow barely hesitated before gingerly stepping, one foot at a time down the stairs and then heading straight for the McKinney homestead.

"It must hurt. I wonder if he has those lumps on his feet."

She watched him climb the fence and then laboriously angle for a horse barn on the far side of the pasture. There must have been a dozen horses grazing. Two deliberately changed places as he crossed. She had to know. She simply had to know what he was up to. No way on earth was she going to cross that pasture, however. She kept an eye pegged to him as she hurried, something shy of a trot until he disappeared. And then her approach was something akin to a high school kid plotting a prank that might harm. Down the road to the McKinney lane and then a cautious eye glued to a cedar-paneled home that felt brim hidden, yet cozy. Doors stood wide open when she pressed a hand simply to steady herself as she leaned to peer inside the barn. There they stood. On the far side. Silhouettes. Two buckaroos, gun-slinging with a few hearty laughs. A saddled horse stood there at the side of a stair-step wooden box.

"Okay, Puncher," Kip laughed. "What did I show you last time?"

"Respect," sounded garbled.

"Yes. But what first?"

"Let her know I'm not gonna kill her."

"Hah. Close. She knows you're no threat. Rub her mane, take the reins and she'll move in and wait for you to get on." The horse didn't exactly comply. A moment of whispers drew Erica in. She stood there, folded her arms, and watched. Slowly, the horse complied and then stood still until Ick sat atop.

"Now what?" Kip said.

"Respect."

"And how?"

No words, Ick took the reins and lightly pulled left. The horse laterally flexed its neck until it touched Ick's left leg. He held it for a moment and then did the same on the right. "I think you're good to go. She's ready for you. Where are you going to go?"

"Same as last time. Down by the creek. Be back soon."

"Okay. You going to be okay without me?"

"Savanah will take good care of me. Always does."

"Okay. Have a good ride."

It shocked Erica when the horse set off in a trot. So much so that she tripped, backpedaled, and fell flat on her butt. She rolled over and covered her face when Ick trotted by and then headed down the lane. She didn't move until Kip touched her shoulder, chuckling. "He didn't hit you, did he? Are you okay?"

Erica rolled over and vacantly stared for a second. She then pushed away from him, stood, and brushed herself off. He stood there grinning. "Don't you ever sleep?" the single words she thought to muster.

"Hah. I got a good night's sleep. Once I got there. Are you okay?"

"I'm fine."

They stood there silent for a few seconds. "You a horse fan... or just out stretching your legs?" he asked.

Erica suddenly understood the disarming effect this man possessed. "Just curious. I saw Ick. I wondered what he was doing."

"I let him ride every Sunday afternoon. If I'm gone and Nuts can't show up, he thinks the world has come to an end."

"Is he disabled? What?"

"Just a victim of disease. He's quite a brilliant guy, actually. Horses put him in an innocent, vulnerable state of mind. He thinks the horse can tell and then they're gentle with him. I wouldn't put him on a horse that wasn't compliant."

Erica looked around, a bit confounded about what to say next. "What kind of horses are those? Is every horse that big? They're so big."

"They're not that big."

Erica raised her brows dubiously. Kip stood there amused. "According to Kallie..." he said, "best horses on the planet. Quarter horses. It was Kallie's dream. Sometimes I wonder if I shouldn't get rid of them. I have Jorge, my hired hand, and Nuts helps out, but he prefers a garage. Even though the horses keep him sane. However, they take a lot of time if you want the best out of them. How light you want them. When I get other things to do, they don't get what they need."

"You both ran off."

"Like I said, I have a ranch hand."

"They're beautiful. What do you mean, light?"

"You got a minute? A brief demonstration if you're interested."

"I'm not getting in that field if that's what you mean."

"Nope," he nodded. "Tabitha is in her stall. We'll go into the arena."

Erica held her smile hidden, shrugged, and stuck her thumbs into her back pockets. "I've got time. Meghan is sleeping."

"Meghan? You mean Jacklyn? What does she do, choose a different name for everyone?"

"Why did you call her, Jacklyn? I've never…"

"That's what she said. Said to call her, Jacklyn. Doesn't matter to me," he shrugged, turned, and ambled for the stalls. Erica, with interest, cocked her neck before following. A half a dozen stalls away a beautiful chestnut mare pricked her ears, stood tall, and whinnied. She nickered when Kip got to her stall. No halter, no reins and yet she snorted when he opened the gate and led her into the arena. He stepped sideways and made a clucking sound. Instantly, the mare began trotting around the edge of the arena. Erica stepped up.

"How do you know that's light? I can't tell that that's light."

"I'm just letting her expend a little energy."

"And she knew to do that? Just because you clucked?"

"She responds to several commands. Horses are prey animals. Once they learn to trust and respect you, they'll do anything for you. We're great mates. She loves to please and I try to give her plenty to prick her interest."

"Huh…"

"Easy, Tabitha," he called out. Tabitha instantly slowed to a trot. She rounded the arena, passed by, and kept going. "Notice her ears. She's always giving me an ear. No distractions. She's focused on me." Another pass and Kip stepped forward. "Watch from here," he said strolling for the center of the arena. Another pass, three-quarters around, and, "Whoa," he gently called out. Tabitha halted, turned, and faced him. "Notice. She's giving me both eyes, both ears, and is facing me directly. One thing you try to do is make her move her back feet. You've earned their respect when they realize that you have that much power. You don't force them. You don't brutalize them. Put them under a little pressure and then release the pressure when they do what you want. Horses learn from the release of pressure, not by trying to pound it into their brain with a rock."

"Amazing. She does whatever you say?"

"Hand signals. Vocal commands. It gives her a job to do. Keeps her interested and engaged. Lucky for me, a small town funeral home gives me a lot of free time. Well... more free time. I have plenty to keep me busy without this. I enjoy the interaction. I guess I do it more for Kallie than anything. Tabitha," he curled his fingers. The white-socked beauty strode straight for him. She halted when he lifted a finger. He then stepped and rubbed her between the eyes. "I ask her to dance. She dances. I ask her to side-step, she side-steps. The more I give her to do, the better engaged she is. If I get busy, I have to spend more time, reestablishing our bond. I don't think that's fair. I'm always debating over it. For now, we're good."

"So light means how well she cooperates?"

"Sort of. I heard about a Mexican horsemen who would use five horse hairs, tied from the bit to a lead rope. That's light. They wanted to prove how light their horse was by how little force they needed to get a response. I did that with Tabitha, reducing the hairs until she responded to just me. Watch..." He stepped around and again curled a finger. Tabitha flexed her neck until she touched her belly. "Hold," he said and she did. He then rounded her and flexed the other side. "Now that's light. As light as you can get. Isn't she wonderful?" By now he'd returned to face Tabitha.

"Unbelievable," Erica uttered.

He stood there for a moment. Tabitha stretched her chin, folded it over his shoulder, and pulled him in.

"Huh!" Erica laughed. "What now... a hug?"

"I guess you could say that. If I stand here long enough she'll cock her back leg, resting the leading edge of her hoof on the ground and dropping her hip. That will show you how relaxed she is around me. Watch her nostrils. They should be soft and round. Her lower jaw is loose when she's happy. When she's learning what you want her to learn, she'll lick her lips. I could go on and on. I think you understand what I mean by light though. Would you like to meet her? Come over here and let her have a sniff."

"Agh... I'm okay right here. I've never been around animals. They terrify me."

"Nonsense. We'll come meet you." Erica tensed up when Kip turned and led Tabitha over. She was breathing hard when Tabitha stretched her neck and sniffed her face. "Oh… oh, my gosh," Erica fluttered. "I didn't think she'd have such warm breath. Is she going to bite me?"

"I doubt it." Kip took Tabitha by the jaws and kissed her right on the nose. "She's not a biter. Some are. It's a sign of aggression. Of course, sometimes it's a sign of affection. She knows I don't approve. I guess that's why she hugs."

Erica nervously giggled. "She's so big. I never dreamed of standing so close." She then reached and touched Tabitha's nose. "Soft. It's a lot softer than I thought it would be."

"Would you like to ride her?"

"What? No! I wouldn't dare. She probably knows how frightened I am. She'd toss me like a rag."

"Don't be silly." No waiting for approval, Kip led Tabitha to where tack lined a wall. He chose a nylon halter, a cream-colored numnah, and a ranch-style saddle. A few minutes later he stood there inviting Erica with a tuck of the chin.

"No. I really don't dare. What is she going to do with me?"

"Whatever you want her to do. Try this. Come over here and I'll toss you up. Just sit there and get a feel for it."

"You? Toss me? Not on your life."

"Then we'll walk to the box. That's how Ick does it." He didn't wait. He led Tabitha to the box and waited.

"O, my God," Erica uttered. "I must be crazy." She hesitated, while her heart raced. She didn't move until after running her fingers through her hair. "I can't believe I'm doing this. I must be totally out of my mind."

She tried to prove it by feigning her begrudging walk, dragging her feet. But then she even shocked herself when she rounded Tabitha and stood there as if anxious. "I'm just going to climb up to see how high it is. I'm not getting on. If it's too high… no way."

"Fine. She's patient."

Erica placed a hand on Kip's shoulder climbing the two tall steps. She held on, now standing there, partly crouching and fully nervous in her titter. "No wonder people hate your guts," she softly demurred.

"What?" raised brows.

"I don't know what it is about you. Suddenly, up here and I don't know why."

"Deep down, everyone wants to conquer their fears. I suppose I make it easy for you. Touch a hand to the saddle. Press on it. See what she does."

Erica gave him a stubborn glare. He smiled. "Damn you," she grumbled. He laughed. Nervously, she reached down and merely touched the saddle. Once, twice, three times she pressed slightly firmer. "She didn't do anything. Isn't she supposed to go or something?"

"No. No one told her to go. She's still waiting for you to get on."

"Shoot. I can't believe I'm doing this. If I fall off and break my neck, I'll haunt you for the rest of your life."

"Good for me. Put a foot in the stirrup. Put all your weight on it. When you're comfortable, throw the other leg over and sit."

"You're a sadist."

"Tabitha says you're lucky it's her standing there. Others wouldn't be so perfectly patient."

"She said that to you? How do you know she said that?"

He laughed. "We're soul mates. Our minds are connected."

"Damn," she said, put a foot in the stirrup, and didn't wait to throw the other over. A brief hesitation and then she settled in like a butterfly with sore feet.

"Beautiful," Kip said. "Now. Don't squeeze her ribs too hard or she'll take off like the wind."

"What?! Don't say that. Don't tell her to go. Don't tell her anything except to stay right here. This is far enough."

A mild chuckle and the next thing Erica knew Kip sat propped up there right behind her. He reached for the reins. With his strong arms around her, he barely wiggled the reins and suddenly they were moving. Erica cringed and gripped onto the saddle horn as if dangling from a jet at liftoff. That was how it started. She would relax, in time. They would talk. Pleasantly. As the gentle rocking of an easy pace put her heart and mind at ease. It would become far more than that as well. Far, far more. What soon became brewing trouble; however, were the witnessing eyes. Multiple eyes. Most notably, those belonging to Judge Meghan Jacklyn Bailey. Who awoke, stirred, and then came looking. And who now spotted the two from Dana's front porch. Never had these kinds of emotions erupted in her like this. Never has she had an ill feeling towards Erica. Instantly, the impact of unknown emotional explosions sent fragments of feelings flying like tactical missiles through the air.

CHAPTER SIXTEEN

ONE SNAKE, TWO SNAKES, THREE SNAKES, FOUR

The best way to describe the hard cocoon, intentionally constructed around Judge Bailey, was supercilious—a scornful, hard-packed barrier erected for protection when Erica later found Judge Meghan secluded on the back porch. "Oh, there you are," Erica sounded Arcadian, coming out of the kitchen door. "Did you have a good sleep?"

Judge Bailey glanced curtly but didn't respond.

"I feel terrible," Erica said, sitting on the edge of a chair.

Judge Meghan didn't know fully how to interpret that. She inquisitively cocked her neck.

"I've had such harsh, awful feelings and thoughts about that man. I think you're right. You saw through it much sooner than I did. He's a decent fellow. I should have listened to you."

It sounded innocent enough. Sounded like he hadn't affected Erica the way he had her. That idea brought a slight simper. "I've been thinking," Judge Meghan said.

"About?"

"About what the FBI agents said. About the many defendants. Which one… I can't imagine which one. There are so many choices. Who would be so vile as to kill my sister to get to me? How would they even know I had a sister?"

"Any standout?"

"Yes. No. I don't know. Don't take this wrong. I know I asked you to come with and you deserved the time off, but I wonder if you couldn't go back and look through the files. Look for anything that stands out. I should stay here and take care of whatever business I have to."

It was easy to read the disappointment in Erica's face. Her shoulders slumped. "Ahh… I guess I could. When?"

"Tomorrow, I guess. You could take my car. Either I'll find a way home or call for you to come back."

"Well… I can do that. One thing is bothering me, though."

"Please share."

"Prince Lowe. I know this makes me sound childish, but someone has to tell him off. Someone has to confront him. He twisted me around his little finger. I thought Kip McKinney was the devil incarnate. He's not. I feel sick about that. If I can get that out of my system, I'll feel better."

"I wouldn't mind ambushing him with you. It's disgusting for an officer of the court to act like that. To say the things he said. First thing in the morning? Get to his office before he does?"

"I think that would be good. He ought to know we're not pushovers. Maybe it would stop him from ever doing it again."

"We'll do it then. We'll then get you on the road. I'll make sure you get paid time and a half for everything you do."

Erica kindly smiled before relaxing in her chair. They sat silently for a moment. "He just put me on a horse," she then pensively said. "I would have wagered anything that he couldn't do that."

"You mean, Kip?"

"Yeah. I saw him put that Ick fellow on one. I was curious. He has this incredible power. He can make his horses do things that boggle the mind."

113

"Really. I thought you were afraid of animals."

"I am. I wasn't by the time he finished with me though." She had the most judicious, yet guileless look on her face as she said it. Another quiet moment before she locked eyes with Judge Meghan. "Do you know what sickens me?"

"What?"

"The idea that a man like that might die alone. It wouldn't be right."

By the look on Erica's face, it was hard to tell if she hinted on the Judge's behalf or her own. It felt as if fairy-tale justice when Erica then stood and opened the screen door. "I'll start dinner," had a languid tone and made Judge Meghan feel at ease, knowing she would soon depart. She knew too well where her heart had wandered and knew the competition presented by Erica was far more threatening than some two-bit criminal out for revenge.

A light early morning rain fell. Two elderly women, plastic bonnets protecting their heads, shuffled up the walk at the church where Judge Meghan and Erica sat parked. "It feels like autumn is coming, doesn't it?" Erica softly muttered and checked her watch. "Do you think this is dumb? Think we'll get in trouble for doing this?"

"For confronting him? Heavens no. I hope it strikes a chord. I hope he self-reports. I'm not sure of the rules and laws in New York State, but his behavior is very unprofessional. If he doesn't do something about it, I'll report him."

"Hm... he might have friends and allies higher up. You know how that works."

"Yes... I know. But it's our obligation too, isn't it?"

"I hope he keeps the hours we're thinking. It's going on eight o'clock. I'm not sure if I want to hang around if he comes in later. He's not worth it."

"What time are you going to leave? It's a four-hour drive home, you know."

"I was thinking this afternoon. Maybe evening. Six o'clock at the latest."

"Mmm…" Judge Meghan nodded with approval. She then touched Erica's arm. "I don't want to miss him. I'd rather do it outside than in his office. I don't want him trying to hide behind a closed door or something. I'll go conceal myself near the doorway. You do what you want. Either way, we'll have him surrounded… so to speak."

Erica smiled. "Thanks for coming with. I'm glad I don't have to do it alone. I would. He has me fuming, but this is better, isn't it?"

A confirming smile before Judge Meghan quickly stepped out and walked for the corner. Erica waited until Judge Meghan disappeared around a hedge and then crawled out. She headed for the opposite corner where a park would provide cover as she waited for his car to arrive.

At precisely seven fifty-five A.M. Lowe's Audi skulked into the parking lot and slowly searched empty spots as if perusing luxury brands. There were merely three cars already parked in a lot that could hold more than fifty and still he had a hard time committing. He stopped, backed up, pulled forward and delayed as if wearing Versace diapers and thus there was no rush. He finally wheeled in and then backed up and pulled forward again, ensuring he sat centered between the lines. When white lights flashed, indicating he'd shifted past reverse and into park, Erica set out at a fast pace, hoping to cover the sixty yards and meet him just as he slinked out. If he was like most attorney's she knew, he'd delay briefly, gathering up folders or reaching for a briefcase or finalizing one last call.

She timed poorly. She wasn't even half way across the lot when he spiraled out, hugging a stack of folders in his arm. And he spotted her instantly. You could see him cuss under his breath. He quickly shoved his door shut, pushed the locker button and scooted like a woman in six-inch heels. He clearly wasn't anticipating Judge Bailey. She emerged from behind a car parked nearer the entry and hurried over, quickly blocking the keypad. He was still twenty paces away and instantly reacted as if caught with no other options. He stopped, took a huge deep breath, looking heavenward and then stomped a foot. He turned to Erica just as she caught up. "Look," he said. "I'm sorry. I'm sorry, I'm sorry, I'm sorry."

"What in the hell is wrong with you?"

"You don't understand. I have problems. I know I have problems. I just don't deal with them very well."

Erica wasn't expecting that. She gave him an agonized glower. Her mind raced, searching for the surgical prose to cut this man down to size. None surged to the end of her tongue at the moment. He already seemed dissected.

"Look, can we go in. I'll ruin these folders. They're getting wet."

"It's not raining that hard," Judge Bailey stepped up behind him. "You know there are rules and laws that govern the legal profession. How are you going to handle this? What are you going to do?"

"Look. I'm sorry. I have issues. I'm so lonely. I've been rejected so many times, I'll do anything to get a beautiful woman's interest. It's your fault. You caused these feelings inside of me. I exaggerate. I know. I know I do. I can't help myself."

Judge Bailey and Erica exchanged a shocked look.

"Apologize!" Judge Bailey retorted. "Apologize to her."

"I did. I'm sorry. I know I'm a jerk."

"What about Roger McKinney," Erica added. "I think you owe him a huge apology too. How could you do that to someone? Have you no decency at all?"

"I don't. Well... I do when it comes to the law." He dropped his chin in shame. "It's me and my personal life. I... I came... I felt terrible. I knew I did something wrong. I came yesterday to confess and apologize. But then, I just couldn't. I saw you. I saw you on the horse. You have to believe me. I've been sick about what I said and did. I just don't know what comes over me. It's a sickness."

"It's a sickness all right," Judge Bailey barked. "Get help. Talk to the authorities about your unethical behavior and get help. If I learn you haven't done something about it, I'll report you. And I won't go easy."

"I understand. Thank you for helping me. I know I need help. I don't know what else to say except, thank you."

Judge Bailey and Erica again exchanged a look. It was obvious they had nothing more to say. "Get out of here," Judge Bailey sounded just like a judge ought to sound. "Take your ineptitude and get out of here."

He gave Erica a sad pout and then turned and shuffled away. Erica and Judge Bailey put their heads together. "How pathetic," Erica murmured. "I never… how can he fill a position like that with such… I don't know how to describe it."

"Pitiful. Absolutely pitiful. And tragic. What an embarrassment. Come on. Let's get out of the wet. I'll have you help me clean the house before you go."

Prince Lowe stood inside the doorway, watching. The single thought chugging in his brain was this. I wish I had that kind of courage. Just once I wish I could exact a little revenge or at least show courage in the flesh myself.

It was a nasty drive. Blinding headlights. Taillights masked in a foggy wash of road spray and Erica in the mood to cry icicles. The clock on the dashboard read 9:03 P.M. when she raced off of the 476 onto the Schuylkill Expressway, nine miles in the rearview mirror now. Despite listening to her preferred smooth jazz station, it didn't smooth anything out at all. A million thoughts felt as if a washboard of commotion on her emotions. Already she was missing him. Already lonesome for Judge Meghan. Already worried about pointing a finger at someone who might exact revenge upon her. Beyond that, and although her pleasant, safe Fairmount high-rise apartment felt inviting, she dreaded walking in and feeling isolated the way she now did.

On the favorable side, from her north-end balcony, she had a view of the Philadelphia Museum of Arts and the Schuylkill River Rowing Basin. On the other hand, across the river, a dozen rail lines felt a constant rusted sliver of blight. The night view toward the east produced a ghostly feeling where the crumbling remnants of the historic Eastern State Penitentiary always felt a black ink stain on her soul. It was easy to hear pained souls screaming out in their anguish. Easy to imagine the drudgery, the endless hollow void of hope. Other than that… oh, I hate feeling discarded. Hate sideline duty. What am I going to find? How can I tell if any of them fixate, determined to kill in the name of reprisal?

So consumed was Erica that as she coursed along, she paid little attention, to the Philadelphia skyline slowly emerging above the tree line. So consumed that she failed to note how much traffic had thinned and that one single set of headlights had pulled in and followed her ever since flying by the Twin Bridges exchange. Past Greenland Dr. and Peter's Island. The Philadelphia Zoo sat just up around the bend when the headlights pulled out and then raced ahead. For some distance a

117

boring, unremarkable, dark colored Mitsubishi Mirage matched her speed exactly and couldn't seem to muster the power to pass. It finally retreated just before passing under the highway signage demarking her exit at Spring Garden Street. Two tenths of a mile to go and all she remained focused on was the stately image of the museum across the way.

Chris Botti and "Good Morning Heartache" aptly played as she eased off the gas and yoked herself to the exit ramp. Then her focus turned to the cement barrier ahead where, in the dark, a menagerie of bizarre graffiti looked more pronounced in headlights than in the bright of day. A stop sign and she paused just a moment to take in the beauty of the skyline at night. The wait was brief. It was then shocking, sudden and violent. The Mirage whipped around her and nearly clipped her front bumper slamming on its brakes. What was violent, sudden and shocking was when a bald black man jumped out and—Bam! blew her side window out with a quick punch with a spiked hammer. She saw and knew the man who climbed from the driver's seat had long, long blonde curly hair and the third who came out of nowhere was dark and brutal. A calm stroke and he drove a needle into the side of her neck. A breath later, the world spiraled wildly just before it evaporated into a void of darkness.

CHAPTER SEVENTEEN

DOUBLE EXPOSURE

Judge Bailey groaned. Not that she sensed anything. It sounded as if a reaction to the incredibly quiet stillness of a home sleeping on the edge of nowhere. The burr, though—she could hardly stomach the slim pickings of reading material she had to choose from. Not a stitch left on the shelves here and so she made a quick trip to the grocery store. Stan's Country Market provided everything from hardware, to flowers, to books, to farm implements. No interest at all in all those outdoorsy or mechanical publications. Even less in the array of Harlequin romance novels. And that assortment of books from Fox News personalities might label her in a way she wasn't prepared to handle. The magazine with a floral arrangement and that offered help in designing a country porch now sat in her lap as she stared at empty shelves, the forlorn look slowly giving way to an incoming tide of sleep. But she knew she couldn't give in yet, anticipating Erica's voice any minute now, telling her she'd made it home safely.

At 9:35 on the dot her phone rang, triggering a wave of relief. "Erica," she snatched the phone and answered. There was a brief delay.

"No, Ma'am. Officer Reynolds speaking. Is this Meghan Bailey? Meghan Jacklyn Bailey?"

Judge Bailey suddenly sat erect, a wave of distress causing not only her voice but hand to quiver. "No. Yes. This is Judge Bailey."

"Excuse me, Ma'am, but why have you left your car parked here like this?"

"I'm sorry. Wha… wha… what are you talking about?"

"This is Meghan Bailey speaking?"

"Yes, of course. Where's Erica? Erica had my car."

"Ma'am… your car is sitting here abandoned on the Spring Garden off-ramp. Can you explain that?"

"O my God. Erica! What's happened to Erica?"

"Ma'am?"

"My clerk. This is Judge Meghan Bailey. I serve in the Philadelphia District Court. Erica Dennis is my clerk. She returned home in my car. O, my God. God help me. What's happened to her?"

"Where are you, Ma'am?"

"In New York. Kermit Falls, New York. I'm up here because my sister died. I sent Erica home. O, dear God, what have I done? I shouldn't have sent her. It's my fault. It's all my fault."

"Ma'am… listen to me. Ma'am, we don't know that anything's happened to anyone. Your car is sitting here with no one around."

"Did she crash?"

"Well… no. The side window is missing."

By now Judge Bailey was on her feet. "The FBI. You need to contact the FBI. They're investigating. There has to be a tie. O, God.

119

This is crazy. This is mad. Look…I can't think straight. I'm an emotional wreck. Call and talk to Agent Duggan or Reed. They're working on the case up here. Ties… that Banda fellow. Argentina. O, what have I done? I think I'm going to faint."

"Ma'am. We're on top of things here. You settle down. I'll contact these agents. You just sit tight and rest assured we're on top of it."

No good-byes or any other calming words. He hung up, sounding as if leaping off a bridge. Judge Bailey stared at her phone for just a minute as the gears in her head suddenly kicked in as if triggering Big Ben. Her face turned a mortified color of white when a sudden thought turned her stomach over. "I'm a target," she droned. "O, my God. I'm a target too."

One thought and one thought only came. She hurried to the door and paused to see if lights were on at Roger "Kip" McKinney's. As always a dim yellow porch light looked as if the eye of a lion. She didn't care if she left the lights on or the door unlocked. Tears welled as she then nearly stumbled down the stairs, extremely annoyed that for some ungodly reason even justice was confined and restricted by the frailties of human limitations.

To her, the quarter-mile run felt eternal and an insult. At last, she faltered up the short flight of steps, and to her deep relief, the door sat wide open, the screen door the only thing slowing her as she didn't even hesitate. Kip had been nodding off. Feet up and bare, fingers locked atop his stomach, sitting in an overstuffed leather armchair, the TV in sleep mode. The simplicity of the room shocked her into holding her breath and then she gasped when he suddenly recognized a presence in the room. Not that he was alarmed by it. He reacted far too calmly for her. He merely opened his eyes and reached like he was going for a weapon. It was the remote. He punched the button. "Jacklyn! Well, this is a surprise. We got prowlers or something?"

Jacklyn suddenly buried her face in her hands and burst into sobs.

Kip sprung out of his chair and took her by the arms. "What is it? What's happened?"

Jacklyn couldn't believe she got the words out. "Erica! They've killed Erica. They took her, they killed her."

"What!? Who!? What are you talking about?"

"I sent her. It's my fault. Why did I have to do that? Now they're coming for me. I'm the last one. I'm next."

"Calm down. Where is she?"

Her voice cracked. "I sent her home. The police called. Car's there, she's gone."

Instantly, Kip pulled out his phone. He dialed and held the phone to his ear.

"Who are you calling?"

"Duggan."

"You know his number?"

"They've interviewed me three times. I..." he held a finger up. "Duggan. McKinney here. Are you aware that Erica Dennis is missing?"

"Eddie is on the phone with the Philadelphia Police Department right now. Where's the Judge?"

"She's here with me. Why?"

"Because we're just pulling up to her place and the door is wide open."

"Well, she's over here."

"Be there in a second."

Agent Reed was still on the phone and tagging behind Duggan when he strode in like he owned the place. Reed crossed into the kitchen and kept his voice low. "So, what's going on?" Duggan said. "Are you going to be okay?"

"Those..." Judge Bailey started and couldn't say another word. She covered her mouth and tucked her chin.

"We think we have some leads."

Judge Bailey's eyes brightened as she looked up. "Who?" she haltingly asked.

"Well... we think the tie is to you. Your clerk's sudden disappearance may prove us right. We've been looking at your cases and have narrowed it down to three. We considered anyone who might have ties to Argentina or South America. We considered rare books or art dealings. We considered high-tech connections. That is, of course, unless you've come up with something."

Agent Reed entered just as he was stowing his phone inside his jacket.

"No. Nothing. I can't think of anything. I don't recall any threats. Nothing. And the only person we've had any harsh words with is Prince Lowe."

"The attorney?"

"Yes. We confronted him about his unethical behavior. For the way he tried to play Erica. That's the extent of any conflict I've ever had."

"Huh… That's it huh?"

"That's it."

"Don't take offense… Eddie, call Lowe. Find out where he is. Just to make sure."

Agent Reed instantly returned to the kitchen.

"You think Lowe would do something like that?" the judge asked.

"He has known issues. You never know."

Roger McKinney suddenly seemed to go into a thoughtful stupor. He lowered his head, pinched his lips and began to pace.

"I can't imagine him reacting like that," Judge Bailey said. "He acted like a wet mop when we confronted him. He has mental issues. He needs counseling. He has no backbone."

"And those can be the worst sometimes."

Reed walked back in, a pokerfaced look to his facade. At exactly the same moment both he and Roger McKinney said the precise words. "He's dead. Prince Lowe is dead."

The only difference. "They suspect suicide," Agent Reed added.

Duggan instantly excoriated Kip with a glare.

"No," Judge Bailey reached for Duggan as if he was about to shoot him. "No. He wouldn't. It's just a connection. Right, Kip. Your connection, right."

"Can't explain it," Kip said, shaking his head. "He's dead though. Whenever I get that feeling, I always know they're dead. First time I've ever recognize the exact person though. Strange."

"Ugh!" Duggan grunted with consternation. "Problem here. Judge Bailey needs protection. McKinney... you bother me. You bother me bad. All right. No other choice. Everybody in the car. I've got to check this Lowe issue out."

"Who cares about him," Judge Bailey said. "Do something about Erica."

"And what do you propose? Philly Police Department is there and covering that. I have to worry about issues in my neighborhood. Try not to fret about it. Still... in my car. You're better off there anyway."

If you drove the speed limit, time to Ithaca was normally twenty-six minutes. Most folks did it in twenty minutes. Pushing the FBI sedan the way he did, Agent Shaun Duggan got them there in seventeen. Five more to find Prince Lowe's apartment, which sat ideally situated with a view of Stewart Park and Cayuga Lake. It was a quiet, yet boorish ride, Duggan clearly disgruntled over the whole affair. They found a street cluttered with trees, cars and enough blue and reds flashing that you thought an alien invasion. Police had cleared a spot for Agent Duggan and before braking he sneered at Agent Reed. "You gonna stay with these two or what?"

"I'm an officer of the court. Surrender him into my custody," Judge Bailey said. "He's not going anywhere."

"He magically knows the guy is dead and I'm supposed to trust that?"

Agent Reed shrugged. "We could cuff 'em together."

Sounded really good to Judge Bailey. For the first time tonight, something felt good. And any good, she was willing to take. She had her arm out when Agent Reed reached back to perform the deed. The instant the two sat alone, Kip lowly muttered. "It wasn't suicide. Someone killed him. I'm sure of it."

The words shocked Judge Jacklyn into silence. And so that's how they remained. For now.

Agent Duggan led as the two agents ducked the tape, flashing their ID's and then trotting for a set of cement stairs to a second level apartment. Seventies-era sort of place with darkly stained panels and a flat roof. They walked into a room where three officers stood together. "Gentlemen," Agent Duggan said, showing his ID. "What happened here?"

"Now, why exactly are you guys here?" the tallest of the officers asked.

"This guy is a cog in our current case. Any notes?"

"No notes."

They took a moment to assess the scene. Prince Lowe's body lay on the bed, his feet on the floor, a 9mm Smith & Wesson between his feet, and blood splatter all over the ceiling, wall, and headboard."

Reed spotted wounds before Duggan and stepped over, squinting. "Twice in the chest, once under the chin?"

"Yup," the officer said. "He wasn't a very good shot. Probably hated the idea of shooting the top of his head off, so he tried for the heart first."

"Exit wounds out the back?"

"Haven't checked. We haven't been here long enough."

"When did this happen?"

"Neighbors heard gun shots just before nine o'clock. Weren't sure where they came from until they went around knocking on doors. Twenty minutes later we got the call."

"Mmm..." Duggan scratched his head. "Damn... that would rule McKinney out, wouldn't it?" he frowned at Reed.

"I suppose. He couldn't have made it back when he called us."

Duggan leaned, looking past where the officers stood gathered. "Laptop. You guys checked that out yet?"

"We thought it prudent to check for prints first."

"Phone?"

An officer lifted the bagged phone.

"Let's look under this guy. I'm curious about exit wounds."

Officers were already gloved up. Two stepped over and rolled Lowe's body up. Both Reed and Duggan examined front, back and front again. "Mm... kay," Duggan said and stepped around the officers to check the head wound. "Very strange here. This is very strange."

"I've heard of someone shooting themselves multiple times," one officer said. "Then they get desperate and finish the job."

"No doubt. That's not my concern. Give me some gloves. Let's see if we can get into that laptop."

Moments later, the screen came to life without a password. "Reed!" Duggan barked the instant a website came up. "Look at this."

"Holy," Reed said when he saw what was there.

"What?" the tall officer said. "What is it?"

"Well... we've got several very obvious things here. Too obvious."

"What do you mean?"

"Entry and exit wounds in the chest indicate a right-handed angle. Head wound travels from the left side of the chin to the right side of the skull. That is most likely committed by a left handed individual or someone else... or he really twisted his wrist in a time of panic. Why would he do that? But a bigger issue for us is this news article on this website. Pedro Cain is an organized crime figure currently on our radar regarding another issue."

"Let me see something," Reed uttered and pushed in. He quickly checked the search history. "Gun shots? What time did they hear the gun shots?"

"Two-three minutes before nine o'clock. TV program was just ending so it isn't a stretch to miss the time."

"Well, this search occurred five minutes after nine."

"What are you thinking?" one of the officers asked.

"Well, either he was aware of our investigation or someone else wanted us to know they knew," Reed said.

"Or they know everything and one is trying to frame the other. Who would know and why?"

Duggan stared at the tall officer for a moment. "I'm curious about any prints on that weapon. Is it his? Everything. We'll turn this over to crime scene investigation. Reed... let's step out."

Both Kip and Judge Jacklyn saw when the two agents emerged and stood talking on the deck. It was then that Jacklyn couldn't help but address that which now gnawed on her to the point of indigestion. "Kip?" she whispered.

"What?"

"I need to know. Is Erica dead? Do you know if Erica is dead?"

He shook his head. "It doesn't work like that. I have no idea."

CHAPTER EIGHTEEN

LOW-RESOLUTION THINKERS

Pavement was wet. Boot falls sounded like a sledge hammer against a wet oak trunk on what looked a moon–silvered alley because of light cast from a distant sodium-vapor street lamp. They carried her face down. Two had her by the arms, the third, Blondie, held her ankles as if managing a wheelbarrow. A black pillow case covered her head. A compulsory shoulder to a heavy wooden door forced a deep grunt before the troop looked as if a runner of blood flooding up and through the wall. They moved in and across the warehouse in a very mundane fashion. The floor was empty except for several pallets stacked with unlabeled boxes. Light cast from an upper office window led them straight to the back wall where a long work bench and sink stood dark. They draped her body, face down, over a half-empty pallet nearest the bench. Plastic wrap circled the floor as if a roadkill snake. The dark one, not the black man, pulled a string, which activated the fluorescent lamp over the bench. Slowly, flickeringly, it hummed to life and its magnetic ballast soon buzzed a sound that spread a feeling of familiarity. Sweet memories of things past. Hours of comfort and delight. From a certain point of view.

The three gathered when the dark one, the bearded one, pulled his phone from his back pocket. "Still nothing?" the black man asked. "Why no message?"

"Call him," Blondie slowly and lowly said.

The dark one gave him a stern look. "That isn't how it works." His accent was strange. Very strange. Like the Far East and Middle East blended in a NutriBullet blender full of rocks. "You know that isn't how it works. You make the call if you're so anxious."

They stood there staring for a moment. "Perhaps he's left us to our own devices," Blondie said. His face was weathered, long and wrinkled. He scowled before turning and walking to the sink where he unzipped his pants and began relieving himself. The dark one turned his back to the other and paced, tapping his phone against his finger. The bald black man glanced at Blondie then the dark one and then at Erica. He raised a lip, grimacing and then reached under the bench and retrieved a small medical pouch. He donned latex gloves before zipping it open. He then selected a small gauge syringe and a vial of military grade nerve gas in liquid form. With the syringe full, he crossed back to Erica, pulled her blouse out and hiked it up close to the bra line. He was about to jab the needle when Blondie suddenly grabbed his arm. He cocked his neck and unbuckled his belt with his free hand. "I don't like doing it to a corpse. Wait until I'm done."

"And you won't do that either," the dark one abruptly growled. He had his phone to his ear as he crossed over. He put it on speaker and laid the phone on Erica's back.

"Say that again," a whiny voice said.

"I said we got the girl. Do like we did the last time?" the dark one asked.

"What girl?"

"The clerk. The judge's clerk. Dennis."

"Who told you to do that?"

The three exchanged a look. "We thought it came from you," Blondie said. "We're going to kill her. Didn't you want her dead?"

127

"I didn't want her. Not now. Later maybe. I don't like this."

"Dump her?" the black man asked. "Kill her and dump her?"

"No. How stupid can you people get? What? What's the status?"

"We knocked her out," the dark one said. "High dose. She's asleep."

"Just like that you were going to kill her? No questions asked? No extraction of information."

"The order was to eliminate her."

"Not from me, it wasn't."

"What do you want us to do then? Just dump her somewhere and walk away? She might have recognized us. Well, at least one of us," the black man glared at Blondie. "He'll have to shave his head or something."

"Don't be fools. Wake her up. Disguise yourselves and wake her up. I want to question her. Use buds. I don't want her hearing my voice."

No delay, the dark one removed earbuds from his pocket and inserted them. The bald one began preparing a dose of naloxone. Blondie opened a door and removed three black balaclava masks. Moments later, hood removed, Erica sat propped inside the boxes as if Queen Victoria waking up on the throne. She swooned coming to, her head coming upright and then back against a box. Limp, dizzy, confused, she merely blinked. She thought it was a dream. Garlic and onions nightmare actually. Until one leaned into her face and his grizzly-bear breath jolted her. "Awake," the dark one acted as a medium.

Erica's bottom lip quivered as she strained, fighting off the terror.

"What can you tell us about the book?"

Erica squinted hard and then pinched her eyes closed. She slumped like she was going back to sleep. Blondie took her by the jaw and straightened her out. "Answer," he commanded.

She wrenched her jaw out of his grip and forced her chin to her chest.

"The book," the dark one forcefully commanded. "What did you find out about the book?"

"Uh… book? I… I don't know about a book," she groggily and lowly uttered. "Uhhh…" she moaned.

"Yes you do. They went looking for the book. Did you get it? Do you have the book?"

"Books. She had lots of books." She kept her eyes closed, her head now back. "I don't… I don't know what book you're talking about. Where am I? What's wrong with me?"

"The man who wrote the book. Where's the man who wrote the book?"

Erica's face twisted into a knot, concentrating. She didn't answer.

The dark one suddenly stared at the others with the next question asked. A slight shrug. "Okay… You left the judge, didn't you? Walked out on the judge. Big mistake. You never know what might happen when someone like that is left vulnerable. Who knows what certain deceiving people will do with her. She's vile. She's not a morally stable woman like you think she is."

That caused Erica to open her eyes, but a sliver.

"The holiness Judge Meghan Jacklyn Bailey. Not a seed of sense in her head. All that time. All that time spent with her and you can't see it. What a sham of a woman you are. She's back there riding the sheets with that undertaker about now. Scummy undertaker. Maybe they're kinky. Maybe they're doing it on the embalming table. Think about that, woman. Or maybe she is a decent thing. Now he's polluting her. Which is it? Is she the scum or is he the scum? Hard to think of both of them as scum. What do you think? What do you have to say?"

Erica sat there unresponsive.

"If you could just get your hands on that book. Now, that would explain a lot. That would help a lot. Tell you the truth that book will. About everything and everyone. You need to get that book. That's enough," the whiny voice then said. "Take her somewhere and dump her. Don't get too rough. Knock her out again. I don't want her future use compromised. Understand? A woman like that could prove herself far more valuable than you think. More so than that last one."

No response. He simply cut the call off.

The black man then vacantly stared at Baldy. He pushed Blondie toward Erica. "Don't let her go anywhere."

Baldy then pulled the dark one out of earshot. "What the hell was that? He sounded like some two-bit spy novel or something. Like hell if I'm taking commands from someone like that again. Is he on drugs or something?"

The dark one mulled a second. "I don't know. Head games. Maybe he's playing head games."

"With her or with us?"

"Possibly all of us. You never know with him."

"I don't like it. I say we kill her and wash our hands of it."

"You do that and you'll share a grave with her. You really that stupid?"

"Ugh..." he groaned. The two stood there for a full sixty-five seconds. "Fine," he then hissed and spun on a heel.

Ten minutes later, a hooded and sleeping Erica Dennis rode slumped in a back seat, shoulder to shoulder with the black bald one. The final location was still undetermined.

CHAPTER NINETEEN

BLIND MICE

Judge Jacklyn couldn't accept what Kip had said. If justice truly governed justice, justice demanded he know. Her mind slipped and scrambled, running through the barrier of pang, bitterness and guilt. The release came when Agents Duggan and Reed came striding back. A gruff look from Duggan and smirk out of Reed when he reached over the seat and removed the cuffs. Duggan then wrapped his arm over the seat and glared. "All right. Fess up. How do you do that? Who tipped you off?"

"I doubt I can explain it in a way you'd understand."

"Try me."

"It's a curse."

"For the dead?"

"The dead are lucky."

"Hah!"

"Tell him," Judge Jacklyn nudged Kip. "I'd like to know myself."

Kip shook his head. "I didn't have a clue what I was getting into. I didn't even know I was getting into it."

"Don't stop there."

"A feeling. Anxiety. A thought. Something you deny. Something you don't want and refuse to believe. You have the premonition once and you think nothing of it. Again it happens. About the third, or fourth time you begin to realize something is going on here and you'd better pay attention. Because suddenly it affects the people you love. Maybe if you had been paying attention, you could have prevented a nightmare. I hate it, but I pay attention to it. There is nothing I can do to prevent an upcoming event. I'm only aware when it's imminent or just occurred. I figured some unseen force wanted me where I am. It has something to do with what I do. Nothing more."

"And this happens every time somebody dies?"

"No. Sometimes it happens, sometimes it doesn't. I wish it never happened at all. I can't stand it."

Duggan and Reed exchanged a look. "Bull crap," Duggan said and turned away.

"Suicide or murder?" Judge Jacklyn asked.

The Agents turned and looked over their shoulders. "What did the prophet say?" Duggan asked.

"Murder."

Duggan gruffly rammed the shifter into reverse and nearly clipped a police cruiser backing out. A backward growl up some crumbly driveway and seconds later he was in no mood, racing ahead.

Something happened to settle him down by the time they pulled up in front of Dana's place. Probably something to do with two phone calls.

The one Agent Reed made to the Philly field office and the one Judge Bailey received from the Philly officer who had called her prior. Assuaged, he merely stopped and sat there staring ahead. "This isn't going to work," he said.

"What?" asked the Judge.

"You need protection. We need a female agent here. I'm not going to sit out here all night."

"I'll house all of you," Kip offered. "I've got plenty of rooms no one uses. That is if you feel you must."

Reed and Duggan looked at one another. Reed shrugged. "Sounds alright with me."

"I need to lock my house up," Judge Jacklyn said.

"Eddie… go with her. Might be a prowler waiting."

Once the two were out, Duggan turned and eyed Kip with a tormented look. "You're screwin' with my head. Why you screwin' with my head?"

"Not my choice. You're the one with the problem." A moment of silence. "Now let's get real. Who's behind this? Who are your suspects? Who's most likely to show up here and put a bullet in our heads? Don't you think the Judge has a right to know that?"

Duggan sat there as if now pumped up equal to Erica. He didn't move, he didn't offer a word. Minutes later, once inside Kip's home, Duggan contritely motioned to Judge Bailey and avoided eye contact with Kip. "Let's sit. Let's get your input on who we're considering."

They gathered around the dining room table. "Pedro Cain. Forty-two years old. Now locked up at Allenwood for three and a half years. Thirty-five years left on his sentence. A man with a bland expression. Small, deep-set eyes. Crafty. Meanness hidden under a thinning head of black hair. Kingpin of the Cantu Family organization. That's his real last name. How he got Cain, I don't know. Money laundering. Drugs. Extortion. Gambling. Racketeering. Loan sharking. Prostitution. You name it. Organization is splintered, but working behind the scenes somewhere. His right-hand guy was Raul Guzman. He had connections to the CJNG. Jalisco New Generation Cartel in Mexico. Last we knew of him he flew to Mexico and then disappeared. Some think he's dead. Others believe he ended up in Europe, orchestrating drug trade with all the big cartels there. Cantu originally came from Paraguay at thirteen. Of course, we nabbed Cain on murder. He's a ruthless soul without a conscience."

"Is that your prime suspect?" Kip asked.

"Judge… you received any threats from those people? If anyone, it would be them."

She splayed her hands and her brows turned quizzical. "It's a vague memory. I can see him standing there in the courtroom. If he made threats it was subtle and concealed. Now… there were a few faces in the crowd, who like a gunshot to the chest, could have bled me out with a mere look. I've never received any verbal or written threats, however. Not from them. That I'm aware of. Some things get flagged and intercepted. You know that."

"That's your prime suspect? You think his group is behind this?" Kip said.

Duggan sulked.

"We doubt it," Agent Reed said.

"Why say that?" the judge asked.

"We have our reasons."

"Who else?" the judge added.

"Well, after seeing what we saw at Lowe's place, I'm not very confident with these two either."

"Who?" Judge Bailey asked.

"Wayne Fuller and Boyd Sherman. Anything ring a bell with those two?"

"Um… Wayne Fuller. I remember him. Callow self-confidence. Ashen gray fellow who looked so bad, he looked good."

"Looked good?" Kip raised his brows.

"Had a priestly look. Like he'd never seen the sun. Dark hair, oiled back. Poisoned a business partner. They had mining interests in… where was it? Bolivia?"

"That's right."

"That's not exactly Buenos Aires," Kip said.

"Search criteria was South America or international connections. He also had an interest in a mining outfit in the Congo."

"The fangs," Judge Bailey mulled. "That would make sense."

"Did he have any sort of organization to carry on?"

"No. Lots of extended family though. They all seem legit, but you never know."

"Who stands out?" the judge asked.

"Nobody yet."

"Boyd Sherman," Judge Jacklyn purred. "The memory is vague. Probably ten years ago or more. I don't remember his crime. He was an angry, stocky fellow with a buzzed haircut. Yellow blonde hair. Huge jowls."

"He thought he was some sort of angel. Had been a missionary in both Africa and South America. He now has brain damage. Attempted suicidal hanging. No blood and oxygen supply for a good while. Killed the family in a moment of rage. They were a bunch of sinners and needed to pay the price."

"Oh… yes… I remember now. He had a cult following. They threw a few threats around. Condemned me to hell. That kind of thing. That's been a long time. Does he still have followers?"

"Now… he may, he may not. Some we can't locate. Dropped off the face of the planet. Others have pursued other sources of worship. He's our weakest suspect. We could see a religious fanatic taking out revenge. Plotting-for-years sort of thing. We still have work to do. Sometimes it takes a while. I thought we were well ahead of the game until tonight. Can't make a connection to Prince Lowe if he's connected. It doesn't make sense."

"Can I ask a question?" Kip asked.

Duggan rested his chin on an open hand and said nothing.

"How long has Prince Lowe been the DA?"

"He's not the DA," Agent Reed said. "Filling in. Burk was the DA. When she died, he was simply one of the assistant DAs appointed to replace her. He wasn't elected."

"How long had he served in that office?"

"Five years. Before that, he worked in a law office in Alexandria, Virginia. Did some work for the Federal government, some private."

"President of the Lonely Hearts Club," Duggan sniped derogatorily.

Silence prevailed for a moment. "What do you think?" Agent Reed asked Judge Bailey. "Anything else coming to mind?"

"No. I'm so worried about Erica that I can't think about stuff like that. Granted, you bringing things up triggers memories, but I can't come up with an original thought."

"Well, sleep on it," Duggan said. "Try to get some rest. Agent Reed... you take the first watch. Mr. McKinney, I'd appreciate you showing me where I can get a few winks."

One hundred and ninety miles away, the Mirage was just then crossing over the Benjamin Franklin Bridge into New Jersey. An idea percolated in the dark one's head as he hotly gripped the wheel—somewhere nasty in or around Atlantic City.

CHAPTER TWENTY

GREEN FISH, LITTLE REAPER

Judge Bailey didn't move when Kip led Duggan to a bedroom in the back. Agent Reed drummed his fingers on the table and reached over as if to comfort. "Sorry about Agent Duggan. He normally isn't as gruff as he is tonight. This case has got him twisted inside and out."

"Kip rubs him wrong. It's obvious."

"He doesn't know where else to direct his frustration. McKinney will handle it just fine. We've researched him inside and out. He takes aggression and the like pretty well."

135

"Yeah. I know. I had a little of my own. Get to know him and it ruins your pity party."

"Hum…" Agent Reed smiled and laughed. "Are you okay here? I ought to get a lay of the land. I want to know the perimeter and get an idea of tactics if any uninvited guests show up."

"I'm okay."

Kip returned just as Agent Reed stood. "Jacklyn? How about you?" Kip said. "I've got another room I think you'd enjoy."

"No. I'm not going to get any sleep. I'll sit in a chair or something."

"Is there anything I can do for you? Hungry, thirsty? Anything?"

"No. Thank you." She gave him a fond smile.

"Well, I need to sleep every time I get a chance. I need to meet with the Sarah Williford family first thing in the morning. I usually don't get this busy with the funeral home. We're a small town."

Agent Reed patted Kip on the back as he stepped around and headed for the front door. A two-finger salute before Kip headed for his bedroom.

This is the exact moment Judge Bailey feared. How she would react once alone with her thoughts and emotions. She felt she deserved it, however—the self-inflicted torture. In the depth of her, she felt for certain she had doomed Erica to death. All because of a sudden selfish eruption. Getting and keeping Erica as far away from Kip as possible seemed rational and fair at the time. But denying the hidden darkness in your own heart is a breeze when you've always felt your instincts perfect. Doesn't common sense require those traits bred into becoming a judge after all? But once that call came regarding Erica, contrition felt a self-imposed guilt purge that she deserved. Self-condemnation became the first weight that bore down, the flow of adrenaline a torturer's thorns across her back. In spirit, the essential question felt settled, and irrevocably settled. In her mind, whatever punishment came her way she deserved. The question now was when and how.

This was her exact state of mind and never altered. The midnight hour came. Agent Reed came and went as well. He'd enter, pause as if expecting something from the judge, and then continue his routine, dutifully excelling as far as she was concerned.

As bitter as the ascent to Golgotha, she continued her flagellation until the sudden and shocking ringing of her phone seven minutes after the one o'clock hour. And then she feared the worst when she snatched the phone. "Don't pussy foot around. How bad is it?" She answered.

"Ma'am... Officer Reynolds here. This is Judge Meghan Bailey, isn't it?"

"It is. What happened to her?"

"Ma'am. We just got word... your clerk... Erica Dennis... they found her in Atlantic City. She's on her way to the hospital right now."

"Oh, my God. Serious. She's okay? Is she badly hurt?"

"I don't have all the details. They discovered her next to a trash bin behind the Convention Center. Maintenance crew found her. She was unconscious. No outward signs of injury. Her status is still undetermined."

"But she's alive."

"Yes, she's alive."

"My God... thank you, Lord."

Honestly, Judge Bailey couldn't recall the exchange after those words. The elation that came over her dwarfed the prior anguish. She jumped to her feet, started, and stopped twice before hurrying out the front door where she found Agent Reed covering his eyes and squinting toward the Bowen home. "They found her," she elatedly said. She almost threw her arms around his neck and then sighed deeply. "I can't believe they found her." When she realized the smile on Agent Reed's face, she threw her arms around his neck and squeezed tightly. Moments later, she gleefully paced, one moment thinking to find Kip and wake him, the next feeling the need to drive to Atlantic City. Fifteen minutes later, she dialed the hospital. A tired nurse refused her since she wasn't family and then insisted she call Francis and Kathryn Dennis of Danbury, Connecticut.

By three-thirty and the hour when Agent Reed woke Agent Duggan she contentedly sat in Roger's arm chair, eye's closed and slowly gliding off the slope of a dopamine high. Relaxed, exhausted, at peace. Until an abrasive sound startled her just after the six A.M. hour. She had fallen asleep and dreamt. Dreamt of funeral homes. Odd dreams. Dreams of a fat old couple joining hands, running and then jumping together and landing foot first, sliding into a casket. Together forever and Roger McKinney tucking them in after they laughed and smiled at him. She thought the sound she heard was when he buried them prematurely and then they frantically dug, clawing their way back out. It shocked and relieved her to awaken and realize the bizarre dream. And then the scratch and rattle. Scratch, rattle and then a bang. "The door. Front door," she groggily muttered. She wiped spittle off her chin. First thought was of Philly policemen with bad news. That they had lied to her. She suddenly believed they had lied to her.

The inside door stood wide. She crept and leaned and then didn't know whether to feel relief or aghast. There Ick Bowen stood, moaning, pacing in place and acting like he needed a bathroom. He frantically pointed and mumbled something she couldn't understand. Grabbed her hand when she opened the door. "Um… Um…" he grunted. "Um w'th mah."

She seriously expected to find a dead Agent Duggan hanging from a tree or something. Instead, chugging up the lane came Tony "Nuts" Ford and some small Mexican-looking fellow. Ick continued to tug. She dug her toes in and waited. Tony panted, rested his hands on his knees, and said something in Spanish. "Vaya," he said. "Jorge, Vayate y llama el sheriff!"

"What? What is it?" she panicked, watching the fellow scamper for the barn.

Tony shook his head, avoiding eye contact.

"The Agent? Agent Duggan? What happened to Agent Duggan?"

No jovial French insult like usual, he vacantly stared at her. "Agent?"

"The FBI agents. Did something happen?"

"Something happened. Don't know anything about an FBI agent. I guess that's who belongs to the unfamiliar sedan parked out front.."

Judge Bailey quickly glanced. "Where's the Agent? He's supposed to be guarding us."

"Is Kip up yet? I need Kip."

"No. I haven't seen him yet. What's wrong?"

"Foul play. Four dead horses. Valuable horses."

Judge Bailey was speechless. She covered her mouth and stared vaguely. Ick followed Nuts through the front door. Judge Bailey felt weak, finding her way back to the hood of the sedan. A moment later a puffing Agent Duggan came huffing around the front of the house, his phone to his ear. He was soaking wet from the waist down. "I know!" he shouted. "It was headed due north. One of those Mosquito ultralight helicopters. Quiet as a lawn mower. I didn't hear it come in, but I heard it going out. Get some eyes out there and watch for it!" He ended the call and painfully glared at Judge Bailey. "Damn!" he said. "We're outclassed and outnumbered here. Have you seen Agent Reed yet?"

"No. I just… the neighbor came to the door. I came out… I don't know. There's a guy in the barn, Tony is in the house. I'm confused."

"Little Mexican guy?" Agent Duggan held his hand just above his belly button. "Yeah. The guy was here at five o'clock. I knew about him. Jorge somebody or other. We interviewed him the other day. He's the hired help. He found the horses and tipped me off about the helicopter. Damn thing was too damned quiet. Buzzing above the ground, masked by trees. Ticks me off royal. Don't worry, I've sicced the highway patrol on them."

"How'd you get so wet?"

"Bustin' my butt to get down there through that creek. They were long gone. I don't even know if I spotted them."

Seconds later, Kip came busting out of the front door, shirtless, Levis and unlaced sneakers. He ran past them and kept on going, Tony and Ick on his heels.

"Hey!" Duggan shouted. "Don't disturb things. Evidence! I need evidence!"

Judge Bailey set off the instant Agent Duggan took a long stride. He was still panting. "Damn out of shape old grunt me. Pisses me off royal."

Judge Bailey stayed quiet. She worried he might collapse of a heart attack he was so red in the face. Other than that, the dread of what awaited them felt another Golgotha. This time not for her, but for Kip.

About a half mile later, you could see the three standing out in the field. Agent Duggan was grumbling under his breath and didn't quiet until he realized they stood a distance out from where the horses lie dead.

139

A bay nearby, a gray several strides further. A palomino and black beauty further off and hard to see in the dim of morning light. Judge Bailey ducked through the rails and sidled up where Kip stood, his hands on his hips. No words. Agent Duggan walked slightly further to climb over at a post. "Thank you, for respecting the scene," he said when he stopped next to Nuts. "Don't get any closer than this. Footprints. Gotta be footprints."

A moment of silence and then Agent Duggan stretched his neck higher, despite being at least four inches taller than anyone else. He then disregarded his own warning. In long strides he approached the bay. He snapped a handkerchief before guarding his distance. He gingerly reached and plucked something the rest of them couldn't see. A moment later, he returned, a stolid look on his face. He held a small fold of paper in his handkerchief.

"What is it?" Nuts asked.

"Fangs and little green fish. Some kind of snake fangs and little green fish."

CHAPTER TWENTY-ONE

THE LAST STRAW

"That Red fellow," Judge Bailey bit the air. "I think you now know your perpetrator. It's suddenly perfectly clear. You need to find out who that is. And fast!"

For the moment, Duggan stood there staring at what he held. Sirens in the distance began to wail. You wouldn't think a man like that would react the way he did when he looked up. His face turned suddenly crimson. "Ho-ly crap!" he howled, and then practically bowled them over charging like a bull. Stunned silence when the others turned to look. There, in the distance, they saw flames licking the air. Dana Bailey's house was now fully engaged in flames, a tall column of black smoke pumping its victorious fist. First thing, Kip looked to see how high the smoke rose. Not high at all. Minutes or less since ignition, he estimated. Ick took off running.

"Like he's going to stop it," Nuts said. "No point in racing like that."

Kip glanced at Judge Jacklyn, fully expecting to see emotion erupt. Not a bit. No emotion of tears and anguish anyway. But there was something different. Something very different. Something grim. Something black. Something grave and sanguine. "That's enough. I've had enough," she resolutely said, and marched off.

Kip turned to Nuts. "I want you to call Bob Simonson. Ask if he'd be willing to take what's left of my horses."

"Selling them?" Nuts said with shock.

"No. I just want them safe somewhere else. I doubt they're safe here anymore."

"I understand. Not that it's a lot of money to lose. Despite the insurance. I feel like someone ripped half my soul out of me too. What else do you want to do?"

"I've got a good idea. I'll wait and see what Duggan and Reed have to say." He then stared Nuts in the eye for a minute. "Think Tracey would let you go for a few days?"

"For you? She'd let me go for weeks or months... if you asked."

Nothing else said, Kip walked off like he hardly cared.

They didn't instinctively gather in the McKinney kitchen until all that remained of Dana Bailey's home was smoldering black rubble. Kip emerged, dressed in a white shirt and tie to find Judge Bailey sitting at the kitchen table. Agent's Duggan and Reed had stood head to head briefly and then gave Kip a veiled look before flanking the judge and leaning on the table. "We'd like to get you out of here," Agent Duggan said. "Federal protection. You can't stay here."

"I want Erica with me. I don't know what you have planned, but I want Erica with me," the judge said.

Nuts stood leaning against the sink, his arms tightly folded. "You know. This used to be such a peaceful, quiet place. Years and years and years and now this. Take her a long ways away."

"I know I can't ask where… but can I make a suggestion?" Kip offered.

The only waned look he got came from Judge Jacklyn.

"What would that be?" Agent Duggan asked.

"Let me take them. From what I can tell, I'm suddenly a target too. I'll take them somewhere completely off the map or radar. No one will know. I can do it so we're not tracked or trackable."

"Yeah, right," Agent Duggan sarcastically cocked his neck. "In today's world. What? By foot?"

"In the meantime, you set up a ruse. A Canary trap maybe. Subtly link information or something. Wait to see who shows and take it from there."

Agent Duggan and Reed stared at one another for a minute. "I wouldn't feel comfortable just turning you loose with her. You were once a suspect, you know."

"Because we were all idiots," Judge Bailey groaned.

"If you use people like Twyla MacDonald as a resource, half the town would be in the clink," Nuts cynically muttered.

"I'm not going to cut the reins completely," Duggan said. "How are we going to know if you're keeping your noses clean?"

"VPN. Secured lines. Whatever. I have no problem with that. Unless you're a security risk."

Duggan bit his lip and knotted his face biliously. Agent Reed smiled and looked away.

"I have ten minutes to get to the mortuary. I'll make arrangements with this family and then turn them over to John Jenkins. He's got staff help, I have Nuts. Won't be a problem. Keep an eye on her until around ten to eleven and then we're out of here. I'll take Nuts with me. I like a co-pilot and I don't mind his protection. He's ex-military, you know. All we need out of you is a ride to the airport."

Agent Duggan nodded at Reed. Judge Bailey stood just as they stepped away. "I'm going with you," she said.

"We're just going right here," Duggan said.

"Not you. Him. Where he goes, I go. I feel safer with Kip than with you."

"And they're not going to hang him by the… he's not going to suffer the consequence if… Judge… please just wait here a minute. We need to consult over this."

"I'm not worried. Whatever happens, happens. I'm staying with Roger until this is over. Let's go, Kip. I'd hate to keep your family waiting."

Judge Bailey led Kip and Nuts out the door. Agent Duggan had Reed by the arm and stopped him when he tried to follow. "Look," Duggan said. "I'd just as soon they drop off the planet. What do you think?"

"I'd say you're more worried about consequences to you than to them. Let 'em go. Technically, we haven't assumed responsibility. We're not running Gulags yet. Private citizens doing private citizen stuff, right? Besides, I like the idea. Best to keep them who-knows-where while we're free to do what we do best."

Duggan scoured Reed's face for a moment before getting a sly grin. "All right. Stay with them. At least appease me that far. I'll get them a phone and you get them to ten or eleven safely."

Seconds later, Agent Reed was trotting to catch up. Duggan stood there wondering, first, why such a wealthy man lived so modestly and, second, where on earth he was planning to take them.

A brown plastic box sat on the front desk when Judge Bailey entered the mortuary office. Roger McKinney had greeted three carloads of Williford family members—common, simple folk—out front and now had them in a light mood inside the chapel. Agent Reed stood just outside the front door. Tony "Nuts" Ford had continued to home with a promise to return by ten. Judge's plans were singular and simple. Call and arrange a way to retrieve Erica, while hoping there would be no need for arm twisting. She sat, held her phone, and tried to clear her mind and settle her heart. No reason to frighten the girl. Yet she needed to understand the gravity of it. And while she sat, she read the label on the box. Bailey—surprisingly jolted her.

It quickly struck her that that was Dana. Those were Dana's cremains. And yet, as she carefully and suspiciously examined this unexpected visitor, she couldn't help but feel as if some, if not all of her, lived inside that box. "How cruel. That's the summation of life?" she said, envisioning the charred remains of a home still smoldering as if symbolic of these ashes placed in front of her. It was the same thing. Once lovely, yet complex and mysterious, snuffed out just like that. What surprised her more was the sorrow she felt for those who would commit such an act. She'd grieved. She'd cried. She'd accepted it. Some parts needed abandoning. The good, she understood, lived on. And yet, some bitter, hateful soul remained determined to inflict pain interminably. She refrained from embracing the tinge of moral superiority now tempting her. A brief moment and then she dialed, anxious to hear Erica's voice.

Minutes before noon, Agents Duggan and Reed stood on a tarmac, watching that sparkling little jet race down the runway, lift gracefully, and then climb at a sheer angle. At the time Duggan thought of forcefully pulling Agent Reed back to their car. But some curiosity, even some sort of prudence made him linger for a moment.

"Are you hoping they don't come back?" Agent Reed carelessly asked. "You look like you hope to never see them again."

"No, not really," Duggan calmly answered. "But I can't help but wonder if they can outrun this thing. I have a sneaky suspicion this is much bigger than we think. Consider those ramifications."

Agent Reed didn't realize it, but he stopped breathing at the horror of such a thought.

CHAPTER TWENTY-TWO

THE INTERVIEWS

Agent Reed ended a call seconds before Agent Duggan turned off of Pennsylvania State Route 296 and onto the drive leading to the United States Penitentiary, Canaan. The prison sat situated in a wide clearing and was a neatly rectangular concrete complex with six tall guard towers around the wire fences and one in the center. The welcoming facility looked something close to Kip McKinney's horse barn. "That was the New York State Police," Agent Reed sounded chipper. "Found the mini helicopter."

A quick querying look from Duggan. He waited.

"Found it abandoned in a field south of a place called Brooktondale. Ends up the thing was stolen."

"Makes sense. Anything else?"

"No. Unless you consider the advanced planning."

"How advanced?"

"The guy swiped a tractor and parked it where he intended to set down. A tractor was found on a country road a couple of miles away."

"A stashed vehicle. Parked on the pavement?" Duggan contorted his lips.

"Parked on the pavement. No chance of tire imprints."

"They're a clever lot, aren't they? Resourceful, determined, malevolent. I'm very interested in knowing if it was the same one who set the fire. Any word on that yet?"

"No word. I'm more interested in how McKinney's horses died. I think that would reveal a level of sophistication."

"No doubt."

"Which makes me question why we're coming here. Sherman seems the weakest link. Can he even communicate with that brain damage of his?"

"They said he can communicate. I'm more interested in visitors and his contact with the outside world. Besides, this is closer than Allenwood. It's a slight detour at the most. Just as well cover all the bases."

A comfortable nod out from Reed and the two didn't exchange another word until they saw Boyd Sherman sitting behind a table in an off-gray interview room. The guard who accompanied them cleared his throat, "If you're wondering why we let him have the books with him, he won't go anywhere without them. Kind of a security blanket. Plus... that's how he talks."

"What's he holding?" Reed asked. "It looks like a Bible."

"Bible and Book of Mormon."

"Is he a Mormon?" Duggan asked, surprisingly.

"Don't think so. No. He's particular about his Bible. He has all kinds of other religious books. That was his choice today for some reason."

Duggan eyed Reed quizzically. "Now, there's a link to that Buenos Aires fellow. Remember that quote?"

"Yeah. Maybe."

They delayed a moment, studying the man. Boyd Sherman sat tilted sideways like he had had a stroke. He looked bony and frail. His yellowish-blonde hair had turned angel white. Duggan wondered why Judge Bailey hadn't said anything about his Max-Klinger kind of nose. It was a honker, but couldn't hide a dark eye when Sherman cocked his neck to look. He still had big jowls. The guard then handed them a folder. "That's a summation of the communique. I can get you the details. Said that's all you wanted."

"It will do for now," Duggan said and stepped to enter. He pressed the folder into Reed's chest. "Check it out, while I make friends."

Duggan didn't notice the palsy-like shake until he sat across from the man. Sherman formed a tight line on his lips and waited. "Boyd Sherman. How are you today?"

Sherman lifted a quavering hand and made the okay sign.

"Hum... doing good, huh? I'm Agent Duggan. This is Agent Reed. We're with the FBI. Wondering why we're here?"

A slight shrug.

"Get many visitors, Mr. Sherman? Have many family or former parishioners shown up? Sort of a way to comfort the downtrodden?"

A not-really flutter of the hand.

146

"Do you like to send out any messages now and then? You know, keep-the-flock-in-line kind of thing?"

Sherman stared for a second before folding his Bible open. A brief search before he slid the book over. He held up two fingers.

Duggan read the passage from 1 Timothy. "Now the Spirit speaketh expressly, that in the latter times some shall depart from the faith, giving heed to seducing spirits, and doctrines of devils; Speaking lies in hypocrisy; having their conscience seared with a hot iron;" Duggan grinned. "Is that meant for me?"

Sherman again slightly shrugged.

Duggan kept his eyes cemented to Sherman. "Finding anything there, Eddie?"

"A lot of apocalyptic threats. Back and forth."

"Tell me, Boyd... Mr. Sherman. Do you remember the judge who put you in here?"

Sherman pulled his Bible back. Another brief search before sliding it in front of Duggan. Duggan read again from Proverbs: "Do not let your heart turn aside to her ways, Do not stray into her paths."

Another search.

From Jeremiah: "Why should I pardon you? Your sons have forsaken Me and sworn by those who are not gods. When I had fed them to the full, they committed adultery and trooped to the harlot's house." Duggan nudged Reed. "He has his opinions, doesn't he?" He eyed Sherman briefly. "Is that how you see the Judge... as a harlot?"

Again Sherman made another search.

From Revelations: "...and on her forehead a name was written, a mystery, 'BABYLON THE GREAT, THE MOTHER OF HARLOTS AND OF THE ABOMINATIONS OF THE EARTH.' And I saw the woman drunk with the blood of the saints, and with the blood of the witnesses of Jesus. When I saw her, I wondered greatly. And the angel said to me, 'Why do you wonder? I will tell you the mystery of the woman and of the beast that carries her, which has the seven heads and the ten horns.'" Duggan then sighed deeply. "I think I've had enough of this. You'd think the man is penitent. Anything but, I'd say."

Sherman slapped his hand down on his Bible, wrenching it back. He began to drool as he wildly flipped through the pages. His lips turned white and his face cherry red. He hotly shoved the Bible back at Duggan. Duggan winked before again reading from Hebrews: "Vengeance is mine, I will repay, says the Lord."

The instant he read the last word, Sherman again slapped his hand down on the open pages. He was now practically fomenting, hotly breathing through his nostrils. The guard suddenly entered. "Problem in here?" he simply asked.

"No," Duggan said. "I think we're finished." He stood. Before leaving, he pressed his hands to the table and leaned toward Sherman. "I can't quote you scripture, but I think there is something that says only the humble and meek are acceptable to God. I think you've got a ways to go, Mr. Sherman. Think about that."

They gathered outside the interview room where Agent Reed dubiously stared at Duggan. "Was that for real?"

Duggan winked at him. "Not from me. I'm sure it was from him. I could see him going off the deep end and committing what we see going on. The question is, does he have any followers with that much vigor? What did you find in there? Any connecting tissue?"

"Most of his exchange is with a fellow named, Alex Gerhardt. Lives in Eustis, Florida. From what I can tell, the basis of their relationship is calling each other to repentance."

"Well… it might go deeper. I can see a motive here. No doubt about that." He checked his watch. "Let's get out of here. Another two-hour drive to Allenwood and it's already been a long day."

Afternoon sun oddly broke out on this dreary overcast day when Duggan and Reed rolled through a green traffic semaphore and into the much larger Allenwood prison complex. A column of sunshine cut across the sky and strangely lit up the pretty green roofs. There were three separate complexes. Low, medium, and high. A roundabout and somewhat smaller parking lot awaited them when Agent Reed shifted, stiff in his seat. "I suppose you have a reason for interviewing Fuller first, Cain second?"

"You would think. Wasn't my choice. But it makes sense."

Once parked, Duggan eyed the high-security area briefly. High walls, guard towers on the corners. A welcoming building that looked more like something designed for a national park. "What are you thinking?" Reed asked.

"About going straight for the obvious. I'm tired. I'm afraid I won't be so sharp with these fellows."

"Let me handle it. I know you hate losing control, but I'm pretty feisty when I have to be. They see diminutive me with my oversized bodyguard and it might affect them in the knocker. Can't hurt. You jump in if you feel I'm going down the wrong road."

"Eh…" it looked as if huge hands were wringing Duggan out. He sat quietly for a minute, before lifting a lip. "All right. But if it's not going the way I like, don't get pissed if I butt in."

A wink from Agent Reed and he stepped out.

Some twenty minutes later they stood looking in on a gray-faced, gray-haired pillar of salt who seemed locked in a trance. The way he sat there, arms folded, chin up, intense stare you could see his ego as clear as the glassy eyes of a deer, hanging above the mantel. This was a man who saw himself as the center of attention. One who thrived controlling others. Reed turned to Duggan after his brief assessment. "He looks a little bit like you. Maybe I should let you handle this."

Duggan gave him a sour grin. "No way, man. You wanted it, you got it."

Agent Reed wryly raised his brows and led the way in. He merely gripped his hands to a chair back and stared. Duggan sat. "What do you want?" Fuller grumbled. "Now what are they accusing me of?"

"Nothing much, really," Reed calmly and slowly said.

"Then why bug me? You know they went down the wrong hole in the first place. You people are so dense."

"You may be right. I'm Agent Reed. This is Agent Duggan. We're with the FBI."

"What? I mean… right about what?"

"We decided to put some fresh eyes on your case. There are strange things going on at those mines of yours. Seems somebody else might have killed your partner. At least that's a suspicion we have. There is a long trail of death and destruction going on right now."

"I told them," Fuller pointed a finger. "I told them a million times. That Freddie Marcia… he's the one you need to look at. That conniving little monster would just as soon cut your throat than get rich off ya. The little bugger. They wouldn't even corner nor ask the bum a single question. He had Gilbert twisted into knots. Gilbert barks and the guy strikes back. Framed me! If I could just get my hands around his throat."

"Care to divulge. Tell us more about Freddie. What was his nickname? Was he involved with the Bolivian mine or the Congo mine? Or both."

"He's still at the mine, is he? I thought he would have looked for someone else to rob blind."

"Why don't you fill us in a little?"

"I don't want to answer any questions. How did you get the idea that Freddie was trouble? What's he been up to?"

"What I said… death and destruction."

"Um…" Fuller formed a crooked line with his lips and leaned back.

"What's the matter?" Agent Reed asked. "Worried about exposing someone you might fear? Someone who might find a way to strike back. We view Freddie as quite resourceful and determined. I know I'd hate to cross him. Wouldn't it be nice to stick him in front of the same judge who stuck you in here?"

"Now that…" Fuller rammed an elbow to the table and pointed again, "That little twit. Wouldn't listen to a bit of reason."

"Now, who was that? Refresh our memories. Was that Judge Stone?"

"Judge Stone. You mean the little cue-balled guy. That's the one. Made eyes at the missus all through the trial. Had a thing for her. Don't blame him. She's a looker."

"So… that's how you're going to play this, huh? Not at all interested in the chance of freedom?"

Fuller leaned forward, the veins in his neck bulging. "No way in hell!"

Nothing else was said, Agent Reed turned and walked out. Duggan sat there a minute in disbelief. A moment later he met Reed out in the hallway. "I was waiting for feisty. You didn't even get going."

"I could tell it was a waste of time. He was lying to us the second we walked in. Sure, my technique was a bit archaic. But even modern-day tactics wouldn't work with him. At least not in a brief interview like this. I reviewed the case. No mention of any Freddie. He knew there was no Freddie. Went along with the Judge Stone lie too. He could have written an entire novel right in front of our eyes. The only other option I see here is to show up at those mines and ask around. See if anyone knows anything about a Red."

"Yeah... I'm afraid you're right. Unless we get any leads out of Cain. No easy answers here. That's for sure."

"No direct questions with this one. No yeses and nos. Non-confrontational. Get him to tell his story. Sitting around the campfire, talking old-times kind of tactic."

A wink out of Duggan and fifteen minutes later they walked into another interview room where Pedro Cain sat waiting behind a table. The man was just as described. A man with a bland expression. Small, deep-set eyes. Crafty. Meanness hidden under a thinning head of black hair. "Good afternoon," Agent Reed greeted him. He paused, looked around the room, and sighed deeply. "How about we get away from that table? I don't like tables." He pulled two chairs out and positioned them near the door. Not too close to one another, but near the door. Duggan played the role of subordinate. Reed sat after Duggan did and then comfortably crossed a leg. Cain didn't budge. "I'm Agent Reed. This is Agent Duggan. We won't take long. We simply have a couple of questions. Not really about you. About people you may have known," he lowered and slowed his voice.

Cain still didn't move.

"Pedro Cain. That's a curious name. Tell me why you chose to make the change. It was Cantu, right."

"Didn't like Cantu."

"Does it have some kind of meaning? Was there a family issue? Wanted to break ties somehow?"

Cain looked down and began picking at a fingernail. Agent Reed stared at the ceiling briefly. "Did I hear you first lived in New York? Now that's a place I know. You can probably tell from my accent. Brooklyn born and bred. What I couldn't tell you about what I learned there. Man... what a history."

Cain glanced.

"Ever spent a summer day at Coney Island? I practically grew up on Coney Island."

Cain pushed away from the table, crossed over, and sat. He leaned against his knees and rubbed his hands. "I don't get what you're after here. What are you saying?"

"Just reminiscing. Not pressing any issues. I thought I'd connect with a former New Yorker. I have to bum around with this horse all day."

Cain sneered at Duggan for a moment. "What did you want to know?"

"Where'd you live in New York?"

"You're cops. You should know. I'm not going to play your games. I know what you're doing."

"Okay. How's Raul Guzman? Do you know where he is? Would it bother you to know he's souring your name?"

"I'm not going to play your game. I'm not going to say anything about Raul."

"You know about him though. Where he is? How he's doing?"

"I'm not an idiot. You won't get anythin' out of me. I don't have to tell you anythin'. Look..." he leaned in. "I've been through this before. Whatever you call the tactic... you suck up. Try to pretend interest. Get me into a narrative. Same thin' they did to me a dozen times. You're idiots."

"Come on," Duggan grabbed Reed by the arm. "I'm not wasting my time with this guy. Let's go talk to Monica. She's probably in up over her eyeballs. Maybe well on her way to a nice retirement like Pedro here."

Cain's tight-faced, derisive glare morphed into a shade of somber. "No! You leave her alone. She didn't do nothin'. She doesn't know anythin'."

"We have a problem here, Pedro. Someone is causing a hell of a lot of trouble and we need to get to the bottom of it," Reed said. "We don't want to trouble you nor trouble her. We need answers."

"Look," his face twisted with anguish, forming a claw with his right hand. "Nobody's doin' nothin'. Nobodies carryin' on. It's finished. It's done. You gotta believe me. Don't go givin' her no nightmares." His face was now purple with anger. "I don't get no info from no one. I don't send out any orders. I'm a nothin' and they're a nothin'. Just leave her alone."

Both Reed and Duggan let out a cathartic sigh. They studied Cain briefly. "Tell you what," Duggan said. "We'll leave you alone. For now. We'll be back. We have a few things to check out. If we don't like what we see, I'm afraid Monica may get a visit. But I'll make this promise, we'll talk to you first. If there's anything you know or want to share, we'll listen. For now, we'll let you think about it. Have a pleasant day."

That said they stood and walked out. Reed pulled Duggan to a stop a short way down the corridor. "He doesn't know anything. Well... I don't think he's hiding anything."

"You caught his nonverbal signals too, huh? You know that doesn't mean much."

"I know. But I think he was sincere. The funny thing is, I think we got more out of the guy who couldn't talk. At least as far as avenues we want to pursue."

"I think you're right. Let's arrange a flight to Florida. I want to know what this Gerhardt fellow is like. Even more, I'd like a BAU report on everyone involved."

CHAPTER TWENTY-THREE

FRIEND OR FOE

Air rushed along the sleek body of the Pilatus PC-24 as it plunged ahead. Flying at 40,000 feet Judge Bailey leaned forward, seeking for Erica's eyes. Erica still sat in a trance as if pulled there by resistance fighters. A pale canopy of light from a tiny overhead light washed over her and blended angelically, almost melting Erica into the eggshell background. In Meghan's mind, an arctic current flowed inside the poor girl's veins. A resentful current. A bitter current. A current meant for drowning. Accommodatingly, Judge Meghan accepted the bleak, black Northern Atlantic, brewing below, as symbolic in the least, and predestined justice at the most. What was worse, she had no idea how Erica felt. The only comfort, at the moment—if flying east—she could live with. If somewhere north, stark unadulterated doom seemed the only option. Either way, the sky forward was black. The arc of the western horizon, though still in sight, was fading. An eerie, orange, purple, dying thumbnail of malice. The quiet chaffing of air seemed to pull Erica further away from her as if lulling her into prison sleep. The judge felt uncertain and cold. She felt the time already far spent and if delayed much longer, irretrievable. She not only needed answers but also reconciliation.

"Erica?" Judge Meghan reached over and touched Erica's arm. "I'm sorry. I had no way of knowing. If I had any idea… Please forgive me."

Erica absently glanced at Meghan and cocked her neck. "Please stop apologizing. I'm not stupid. I know it's not your fault. How could anyone know what those people had planned? I'm not sitting here, filled with rage and anger. I'm in a stupor. Who were they? Why me? What did I do?"

"They probably thought you were me. My car. My directive. It was my fault."

"Stop saying that. Please, stop saying that. I don't blame you and I never will. You've got to get over this guilt. Just because I'm so closed up, doesn't mean I'm mad at you. I keep reliving it. I'm trying to remember the details. Odors. It's all such a foggy blur. I'm confused.

I'm angry at them. Mostly at myself for not paying attention. I should know better."

"Are you hurting anywhere? Physically, I mean? No pains? No injuries?"

"I'm fine. I've still got a headache. They doped me up."

They both sympathetically reached for one another and embraced. A long embrace. Long and fulfilling. Once settled, Erica glanced out the window. "Where are they taking us?"

"I have no idea. Kip won't say. Bon vol… bon vol, is all you get out of Tony. He's all chipper about it."

"We're flying north, aren't we? What would you guess?"

"I have no idea. Maybe Canada. Maybe he's going one way with another objective in mind. A diversion or something, flying until its pitch black."

"What are our options? Alaska maybe? Russia? I don't want to go to Russia. Iceland. I could see them taking us to Iceland. Just to see the look on our faces." Erica smiled.

"I doubt that. He's probably looking for a big city. I wouldn't mind London. I like London. We could hide in London. It's such an international draw."

"I've never been to London. I wonder if these people haunting us have the wherewithal or sense to consider that."

"Seeing what we've dealt with so far, I wouldn't put anything past them." Judge Meghan got a grim look on her face as she turned to look out a window. "You just have to hope those FBI agents can figure this out quickly."

"Sometimes they get lucky. Sometimes things fall in line right away. They have a lot of bright people."

"And sometimes it takes them years to figure it out."

That thought landed the two somewhere outside of the here and now. As if dangling by a rope and whipping about in the turbulence.

Day-dawn gray held the world pinned to the ground. Or so it felt. Especially for the 62-year-old man crawling through the wild brush. He repeatedly blinked before wiping the sweat from his brow with the back of his trembling right hand. His heart was racing, his mind tormented by images he dared not describe. He reached a small promontory—high ground—in a forest clearing that felt as if land's end. Horror felt burned into his memory from years ago. The terminal point of the beginning. The grassy point sealed his fate and infused the nightmares with meticulous pain.

The grassy point overlooked a peaceful vale where a happy cottage sat hidden among the trees. A flagstone path bordered by yellow daisies led to it where a yellow sconce glowed with a sparkle. A wide, long spread of grass separated them and sat one hundred meters below. Gripped in the man's left hand was a twelve-gauge shotgun. He was dressed in black, his face smeared in chaotic swipes of soot. If things repeated as they always did, no one would appear. No one would surface and no one would stop them when Tolkien's demons suddenly flow out from brush lower than him and then chew the life out of him.

Then it happened. Precisely seconds before the screams started. The unexpected. Rescue? Or so he thought. Or wished… and then quickly denied. Out of the gray, a bright light appeared. "O, my God!" he said with an expensive, refined voice. "They're coming. Why have you abandoned me all these years and coming now? Blimey!" He stood and squinted. "Unless… unless the incubus has another torture planned for me. Not on my watch," he swore, swinging his shotgun up to his shoulder. "This time… you will die."

Ignoring the light, he bound off the knoll and dodged black oak trunks as he forced his way through the underbrush. Halfway down he halted to assess. Still… still… still… one can hear a hush. "No blades. I can't hear the blades slapping the air. There should be blades. Turn the .50 cal on them. Blow them to bits. Rescue helicopter. Hold on… that's not my rescue helicopter?" He had to lean, peering around a tree to see the light touch down and then race, kicking up a trail of brown dirt.

He felt he had no other choice. Shotgun leveled against his shoulder he continued bounding down and eventually emerged just as the Pilatus turned in a graceful arc. Roger "Kip" McKinney and Tony "Nuts" Ford weren't aware and didn't see him until he tromped out in front of them and kept the shotgun leveled at their windshield. "Sainte merde!" Nuts blurted. "Don't blow a hole in our shield. Who the hell is that?!"

"Don't move. Just stay calm. Commander Allen!" Kip shouted. "It's Roger. Roger McKinney. Commander!" Kip quickly unbuckled and piled out. By the time he opened the door and lowered the stairs, he could hear the alarmed voice of Lisa Allen calling.

"Edward! For heaven's sake, Edward put down the gun!"

Kip ducked, crouching once at the bottom of the stairs. He saw Commander Edward Allen still positioned to kill. In a flowing morning robe Lisa Allen, a slim woman with short blonde hair, in a panic, ran straight for Commander Allen and didn't stop until she forced the shotgun barrel heavenward. A breath later, the gun weakly fell out of his hands. Commander Allen then got the most vacant look on his face before suddenly looking as if the Gods had knocked all the wind out of his lungs. A moment of recognition and he nearly collapsed, sobbing into his cupped hands. Lisa had him in her arms when Kip hurried over. At first, her single concern was Colonel Allen. She stood stroking his hair, consoling, whispering in his ear. Kip placed a hand on each of them. She took a double take before realizing who stood there. She then began to whimper. "Oh, Roger, I'm sorry. I'm so sorry. He's been having episodes for a week or so. I can hardly keep track of him. How did you know to come?"

Kip said nothing. He merely wrapped his arms and quietly held them for a moment. It was Nuts who stepped around Lisa and got a firm hold on Colonel Allen's arm. "Let's get him inside, Lisa. Do you have anything to calm him down? What's he been on?"

Lisa turned to look at Nuts. She wrapped an arm around his neck before chittering mildly. "You two. I should have known you two would show up."

Kip stood there as Lisa and Tony shuffled the Colonel toward the path. He turned to find Erica and Jacklyn clinging to one another, expressionless. Kip crossed to fill them in. "That's Commander Edward Allen. Former RAF Wing Commander. We met during a joint training exercise years ago. Hit it off and have stayed close."

"What's wrong with him?" Jacklyn asked.

"PTSD. Never shot down. Never captured. Took a lot of heat though. He flew a Tornado in Bosnia, patrolling the 'No-Fly Zone'. So to speak. Violated over 6,000 times. Constantly fired upon. A duck in a shooting gallery is what it came down to. Now it haunts him. Not so much because of the attacks on him, but because they tied their hands while those who they supposedly protected lived in a slaughterhouse. Cleansed," he made air quotes. "He probably forgot to take his meds. Or refused to. We'll find out."

"This is England then. We're in England?" Jacklyn said, relief in her voice.

"Yes. Won't tell you exactly where. Not that I don't trust you, it's just a habit. I get into a military frame of mind and I'm careful. Sorry, we plucked you out of there with only the clothes on your backs. We'll see what Lisa can do for you. She's a hoot when you get to know her. Don't let that saucy face and loaded eyeballs fool you. She might even have some costumes you can wear." He grinned wide. "She and Edward are members of a local theatre club. Half the time you can't tell whether she's in character or not. She's a charmer either way. Shall we go?" he extended his hand.

Judge Meghan seemed pleased about the whole affair. Like it was a long-awaited vacation. She inhaled, smiled, and hurried off. Erica delayed briefly. "Thank you," she sincerely said.

"What? Smooth landing? Enjoyable flight?"

"No. For doing this for her. For both of us. You don't know how frightening it suddenly is."

"I have an idea. Besides, with you two around, it seemed nobody was safe."

"You mean Prince Lowe?"

"I mean all of us. They started attacking me. Well... my horses."

Erica went palely vacant. "Tabitha?"

"Thank God, no. A few of my five-year-olds. We were planning on breeding them soon. Granted, they don't mean the same to me that Tabitha does, but it hurts still the same. Who knows if I wouldn't end up a target as well. I'm protecting my hide when it comes down to it."

The look on Erica's face was of disbelief. A gentle nod and Kip waited for her to lead the way. Moments later, they walked into a thatched cottage to find a front room contemporary, yet charming. The

158

room was light and pleasant with a stone fireplace dominating the far wall. Everyone stood gathered around a recliner where Tony seemed medic on demand. He knelt on one knee, examining the Colonel, pulling one eye open with a thumb. Colonel Allen now sat there clear-eyed and present. "What's he on?" Tony asked. "Zoloft, Prozac. Effexor perhaps."

"Uh… He's supposed to take his Paxil every morning for another week. I don't think he's been taking them. I see him with the bottle. I don't remember seeing him taking them."

Kip pushed in, knelt, and gripped Colonel Allen by the knees. "You need to do what Lisa says. You hear me, Edward."

"Damnit! I take them. I take them every Godawful day. I think they send me loo-loo."

"Has he been depressed?" Tony asked Lisa.

"I'm not depressed!" Edward barked. "I get antsy. Antsy as hell. I feel like I'm coming out of my skin. My heart races. Then the nightmares come. Along with those gorillas, hunting me down."

"He's doing better. Much better," Lisa said. "He hasn't looked this clear-eyed since the play ended. He does a lot better when we're busy. Give him time off and he goes bonkers. I think seeing you people knocked him bodge."

"Lord, I'm knackered," Edward sighed.

"Well… you ought to be," Lisa said. "Up all night, hunting demons. What I wouldn't give to get you back to your cheeky self."

"We'll take him up in the bird," Tony said. "That will straighten his brain out. Does me a hell of a lot of good. That and hangin' with Kip. It's been two years since I took my Prozac."

"Blimey!" Edward said, gripping his head. "Feel like I've been three years in a concentration camp. Look at me. I'm reduced to idiocy. Psychological jiggle in the noodle. That's what's wrong with me."

"Hah!" Lisa hooted and raked her fingers through her blonde crop. "See… coming back around. Be fit as a fiddle in no time. What a pleasant, if not opportune time for you to brush through like you always do. I'm chuffed to bits, seeing you."

Kip looked Edward in the eye. "Do you still have your plane? When was the last time you flew?"

"It's been ages," Lisa said. "I think it scares him. How long are you going to be here?"

Tony and Roger exchanged a look before Tony inhaled deeply. "Actually, Bella Dame we were hoping this could be more than a 'fancy-a-cuppa' visit. We need a place to lay low for a while."

"Absolutely!" Edward slapped a hand to a knee. "Who's sleeping with whom? Eh!" he threw a hand in the air. "Who cares? Doesn't matter. We'll put you up and have a jolly time. Best thing that's happened in ages. Of course, we'll put you up."

"You don't even want to know why?" Judge Bailey hesitantly asked. "You might regret it."

"Rubbish," Edward said. "Nothing else matters if you can't lean on your friends. Don't even care why you're here."

Lisa looked at him cockeyed. "Well…" she drawled, squinting at Kip. "At least ask. We should at least consider… you know… don't go into this blind."

Kip stood and gave her a reassuring nod. "Meet Judge Jacklyn Bailey. Erica is her clerk. Jacklyn's sister was my neighbor. Ends up she was murdered and we think it has something to do with someone the judge dealt with. Everyone has become a target and so we thought it prudent to move them to a safe distance."

"Hah-hah," Lisa hugged Tony. "I love it when he talks French to me. You'll stay. As long as you want."

CHAPTER TWENTY-FOUR

GIRLIE STUFF

A white orchid stood next to the sink where Kip stood washing carrots and potatoes. Lisa had a quirky smile on her face as she tenderized and flattened out the chicken for the dinner meal. She glanced out the window where she could see Erica and Jacklyn milling about in the back garden. "It's been a lovely day," she said. "Did you get enough rest?"

"I try not to sleep. But I've rested."

"I saw you out there messing around with that plane of yours. How long have you had that one?"

"Year and a half. It fulfills my needs much better than the last."

"I think it's wonderful," she paused and looked over her shoulder. She could still hear Tony and Edward's muffled voices tiptoeing in from the library. "Is that a fishing trip the two are planning?"

"That was the last word I heard."

"That's exactly what Edward needs. He needs more friends like you. Unfortunately, you live an ocean away."

"I thought he had a lot of friends."

"Not for what he needs. They don't mind meandering about locally. Edward needs that adventure. Keeping him tied down here… granted… it's a lovely place and area. He just needs…" she shrugged and smiled, "room to spread his wings. Exploration. He loves exploration. New places and sites. See how he goes all to pot with so little to do. I know the theatre helps. But the season is short and coming to an end. No one likes an outdoor play when it gets chilly. Speaking of which, those friends of yours need new clothes. Couldn't you have at least accommodated that?"

Kip gave her a coy look. "The judge's burned up in a fire. I had nothing to do with Erica getting ready. We had a schedule to meet and that was that."

Lisa paused long enough to watch how Erica and Jacklyn now stood surveying the countryside. It was easy to tell because of the way Erica stood pointing. "No love interest there then?"

"No."

"You've been alone a long time now. How long's it been?"

"How does Edward fuel his plane? I see the sheds and the hanger out there. No fuel tank."

"Oh… you goat! Don't change the subject. I'm not pressing."

161

"I know. How does he get fuel? If we're taking him on an adventure, I need to know."

"I don't know. He calls someone. A lorry comes."

"The plane... what kind of plane does he have now?"

"I don't know. Something that does aerobatics. If he could get his hands on a Spitfire he'd go dizzy with glee. I know that."

"I like this place. I like it a lot. Feels a lot like home. We're in a rural spot with wide open spaces. It's the way it ought to be."

Lisa now seemed over-energized with the meat. A slap and a pound as she flipped them over. "I know I might get ice," she said, "but just consider this. I know you were transitioning to a cowboy or something. And those two might not fit in that picture frame. A buff bloke like you... Heavens... the one is very lush. The other is quite tidy, isn't she? You couldn't go wrong either way. Just think about it. I won't say another word."

"Hah," Kip laughed, throwing his head back. "I'm not transitioning to a cowboy. I own and breed horses. The Queen was not a cowgirl, was she? Just because she had horses."

"You know what I mean."

"No, I don't. Maybe you should just worry about your shopping trip and leave me out of this."

"You're just being dodgy."

"No. I'm being reasonable. When you do take them shopping, go incognito. I don't want to take any chances. With CCTV everywhere, they'll be exposed. I want to keep them safe. I don't know the reach of those interested in Judge Bailey. That's all I'm worried about."

"Now if I ever saw dodgy, that was dodgy. You just don't want me talking about matters of the heart. And as far as I'm concerned, those are the only things that matter."

Kip sighed. "This is how I see it. Love and romance never go unpunished. Everyone I get close to dies. I don't want to live as a prisoner of pain. I've had my share and I don't need more."

Lisa paused for just a moment. She then pounded on the chicken so hard the mallet dented the tenderizing board.

After dinner—after listening to Tony and Edward bantering about where and how far to go for fishing—nearing the nine o'clock hour, Lisa escorted Jacklyn and Erica up a narrow staircase and down a hallway to a comfortable little room with twin beds. "This is where I put the grand-kiddies," she said. "It will be quiet. I'll put Kip and Nuts on the far side. I've heard them snore. They blame it on my beds. I blame it on a couple of blokes that can sleep through an earthquake."

They all laughed.

Erica tested a bed, sitting and bouncing. "Soft," she said. "Really soft. That's why they snore."

"Oh… don't be like them. Soft beds are hunky-dory for most around these parts. Only a dim wit sleeps on a rock."

Judge Jacklyn sat. "Tony and Edward get along well."

"I think their battle wounds cement them together. They understand each other. Does them good."

"You know them well. I mean Kip and Nuts. That's a weird thing to call them, isn't it?"

"Call names. Or signs. Whatever they call it. What else are you going to do? I didn't know who Edward was talking about one day when he kept referencing Roger. I didn't know Nuts was Tony until a few months ago."

"Those two get around, don't they?"

"You know what Kip does, don't you? I don't mean the horses and dead people. I mean his real work."

"Oh… I know all about his real work. Nearly got us killed," Jacklyn raised her brows.

Lisa gave Jacklyn a grave look. "Now what's he been up to? Does he need a good scolding? That's one thing about Kip. He's as cool as a cucumber and as bright as a button. But if something goes haywire, you'd never hear it from him. What did he do?"

Jacklyn raised her brows even higher. "It wasn't his doing. I guess it was more my fault."

"Do tell. Unless it's going to twist your knickers."

"Hah… no. Actually…" Jacklyn seemed caught off guard as she thought back.

Erica jumped in. "We both thought Kip was a criminal. Thought he was the devil himself, at first. Luckily we got our noses rearranged."

"And our butts kicked for misjudging. I guess you are referencing his charitable work when you say real." Jacklyn paused while Lisa nodded. "I was so suspicious of him that I thought for sure he was behind my sister's murder. Thought he was behind everything awful. It's a long story."

"Are you talking about his gift? His premonitions. What a gutted burden. I don't know how he lives with that nightmare."

"What do you mean, gutted?"

"Sad. Devastating. You'd have to be a Brit to understand half the things I say."

"Well… that's only part of it. Let me go back. When we first walked into Dana's home… that's my sister. Dana…" she formed a straight line with her lips and shook her head. "We didn't know someone had murdered her. We went in and found hints."

"Hints?"

"Fangs!" Erica went wide-eyed, clawing the air. "Big ones."

"And a note identifying a fellow in Buenos Aires." Jacklyn reached in and pulled the same note out of her bra. "Antione Banda. Rare book. Buenos Aires. When I found out Kip was flying to Buenos Aires the next day, there was no way I was going to let him go alone. I wanted to know what he was doing and why. I'm so ashamed. He was picking up a kidney patient. I'm surprised he even paid any attention to me. He took me to this marvelous bookstore where we met this fellow. Odd, creepy man. Rings all over his fingers. Long face. Ashen. We walk out and next thing you know we're just about gunned down. The judge inside of me wanted to stay. He forced me to run. He didn't want anything interfering with getting his patient back and here we are. Except the FBI thinks it has something to do with all my cases. I don't think they want to dig into this."

"Can I see that?" Jacklyn handed the note over. "Hm... you say rare book?"

"We think."

"And it goes deeper than that. Someone most likely killed the District Attorney who was trying to poke his nose in," Erica added. "He was creepy too."

"And then they burned my sister's house down... and killed four of Kip's horses... and abducted Erica before letting her go... they took our phones from us so no one could track us."

Lisa's chin lowered with each indictment. "No wonder Kip wants me to keep you two incognito. I've got plans for that." She then got a sparkle in her eye. She stepped into a corner armoire wardrobe closet and threw the doors wide. "I've got costumes galore. Kiddies love dress-up time. Wouldn't be necessary at all if we gave in to Wilhelmina Stanley. I call her the Cro-Magnon Romanian cheerleader. Kind of looks like that. If you can imagine. She'd have us do every play in the nude. Hah... You should see the way Edward's face twists. He's so proper. One time she almost had us doing Shakespeare dressed as farm animals. Midsummer Night's Dream. But that's neither here nor there."

"I'm not wearing a costume," Erica sounded alarmed, leaning and peering in, spotting a King Henry V outfit right off the bat.

"Don't be miffed... unless you want to go posh. I'm talking about this..." she pulled a shoebox out. She then donned a face mask with the image of Sylvester Stallone. She batted her eyelashes, eliciting a rich rolling chorus of laughter out of Erica and Jacklyn. She changed costumes to Madonna, Cher, and Barack Obama before they sat there giddy with giggles. "We could be side-show wiggle dancers." Another chorus of laughter. She then got a serious look. "And as far as that note... I know someone. If you'd like, we can visit. He knows all kinds of things about books. Especially rare books. What do you think?" she raised her brows.

Erica snatched a random mask and quickly morphed into Bill Clinton. "We can do anything you want. No one would know it was us. What a wonderful time in history to be a bank robber, right?"

CHAPTER TWENTY-FIVE

OF ALL THE GIN JOINTS

Minutes before 8:00 A.M. the next morning Kip paced with a phone to his ear while Tony and the Colonel loaded gear in the plane. "He'll be too warm," Lisa said to Jacklyn and Erica. "Those wool pants. That tweed jacket. It's not that cold yet. Even… well… maybe not. Northumberland gets chilly all year long. I'm a bit jittery. I hope he'll be okay."

"He's in good hands," Jacklyn said. "I wouldn't worry."

"I know he's in good hands. It's just… he snapped out of it so fast. He might snap back just as fast. Of course… they'll banter all day long. I guess I've become protective. You're right. No need to worry."

A moment later, Kip stuffed the phone inside his cargo pocket and stepped over. "Left a message on Agent Duggan's phone."

"Did you tell him where we are?" Erica asked.

"No. Just that we're in an isolated location and all is well. So, what are your plans?"

"How long will you be gone?" Jacklyn asked.

"Be back before dark."

"Hmm…" Erica chortled mildly. "The life of the rich and famous. I can't believe how this seems suddenly normal to me. Most people don't fly off for a day of fishing."

"It's a day of rehabilitation," Kip sounded serious.

"Always purpose behind what he does," Lisa said. "That's what keeps him sane. You boys have a tidy knees-up. We'll look forward to seeing you before dinner. That will be served at precisely 5:30 sharp."

"You didn't say. What are your plans?"

"Shopping. One blessed day of shopping. Nothing more." Lisa smiled wide and batted her eyelashes. "I better go say goodbye to Edward. He needs a hug."

Lisa was over and back in less than two minutes. They stood there until the Pilatus raced down the undulating airstrip and then lifted abruptly into a sky of broken white clouds. "Ta-ta!" Lisa wiggled her fingers. She then got a brilliantly radiant glow on her face. "Now, we get down to serious business. At this hour we'll get there early, but who cares."

Giggles fluttered like excited finches in a tree of ripe cherries. Around the house and up a gravel patch to the shed next to the hanger. Lisa pushed the door open to reveal a silicon-silver one–year–old Jaguar XE. Another chorus of giggles and soon they were off, cash seemingly swirling like dead leaves in their tracks.

The lane was narrow, twisty, gravel, and lined with hawthorn and blackthorn hedges. Tall beech trees stretched over short, leaning walls of field stone mixed with Cotswold lime. Lisa kept the speed down until the gravel changed to the pavement. Then she got a sly, ruby-red grin and drove like one of those side-show wiggle dancers. A bit out of control. For a little more than a mile and then slowed at a sharp turn. Hedges thinned enough to see a field dotted with shiny black cows. And then instant order came. A neat, tall, and exact Headington stone wall marked the edge of civility. A curve in the road and an idealistic English hamlet emerged where a row of one-story buildings lined the right side and a tiny square on the left presented a small church. Down the way where the road curved opposite, a stately little pub bookended an Inn that looked 17th Century Shakespearean timber frame. An old gentleman wearing a dark blue jumper walked there with a cane. Lisa raced ahead and then braked next to the fellow. The judge's window solidly purred, lowering. "Charlton… morning," Lisa raised her voice.

"Oh, sweet Lady…" the white-haired fellow's voice was squeaky and genteel. "My sweet Lady." Lisa reached across the judge and the gentlemen reached in. He gripped with both before patting. "On a jolly outing?" he asked.

"Yes, we are."

"So lovely. Always so lovely. How good to see you."

"Charlton… Alright? Has my brother looked into your roof? What about the pipes?"

"Not as yet," he said. "No worries. Surviving we are."

"No. Rubbish. He said he took care of it. You wait right there for just a minute." Lisa made a call over the Jaguar's phone system while the gentlemen looked in on Jacklyn and Erica.

"Haven't seen you before. Tourists?"

"Friends."

"Oh, Americans. Who she doesn't know. Well… aren't you a lush sight for fading eyes."

"Charlton," Lisa then interrupted. "I've left a message. The bloke isn't answering his phone. If he doesn't have somebody on it by the end of the day, I'll see to it."

"Oh, isn't she sweet? Thank you, my Lady."

Lisa pulled away while the gentleman remained watching. Jacklyn gave Lisa a jesting look. Lisa seemed to ignore her. "Lady? My Lady? Royalty?"

"Royalty!? Hah! Tosh. Not even."

"Then why Lady?" Erica asked. "Doesn't that mean something?"

"It's a courtesy title. Lord Muck… My brother… the Earl of Godsham likes it. Me… not so much. I could care less. I'm a Lady because of the family tree. Didn't do a thing to earn it. Comes with being land owners. You know… the Gentry class. Means a lot to James. Right up here around the next bend, if you look off to your right you'll see a stately manor house. He's good at playing certain roles, but doing his duty to his tenants takes more than kibitzing."

"Wow!" Erica said. "Impressive. You own all this land?"

"Not me. The James George family. I might make a claim indirectly. Of course I live rent free and get a pittance allowance. There's a caravan park up that way behind those trees. I get a portion of the rental and fees. And it's going to buy to your hearts content this morning."

"I'm still impressed. Not because of the wealth. Because of how you handle it. You're so…" Erica looked dizzy, "down to earth."

"Ha-ha… not how James would describe me. I'm a daft mug."

"Meaning?" Jacklyn asked.

168

Lisa winked and giggled. "A stupid idiot that goes along with anything. Says I'm more common than a commoner. And I love it," she emphasized. "In all of Wessex you won't find anyone more pleased at being mental than me. At least according to James. I put on for him and him only. Everyone else gets the real me."

"And I think you're absolutely wonderful," Jacklyn said. "I've never been so comfortable and pleased in meeting someone. I can see why Kip wanted to come here. I guess I'm a loony bird too."

"Count me in," Erica said and laughed.

The passage of forty minutes found them in front of a stylish dress shop called My Fair Lady, Jacklyn wearing a Tony Blair mask, Erica a Betty White and Lisa as Donald Trump. Lisa immediately climbed out. "Is this Oxford?" Jacklyn asked. "This feels like Oxford." She glanced over the seat at Erica. Erica shrugged, and practically bounced out. Jacklyn asked again at the trendier chic place called Cotton Bottoms and got no answer. Same cold shoulder at a covered mall simply labeled Market. But when, with a boot full of packages, they pulled into one of four stalls not far from the Hume-Rothery Building she boldly declared, "This is Oxford."

Lisa pulled down her mask and stuck out her tongue. "Kip said not to say. I didn't tell him we were coming this far and especially considering all the CCTV around here. And that insult was for him, not you." She giggled. "I have to get a parking sticker and then we walk. Not far. Right on the far side of these buildings."

The day had turned pleasantly warm. The noon hour had sauntered by, evidenced by a lull in the afternoon traffic. Short walk on Parks Road to Keble and then to St. Giles'. The tree lined A4144 held a smattering of cars, a line of buses and darting students. Less than a half mile later, Lisa darted, leading them over and under a flat tarnished arch with an etched, yet cacographic seal. Almost instantly, she turned right, cutting through an open door and then left again up a creaky set of well-worn wooden stairs. A right, a left and down a corridor that soon dipped where old met new and then a short walk where she paused to peek into a lecture room. "I knew it sounded too quiet. You can usually hear the professor's adenoidal echo."

No worries, she spun back. New back to old and then a left and up two flights of dark creaky wooden stairs before the unspoken sense of familiarity slowed her pace. Straight to the front of the building where a door stood half open and where the bright light from two narrow arch-angle windows briefly blinded. Jacklyn and Erica merely poked their heads in far enough to see a rotund man sitting behind a cluttered desk. He had fluffy white hair on the sides. He sat peering over his round spectacles with a hostile glare. The room was of dark stained wood, overburdened with bookshelves and books galore. No response until Lisa tugged her mask down. "Hoooo…" he howled a sophisticated howl, throwing his arms in the air. "Lisa, Lisa! What a wonderful surprise. What's with the get up? Jump started my heart for a moment." He moaned getting onto his feet and then reached for Lisa. The two embraced. He kissed her on each cheek and then straightened his bow tie before running his hands down his knitted charcoal sweater vest. "My goodness…" he squeezed her cheeks. "It's been too long."

"Sorry about that. I know I should come more often. It's only been about seven or eight weeks."

"Really? Feels ages. Didn't come, expecting lunch, did you? Tummy's a bit out of sorts. Doc's got me on a new pill. Gerd and all."

"No. No lunch plans. Least not for you. I'm taking my new friends when we finish here."

He lowered his chin, glancing. Jacklyn and Erica removed their masks. "What's with the ugly get-ups? Hiding such lovelies. My, my. Such lovelies."

"Professor. Meet Judge Meghan Jacklyn Bailey and her clerk, Erica Dennis. They're visiting from the United States. This is my dear, dear friend, Professor Dexter Cowen. Anthropology, religion… all that stuffy stuff."

He extended his hand and heartily shook. "Don't let her fool you. Everybody is her dear, dear friend. Nothing special about me." You could tell he had a bad hip when he settled back down into his chair. "Just lollygagging?" he asked. "I doubt that. Even if she's playing tour guide."

"Actually…" Lisa looked over her shoulder before her face turned purposeful. "We're playing detective. I'd like your expertise… or at least your opinion on something. It nearly cost the judge her life. I'm hoping you might shed some light."

His eyes brightened. Lisa held her hand out. Jacklyn passed the note over. "The judge's sister was murdered and we think it has everything to do with this note. Best we can tell, she traded in rare books."

"Let me see that." Cowen's face turned quite grave the moment he glanced. He then nodded and lowered his voice. "Close the door."

"You know who that is?" Jacklyn asked. "You look like you do."

"I know about him. Have you had dealings with this man?"

"In Buenos Aires," Judge Bailey said. "We nearly got killed after meeting with him. It happened so fast. It was terrifying."

"Really. Um…" he covered his mouth, thinking. "Interesting. Very interesting."

"What do you know about him? Do you know about some book he refuses to sell?" Lisa asked.

"I don't know that much about him. I know his name is tied to something I don't dare talk about. I've considered it rumors and questionable. Others believe it true. If it is… I'll have to completely change my thinking. I know that much."

"What?"

"This saying. It's from the Book of Mormon. Have you heard of the Book of Mormon?"

"Yes. My sister had one. That section was highlighted."

"Do you realize what it is saying?"

"Didn't really delve into it."

"If you read it, it talks of Christ appearing in the Americas following his death and resurrection in Jerusalem. He called apostles. Three wanted to remain alive until his return. There are some—aside from Latter-Day Saints—who believe it to be true and that one of them has a written record, identifying modern day people and events that could topple power structures." He then looked up, studying them.

"What do you believe?" Lisa asked.

171

"I have no idea. Until I see a book or meet the man and he can prove who he is, it's a conspiracy theory. Although, for some… and if they take it seriously… I would consider that extremely dangerous."

"Some religious cult maybe."

"Maybe."

"Well, this doesn't settle me very much," Judge Bailey said.

"Makes it worse," Erica added.

"Why Banda? What's his role?" Lisa asked. "Is he some kind of a religious leader?"

"Hah! Hardly. Rare book dealer. Among other things. Deals with lots of international clients. A good way to launder money if that's your game."

"Well… maybe it isn't me they're trying to kill then," Judge Bailey said. "At least from one of my cases."

"Unless they're tied to this Banda fellow," Erica said.

"I can't believe you ladies would handle this on your own," Cowen said.

"We're not. The FBI is involved. We escaped here to preserve our lives. You've shed more light than anybody else has. That's for sure. It was like providence, meeting Lisa."

"Lisa is providence," Cowen said and laughed. "When she's not playing one of her intriguing roles. Right fine little actor, she is." He chuckled.

"Well…" Lisa sighed heavily. "I think we've accomplished what we've needed. You've helped so much. Hate tying you up. I'll come back and visit when I have more time. I want to feed my friends and then get them back before the army comes marching home."

"Army?" Cowen raised his brows.

"Just Edward and his mates. Fishing trip."

"How is Edward?"

Lisa waffled her hand and grimaced. "Good days and bad days. Right now, brilliantly. Providence is a two-way street. Ta-ta for now," she wiggled her fingers and nearly pushed Jacklyn and Erica out the door. "Sorry," she said once walking the corridor. "I have to force myself out. If not… we go on forever."

Once on the street, Lisa pointed. "Down past St. Mary Magdalen church and around the corner. I know a little place to satisfy any appetite. Masks on. March," she said, giggling.

Jacklyn quickly became lost in thought and trailed a few steps. Soon she walked engrossed. She could see the long folds in Banda's face. Could see silver rings. Gaudy rings. Heavy rings. Past the Balliol College Library and Porter's Lodge. Past decorative posts where hanging red geraniums brushed her shoulder when she walked by. Currency exchange shop across the way could have been the doorway to hell with demons emerging and they would have gone unnoticed. College shops, coffee shops, café this and café that. All went unseen. Everything until a shiny black façade with its captivating window-display demanded she look. Because of the books. Books stacked and neatly arranged to trap anyone. Especially those with books on their mind. Call it subliminal. Call it the mischief of a predisposed mind. The moment she looked up and in beyond the display her heart erupted. Her knees buckled slightly. She couldn't move except to spiral on a heel and bend her knees, slumping down against the façade. "Impossible," she whispered. "No way on earth." Closing her eyes she could barely breathe. One thing she knew. If God was providential, not only is evil inopportune, it was difficult and grossly rude as well.

CHAPTER TWENTY-SIX

LADY LISA PLAYS THE BARD

It felt ages, but was twenty, thirty seconds later when Erica and Lisa quickly returned. "What's happened? Are you alright?" Lisa sounded a lot like Twyla MacDonald. "What? What?"

"He's in there. I saw him. O God. I don't believe it. How would he know? How could he do this?"

"What? What?" in a panic.

"Banda. Antione Banda. I saw him. He's in there."

"No way. You're mistaken. It's just because you had him on your mind. Couldn't be," Lisa said, squinting with a hand over her eyes. She nearly pressed her nose to the glass.

"That's him. I swear that's him. I'd recognize him anywhere."

Erica quickly ducked and moved away from the window. Lisa cupped her hands and stared. "There is a customer in there at the counter. A few students too. You sure?"

"Positive."

"Hah. We'll see about this," Lisa snorted and stormed in.

Jacklyn could barely muster the strength to turn her head, let alone go after her. "We should get out of here," Erica hissed. "We can't just sit here. What if he comes out and sees you? Then what?"

"Oh..." emptied her lungs. Curious about how certain images and threats affect the human condition. No problem moving now. Jacklyn took Erica by the hand, rose to a crouch, and pulled her down the street until they found the first doorway that felt antithetical to Banda. A narrow, trendy pizza place, in shades of black and hot pink and marketing to a much younger crowd, the teen pop music playing the giveaway. A waitress dressed in white-hot, butt-short, and tight coveralls and big black boots gave them a crude look and dully droned,

"Seat yourself. Any table." She then pouted her black lips before swishing her pink, purple, and blue hair as if offended.

"We'll wait here," Erica answered. "Waiting for a friend."

Lisa coolly walked into the bookstore, pulled her face mask down, and paused as if browsing. No problem noticing Banda's long gray hair. Even easier spotting his rings. He stood there turning a page and fully occupied with text. The clerk behind the counter, a slim, young, book-worm-looking fellow with large-rimmed black glasses and greased hair, stood chewing on a fingernail, either full of self-doubt or terrified. Lisa calculated briefly. This seemed to call for a coy Hamlet mistress character or something of that order. Seductively strutting, she ran a finger along a row of books before pausing. No embarrassment at all, playing off a title about British battlefields.

"A horse, a horse! My kingdom for a horse!" she said, reeling and crossing an arm over her forehead.

She changed positions, pretending Catesby. "Withdraw, my lord:" she lowered her voice deeply, "I'll help you to a horse."

Back to King Richard: "Slave! I have set my life upon a caste, and I will stand the hazard of the die. I think there be six Richmonds in the field; five have I slain instead of him. A horse, a horse! My kingdom for a horse!" She closed her eyes, leaned her head back, and peeked with one eye as if expecting an Academy Award. A few giggles out of two girls in school uniforms and then a light smattering of applause. Lisa cracked both eyelids just as Banda grilled her with a look. She lifted and showed off the battlefield book. He looked away.

She continued perusing. She came to a title regarding famous British shipwrecks. She removed it, fondly smiled, and flashed it at the clerk. "I warrant you, sir," she dramatically said, "the white cold virgin snow upon my heart abates the ardour of my liver." She expected a look out of Banda. Nothing. She tried another line and approach. This time clutching the book to her breast, amorously advancing and eyeing the clerk, increasing the drama in her voice with each line, "You do look, my son, in a moved sort, As if you were dismay'd: be cheerful, sir. Our revels now are ended. These our actors, As I foretold you, were all spirits and Are melted into air, into thin air:

And, like the baseless fabric of this vision, The cloud-capp'd towers, the gorgeous palaces, The solemn temples, the great globe itself, Yea all which it inherit, shall dissolve And, as this insubstantial pageant faded, Leave not a rack behind. We are such stuff As dreams are made on, and our little life Is rounded with a sleep. Sir, I am vexed; Bear with my weakness; my, brain is troubled: Be not disturb'd with my infirmity: If you be pleased, retire into my cell And there repose: a turn or two I'll walk, To still my beating mind."

She tucked her chin to her chest and exhaled as if exhausted. The clerk gulped. Banda stared at her like she was crazy. "I act," she said. "It's in my blood. Sites and words inspire me." She batted her lashes at the clerk. "How'd I do? From The Tempest."

"Ugh, ugh, ugh," he sucked for air. "Good. Really good."

Banda looked back and turned a page.

"My... how curious. What beautiful rings. Those are something. May I ask where you got them?"

"No," he coldly said without looking.

"I'm Lisa Allen by the way," she extended her hand.

He ignored her. He then seemed to cut the heart out of the clerk with a simple caustic glare. The clerk again gulped. "Sorry, Mr. Banda. I don't know who she is."

"Well... aren't we the rude lot," she puffed. "Maybe I'll just take my act... and business elsewhere. Some people appreciate what I do. Some people are friendly. Umph!" she huffed, left the book on the counter and marched out.

She instantly panicked once out the door. Not a soul in sight. Well... those souls that mattered. Lisa hurried out into the street to look up and down, but before she could look she heard the, "Psssst!" hiss from down the way. She quickly spotted Erica emphatically waving. She ran to her.

"It's him. It's actually him. I can't believe it."

"What do we do?"

"We call the coppers. That's what we do," she said, tugging her phone out of her pocket.

For thirty-five agonizing minutes a female officer sat with them while they waited. She stood at the doorway, while the three locked ranks and suffered. "We've got extenuating problems as far as I can see," Jacklyn whispered. "We shouldn't have called the police. We've compounded a problem to who knows what reaches."

"Don't get your knickers in a twist," Lisa said. "There are ways to smooth things over. When you know the right people."

"Yes. But we're in the country illegally. What are they going to do about that? Then they contact the FBI and suddenly we blow our cover tenfold. What a mess this is. Kip is going to kill us." A middle-aged officer with a gut walked in. They had pretty much closed down the pizza shop and so he took his pick of chairs before sitting across from them. "Now," he sounded gruff, "who is this Banda fellow again?"

"Did you get him?" Lisa punched. "Don't let him go."

"The man must have slipped out a back door. Besides, what crime has he committed?"

"Crime? Who cares about a crime here?" Lisa honked. "He tried to kill her in Argentina. What do they say in Argentina?"

"You know how strained our relationship with Argentina is, don't you? Be lucky if we get any word at all out of them."

"Well, that makes a bloody hell lot of sense. Couldn't muck this up worse than it is."

"We have this issue with your illegal aliens."

"That won't be an issue. I'll make one call and get this cleared up. The problem is… now these sweet ladies are exposed. You do realize that, don't you? Did you call the FBI?"

"You should have gone through channels. No permissions. Should have done this properly. Don't get on my case for your poor judgement. Tell me… where is the Colonel right now? We'd like a word with him."

"He's out somewhere fishing. I'll have him call you the minute I get home."

"I hate to imagine the trouble if we had arrested this Banda fellow for no feasible reason. Tell me… what did he do here that's illegal?"

"Well… who cares about here. It's what he does everywhere else."

"Unless I have something in hand that gives me that authorization, I can't do anything. Do you understand my position?"

"Are we free to go?"

"I'd like you to make that special call of yours. You know your friends could get up to four years for illegal entry."

"And they can apply to stay here legally. I'm not stupid. Good heavens," she shushed, before taking her phone and angrily punching an autodial number. A ticking clock marched off thirty miserable minutes before all the connections made. Lisa contacted James, James contacted Arthur—a member of parliament—and Arthur called the Department for International Development who in turn spoke with the U.S. Embassy, who in a line of calls spoke with Agent Shaun Duggan at 7:00 A.M.

177

Florida time. A call then to Immigration Enforcement, who finally rang Officer Bennion. Officer Bennion merely nodded and let them go. By four o'clock a very grumpy Lisa pulled her Jaguar to a stop near the back garden and didn't say a word until Jacklyn and Erica found her finishing off a shot of Somerset Cider Brandy in the kitchen. "Sorry," she said. "I'm normally quite pleasant. Injustice simply riles me to the core."

"No. It's our fault," Jacklyn said. "We should have never put you in such an awkward position."

"And I understand how a military mind works. They're not always thinking about hoops you have to jump through. They have a mission and they're going to fulfill that mission no matter what." She checked her watch. "I'll whip up something to eat and hope no one has put a burr under Edward. He won't like the trouble."

"All we have to do is tell him about Banda and that he was here. That's enough, isn't it?"

They searched eyes for a moment. "Hope so. Yes. Why not."

"What can we do? We'll help you fix dinner."

"Won't be a problem. We'll prepare bangers and mash. Plenty of time to do that." Lisa looked at the way Erica had her head down. "Don't fret. We'll be fine. Hardly any trouble when it comes down to it."

"Yes. I'm just worried," Erica muttered. "Banda shows up here. That's weird. Really weird, right? Now that others know we're here, would they show up like he did? We don't know the depths of this."

Lisa studied her glass like she needed another. The look on her face appeared as if blighted rosebushes awaited her when she said nothing and stepped to the pantry where a sack of potatoes awaited her on the floor.

CHAPTER TWENTY-SEVEN

AGENT DUGGAN COMES CLOSE

Agent Shaun Duggan tossed his phone onto an unmade bed in his room at a Holiday Inn Express in Eustis, Florida. A rush of steamy anger spread over him, compounding the sticky feeling in a world that had gone mad. What he wouldn't give to simplify things, at least by a fraction. Perhaps, confirmed bachelorhood, as Eddie Reed enjoyed would help. He considered that briefly and quickly regretted it, knowing how hurt Debbie would feel. At least she understood and accepted his life as an FBI agent. A role to which he quickly returned. "You're not going to believe this!" he barked through the wall. He wouldn't have except Reed had turned the shower off seconds ago and so he felt certain he could hear him. A breath later, Agent Reed appeared in the doorway, a towel around his waist and a toothbrush in his mouth.

"Wha...?"

"They're in England. They go over there, don't clear it with anyone, and expect it to go unnoticed. What a bunch of idiots."

"Wha' appen?"

"Ladies march off to Oxford for some moronic reason and end up... get this... running into Antione Banda."

Agent Reed quickly returned to spit in the sink before reappearing. "You've got to be kidding. What did Roger McKinney say about that? I thought he was reasonably competent."

"Haven't talked to McKinney. I called, but no one is picking up."

"England. That's a long way away. Should be safe there, shouldn't they?"

"Yes. I hope, but what about this Banda guy? Did he know? We need to find out about him."

"The Brits are aware. Are they providing protection?"

"I don't know. I'm so mad I almost don't care."

"What do you want to do?"

"What am I going to do?" Duggan threw his hands in the air. "They have lives. They make choices. More important to me right now is finding out if there is any connection here. We need to track this Gerhardt fellow down and fast."

"That mobile home... that looked pretty much abandoned. We should have asked around last night."

"And who were we going to talk to that late? Neighbors didn't want to be bothered. A good portion of these people are over 65. They go to bed early. One question we haven't answered is, who's his employer?"

"Let's get back out there and dig. We'll set up camp and watch for activity. I'll get dressed. Find us something to eat. Wasn't there a Denny's around the corner? Call. We'll pick up on our way."

In the ten-minute drive from Denny's, Agent Reed studied his phone. "Lake County," he muttered. "Two-hundred and fifty named lakes. Seventeen-hundred and thirty-five other bodies of water. That's a lot of water. They get sinkholes around here, don't they?"

"Possible."

"Used to grow cotton. Citrus was king for a while. Suddenly, I wish I'd ordered a glass of orange juice."

"Why?"

"Cold wave in '89 destroyed most citrus groves. Feel like I missed out or might if I don't do something now."

Duggan passed Reed's curiosity off and soon wheeled into the side lot of a Dollar store whose back wall faced Trout Lake where the mobile park sat a third of a mile opposite. Seconds later, they both sat in silence as they scanned through binoculars. For five minutes Agent Duggan scoured the Gerhardt's mobile home and how it abutted the nearby woodland of mangroves and cypress trees. He finally laid his glasses aside and expected Reed to do the same. "What are you seeing?" he asked.

"A lady we ought to be talking to. That middle unit… where the road turns. I've seen a half-dozen dog walkers already. Every one of them stops to visit. If anybody knows anything, that fat, purple-haired lady does."

Duggan picked his glasses up and scanned briefly. Nothing else said. A breath later they were on their way.

Mrs. Anita Clayton's double-wide sat perfectly situated with a view of Trout Lake, plus an ideal location if you were the nosy sort. Her place had a low, white-picket fence, a single palm tree, an older model Champaign-colored Cadillac, and rose bushes aplenty. She sat in a lawn chair, near the road, and running a hose when the agents pulled up in their Chevy Malibu rental. She dropped the hose the second they stopped, a wash of either guilt or derision washing over her face and turning a pleasant smile resolute. Agent Duggan called out to her the instant he stepped out. "Good morning, Ma'am. Beautiful morning, isn't it?"

"Look… they needed a little water. You can't come by here harassing old people like this. You're giving me ulcers."

Agent Reed was already chuckling. "Ma'am," he lightly said. "We're not from the water department… or the city… or whatever."

"Health Department?! Are you from the Health Department?"

Agent Duggan flashed his badge. "Actually… FBI."

A determined look suddenly turned near ecstatic. She wiggled out of her chair and moaned an arthritic groan before beaming. "My… who ya after? Drugs? Murder? What?"

"Hm…" Agent Reed chortled. "Who are you? What's your name?"

"Me? I'm Anita Clayton. What then… murder?"

"No. Just wondering if you know anything about your neighbor. Hasn't done anything wrong. We're just following a lead."

"Which neighbor? Gary? Is it Gary and Lolita? They do funny stuff."

"No. Do you know Mr. Alex Gerhardt? Lives in the last unit down here along the lake. The shabby green and silver place. Has plywood and a padlock on the door."

"That's his name all right. Bum! Come in! We'll have a cup of coffee."

"Ma'am," Agent Reed said, "here is fine. What can you tell us about him?"

"Let's not be rude Agent Reed. By the way, I'm Agent Shaun Duggan. This is Agent Eddie Reed."

"He's a New Yorker. Recognize that wind-song accent anywhere. My Wayne was Brooklyn-bred. You don't know what it does for me to hear that."

Agent Duggan exchanged a wink with Reed. "Alright," Agent Reed smiled wide. "Let's go in for a minute."

It was a pleasant setting around a small corner table by sheer curtains touching the floor where the agents settled in. "I've been wondering why someone doesn't do something about that man," Anita huffed while preparing instant coffee.

"What do they need to do?" Duggan asked.

"Have you seen his place? It's an embarrassment."

"Isn't there an HOA or something?" Agent Reed asked.

"For us there is. He was a squatter or something before we came in. I think that junk yard is a decoy or something. I think he lives out there in those woods."

"Squatter? Doesn't the city or county do anything about that?"

"They don't care. You've got to have money for anyone to care."

"Do you see him often?" Duggan asked. "What does he do for a living?"

"Hardly ever see him. Comes in here with an old green Dodge pickup. Sometimes has a lawnmower in it. Sometimes other equipment."

"How old is he?"

"I don't know. Looks forties maybe. Scary guy. Has big red whiskers. Always wearing army garb. I keep thinkin' he's gonna pull a big-bladed knife on someone and slit their throat."

"He makes threats?"

"Not to folks around here that I'm aware of. I don't remember ever hearin' him talk to anyone. Tries to lure kids in there though."

"Kids? What kids? Are there kids living in here?"

"No kids allowed. 55 plus only. I mean them missionary sorts. You know... The Mormons."

"What do you mean lure?"

"These young lads show up now and again, askin' directions. Says he wants them to stop by. Sharp fellers. Kind of like you two. You know… clean shavin'. Smartly dressed. White shirts and ties. Black badges. Pleasant as fuzz on a peach. What were their names…?"

"Has there been a mishap?"

"Oh… Lordy no. They're too clever for that. Been in here three, four times. Six different ones. Davis!" she brightened up. "One was named Davis. And Ralph. Something Ralph. Davis, Ralph, and Kirk. I remember those names now. Only got as far as Melba Squires. You get there and you get a good view of his pig sty. That's as far as they go and then they hightail it out of here. Those last ones… Davis and Ralph… they told me that if any other missionaries come in here lookin' for him, to turn 'em away. Said they're not to visit that place, they did. And I don't blame them." She shivered, placing a cup of coffee in front of them.

Agent Duggan stood. "I think we'd better check on this place before we entertain ourselves. Don't you think that would be wise, Anita?"

She touched a finger to her lip. "I suppose it would. Well… yes. Go on. I'll keep the coffee waiting if you change your minds."

They knew the white mobile home with yellow trim belonged to Melba Squires as they eased around the bend, leading to Alex Gerhardt's place. A chain-linked fence separated Gerhardt's lot from the mobile home park called Haven Creek Manor. The pavement ended as well. The Chevy rocked, rolling through a few mud puddles before coming to a stop. Another chain-linked fence reached about chest high and surrounded the home. A gate stood reinforced by steel posts. Tall grass and weeds felt the oppressive camouflage of choice. Same rusted padlock declared the dwelling off limits. Agent Reed climbed out and stood there as if the place had fleas. Duggan pranced around a few mud puddles before standing back and assessing. "Hey," he said to Reed. "Look at this?"

"What?"

"Power pole back here. I think it's got more than power coming off of it. It could be cable. Could be internet. Could be a direct line to the president." He laughed. "Strange." Duggan tiptoed like he intended on rounding to the back of the lot.

"Wait!" Agent Reed suddenly shouted. "I wouldn't do that."

Duggan froze and stared. "Why not?"

"Come get a look at this. If I'm not mistaken there's a trip wire up there in front of that bottom step. Looks like we need some SABT fellows out here pronto. I'm not going in there. I know that much. At least not until those boys get a look at this."

CHAPTER TWENTY-EIGHT

WHAT WEBS WE WEAVE

Considering the entire Gerhardt mobile home could be a bomb, local police, and sheriff's department assisted in evacuating all of Haven Creek Manor trailer park and everyone else within a one-mile radius. An FBI CRIG (Critical Incident Response Group) had also assembled. Agent Duggan and Reed stood outside a sheriff's mobile command center on State Route 19 when two bomb squad vehicles rolled through the roadblock. An accompanying unmarked, dark-colored sedan wheeled to a stop, and a dignified man with a gray mustache stepped out. He wore a light green T-shirt and dark cargo pants. He approached Agent Duggan. "They said to look for the tall one. Are you Agent Duggan?"

"I am."

He extended his hand with an amiable smile. "Victor Stewart. I'm the Unit Chief of the Hazardous Devices School. Mind filling me in on what you saw in there."

"Unit Chief? We're climbing the ladder on this one, aren't we?"

Stewart chuckled mildly. "I was down here in Gainesville, conducting a little training. Thought this would be the perfect opportunity. What did you see in there?"

Agent Reed spoke up. "Saw a trip wire. In front of the stairs. Didn't take time to poke around. We're not stupid."

"Also noticed that the place seemed to have a larger power source than may be necessary," Duggan added. "I've never dealt with an IED. What are you going to do?"

"Assess. How far back are we?"

"We figured a two-thousand-pound bomb... possibly. Consulting with the local boys, we figured a mile."

"We may change that. What's the ground like? Can I get a robot in there?"

"Ground was uneven. Muddy pot holes everywhere. Everything sits behind a chain-linked fence and is buried in weeds. How long is this going to take?"

"Depends. We make an assessment, we'll take X-rays. We want to do this right. Last thing I want is a post blast environment inspection. Understand? I'm not going to rush this."

"That's not an issue. I was just worried about the folks. In case anyone asks. Plus... I'm really hoping to find out a lot more about this fellow. Plus, we suspect or have reason to believe he may be living inside the woods next to the trailer park. That's all within the danger zone. Can't go in until we get this done. I don't want him getting away from us."

"You have men posted, don't you?"

"Entire area is surrounded, but there are limits."

"We'll do the best we can. My men's safety is priority. Let me ask one more question... this power source... could you tell if it split or anything of that nature? If we're dealing with a victim initiated device that's one thing, if I'm dealing with a timer or radio controlled device it's another. You best be ready for a long wait."

"I understand. Like I said, I've never dealt with an IED before. However we can help."

"All right. If we get in there and assess things differently, we won't narrow the evacuation zone, we may extend it. Depends on fragmentation and overpressure estimates. Be ready for that."

"Very good. Thank you, sir."

An acknowledging nod before Stewart climbed back inside his sedan and raced off.

Duggan's phone rang seven hours later. "All right. Agent Duggan. Victor Stewart here. You can do your search."

"What was it?"

"Victim initiated. Trip wire attached to two propane tanks. Very simple, but clever devise. Initial charge alone could have leveled this baleful, yet dowdy castle. All we had to do was disconnect the trip wire. Had to go through the entire place though. What a rats nest."

"Was he living in there?"

"Somebody was in here recently. One week old copy of The Ithaca Journal on the computer keyboard."

"Does he have a lot of computer equipment?"

"Just the basics. Single screen and tower. Looked well used. I'll leave that to you. We left it as clean as we could."

"Thank you," he said nodding to Agent Reed. "We're in. Turn the sheriff loose and everybody else we can onto those woods. Let's get a team inside that mobile home and see what we can find."

Within the hour this was the information gathered:

Real name—Donald Edwin Gerhardt

Supposed occupation—self-employed handyman/lawn care.

Pertinent software applications—Linux OS, VPN, JTR, Keylogger—are all necessary for basic computer hacking.

Other significant information—Army vet, dishonorably discharged. Hides behind religious fanaticism—faith substituted with delusion, good works substituted with revenge, compassion substituted with hatred. List of contacts designated by code names only. Peter, James, Matthew, John, etc. Every one of the twelve apostles plus Lazarus, Simon, Ananias and Uriah. Envelopes containing a selection of six different species of snake fangs.

Within an hour and a half, Donald Edwin Gerhardt himself was found hiding inside a "spider hole" some four hundred yards away and stunned that anyone had found him. For Agents Duggan and Reed, they felt satisfied and certain they were well on their way to wrapping this whole nasty affair up. Just a few rogue apostles out there, waiting for the fisherman's net cast upon the waters, which seemed a minor complication and then accolades. Judge Meghan Jacklyn Bailey, Erica Dennis, and Lisa Allen wouldn't agree in the least. Especially in their current state of mind. It would be some time before, if at all, when such declarations even seemed feasible.

Jacklyn roused herself with a slight start. Her eyes darted from the dinner table and back out the front window, recognizing the Pilatus as it slowed before turning. Kip didn't park it in the middle of the airfield like he did the first time. He steered up and positioned it out of sight and Jacklyn presumed in front of the hanger. She retreated to the kitchen where Erica and Lisa pensively stood. "What are we going to tell them?" Jacklyn asked.

"Not a thing," Lisa said harshly, bringing both hands up to her temples. She scowled. "Not one bloody damn thing. The less they know the better. Besides, what good is it going to do them to know anything about this? What good would it do anybody? He was there, he is gone. If Dexter is leery of him, I'm leery. We'll bring trouble if we pursue this. If he has the ruthlessness like you said. I don't want that at my door."

"I can stay quiet," Erica said.

"None of you were nearly gunned down. I feel an overwhelming obligation to justice. I can't just toss that aside," Judge Jacklyn said.

Lisa smiled. "Forget about that. Look at that must-have, sleek outfit of yours. They'll notice that and wouldn't hear a word anyway."

Jacklyn looked down at the blue pant suit with black tiger stripes. "I'm actually shocked. I've always obeyed the green and teal-tints philosophy. This does look good on me."

"Brilliant," Lisa said and winked. "Especially with that darling figure of yours. Wouldn't dare compare us to Erica. Mother Nature cheated with her. We can't compete.

A mere sheepish simper out of Erica before she deposited her thumbs inside the pockets of her skinny jeans. No interest at all in noting her mauve blouse with dark purple stripes. And the bellowing voice of Tony "Nuts" Ford took all the angst out of the air a breath later. "Mon cher ami! Mon cher ami. Nourriture. Nous avons besoin de nourriture. Nous sommes morts de faim." [My dear friend! My dear friend. Food. We need food. We're starving to death.]

"He's starving to death," Lisa said. "I knew that's the kind of greeting we'd get. Same thing he always says when they come back from an adventure."

He appeared in the doorway with a fishing rod in hand and a toothy grin on his face.

"Where's all the trophies?" Erica asked. "I don't see slimy, stinky things flapping around in your other hand."

"All loose and swimming… with gratitude in their hearts and a sore jaw to remind them. Dang that was good. Dang, dang good. We need to come more often. Talk about clearin' out the brain cells. Holy Mackerel!"

Just as Nuts stepped to rest his pole in the corner next to the cabinet Edward entered. With a broad grin on his face he went straight to Lisa. A big kiss and a big hug.

"Wow!" Lisa hooted. "That was a surprise."

"I haven't felt this good and clear headed in days and days. Did me wonders."

"And I see you had a successful wardrobe safari," Kip's calm voice seemed to wash the air as he entered. "Everyone looks good. About what I'd expect."

"And enough of that," Lisa said. "Wash your hands. Dinner is ready. The last thing I want is a fishy odor while I eat."

"Strange words from a lady that loves her fish and chips," Kip said.

"There's a difference between aroma and stench. Get on with it," she clapped her hands. "No more pussy footin' around."

Lisa seemed determined to focus the conversation on anything other than their day. Once seated around the table and passing dishes around she started in, "Where exactly did you go?"

"Told you," Nuts said. "Northumberland. Just outside of Newcastle. Lovely little airstrip near the River Tyne and it couldn't have been any better."

"How long of a flight is that?"

"About thirty minutes each way," Edward casually said.

"Who caught the most? The biggest?" Jacklyn exaggerated a look on her face. "Any tall tales to tell?" she feigned a laugh.

"Who do you think?" Edward said, grinning. "Creatures know when there's a Brit on the other end of the line. It's an intuitive behavior."

"Or they recognized a familiar scent," Nuts groused. "Poisson muet."

"Hah!" Edward hooted. "You can tell who got skunked. Poor lad."

"Not totally. I had a good honker on. Landed two others. Not monsters, but at least I landed them."

"What kind of fish were these?" Jacklyn asked.

"Salmon. Blessed salmon," Edward added.

"Speaking of getting caught," Kip said.

"Leave it! Just leave it!" Lisa snapped, interrupting and instinctively knowing. "We don't want to talk about that."

"I think that's a rather serious matter," Edward said. "You mean, you were never going to say a thing?"

"No need to say anything. Nothing happened. Nobody got hurt. Just forget about it."

"I think damage is done," Kip said. "Half the world knows we're here now. Plus, I didn't appreciate the half dozen calls I got, ripping my hide off for what we did."

"I straightened them out," Edward boldly declared. "Once they knew who was on the line, they acquiesced. Dolts!"

"They still want to see our passports. Still want us to go through the proper channels. Act like we did it right the first time. We do that and we're out of here. I don't think we can stay here any longer."

"Well, who exactly do you think is behind this?" Lisa tooted. "It's not like its some well-funded terrorist group. Unless Jacklyn dealt with them." She gave Jacklyn a querying look, hoping she was right.

Jacklyn shook her head, a dubious look on her face.

"We won't talk about it anymore. It's ruining dinner. Eat! I don't want another word out of any of you." A stern look put everyone in line. They quietly ate, Lisa, Erica and Jacklyn uncomfortably rushing with cause. Lisa finished just before Jacklyn. Jacklyn couldn't stand to sit and wait for another scolding. She stood, took Erica and Lisa's plates and headed for the kitchen. What was most disturbing about what happened next, was the suddenness of it. The sharp, horrid sound of stoneware crashing down on a slate kitchen floor. Copper, rust and broken tile all screamed as if their random pattern a discordant song. Everyone exchanged a shocked look before pushing away from the table and rushing in. Kip led. It was him who first saw what still held Judge Bailey petrified and shaking. There, outside the kitchen window, in the middle of the back patio, dressed in a long black trench coat stood Antione Banda, the most stoic look on his face. He didn't move. He simply stood there, hands deposited deep inside his pockets and staring in.

Kip reacted instantly. He bolted, found Edward's shotgun, which sat propped next to the fireplace and stormed out the front door. Nuts was a step behind as he nearly took the door off the hinges, pounding a fist and then racing for the Pilatus where he had a .40 cal Smith and Wesson stowed. First to appear was Kip. He boldly charged in from the left side where the library jutted out, the shotgun tight against his shoulder and leveled squarely on Banda's head. Banda didn't react at all. "Move a muscle and you're a dead man!" came through the window in a muffled tone. Kip didn't move until Nuts appeared and slid to the four o'clock position, pistol centered on core mass. Kip then quickly stepped up and made a hasty search. "All right. Are you alone? Anyone else out there?"

Banda barely turned his head, looking. He then returned his stare to Judge Bailey and said nothing.

"Inside!" Kip ordered. Snagging Banda by the collar, he forced him forward and soon shoved him through the back kitchen door. Nuts forced him into a chair and then took up the assassin's position, pistol pressed to the back of Banda's head.

They had moved Jacklyn out of the room. Edward and Erica appeared just as Kip removed a phone and a long piece of folded paper from inside Banda's coat. "What are you doing here? What's your business?" Edward demanded. "You have such nerve. Devil! How dare you!?"

"Let me handle this, Edward," Kip calmly said. "Keep everyone calm. All right," Kip stepped and faced Banda. "What ARE you doing here?" he emphasized. "How did you know to come here? Is anyone giving you orders? Why did you try to kill us? I want answers. What are your ties to the Judge? Did you kill Dana?"

Banda's eyes were down. He now looked up. "What did you do with the woman? Bring her back in here."

"Why?"

"Because. I'm reasonable. It's a reasonable request. Would the judge convict a man without witness or evidence?"

"What is that supposed to mean?"

"Bring her in," he mildly said. "What harm can it do?"

"You've done a lot of harm from what I can tell," Edward said. "Heathen!"

"Edward," Kip said. "Bring her in. She's faced monsters before. She can handle this."

Edward begrudgingly moved. Kip crouched to lock Banda's eyes on his. "How did you know we came here? Who informed you? How deep does this go?"

Banda remained just as stoic as before. He looked when Lisa and Edward brought Jacklyn in. They both held her by the arms. It startled Kip when Jacklyn sounded perfectly in control. "You have nerve," she said. "No doubt about that. Certainly, you don't fear anything. So bold and brash. I can only imagine what ties and protections you have. I would hardly dare speculate. But why? Why kill, Dana? Why try to kill us? We did nothing to you and we were nothing of a threat."

"I didn't try to kill you. I didn't kill your sister. I saved your life."

There was a shocking moment of silence.

"Don't insult us like that," Kip said. "We're not fools."

"And I've heard that a million times," Jacklyn said.

"And I can prove it. Let me have my phone."

"Right!" Nuts barked. "Bring in the clowns. That's what you want."

"And you think I couldn't have done that when I came in here? Why do you think I surrendered myself like that?"

"He's got a point," Edward said. "That didn't make a lot of sense. If he was here to assassinate someone."

"Unless this is just reconnaissance," Nuts said. "Get a lay of the land. Determine the level of resistance and then bam! we're dead."

"I don't think so," Kip said. "What do you want the phone for? Who are you going to call?"

"You call. Or better. Go out there. Wave my phone overhead. My proof will come running."

"Who?"

"My proof."

"What do you think?" Edward said. "Should we trust him?"

"No," Jacklyn said.

"Absolutely not," from Lisa.

Nothing else said, Kip grabbed Banda's phone and determinedly walked out into the back patio area. He looked around briefly before raising the phone over his head. It didn't happen instantly, but some lengthy seconds later, a dark figure emerged from a hedge bordering the left side. He took a few steps, paused, looked around, and slowly approached. He wore a black hoodie, which helped disguise him. Kip held the shotgun on him until he stopped short. "Name?" Kip asked.

No response.

"Kay. Take it easy. Banda has a gun to the back of his head. You try anything and he may regret it. Understand?"

No response.

Kip stepped forward and removed the man's hoodie. The man was salt and pepper bearded and submissive. It was a quick search that brought a look of utter astonishment to Kip's face. The man sadly looked him in the eye when Kip revealed what he'd found. A look over his shoulder, before Kip simply turned and let the man follow him in. A few steps in and he tossed what he'd found at Jacklyn. It bounced off her chest before she caught it. A gobsmacked look caused her jaw to drop.

"De vo-man... Vye she no like me? She like me to die?" Kip said. "Recognize him?"

192

She shook her head vacantly.

"Isn't that your cap? Apricot cap. Remember the beggar?"

"O, my God," Jacklyn breathed. "They killed him. They shot him down."

"No," Banda said softly. "Emiliano knew to duck. I tell him what they will most likely look for and he saves your life. I saved your life."

Sudden air shattering silence. Pensive silence. Silence long enough for Kip to have a thousand different thoughts. "Who then? We were target. If I'm interpreting you right, we were target and you threw up a smoke screen. Who then? Who was trying to kill us?"

Banda shrugged. "Could have been one of a dozen different governments or some mixture of many. I don't know. Someone with an interest in tracking you. What I know, is whenever someone comes asking about that book, they die. A given clerk gets an inquiry, and they pass the word on."

"You're telling me some government is responsible for killing my sister?" Jacklyn said. "Who? She would have been insignificant. We're insignificant. All over a book. A nonexistent book as far as I can tell."

Banda glanced at the pages Kip had placed on the counter. He nodded. "That book. That might have been the reason. Maybe not. Depends who did it."

Kip quickly grabbed the folded pages and snapped them open. "This isn't a book. This is a photocopy of a bunch of gibberish. This isn't words."

"It is if you know an ancient language."

"What language? What does it say?"

"I don't know. I simply made a random copy. Proof."

"Language?"

"Some form of Hebrew... or Egyptian... or some reformed form of either or both. I'm not sure."

Lisa rushed over, crunching on broken stoneware. She snatched the pages out of Kip's hands. She merely rifled through the dozen pages. She said nothing, glaring as much as she could a death glare at Banda.

Seconds later, all but Nuts stood gathered around. "We need to get this interpreted," Lisa said. "And you're not going anywhere until we know what this says."

CHAPTER TWENTY-NINE

MEET DR. STEPHEN RUSSELL

It was hard to believe that somewhere hidden behind a pristinely trimmed hedge, where a false spiraea bush with its residue of delicate, yet odd-pinnate foliage, stretched over and hung half way to the walk, stood Dexter Cowen's majestic medieval Edwardian home. Kip looked over his shoulder at Jacklyn and Antione Banda before looking at Lisa. "Why did you park here? There's an open gate. Pull in there."

"I should call first," Lisa said. "If Maggie is in one of her bad moods Dexter will refuse to see us now, and then not talk to me for a month."

"Call," Jacklyn sounded like the judge in her.

"What makes you think this man can interpret?" Antione Banda droned. "It's a rare gift."

"If he can't, he will know someone who can," Lisa said and punched the dial button on her steering wheel. Six rings before Dexter's sophisticated nasally voice sounded exhausted.

"Zero one eight six five... six five four one five-five eight," he answered the old-fashioned way. "Alright."

"Dexter... Lisa Allen again."

"Blessed day. Has something happened?"

"You sound tired. Are you alright?"

"A bit knackered is all. Why?"

"How's Maggie tonight?"

"Why do you ask?"

"I'm in the area. I have a rather startling surprise for you. I wouldn't dare intrude if she's not feeling well."

"She's in her room. Hasn't complained of anything. What is my surprise?"

"I'd rather meet you at the door. Can we do that?"

"How soon?"

"I'm parked in the street."

"That will be fine. Give me five minutes. I want to make myself presentable." You could sense excitement in his voice. Lisa turned, giving them all a cheesy grin.

"He'll be chipper," she said.

"I think it would be better if Mr. McKinney stays here," Banda mechanically said.

"Why? What's wrong with him?" Lisa demanded.

"It will go better if he's not there."

"Why? What do you know?" Lisa huffed. "That's ridiculous."

Kip gave her an odd look, before looking back at Banda.

"We need Kip there," Lisa said.

"Why? Or do you just want him there? Believe me, it will go better if he's not there. He might intimidate certain parties who might show up."

"Him intimidate? You intimidate. If anyone does, you intimidate," Lisa said.

"Lisa," Kip said and touched her arm. "This won't help. I'm fine sitting here. You go ahead. If you need me, I'm right here."

Lisa hated that disarming power Kip seemed to possess. One second riled, the next subdued. "Okay. Fine. Don't know what good it's going to do. Whatever!" she gasp.

Minutes later, Dexter flinched when he opened the door to find Lisa, Judge Bailey and Antione Banda. There was a pause as they somehow expected a moment of recognition between Banda and Cowen.

195

Nothing. "Shall I invite you in?" Dexter said. "If this is the surprise I'm a bit perplexed."

"If it's no trouble, we'll just step inside the door," Lisa sheepishly said.

He stepped aside and motioned with his hand. They entered a near cubicle-like entry where slate floors and dark wood felt oppressive. A hanging yellowish sconce cast a pall of darkness at their feet. Dexter merely closed the door and smiled politely.

"Remember our visit?" Lisa weakly said. "From today. Well… you met Judge Bailey. This other gentleman is Antione Banda."

It looked as if Dexter suddenly met death head on. A look of shock and haunt turned his face ashen. He grunted a few stuttering grumbles. Nothing intelligible.

"Are you okay?" Judge Bailey asked. "You look as if you believe he didn't exist."

"Well… are you sure? This is Banda? Antione Banda? What's he doing here? Like that… he's suddenly here. Talk about surprise. This is no surprise… this is murderous to present a man and make a claim like that."

"I am who I am," Banda adamantly declared. "I'm no myth. Why do people always treat me like a myth?"

"Probably because of the reputation you've put out there."

"You know all about him though, don't you?" Lisa said.

"I've heard of him. I don't know anything about him. I know he's dangerous."

"I'm no more dangerous than a dream."

"A nightmare!"

"Calm down, Dexter," Lisa said. "Seems we've been misjudging a good many things lately."

"We thought he tried to kill me…" Judge Bailey said, touching Lisa's arm. "Ends up, he prevented my death."

"And who told you that? Him!? Huh!" Dexter snorted. "That's the surprise, huh? I'm not really interested if this is your surprise. True, it is a shock, but… I'd rather not be a part of this play of yours, Lisa. You should have thought this through better."

"There's more," Judge Bailey said. Dexter glanced and quickly and disrespectfully glanced away. "The book. We have a portion of the book."

Dexter had stepped as if to stomp away. He abruptly halted, spun, and gave them a hideously vacant look. Judge Bailey held a hand out. Banda reached in and pulled the folded pages out of his pocket. The moment Dexter had them in his hand he turned and rushed straight into his adjacent study where a green and burnt orange Tiffany desk lamp burned dimly. Straight to the desk where he donned a pair of glasses and flattened out the pages under the light. The moment he recognized the characters he covered his mouth with a hand and stayed silent. For some time he stayed silent. Then it was as if exhaustion overtook him. He slumped into his chair and again vacantly stared at them.

"What do you think?" Judge Bailey asked. "Do you know what it says? Can you interpret it?"

He cowardly shook his head. "Wouldn't have a clue. I can tell you this. The characters are correct."

"What language? Is it Hebrew?" the judge asked.

"I believe it's reformed Egyptian."

"Is that good or bad?"

"Both. Good if you wanted to authenticate a certain aspect. Bad if ramifications mean anything."

"Can you interpret it?"

"I wouldn't know where to start. This is not my cup of tea… that much I can say." He then got the most demure look before the sun seemed to rise inside of his eyes. They grew wide. "But… this may be a shot in the dark. Let me make a call. Jonathan will know who to talk too. If anyone would know, Jonathan would know."

Lisa exchanged a blithe, yet ecstatic look with Jacklyn. "See… I told you. If he can't, he'll know someone who can."

Nothing said, Dexter got to his feet, wiped the most intense, furtive look down his face and walked out while holding a finger as if in warning. Judge Bailey stepped and snatched the pages up. She held them respectfully before quizzically looking at Banda. "What percentage of book do we have here? You have the rest of it, I presume. In a safe place, I presume."

"You're seeing a fraction. Less than one percent maybe. I won't say a thing about the original. I'll never reveal where that is."

"How did you get your hands on it?" Lisa asked. "Did someone approach you?"

Banda inhaled and closed his eyes. Said nothing.

"Okay," Judge Bailey said. "Have you tried to interpret it before? Has anyone? Certainly someone had to, because Dexter seemed to believe what was in it. Governments will kill for it. Why hasn't any government cornered you… or abducted you… or something to force it out of you. Clearly, if they know of it and you, they would have moved. Done something."

"Some have tried. They know it serves them no purpose to threaten me. Without me, they have nothing. For now, they're content with eliminating anyone curious."

"And clearly," Lisa said. "He has some sort of leverage. Some protection. Perhaps there are translated copies out there. Our question should be, why has he delivered this here and why now. Right? Or he likes the fact that he attracts bait of a certain taste."

"Someone finally beginning to understand," Banda said.

Those words brought an air of auspicious danger. They stayed quiet. The room stayed quiet until Dexter came rushing back in. Instantly, he looked alarmed when he didn't see the transcript. A deep sigh when Judge Bailey handed it over. "Stephen Russell. Jonathan is bringing Dr. Stephen Russell over."

"Who's Dr. Stephen Russell?" Judge Bailey asked.

"I'm not sure. I've never heard of him. Classical philologist who recently transferred here from the University of Santiago de Compostela. An American. Apparently, quite brilliant."

"Where's this University?" Lisa asked.

"Spain," Banda frankly said.

"Do you know this man?" the judge asked Banda.

"No comment."

"Well… doesn't matter," Judge Bailey said. "How soon before he gets here? We'll know then whether they know one another or not."

"Twenty minutes at the most," Dexter said. "May I see that again?"

"Make a copy," Judge Bailey said. "Unless you have another in your pocket."

"I'd make the copy if I were you," Lisa said.

Ten unbelievable short minutes later a knock came to the door. Presented there was a middle-aged man who looked more like a tall Pentagon official than a professor. A keen, penetrating eye, however revealed… or better said, skillfully hid the man's character. A huffing, puffing Jonathan Ryder, a professor who seemed bred from the same mold as Dexter pushed him in and closed the door. He panted. "Where is it, Dexter? Where is this marvel? This could be the discovery of the century. My God, man, where is this?"

Dr. Russell gave them all an analytical look before pressing a hand firmly to Jonathan's shoulder. "Don't butt in. I'm the expert," he sounded callous and arrogant. One characteristic that clearly seemed removed from the man… average. He seemed to stand there peeling away onion layers as he studied them. Banda had already evaporated into a corner. "Where is it?" he choked. "We rush over here as if fire bells ringing and you all stand here like simpletons."

"No need to insult," Dexter grumbled. "This way."

Dr. Russell assumed the same pose Dexter had when first inspecting the pages. One page, two. Then he lingered. For two full minutes. "Interesting. Very interesting."

"What? What?" Dexter said excitedly. "What is it saying?"

Dr. Russell straightened up some and pinched his lips between a thumb and a finger. "I need time. I need time and I need space. I'll be taking these." He folded and stuffed them inside his jacket pocket."

"Well…" Dexter expectantly said. "When will we hear back? It's only a few pages."

199

Dr. Russell indolently eyed him down his nose. "When I have the time to spend with it. Some of it is familiar to me, some is not. I'm going to need time to figure it out. You'll have to be patient."

"Hah!" Jonathan hooted. "Wonderful! Absolutely wonderful."

Clearly, Dr. Russell saw no reason for further discussion. He pushed his way out and even closed the door behind him before a hedging Jonathan Ryder grunted. An apologetic ache filled his face when he took Dexter by the shoulder. "So sorry. He's not exactly sociable. All business. A bit of spit and vinegar. Quite impatient. Believe me, he won't dawdle. The question is, will he become so consumed that he'll forget where he got it. He'll want more. I guarantee you, he'll want more."

The judge and Banda locked eyes. Banda shook his head.

"Well…" Judge Bailey then said, extending her hand to Jonathan. "None of us got introduced. I'm Judge Jacklyn Bailey. I'm not sure whether you know Lisa Allen or not." Lisa waved him off. "We appreciate you coming. We really should be going. We look forward to hearing back from you. Dexter," she acknowledged and politely nodded before leaving. Banda followed right on her shoulder. Lisa delayed.

"Thank you, Dexter," she said. "Sorry if everyone is being rude."

"Nonsense." He winked a twinkling wink. "Go on with you. We'll be in touch. Don't hesitate at all. If I'm at my desk or anywhere else except a lecture hall your time is mine. Such excitement. It's absolutely luscious."

Dexter and Jonathan exchanged a deferring look. It was obvious, to which Lisa responded by respectfully leaving. Minutes later, sitting inside Lisa's Jag the mood felt fragmented. "I'm not sure that was a good idea," Jacklyn said. "Wham, bam… now we don't have the pages."

"But we have copies… right?" Lisa warily looked at Banda.

"I wouldn't worry," Banda said. "They're in good hands. They're in the right hands. Trust me."

"You know him?" Lisa blurted. "You sound like you know him."

"I know of him. People in my circles know very well about that man. Like I said… trust me."

Those words seemed to satisfy Lisa and Jacklyn. Lisa revved the engine and slowly pulled away. Kip not so much. The dominating thought for him… was Banda deceiving him moments ago or now?

CHAPTER THIRTY

A THORNY TRIP TO LONDON

The mood at the US Embassy in London was what you'd expect for a Friday morning and approaching noon. Especially with the young, average-looking woman, consular officer, helping Erica Dennis. This felt her first foreign post and as if she expected Fridays off. As if friends now impatiently waited and she couldn't get out of there fast enough. She hardly said a word. A phone call here. A phone call there. A suspicious, condescending look strategically inserted now and again and then rifling through Erica's passport and papers as if searching for forger tells. Finally, she snapped Erica's passport down in front of her and leaned forward. "I wouldn't be playing those kind of games again if I were you. You're lucky you're not in trouble up past your eyeballs."

"I'm sorry. You do understand the reasons why, don't you?"

"You should have just stuck with the FBI protection."

"Don't take it out on me. I climbed on board a plane with no idea where we were going. Self-preservation was the single motive. I think we were perfectly justified."

The consular officer stared at Erica for a minute, her expression turning a bit tormented, a bit regretful. "You can go," she weakly said. "Have a nice day," felt empty.

Erica stepped out into a stale corridor to find Lisa waiting. Lisa sat on a fold-down chair, a copy of Poetry London magazine on her phone, a crossed foot bobbing nervously. She didn't look up.

"They torture you first?" Lisa asked. "Took longer than I thought it should."

"The others aren't done yet?"

"I'd imagine Nuts is making them take their time. He sure didn't like all of us crammed in my car. Don't know what he was complaining about, he had it good in the front seat. You didn't hear Kip complaining."

"I think he liked it."

"I don't blame him…" she smiled flirtatiously, raising her brows. "Sandwiched in between you two. Tart cream in a sweet pastry. Delish." She giggled.

Erica mildly did too before sitting.

Lisa placed a motherly hand on Erica's knee. "Any vibes between you two. I mean you and Kip. Wouldn't hurt, you know. He's a catch."

"Please. He must be close to twenty years older than me."

"Nah! Why would you let that stand in your way?"

"You come right out with it, don't you? No hesitation at all. Most people are a bit coy about these kinds of things."

"Why waste your time? So is there?"

"Uh…" Erica sighed heavily. "Uh… I don't dare say."

"There is then."

"I sat on a horse. Kip sat behind with his arms around me. I wouldn't dare tell Meghan, but it felt as if life ending when I had to get off. I wouldn't allow him the pleasure of knowing that either. And I'm not about too. Don't you dare say a thing. And…" she stared, "how in the world did you do that? I had no intention of ever saying anything to anyone."

"He's behaving the same way. I have a way with these things. I perceive where others don't."

"He's closer to Meghan's age. I was thinking… I'm not sure what his relationship was with her sister, but… you know… that seems the obvious, doesn't it?"

Judge Bailey suddenly exited from a doorway, terminating that conversation. "That was pleasant," Judge Bailey sarcastically said. "Where are the men?"

"I suppose they're the ones getting excoriated. They should know better, right? Former military guys acting like they own the world."

"Let's move," Lisa jumped to her feet and exhaled. "I've sat here long enough."

"You mean, leave them here?" Erica expressed qualms.

"Eh…" she waved her off. "They're used to the way I do things. They've got a phone, I've got a phone. That will be their last option. You'll see… we'll end up finding them in a pub or something. Or down the street at Vauxhall. Which is another thing. Why did they move the embassy here? Sure they get a view of the Thames, but I think it was to get closer to Vauxhall. You know… MI 5 and 6 and spies and all that stuff. So they could spy on each other through a window. Hah-hah…" she threw her head back. "Let's go," she said and strutted down the corridor.

"Here we go again," Erica leaned on Meghan as they walked, whispering. "She's going to get us in trouble again."

"I like her. I like her a lot. She's harmless."

Before they got to the end of the corridor Lisa swept through a restroom door and vanished. "I'm glad she stopped," Erica said. "I need to powder my nose too."

Judge Bailey skidded to a stop. "I'll wait out here," she said. "If the guys come out, they'll know we haven't abandoned them." They were on the ground floor where around the corner elevators carried non-citizens for visa applications. The judge wandered to the corner and back and then back again. She heard voices just as elevator doors opened and didn't think anything of it until the men stopped, one raising his voice.

"Look… keep your nose out of it. I'll handle this," echoed.

The judge leaned to see two men. A tall one with his back to her and a short balding fellow with round ghostly jowls and wearing an expensive suit. The short one then poked the taller fellow in the chest and snorted, "Go back to your business. You hear me?"

The stocky one spun on a heel. "No!" the other blurted and grabbed his arm. They now faced one another, giving the judge a clear view of both. Instantly, her heart skipped a beat. There Dr. Stephen Russell stood, towering over the man and looking just as intimidating as the night prior. "We'll discuss this now," he said. "I won't be used unless I have controls."

"Look," the short one said, leaning in, lowering his voice. A brief exchange and they headed for the doors.

Instantly, the judge hurried back to the restroom and burst in just as Lisa and Erica were washing hands. "We've got trouble. I knew there was something strange about that man. I didn't trust him then, I don't trust him now."

A couple of vacant looks before Lisa grinned, "What on earth now, girl? You look like you've seen a ghost."

"Dr. Russell is here. Why would he be here?"

"You're sure?"

"I just saw him come out of the elevator with some other man. They were not happy. I know it has something to do with that book. It has something to do with us. I'm positive of it."

Lisa got a wry look, Erica a wan look. Lisa charged by and out the door.

"Oh, no… we can't do this. Don't let her do this. We should wait for the guys," Erica said.

"A horrid thought just struck me. A consular official and Dr. Russell. Government ties. Suddenly, I understood the way long-jaw was thinking. What if…?"

Those words seemed to suck both out into the corridor. No sign of Lisa. No sign of Kip or Nuts either. "Shoot!" Judge Bailey rustled and hurried around the corner. Lisa stood near the front doors where outside several large artistic pillars felt like a downpour of horror on such a cloudy, dreary day. It seemed they had no choice. Certainly wouldn't allow Lisa the James Bond role alone. They, in unison, walked over, trying not to draw attention to themselves.

Lisa didn't turn her head. "I've got them on radar," she uttered. "Out there. Behind that last pillar. Do you think they had to go through security like we did? If they're parked somewhere else, we're in trouble."

"What makes you think they're going somewhere?" Erica whispered. "This is crazy. If you think they're after us, they might turn around and come right back in. Then what?"

"No. They looked in the mood for a drink," Judge Bailey said.

"And if you want to follow them, we're parked eighteen miles away," Erica said.

"No," Lisa quipped. "That was Eighteen Miles Street, not eighteen miles."

"I know that. I'm just saying. It was a decent walk though. Five-six minutes. Maybe a little more."

"Uh…" Lisa grunted and pushed out the door. Erica stepped to follow. Judge Bailey grabbed her arm.

"I've never seen Dr. Russell. He's never seen me. I can go out there," Erica said excitedly.

"Unless they have pictures of you or something. You never know. We have no idea what we're dealing with anymore."

A reassuring look from Erica before she left Judge Bailey standing there. She got three steps before she stuttered to a stop. Dr. Russell and Ward Stelter stepped out from behind the pillar, said a few harsh words, and then stormed off. A breath later, Lisa came clattering back, glee on her face. She caught Erica by the arm and scooted her back inside. Lisa wrapped her arms, putting their heads together. "Dr. Russell is on his way somewhere. I think he said Fleet Street. The other guy… he's staying at the Chelsea Bridge Hotel. I have a bad feeling about him. Really bad."

"We're not going to follow him, are we? We'll wait for the guys," Erica uttered.

"Of course not," she cleared her throat and stood erect. Both Erica and Judge Bailey turned just in time to see Kip and Nuts approach, walking around the corner. Nuts and Kip were trying to interpret the looks they were getting. It was a mixture hard to decipher. A certain level of appeal on Lisa's face, mild blithe on Erica's, and fixed on Jacklyn's. All wrenched with an underlying level of brooding. "Now what's up?" Nuts asked. "Something's happened."

The gals exchanged a look. Lisa shook her head. "Nothing's happened."

"Like I believe that," Kip said and motioned for the doorway. They hadn't even cleared the last pillar before Lisa spiraled around and fronted them. "All right!" she emphatically declared. "They're going to get it out of us anyway. We've got to say something."

Neither Kip nor Nuts had a chance to ask. "Dr. Russell," Judge Bailey blurted. "We saw Dr. Russell. Why would he be here?"

"Say what?" Kip said.

"He was with another fellow. Short, bald, stocky guy. Expensive suit," Erica said. "They were arguing. I know it was about us and that book. Now what's going to happen? Something is bound to happen."

Kip quickly pulled his phone out and dialed. A breath later he held the phone among them while on speaker mode. "Loser here," Edward answered.

"What?" Lisa brooded with alarm. "What do you mean loser?"

"That you, Lisa? Everything okay with you and your troop?"

"Uh… we're okay."

"What's going on there?" Kip asked.

"Well… my ego is bruised. Antione keeps out strategizing me. Emiliano keeps chuckling. The third game in a row and I'm about to go down again."

"What?" Lisa said, her nose scrunched.

"I've lost at chess, but never been beaten three times in a row. Don't want to say four. I'm dreadfully wounded here. I don't know how I'll recover from this. The only positive is that he isn't some pedantic boob."

Lisa laughed.

"So… get your legal issues straightened out? Both governments contented with you scoundrels?"

"Things are cleared up," Kip said. "We're on our way home. I just wanted to call and see how it was going."

"I couldn't have done worse at Versailles. I'm burning in ashes here."

"Alright. We'll see you in a couple of hours." He hung up.

"You were worried," Lisa gave him a stern look. "About Banda... why?"

"Um... just curious."

"No," Judge Bailey said. "He was digging. He wanted to know... maybe he was suspicious about Banda setting us up or something. I'm right, aren't I?"

"Hard to know anybody's motives, isn't it? I'm not sure what to think. And as far as another fellow... we have no idea what Dr. Russell was doing here. We don't know all his dealings."

"We need to check out this fellow Dr. Russell was talking to," Lisa said. "We need to go to the hotel. We need to find out who he is and what he's doing."

"No we don't," Kip said. "Ask these two." He pointed a thumb at Erica and Judge Bailey. "How many times have they gone down the wrong rat hole lately? Am I right?"

Erica and the judge gave each other a sheepish look.

"That was then. This is now," Lisa said defensively.

"Fine. Have a good time. Nuts and I will find our way home. We're resourceful. Won't be but a minor headache." Kip nodded and Nuts followed as they headed for the south entry security building. Lisa scowled before sort of moping. She lowered her chin while studying Erica and Jacklyn.

"What do you think?" Erica asked. "I don't know about you, but I'd rather stay with them."

Judge Bailey nervously bit a fingernail. "I hate to say it, but I think Erica is right. We don't know who the man is, or anything."

"I'll call someone," Lisa said. "I know all kinds of people."

"I'm sure you do, but I'm not very comfortable about playing secret agent again. It caused more headache than it helped."

"Or did it?" Erica added. "We know a lot more about Banda. And about that book. At least initially."

"Augh…" Lisa groaned. "I don't like it. I don't like it at all. We have the opportunity now. I don't like letting something squeeze out of my fingers."

"And I guess that all depends on what you're squeezing," Judge Bailey said. "If you're totally in the dark, you might be squeezing something different than you thought you were. I'm staying with Kip and Nuts."

Erica and Judge Meghan walked off. Lisa stood there brooding for a minute. A glance and a sharp, "Blimey!" before following in line.

CHAPTER THIRTY-ONE

SOMETHING DOESN'T SMELL RIGHT

The interrogation room was small, stark, and poorly ventilated. Donald Edwin Gerhardt sat slumped, one elbow on a table, his legs spread and eyeing Agent Duggan as if he couldn't wait to skin him alive. Gerhardt's clothing was ragged Army surplus. He looked like he'd spent a year in the jungle, alone and starving. Agent Reed stood leaning against the wall next to the door with a paper sack in hand. "You've been read your rights, you sure you don't want an attorney here?" Duggan asked. "They could get you a public defender here in no time. We're patient. We'll wait."

Gerhardt moved his focus onto Reed. Reed wrinkled the sack briefly before gesturing. "Change your mind? I've got water. Energy bar. Apple."

Gerhardt looked away, extending a hand and snapping his fingers. Reed stretched from where he stood, as if wary of the man's horrendous odor. Gerhardt snatched the sack away and instantly rifled through it. He threw his head back, slowly chugging on the bottle of water, eyeing the two. Agent Reed leaned down to Agent Duggan. "Six months at the least without a bath," he whispered. "How much do you want to bet?"

"Hey!" Gerhardt cut, "What gives? What'er ya whisperin'?" Water ran down his front when he suddenly spun in his chair and looked at the wall behind him. He spun back and straightened up.

"Agent Reed was just wondering if he should get you another bottle of water. Do you need another bottle?"

Gerhardt eyed him briefly before taking a few more chugs. He pulled the apple out of the sack and placed it aside. He nearly had his face inside the sack, tearing an energy bar open and half devouring it.

"Pretty hungry, huh?" Agent Reed said. "You let me know when you need more."

Gerhardt wiped a hand across his mouth. "Famine's wiped it all out. How'd you git this stuff?"

"Famine? What famine would that be?" Duggan asked.

Gerhardt stopped chewing briefly and then peered into the sack.

"Take your time," Duggan said. "When you're ready to talk we'd like to know what you can tell us about Boyd Sherman. Remember Boyd Sherman?"

Gerhardt gave them an impassive smirk. "The man's a killer. He'll rot in hell forever."

"Haven't you called him to repentance? Doesn't he have a chance of repenting?"

"Not him. Faked it."

"Who has to pay the price then? Somebody else is paying the price."

"Jesus paid the price. You don't get paid for, 'less you change," he barked. "He ain't changed nothin'."

"You bring up Jesus. Jesus had apostles. Do you have apostles? Who's Peter, James, and John?"

Gerhardt had a cheek full of energy bars. He stopped chewing, and stretched forward, a blood-red expression growing intense. He spit food everywhere when he shouted, "They're all dead. What the hell's wrong with you? Don't you know nothin'?"

"How much time do you spend on that computer of yours? Are you a wizard on that thing?" Agent Reed asked. "Know all about hacking, do you?"

Gerhardt squinted for a good thirty seconds. "Don't let it in yer brains. Hallucinations," he calmly said. He swallowed what he had in his mouth and seemed to become quite docile. He belched long and deep. "I need a nap," he said. "You find a quiet place in the sun, lay down on the brown forest floor, and watch the white fluffy clouds. A good way to take a nap. Birds sing. The wind blows through the pine boughs. Ants will eat ya alive. Gotta watch out fer them."

Agent Duggan sighed and stared at Agent Reed briefly before nodding. They stepped out into the hallway. "Think he's faking it?" Duggan asked.

"I know what you mean. Showing all the signs. You can fake insanity. I have my doubts about this one. What do you want to do?"

"I'm not sure. I guess we can sit in there and twist him in the wind forever, trying to determine just how insane he is. It might take forever to get your Brodie on. I could see him tugging our chain forever. Problem is… I don't think he'd have a clue at what he was doing."

"He had to be rational at one point to rig that bomb."

"True. But judging from appearances, I'd say he's been applesauce for a good long time. This all felt way too easy. And I'm not all that sure he's the one who put the bomb in there."

"What do you want to do then?"

Duggan cracked the door and looked in. "Get him some more food and a bath. Beyond that… it feels wrong. Do you think someone would frame him?"

"Feels more like they framed the crime around him than framing him for a crime. The question now is… who on earth would do that?"

Similar angst wouldn't come for Kip McKinney until taking the A4142, which circumvented Oxford on their way back to Godsham. Misery seemed to pull the clouds down to the ground, their weeping drizzle an added weight neither Erica nor Judge Bailey could decipher. They knew Kip had become quiet, but they were essentially oblivious to the inexplicable, slowly growing, inflated, and near calamitous disquiet going on inside the man. How he hated it. Now this wretched pressure which brought with it such brilliantly, yet brittle efficacious results. He sat between Erica and Judge Bailey, pulling his arms tight as if that alone could suppress the sadness. No one noticed until Lisa pulled to a stop near the Jag shed and they all climbed out. Kip didn't move.

"Are you coming?" Judge Bailey delayed and asked. She looked in on him and saw a man slumping as if overcome with a stroke. "Kip!?" He began to fall over. "Nuts! Help! Something is wrong with Kip," her alarmed tone brought everyone back in a rush. Nuts rounded to the other side, Lisa piled in over the driver's seat, and Erica sidled in next to Meghan.

"Kippers," Nuts climbed in, wrapping an arm around his shoulder. "Kippers? What's with ya man? You sick?"

Kip moaned, slumping into Nuts' side.

"Kip! Kip!" Lisa raised her voice, reaching back and slapping his hand. "Come back to us, Kip."

"Hold off," Nuts said. "Hold off just a second." He braced Kip and studied his face briefly. "Oh, no. Not that."

"What? What's wrong with him?" Lisa said.

"Oh… I've seen this," Judge Bailey said. "I've seen this, haven't I? Not to this extent, but I've seen this."

"What?" Lisa exclaimed. "What is it?"

Nuts gave her a bleak look. "It's that curse of his. I've never seen it this bad, but it's that curse."

No one dared say it. No one wanted to. It was Kip who said the unwanted. The unspeakable. "Why God?" he moaned. "Why now… of all the times, why does someone have to die now?"

A fit of anger seemed to come over Kip. He pushed Nuts out of the way and quickly climbed out. He paused momentarily, resting his hands on his knees, and then charged off, swatting Nuts away as he went. The girls stood watching until Kip disappeared through the back door. Nuts gave them a hard stare before following. A breath after Nuts entered Antione Banda appeared. He stood there, under the small thatched roofing covering the porch, blowing as if to see his breath.

"That's terrifying," Erica said.

"No kidding," Lisa added, looking heavenward and holding a hand out. "Skies even know when to cry over him."

"Which one are you talking about?" Judge Bailey asked. "Kip or that one?"

"I was talking about Kip," Erica said. "How could you live with yourself? Besides… who's supposed to be dying?"

"Not me," Lisa said. "I think I'd know if I was about to die. I think we all get that inkling. Mr. Banda there gives me the willies. Maybe it's him."

"I'm having my doubts…" Judge Bailey said. "About all of it. Besides, I don't see the point in standing here getting wet. I'm going to go talk with Kip. I want to know what he's thinking."

She avoided eye contact with Banda. Even had a small blemish on the door jamb set as her focus as she marched up and kept her right eye half closed. Lisa and Erica were right on her heels and even bumped into her when Banda suddenly stuck his arm out, impeding them.

"Do you mind?" Lisa cracked. "How rude."

"I know what you did. I know who you saw," he cleanly said.

"What is your game?" Lisa again cracked. "You know, I'm sick and tired of you already. Why do you put up such pretenses? What are you trying to do? This isn't a game. This isn't some fool's play. I know when I'm seeing an act and I'm sick and tired of your act."

"Calm down," Judge Bailey said, grabbing Lisa's arm. "Just what do you mean, you know who we saw?"

"What I said. I know who you saw. I believe it's time you fully understand what's going on here."

"Hah! I don't trust you," Lisa declared. "Not one bit."

Banda's face became a bit adroit. He shrugged. "I recognize what an oddity I am. But that isn't the point. You saw Dr. Russell today. You saw him with a man who, when it comes down to it, is one pillar of all that is wrong. He's not ultimately responsible, but he is the reason why your sister is dead."

212

Every countenance changed with those words. Words that suddenly seemed to suck the oxygen out of the air. Changed scorn to sudden curiosity. "Did I hear you right?" Judge Bailey asked. "Did you say, my sister? Why haven't you brought this up before? Why haven't you done anything about this?"

"It would have served no purpose. You can't bleed justice from that stone."

There was a moment of boorish silence.

"Explain," the judge demanded. "You've got my full attention."

"Years ago. Many years... one world leader ordered a military strike on a given target in a given land. Killed in that strike is the son of another world leader. That leader, of course, is outraged and demands reprimands. His burdens go ignored. Subsequently and continuously he demands the same out of the following leaders. He gets no satisfaction until a sympathetic ear comes along and one whose moral backbone is nothing more than a narcissistic pillar, buried in the sand. The one leader offers to pay, not for the head of the man who killed his son. But for the heads of select people surrounding that man. The longer the suffering, the better. Keep it random and disconnected. Understand? The new leader sees an opportunity for easy profit. He fully recognizes no one can rightfully identify who dropped a bomb and so he creates layers of protection. Plausible deniability, you see. And so he creates layers. Asks a trusted associate to create a mechanism in which he can satisfy his new cash cow and yet keep the separation clean enough that no one could ever find connecting ties to him. The associate is clever enough to not only protect the leader, but himself as well. They have one problem. Who dropped the bomb? They have no idea so they choose. Not arbitrarily, but one whom this given associate disdains. Because the man is so successful and what's more... he represents everything the man deems as loathsome. These men are clever. They're shameful. They're weak and have mental misgivings. They do everything they can to misguide and misdirect. Soon it ends up in the hands of the most heartless of souls. A creature without a soul and yet is so brilliant it's frightening. You can't imagine the conniving possibilities. And so the killings begin. Well camouflaged killings. Soon the family begins to die. In no time the man's wife and children are dead. They're in no rush. They choose another who becomes too friendly and she dies. This woman's sister shows up. With her comes one that stirs the pot in a way unanticipated. When one layer of eyes and ears is rebuffed, he tries to take matters into his own hands and subsequently pays the ultimate price. Are you following me?"

"To the letter," the judge says. "How can we believe you? How do you know this?"

"Because it's in the book."

"Then they're going to know. They're going to know all about this," Erica said. "Now, just so I understand… you're talking about Prince Lowe, right? The one rebuffed? I'm not fully putting that together."

"He violated the strictest of rules. It wasn't his place to order a killing. It wasn't his place to reveal identities, places, and times. He paid the price."

"Are you telling me they don't know who we are?" the judge said.

"I'm telling you that most don't. There are eyes and ears. Lowe was eyes and ears. They will need new eyes and ears. Those who pull the trigger, so to speak, have no idea who gives them the order. Every component is strategically hidden from the other. Plausible deniability for all."

"So they have no idea… Kip is simply an innocent target."

"A convenient target. Well… better said. Those around him are the target. No one is safer than he is."

"And he doesn't know. He has to know this," Erica said. "That's not right."

"You tell him and what do you think he'll do?"

Silence.

Until Lisa sighed heavily. "Knowing Kip the way I know Kip, he would kill himself," she sadly said. "I'm hearing this. I'm not sure I'm believing this." She gave Banda a stony stare. "I'd like to read that book."

"You won't get anything out of Dr. Russell. He's eyes and ears."

"Hunting for that book… right?" Judge Bailey said. "He was eyes and ears, hunting for that book. So what's the tie to Kip and that book?"

"Circumstantial. Aside from being a key figure subject to the snakes, he's clueless."

"We need to get those pages back… From Dr. Russell," Lisa said. "He shouldn't have those. Why did you give them to him in the first place? That was crazy."

"He won't get far. I gave him a section with characters that will stump him to no end. He'll never figure out what it says. Or his interpretation will turn out so flawed, he'll be a laughing stock."

"Why are you telling us this?" Erica asked. "Why now? Why not before? You could have told us a long time ago."

"Because it would have ruined the setup."

"Setup? You're setting us up?" Judge Bailey sounded winded.

"No. I'm setting them up. The timing is near perfect now. You only have one serious problem."

"Meaning?" Lisa said drably.

"Me," Erica said. "I'm the problem."

"What?" Lisa dubiously cried. "Why? How?"

"Because he identified me. Lowe identified me. They'll know who I am. Right?"

"That's right."

"Who is this man?" Judge Bailey asked. "The man who met with Dr. Russell. You say he's the key to everything."

"He's not particularly the key. But he gives orders. He gets orders. He does not have a clue who's directing this."

"What's his name? Who is he?"

"Name is Ward Stelter. He's a bureaucrat. A low-level one at that. Who gets paid handsomely for what he does and who feels not only superior but isolated and protected. Sometime this evening he'll show up in a hotel restaurant, looking for a certain kind of female companionship. It's about the only chance you'll get to see or meet him while he's here. From then on his full attention will be on that book."

"Are you telling us, if he's eliminated the killings stop?" Erica asked.

"I'm not telling you that. But he is essential for what happens next. They've done such a good job at layering their organization, that if he becomes the target, the repercussions may be devastating."

Lisa locked arms with Jacklyn and Erica. "We need to think. We need to talk. We'd like to see this book. How it describes this."

"Impossible. I'll never expose that book. You can't imagine the good, nor can you imagine the harm. People aren't ready for it."

"This is almost too much to take in," Judge Bailey said. "You're not going anywhere, are you? You can't leave. I have too many other questions."

Banda nodded. "I have a good many chess matches I'd like to play. Edward's ego could keep me going a good long time."

Lisa gave Banda a knowing smirk. She tugged on Erica and Judge Bailey. "Come with me. We'll get in the car. I don't want anyone else hearing what I have to say."

CHAPTER THIRTY-TWO

SEEDS OF A MURDER PLOT

They all climbed into the back seat of the Jag. "We have no other choice," Lisa declared. "I can't see any other way around this. That Stelter man has to die."

"Are you crazy? Do you realize who you're talking with here? I'm a judge. Judge Meghan Jacklyn Bailey. They'd string me up so fast my head would pop off."

"We're speaking metaphorically, aren't we?" Erica said with fear. "You're not going to kill him. I mean, actually kill him. You're just talking about somehow stopping him, right?"

"And if Banda is anywhere near correct, you won't be able to lay a hand on him."

216

"Stop! We're talking nonsense," Judge Bailey groused. "How do we know we can even trust what Banda is saying? He might be manipulating us. Why doesn't he take care of it? If he's the man he says he is… and he's got international connections, I don't see why he isn't taking care of this."

"That's right," Erica said. "How many rat holes have we gone down? He could be playing us, you know, trying to get us to commit the unthinkable. I'm not going to get involved with killing anyone. Not on your life."

"And we didn't say that," Lisa sounded very defensive.

"Yes, you did. You said the man has to die."

Lisa started and stopped. "I guess I did, but I didn't mean that. Maybe you're right. Maybe Banda is manipulating us. Why would he do that? That awful man. He's very good at twisting you around his little finger, isn't he? One minute you want revenge, the next he plays on your sympathies. I feel I've been pummeled by a tsunami wave. Now I'm not sure what to think."

"Don't you have connections?" Erica asked. "In the British Government. Can't they investigate this Stelter fellow? Or something?"

"Investigate him on what? If he's isolated and protected, what are they going to do? Besides he probably has diplomatic immunity."

Silence dominated for a moment.

"Then let's go back to London and look at him better. Just go in and watch him. We'll find this hotel restaurant and wait around for him."

"And get arrested for loitering?" Judge Bailey laughed.

"It's only three o'clock. We can go back in no time."

"Two hours is not no time."

"What do you care? I'm the one driving."

"I don't know."

"We'll just drive back and watch him. We're not going to do anything beyond that… are we? I mean, seriously. We have to get a better look at him if nothing else."

Judge Bailey sat thinking for a minute. "I feel pregnant."

"What?" Erica sounded shocked.

"Pregnant with a million different emotions and thoughts."

"Maybe we could fly back," Lisa said. "Nuts and/or Kip could fly us before its dark."

"Good luck. You saw their state of mind. Consider that too. Do you really think someone is going to die?" Erica said. "Maybe we should talk with them."

Lisa crawled out and climbed into the driver's seat. "We'll go. We'll buy you some clothes and dress you up like a tart."

Erica couldn't believe what she was hearing. She fully expected a protest out of Meghan. Instead, Judge Bailey joined Lisa in the front seat. Erica sat there feeling these two had stepped from the realm of rationality into the bizarre. Lisa started the engine and gave Erica a frosty look. "Get out," she said. "Don't say anything."

Erica didn't move until Lisa shifted into drive. She then hopped out and stood there gawking while the two drove away. A few minutes later she rounded the house and poked her head through the front door. Relief came because all but Kip now stood arguing in the kitchen. Kip sat on the sofa, next to a burning lamp, elbows on his knees and head clutched in his hands. Erica gently closed the door, every minute watching the entry into the kitchen. Comfortable they were alone, she sat close enough to reach and place a hand on Kip's shoulder. He gave her a strained look.

"Look," she said sympathetically. "I know I don't understand what you're going through. Is there anything I can do to help? It's very painful to see you suffering like this."

Kip sighed heavily before slumping back on the sofa. "I never asked for this, you know."

"How long have you had this... I don't know whether to call it a curse or a gift?"

"I can't really say. I slowly became aware of it. Strong, overwhelming impressions, which at first I didn't connect to anything. First time I became starkly aware of it was when..." he paused, and bit a quivering lip, closing his eyes.

"When your family died… right?"

He merely nodded.

"I'm sorry. I'm so, so sorry." She touched his hand. He seemed to cathartically inhale. A moment of silence. "Who's going to die now? Do you have any idea?"

He shook his head.

"What did they say… you know where, but not who?"

"It's not that simple. I can't really describe it. I don't think it would be appropriate anyway. I think it's meant solely for me to know. I vent with Nuts, but wouldn't presume the right to say anything to anyone else. Imagine how it would affect other people if I went about blabbering things like that."

"What an awful burden."

"That's the best way to describe it. It's not so pleasant being a seer, so to speak. Not that I'm claiming some sort of religious right or anything. It is seer-like though."

Erica didn't know what else to say. She folded her hands into her lap.

"Where's Jacklyn and Lisa?" Kip asked.

Erica suddenly looked as if the kid caught with the proverbial hand in the cookie jar. "They went back."

"Back? You mean to London?"

"Yes."

"Why?"

Erica merely shook her head.

"Oh… those fools." Instantly Kip shot to his feet. He stormed to the kitchen door before caustically looking back.

"What? What's wrong?"

"London. It's London. Someone close to me is going to die in London."

Minutes after six P.M. Lisa Allen was a woman rushed, excitable and on the edge as she brushed boxes aside, stumbling over a bed just to get a better view. It was in a business-like hotel room every bit akin to something Doc Martin and that persnickety Edith would run off to. Lisa formed a straight line on her lips and looked with fiery eyes.

"O… this isn't right," Judge Bailey said, frowning at the mirror. She turned sideways to get a better view of her bum. Tight, faux leather jeans showed too much of a middle-aged woman out of shape. Red stiletto heels caused her to wobble and a lacy, low-cut black and red roses blouse made her want to hunch in embarrassment. "I told you this is not going to work. I couldn't pass myself off as a tart or crumpet or Essex Girl… or any of those other words you called me."

"Hah! Don't kid yourself. You could pack 'em in. Punters galore."

"What? He's not going to kick me, is he?"

"Hah-hah… brilliant! You look smashing. We could print you up a bunch of flyers and spread them all around the phone booths."

"What do you mean punters? He's going to kick me? I don't know what weird customs you have over here. Especially when it comes to this."

"Oh, relax girl. They're just like everybody else. That's what they call the clients. A go'ol punter."

"I don't like it," Judge Bailey said, flattening her stomach. "Why am I doing this? We were going to watch, not solicit him. Don't I need a license for that or something?"

"Hah-hah… you're a darling. A judge and feigning such innocence. I'd play the role, but look at me. I'm a wrinkly old goat."

"Are not."

"You're not getting the full Monty. You'd scowl."

"I doubt that."

"Sixty years do a lot to a woman. Besides… I look like a chicken. Pointy beak of a nose, no cheeks, thin lips. I look like a chicken."

220

"Do not," Judge Bailey whined. "You don't even look close to sixty. You're beautiful. Besides, my forty-five years wear on me worse than your twenty-nine."

They both laughed.

"All you have to do," Lisa said, "is set up camp and advertise. Suppose he takes the bait. You might get a confession out of him or something."

"I doubt that. He'll be looking for someone younger. He probably calls a service or something."

"Well, either way, we'll get a better idea of who he is. We're just gambling on vague chances. We'd better hurry. We still have to make you up. I can take fifteen, maybe even twenty years off with the right makeup. You'll see. I'm a whiz. Even Wilhelmina Stanley thinks she's looking at a stranger in the mirror once I conduct my magic on her."

"Ugh," Judge Bailey groaned irritably, giving in.

In a restaurant that felt and looked far too cafeteria-like and not the chic, low-lit moody place anticipated, the two immediately swept behind a corner table, near the entry and sat down like lost change. Now, going on seven P.M. the crowd was modest and the conversation a bit loud if you wanted intimacy. Which suited Judge Bailey just fine. They had menus in hand when Judge Bailey finally straightened up a bit, but still hid behind her menu. She whispered, "I don't remember, did you see him? You didn't, did you? You don't know who we're looking for, do you? It's just me."

"I got a glimpse. Besides, I have an eye for delegate types. You can't hide behind that menu all night long, you know. You're going to have to look sometime."

"Well… can you see anyone now that looks like that? Banda could have been pulling our leg, you know."

"True. But isn't it exciting? I love these kinds of things. Let's you know you're alive."

"Then why do I feel dead? Forget about that. Can you see anyone?"

"No suits. He would wear a suit. You can relax."

"How long will they let us hide in here? We can't just sit here forever."

"As long as we're eating, what do they care? There are plenty of empty chairs. The bar has three customers."

"O…" Judge Bailey moaned.

In the slow, lingering wait they had the seasonal homemade soup. Lisa then had the house prawn cocktail and Jacklyn the avocado and tomato bruschetta. Needing to draw time out, now after seven-thirty, Lisa ordered smoked salmon Caesar salad and Jacklyn the chicken Caesar salad. Dessert decisions leaned toward Apple strudel and toffee pudding if need be. And it was nearing that critical point when it happened. Not Ward Stelter appearing, but another well-dressed gentlemen who had held a keen eye for some time. He was slightly older, had a thin mustache, and held himself very erect. He demurely approached and then subtly turned away as if ignoring them. A moment later, he slipped a hidden fifty pound note from inside his hand and under the edge of Lisa's plate. "If you don't mind," he lowly uttered.

Lisa looked at the note and then up at him. "I beg your pardon."

"Please. Ladies. We prefer not to accommodate your profession here. Other guests find it rather outputting."

"Agh! You're serious. You seriously… I beg your pardon. Are you suggesting…?"

"Please, ladies. Let's not make a scene. That small offering should satiate you. If you don't mind, you could excuse yourselves."

Lisa gave Judge Bailey a surprised look. Judge Bailey felt the embarrassment and wanted to crawl under the table. It was just then when Ward Stelter strolled in, sharply dressed, the unmistakable Dr. Stephen Russell a step behind. The two clearly exuded a pompous, self-assured air. A quick thinking Lisa Allen nearly crawled up the maî·tre d'hô·tel's arm. She grabbed him and spun him around. In her best imitation of James Cagney, she lowered her voice and grumbled, "Listen Mack, you don't know what you've stumbled onto here. My partner and I are working undercover. We're expecting our mark any minute. Vauxhall, mind you. Grant us a certain level of professional allowance and I'll up that tip two fold. Don't blow our cover."

"Ho!" he grunted, shocked and leaned away. He eyed her up and down twice before giving Judge Bailey a toffee-nosed scrunch of the nose.

"What do you say, Mack? Scat. Quickly."

He leaned away as if the unwashed had touched him. He brushed his arm off before stepping twice. He then skidded to a stop, quickly returned and snatched his fifty-pound note with an audible snap. A deep sigh of relief in both Lisa and Judge Bailey. For two reasons. The snob was gone and Stelter and Dr. Russell had deposited themselves at the far end of the bar so that the only way they could see Lisa and Jacklyn was to stand and stretch tall to see over the end of the bar.

"I can't believe it," Judge Bailey uttered. "I can't believe it. I simply can't believe it."

"That they would show?"

"That Banda was right. I thought for sure… I can't believe it."

A few brief seconds later and that disbelief felt swallowed up in a tornado of total repudiation. It tugged on Jacklyn's heart with such force she felt eviscerated. If it had been the first, faint tentative tugs of a fish on the line, it would have been one thing, but this was the complete ingestion of the hook before the young, overexcited fisherman wails back and rips the hook out, stomach and all. There, a very handsome and debonair Roger "Kip" McKinney strolled in with an air of confidence, a hand deposited in the pocket of a charcoal-gray suit and looking as if not a thing in the world could fracture him. No pause or delay, he strolled straight for the end of the bar and sat down right next to Dr. Russell. Judge Bailey shot to her feet, despite the blood completely draining from her face. If Lisa hadn't grabbed her arm and yanked her right back down she would have stood there until exploding with rage. Judge Bailey looked at Lisa as if she didn't recognize her. As if deep underwater, and those still shimmering waters on the surface would never see a hint of decaying life bubbling to the surface again. "We should get out of here," Lisa said as forcefully and as hushed as possible. Judge Bailey didn't respond. She seemed in a trance. Until Lisa modestly backhanded her across the cheek. Judge Bailey suddenly escaped, ducking around Lisa's chair and scooting on out. Lisa didn't count it, but she left a decent wad of cash as she spun away and quickly followed the sweet smell of a reformed Tart's scent.

CHAPTER THIRTY-THREE

Losing the Sacrificial Lamb

The moment Lisa Allen wobbled into their hotel room she dialed Edward. She paced, running a hand through her hair and totally oblivious to the touristy view out the room's wide picture windows. The Thames, and the beautiful smoke stacks of the Battersea Power Station, a smooth 200 meters north. Such emblematic irony when it came down to it. Edward picked up on the fourth ring. "Lisa Luv… what on earth? Why didn't you say you were leaving? The whole world has tipped upside down."

"Sweetie… I don't have time. What's going on there? What's happened?"

"I can't rightly make any sense of it. One moment, things are quite blissful, the next I feel like I've been cleaned off the deck of the HMS Hermes. Tidal wave left us all a bit staggered."

"What happened? What did Kip say?"

"I didn't hear a word out of Kip. You see, there we were… I don't exactly know how it started. I don't actually know what it was about. Antione up to that point had been quite congenial. A mysterious character of course, but suddenly we're in this argument. Peacemaker Tony hauls me out of there and we go up the road to Barneys. Pub was a good place to calm the nerves. We go back, Antione and his partner are gone, Kip and his plane are gone and all that's left is a sobbing Erica."

"What did they do to her?" she asked, now watching a shattered Judge Bailey vacantly staring while finding a bed to sit on.

"She's upset. Keeps going on about Kip. No greater love than this, she keeps blathering. You know what that means, don't you? Is that what she's suggesting. I'm very flustered and confused here."

Those words felt like a wallop to the gut. No goodbyes, she simply hung up and marched for the door.

"What?" Judge Bailey said. "Now what?"

Lisa paused merely long enough to hotly say the words. "That idiot Roger is trying to get himself killed."

It took a few seconds for those words to register. Once they did, the judge's shattered world suddenly self-repaired. "O my God. He wouldn't… no, of course he would. Damn him," she blabbered and quickly hurried out the door. Judge Bailey found Lisa at the bar haranguing a flustered waiter. No sign of Kip, Stelter or Dr. Russell.

"Look, they were sitting right here," Lisa jammed a finger to the bar. "Seconds ago. Don't go telling me you don't know anything. Where did they go?"

"Uh-I-uh…" the fellow with silver on the sides of his head looked for rescue in a waitress who just then came out of the kitchen. "You were serving out here. Did you see anything?" he sort of wheezed.

She calmly gave him a confused look. "Sorry."

"The three customers that were sitting here," Lisa barked. "What happened to them?"

The gal sardonically shrugged. "They walked out. What else are they supposed to do?"

"Which door?"

She motioned where they had entered. A second later, Judge Bailey is stumbling along, almost falling off her heels and trying to keep up. She finally caught up at the front desk. "You sure you didn't see anyone cross by here within the last few minutes?" Lisa demanded.

"Ma'am, please," the young gal of Indian descent was very calm. "This is a quiet time. No one has crossed by here in twenty or thirty minutes."

"Where else could they exit?"

"Out the east side, down around south. Several places actually."

Lisa bolted. Judge Bailey had had it with the heels. She tugged them off and ran to catch up. Judge Bailey held the east side exit door open while Lisa briefly searched an empty street. She handed her phone to Judge Bailey the moment she reentered. "What?"

"Give me a couple of minutes and then call the front desk. Ask for that moronic Ward Stelter's room."

"What?"

"Haven't you seen the Jason Bourne movies? They would never give me another guest's room number. You're going to call and ask for his room. I'm going to spy and catch the number. If he answers, think on your feet and find a way to get there. If he doesn't, we'll still know his room number. Call!" She said and hurriedly walked away. Judge Bailey remained and seconds later stood there with the phone to her ear, not dialed yet, grumbling,

"This is not going to work. This will not work. We're not in a movie for Pete's sake." A breath later and she was trying to count off seconds, but the dominate race of her heart, pounding inside her chest kept tripping her up. She thought to wait longer, but dialed the second she found the hotel's number on Lisa's phone. A controlled request and what felt interminably long before the attendant's voice came back on the line.

"Sorry, Ma'am. Mr. Stelter is not answering. Would you like to leave a message?"

"Thank you, no. I'll try later."

Judge Bailey found Lisa nervously pacing near the front entry. She sidled up and whispered. "Any luck?"

"It didn't work the way it did in the movie. I couldn't even tell where the phone was. What happened when you called?"

"No answer."

"Shoot. Now what do we do?"

"We could walk around. Walk the halls. Maybe they're here. Maybe we'll find them."

"Good idea. Let's be calm about it."

Though safely back inside their hotel room, Judge Bailey sat in a briar patch some two and a half hours later, feeling as if some horrid crow stood there pecking at her skin and she couldn't scare it off. All while nervously sitting and hanging on every word out of Lisa's mouth. Lisa exhaled hotly and stood there exasperatingly staring at the ceiling. "Yes, officer, I know. You've told me a million times and I'm telling you for the millionth time they are going to kill him." She stood there silently for a minute, nervously digging a finger in her hair and squeezing her eyes closed tighter and tighter. She finally exhaled long and deeply before tossing the phone on the bed and giving Jacklyn a chagrined look. "I think they've got my name on a list," she said. "Cued up for the funny farm." She twirled a finger around her ear. "I can see them now. The old dingbat has called again. Nutjob wants her windows licked. Daft nut head. I ought to knock them upside a brick wall."

"Maybe you should settle down. We've done all we could. What more could we do? What are they going to do?"

Lisa got a long face. "It makes me sick. For all we know Kip is already floating face down and headed for high tide."

"Don't say that. Don't talk like that. We don't know anything. At least try to be hopeful."

"And what did hope do for you?" she said and instantly covered her mouth in regret. She dropped to her knees and grabbed Jacklyn's legs. "I'm sorry, I'm sorry. I didn't mean to insult you. I'm so sorry. I'm just so upset."

"Don't fret. You didn't hurt my feelings. I didn't know my sister… when it comes down to it. I know what you mean and I sympathize. I just can't see how constantly badgering the police is going to do any good. You're making enemies. They may ignore you out of spite. What did they say when you asked them about his plane?"

"They located it at the London City Airport. Private jet centre. That's all they say."

"They're watching it?"

"We know what we're doing, they tell me. I should watch my tongue I guess. I've made a few enemies."

"We've been away from the door too long. I'll go back down and keep watch. Are you going to rest or what?"

"Are you kidding? I can't sleep, nor would I dare. We'll do like we've been doing. I'll watch the east door and pace. Then we'll change and you pace."

"We can't do this forever."

"I know. If nothing happens by morning, I think we'll have to conclude they've gone somewhere else. The problem is... well... I'd shoot myself if we left and they walked right back in here. Know what I mean?"

"I do. Come on. Back on watch."

Honestly, by sunrise, with no rest at all both, Lisa and Judge Bailey felt assigned to the lower end of the cognitive distribution scale. Low IQs, low morale, low energy. They slept for four hours before spiraling into a funky drift down what felt like the River Styx. A Pro Forma ritual according to Judge Bailey. Then, like two cloudy-eyed frogs in a specimen jar, they rode that river back to Godsham completely uncertain of what might happen next.

CHAPTER THIRTY-FOUR

WALKING THE RAZOR'S EDGE WITH ROGER "KIP" MCKINNEY

In what felt like a divided world Kip looked back at Erica, keenly aware of the sudden mortification in her face. He then looked in on Banda, Emiliano, Nuts, and Edward. He had thought they would have overheard him. Instead, a red-faced Edward threw his hands in the air and stormed for the back door. Nuts rolled his eyes and quickly followed. A very calm-looking Banda turned and looked at Kip. "Emiliano," he lowly said. "Show him."

The little Beggar meekly lowered his chin before lifting his jumper and unbuttoning his white shirt. He removed a plastic enclosed sheet, secured inside his waistline, and handed it to Kip. Kip looked but didn't read. "What is it?"

"Read."

He studied the first few words. "Part of the book, right?"

Banda nodded. "A translated section. For your eyes only."

Kip slumped against the wall as he quickly read the first few lines, skipped, and read a few more. It was enough. A few simple lines enough.

A brief obscure exchange between the two and Kip beelined for the front door. "Kip!?" Erica called to him. "Kip? What happened? Where are you going?"

He was gone. She quickly followed. In a slightly increasing drizzle, she caught up to him just as he opened and lowered the stairs on the Pilatus. "Kip!" she demanded. "What is happening?"

"Sorry. I have to go."

"You're going after them, aren't you? Take me with you."

"I have other things to do. You stay here."

"Why? What are you going to do? Why can't I come? I need to come."

"No, you don't."

"Why?"

"Because this is deeper and more dangerous than you understand and I don't have time to explain."

He took the first step. She grabbed and hung onto his arm. He turned and locked eyes with her. "No. This is not for you."

"I'll stay out of the way. I need to come."

"No. This is my responsibility, not yours."

"What? What responsibility?"

He pushed her back and began lifting the stairs. "Sometimes a man has to lay his life down for his friends. Especially when snakes target his innocent friends because of him."

She stood there a bit flabbergasted. The words hadn't fully sunk in until the door was sealed tight. "No! Kip!" she pounded a hand on the door. "Open this door! What are you going to do? Don't do this."

Moments later, as the engines whined to life, she defiantly stood directly in front of the plane. She glared at him before stomping a foot. On the second attempt, she suddenly realized the presence of Antione Banda and Emiliano standing off to the side. Banda simply stood there shaking his head. That affected her in a way that shocked her. Tears welled up in huge globules, causing everything to blur. She felt a hand

229

take her by the elbow a moment later and she couldn't resist him as he pulled her away. She knew she stood under a front porch roof, but couldn't recall getting there sometime later when the Pilatus roared and lifted away, quickly disappearing into the low cloud cover. When she turned to look for Antione Banda, he was gone.

Kip had made the proper arrangements before taking the fifteen-minute flight and then landing at the London City Airport. He landed, changed into the suit he always carried on board, and from there took a Taxi into the Paddington neighborhood near Hyde Park. Not far from the Bayswater Station, the taxi swept to the curb in front of a stately-looking hotel. Brass signage against a white façade picked his reflection up but a breath as he climbed out and dashed up the stairs. Just inside the door, a gentleman stood impatiently tapping a business card at the counter where a fair, familiar face quickly looked up. The dark-eyed and red-lipped attendant's name was Sofia. She smiled. "Mr. McKinney. How nice to see you again. I'll be a moment. I'm trying to arrange a room for this gentleman."

"No rooms available?"

"Ah… can you give me a minute?"

Kip hesitated a moment, recognizing that the gentlemen had placed several of his business cards on the counter before impatiently stepping away. In reaching for one of the hotel's cards, Kip smiled and fingered one of each and then palmed them. "Sofia. Why don't I check back with you? I should have called ahead. I may have to make other arrangements."

She got a concerned look, but wiggled her fingers when Kip spun around and skipped out. Once back inside the taxi Kip first studied the hotel's card, which was merely an Arabic greeting card. Embossed golden symbols on satin. Peace, wisdom and love. He simply needed them as fool's gold. The businessman's card was a fortuitous extra and seemed to fit in perfectly for what he had planned. "Well, Mr. Wilson Graham of Baker, Simpson and Raja," he kept his voice low, "Let's hope they're either too stupid or too greedy to question you." He then cleared his throat, raising his voice. "Barclays. Victoria Street."

Approaching five-thirty P.M. the taxi carried Kip over the busy Chelsea Bridge and moments after that it was merely a case of evaluating, stocking, assessing, reading and rereading a tract meant solely for him. By seven-thirty P.M. he stood in the recesses of a seating area that had a clear view of the restaurant's entry. Spotting Ward Stelter meeting up with Dr. Stephen Russell did nothing to rev his heart. He waited briefly, steepled his fingers, touched his lips and then casually walked for the door before depositing one hand in a pocket. No hesitating, he strode straight to where the two now sat. He sidled in next to Dr. Russell and gave them a discreet smile. "Gentlemen. You'll forgive my intrusion…" it was obvious to Kip when Judge Bailey shot to her feet, her chair's feet haltingly stuttering, "but I know who you are and why you're here. I know what kind of business you're conducting." He reached in, removed both cards out of his pocket and placed them tightly together on the bar. "You see by my card who I am. You'll also note my employer. I won't share names for security's sake. Dr. Russell, several hours ago you contacted a colleague in Santiago de Compostela. You don't know this and I regret to inform you, but he isn't as loyal to you as you would suppose. He contacted my employer. My employer is extremely interested in the transcript you recently acquired and is prepared to pay significantly."

Both Stelter and Dr. Russell got a sour look on their faces, Stelter's brows growing tight and furrowed.

"Something else you need to know… the news of that book portion becoming public, as a matter of speech, has ignited a hail storm of interest and activity. Other portions are beginning to surface. A great many people of significance have had their radar peeked and are watching. Now… I have here," he removed a bank note, which he placed on the bar, "one million pounds. You can see the value my employer places on that book. I have other appointments arranged. Once we calculate the value your portion adds or subtracts that value can go up significantly. I'm authorized, without speaking with my employer, to go as high as ten million. Do I have your interest, Dr. Russell?"

"Dr. Russell doesn't own the book. I own the book," Ward Stelter harshly said. "Who has them? Where are these other sections? I'd like to know."

"Sorry. I can allow you to travel with me, but I can't divulge. I'm sure you understand."

"No," Dr. Russell said. "It's not his book. I found it. I came up with it."

"And you were working for me. You don't want to go down that rat hole, do you? You'll get your finder's fee. You don't have to worry."

They all went silent for some time. Kip studied their faces briefly before standing. "I see I'm getting no response." He picked up the bank note and his business cards. "Good day to you Gentlemen. I have other appointments to get to."

"Hold on," Stelter chirped. "You just don't walk away."

"I most certainly do."

"But this hasn't been translated. You don't even know what's in it."

"Thus the options in value. We're not stupid people. We know value when we see it. Right now, as is, we value what you have at one-million pounds."

A few breaths and Kip spun on a heel.

"Now stop," Stelter hissed. "Give a man a chance to consider his options."

"Oh, there will be time to consider. We have to evaluate and compare. It's not like the price has evaporated right in front of your eyes."

"Appointment? With who? Where?"

"You'll have to trust me and come along."

"And who's going to translate?" Dr. Russell barked. "Who? I don't know anyone more gifted than me."

"Well... perhaps we'll contract with you then. We have options. We always have contingency plans. We wouldn't be where we are without that. It's the nature of the world we work in."

"We'll go," Dr. Russell said. "We'll come with you. Do you have a car? How did you get here?"

"I'm more interested..." Stelter said, looking around. "You wouldn't be armed or anything, would you? No thugs waiting to knock us off or something?"

"Do you have the transcript on you?"

"Don't be an idiot. Of course not. It's in a secure location."

"You have your security and leverage then. Why would I jeopardize our interests? Can we get a copy? We need to compare and evaluate next to other text."

Stelter jutted his jaw out, scratching his neck. "I have to get a copy. It won't take long. What do we do?"

"You get us a copy and I call a taxi. Is it in the hotel safe?"

"Dr. Russell… let's go. Mr… what was it, Graham? I'd prefer you don't follow on our heels."

"No problem. I'll step outside and make that call. I'll be waiting near the circle." Kip stepped away and soon exited where he called the same driver who now sat waiting for his call. Stelter and Russell went to the front counter. Dr. Russell stood warily looking around when Stelter pulled the folded pages out of his pocket and then in a hushed voice spoke to the desk clerk. "I need two copies. Promptly please."

A nod from the clerk and an alarmed look on Dr. Russell's face. "You didn't make a copy. There's nothing in the vault?"

"I knew it was valuable. I didn't know it was that valuable. How would I know that?"

"Put a copy in the vault. Don't take the risk like you have up to now."

"Same risk you were taking. Did you make a copy of this?"

Dr. Russell did the best he could at feigning innocence. He frowned, shook his head and then rubbed his jaw. "How many people out there know about this?"

"Obtuse words coming from the leak… wouldn't you say? We'd better take safeguards. Pay the clerk. Tell her she didn't see us and she doesn't know anything if anyone comes asking."

Stelter left Dr. Russell at the counter after he had a copy in hand. He found Kip waiting beside a taxi. It was an awkward moment, Kip very confident and unaffected in any way, Stelter feeling he should warm up to this man, but also overly guarded and nervous on two counts. He felt the fraud that he was and he felt wary. Couldn't trust a soul if they were just like him. Inside and outside sweat beaded up, a hoary reflection in the way rain drops stood proud on the well-polished black paint of the taxi. Moments later, Dr. Russell arrived and the three piled in. Dr. Russell and Stelter on the back seat, Kip facing them on the fold down. By the time the taxi rolled onto Chelsea Bridge, Lisa and Judge Bailey stood querying at the front counter. "Now that we're alone, I'll fill you in. Shortly, a Mr. Laghari will be arriving at Waterloo Station. He's on his way from Gatwick. He can't take the Express directly, so there may be a delay. Dr. Russell, once we arrive, I must ask you to remain outside. People know who you are and if he sees you with us it may alter our negotiating ability. Realize, money is hardly an issue with my employer, but if I can acquire vital tracts at a lowered price, we increase our profits on the backend. I'm sure you won't object to that. Is that alright with you?"

Dr. Russell's conceited, stealthy look confirmed he liked having that kind of clout. Stelter's derisive lift of a lip spoke volumes too. "He'll stay outside," Stelter said.

"May I see that copy? Mr. Laghari will need to see it. Rest assured, I won't give it to him, but he needs to know it exists. I've dealt with him several times before. We'll make contact tonight and he'll have us meeting in some dark, exotic place the next day. Mr. Laghari… well, he won't have possession of his tract until he trusts us. Before then, I have a time arranged after we meet with him to meet with someone else, elsewhere. I'll withhold that information until we're again isolated like this. Any questions?" Kip asked, his hand extended.

The two men looked at one another, unable to form a single thought. At least initially. Stelter finally produced the copy and cleared his throat. "Laghari? That's Indian, right?"

"He's British but is traveling out of Germany. That's the extent I can tell you. For now."

Kip sat waiting for more. The two now looked quite bewildered and didn't produce a sound. Perfect, he thought. Absolutely perfect. His only concern now, that the future-telling text was right. That someone just happens to show who looks the part and is friendly enough, or has the proper ego to succumb to his Bard-like performance. If not, no problem, these two were already hooked. But then Kip couldn't remember once not seeing some smartly dressed fellow of Indian descent, strolling the halls of Waterloo Station. Kip folded his arms and crossed his legs, totally comfortable with what awaited them.

Thirty minutes later, dusk had faded to darkness as they stood on the curb while Kip settled up with the cabbie. "Make yourself thin," Stelter roughly said to Dr. Russell. He then punctually followed Kip into the station. First priority was exposure. No real concern about the chaotic bustle of small crowds, moving in predetermined hypnosis. No worry about the din. Less worry about the suave announcer's voice, echoing arrivals or departures or general information. Yellow-vested security officers paid them no attention. Two students rushing up and embracing an arriving friend pushed Kip to their right where he first feigned interest in the large scheduling board. And then it was an easy spot. A CCTV security camera positioned on the first pillar in front of them. And then one after another after another, hanging from the arched rafters like Halloween ghosts in a tree. Kip took Stelter by the arm and snugged him up close.

"I'm not sure if Mr. Laghari has arrived yet. He was supposed to meet me right over there next to the underground station. We'll walk," Kip muttered and angled towards an escalator for the second level. Stelter seemed the bewildered kid, afraid to leave his side, yet mesmerized by the sheen of white light, reflecting off of well-polished white floors. Kip's intent was high ground where he could survey, spot a victim and then leave Stelter at a distance. A few steps from the escalator, it even shocked Kip to see a man, standing some forty meters ahead, directly under the clock and across from departures. He was on the phone and had a hand up, gesturing.

"There he is," Stelter said. "He's not very shy. You'd think he'd be discreet."

"He likes me," Kip muttered and faced Stelter briefly. "Stay here. If things go well, it won't take long."

Stelter sidled near the escalator and suspiciously stood there, a finger to his chin and watching indirectly. Kip approached the dark-haired man, his disarming and charming smile the single weapon exposed. The man had an overcoat over his arm and a briefcase partly hidden. Expensive Santoni Oxford shoes published enough about the man's wealth that Kip didn't need to see his charcoal cashmere jacket with its velvet collar to make a judgment. He was wondering what to say when the man hung up his call and opened his arms. "Professor Childers. How good to see you again. I was hoping to meet you and thank you," the man said.

"I'm sorry. You have me at a disadvantage." Kip positioned himself to block a direct line to Stelter.

"Last week's conference. On derivative nightmares and the next financial crisis, no one likes talking about. Your comments were very insightful."

"I'm sorry. You're name?" Kip said, knowing he'd hit the jackpot. He could fake his way through any financial topic with a breeze.

"This is very exciting. Very exciting."

"I thought I put everyone to sleep."

"Nonsense. Oh… my name… See… I'm so excited to meet you. Paul Sharma. I'm Paul Sharma. I'm employed with Lloyds."

"I guess you're referencing the new mortgage disaster ahead."

"Foolish politicians, right? How gouch can they act? It's frightful. Absolutely frightful."

"Glad you enjoyed the conference."

While Kip went on talking everything from derivative contracts, to asset groups and underlying assets, to the risk-averse, to the risk seeker, to options, to speculating and new mortgage tomfoolery, Stelter strained and pretended the casual observer. Until his phone pinged a new and urgent message. He turned his back before checking it. Leatherback has a new contact, it read, Leatherback being the code word for Roger "Kip" McKinney.

Not now, Stelter replied.

Following protocol. Unique, new contact. Imperative we contact you.

Contact me later. Not now!

Stelter ended the message and turned just in time to find Kip and Mr. Laghari a few steps away. Mr. Laghari was all aglow, his eyes glittering with excitement. "Very exciting," he said, grabbing Stelter's hand and vigorously shaking. "Yes, sir indeed. Very exciting. Sorry I have to run. I very much like your associate. Very much. Hope to see you soon," he said and hurried off.

Stelter gave Kip an ill-natured look. "You sure about him? I don't like a man that... I don't know," he suspiciously looked over his shoulder, "who's not only demonstrative, but uninhibited. You dare do business with him?"

"Like I said. He likes me. Wait until we see him in a different setting, where millions of pounds are on the line. He has his tactics. As do we."

"Well, that didn't take very long. Now what?"

"On we go. I'll tell you once we're secluded."

CHAPTER THIRTY-FIVE

Polishing the Razor's Edge

They walked out of Waterloo Station into a night demonstrably and suddenly different. Rains had faltered, clouds had broken and the bright light of moon painted the edges of solid, fluffy clouds silver. An almost audible ooh and aah out of a trio of students on their heels caused Stelter to swat as if a dog nipping at his heels. The most obvious change, which Kip instantly observed, was an absent Dr. Stephen Russell. "Perhaps he anticipated a much longer delay or he couldn't control his hunger and thirst," Stelter grumbled.

Either way, Kip wasn't particularly concerned. Not at the moment. Racing through his mind was the next leg in this silly ruse. Primarily, he had considered King's College, a short trip—walk if need be—across the Waterloo Bridge and into the realm of literary studies. Ancillary, he hoped to find either a random book store or cosmopolitan stomp, open late and had little doubts. He recalled an insomniac's guide to late night London and knew well that morose and peculiar creatures needed places to roam and roost. Whether oddballs or Mavericks roved, there was always an eerily quieted universe of wretchedness that needed kept behind closed doors. And if not closed the better. Stelter audibly groaned, sounding as if one of those night creatures, and in sleep, imprisoned there missing out on something wicked. "What the hell happened to him?" he griped. "We were gone only long enough to whizz. You see him anywhere? He's tall enough to sniff a giraffe's butt."

Kip almost laughed—and then did. He hadn't figured in finding anything appealing in this man. In a way, Stelter suddenly reminded him of Nuts. Attitude and junk-yard sense of humor. "How well do you know him?" Kip asked. "What are his tastes? Would he have gone for a pint or something?"

Stelter didn't know him on that level. Not in the least and saw no reason to feign friendship. "I have no idea. Maybe he's feeling betrayed."

"An employee feeling cheated, you mean?"

"Exactly. Doesn't make sense, however. He's always been rather professional about this. He knew he would never own anything. What kind of resources would he have? He wouldn't. He'll get amply rewarded. I don't know what his issue is."

Several seconds passed. "I can't see him anywhere," Kip impatiently said. "We can't wait here all night. Call him."

"No. Let's move on. It's his loss if he doesn't have the discipline to wait ten minutes. Flag down the next taxi?" he looked up at Kip with an eye of self-doubt.

"We can walk. King's College. It's right across the river. Half a mile."

Stelter's self-doubt morphed into something exceptionally anguished. "Walk?" he groused. "Walk? I don't walk anywhere."

"And I don't see a taxi. By the time one comes along or we call one, we could be there. The fresh air will do you good. Walking London streets by the light of the moon… you couldn't ask for anything more romantic."

"Or haunting," Stelter complained as he watched Kip step off the curb. And that's all Kip did. They were nearly eye to eye now. "I'd feel better if you called Dr. Russell. He's more important in this than you and I are. At least when it comes down to it."

"I don't see it that way."

"Can you detect a forgery? Can you even decipher one character on those pages? I know I can't. Call him."

A stubborn Stelter huffed a quick breath out of his nostrils. He formed a downturned line on his lips before pulling his phone out and dialing. He paced. Twice. He paused and looked at his phone. "I'm not getting anything. He's not answering. He's having a temper tantrum. I say we go. He's got my number."

"Fine," Kip said and trotted across the street. Stelter stood there, his protest measured by the time it took to imagine a million dollars stuffed under a bed. Begrudgingly, he looked side to side before stepping off the curb and racing to beat a set of headlights coming on. Nothing was said until they walked by a street-side café where a busboy was out wiping the wet off of tables and chairs.

"You're an American," Stelter said.

Kip said nothing until they stood under the elevated rail lines that not only crossed over the café, but resonated with the strange metallic roar of an approaching train. He paused there until it roared overhead and quickly passed. "So are you. Does that matter?"

"Doesn't. It's just… it strikes me as odd that it's a couple of Americans chasing this."

"Dr. Russell is an American. I hardly see the point. Just about everyone I deal with is not."

They began to walk. A small crowd of young people approached, boisterous and clearly animated about whatever was playing across the way at the IMAX theatre. Stelter waited until the group rushed by, clearly anxious to get down into the tubes and the theatre's entry. "Does your employer have a residence here in London?" Stelter asked.

"You know I can't answer that."

"You have an office here, though?"

"We have offices all over the world."

Stelter scrunched his shoulders before looking back. "What do you think about this book? I mean… do you really think it is what they say it is? You know… tells the future."

"Are you a religious man?"

"Are you kidding?"

"So you wouldn't put any faith in it?"

239

"I don't know. I guess if I read the thing and what it said came true… I could be convinced."

"You know what they say?"

"What?"

"About sign seekers. Wasn't it Moses and Pharaoh? It's an evil and adulterous generation that seeks signs."

"I hardly see that as a sign. It's more like evidentiary facts. In my opinion. Speaking of which…" he looked over his shoulder again. "You know my name. You knew who we are and where we were meeting."

"Are you suggesting I read that in the book or something?"

"I don't know. You tell me."

"Mr. Stelter… Dr. Russell has a loose tongue. He gets excited. He calls a colleague and spills all that he knows. That colleague passes it on. It's not that hard."

"Are you living here in London? You seem to know the city quite well."

"I don't live here. I get a hotel room whenever I visit. I spend most of my time in Paris."

They were approaching the Waterloo Bridge where erected barriers protected the sidewalk and bike lane. Stelter stopped and looked back again. "What's bothering you?" Kip asked. Stelter stood there spying as if attached to a cable. Kip looked around, noting the Hayward Gallery with its glassy pyramidal spikes and row of illuminated orbs, which sat a meter away and just over the top of a side barrier. In the distance, he could see the top half of the London Eye gracefully arching. You couldn't hear the revving engine. Nor could you sense that anything was amiss until a narrow set of headlights came racing from the IMAX roundabout and then jumped the center curb before steering straight for them.

"Holy shiiis…" Stelter hissed and lunged, clawing at Kip, pushing him aside and running. Kip delayed long enough to quickly assess distances. He bolted, caught Stelter in a few short gaits and then lept, part tackling and carrying them both over the cement barrier where the orbs stood proud. They rolled once and shuttered to a grinding stop. A beat later the bumper of a small dark utility van careened off the barrier, rocked and then spun back before glancing off the sidewalk barriers. There was a brief moment of indecision on all counts. Stelter then fought to get back off the barrier. Kip locked onto Stelter's collar and yanked him toward the roof's edge and was instantly assessing the jump down when tires squealed as the van created a cloud of blue rubbery smoke, whipping around. It shuttered, racing away and then shuttered again, screeching to a halt.

"O, God. They're coming back," Stelter objected and nearly jumped the ten feet. Kip restrained him, nearly jerking him back off the ledge. A moment later, the back doors to the van burst open, a dark object rolled out and the van revved wildly racing away. "We've got to run," Stelter said frantically. "Now! O, God. I knew this would happen. Why wasn't I thinking? I'm such a fool."

Kip studied him but a moment. Headlights from an approaching bus soon lit up the roadway and highlighted that left abandoned. Kip jumped, ran down the sidewalk and merely stopped to look over the dividing barrier. By then other vehicles had stopped. By then a crowd was gathering. Kip was shocked to find Stelter still standing where he had left him. Kip pulled him down off the side barrier and leaned into him. "I can't stay here. I can't get mixed up in the middle of this."

"You can't!? I can't! Was that him? Was that Dr. Russell?"

"You knew?"

"O God, I'm a dead man. Why wasn't I thinking?"

Stelter now seemed a paraplegic, locked inside a body cast. The classic battlefield freeze response. He didn't move when Kip tugged. Glassy eyes remained cemented where Dr. Russell lay dead. Short rapid breaths seemed impossible with Stelter's clenched jaw. "Stelter?" Kip growled. "Are you hearing me?"

Nothing.

Kip glanced once before circling behind and giving Stelter a few sharp Heimlich-like maneuvers, simply to alter his breathing. He then dropped to his knees and wildly massaged Stelter's legs. He knew to stop when Stelter's knees nearly buckled. He again fronted him, taking him by the shoulders. "Stelter? You with me?"

"O God," he said. "I'm terrified."

"We'll get you out of here. Move with me."

241

Stelter was now like a stumbling bag of cement. Kip guided him forward where the jump over the side barrier was a few short feet and the entry into the Hayward Gallery a short distance away. Kip slid Stelter over the wall and held on until he was solidly down. He then had to practically carry him. Through the Gallery's glass doors, down a flight of stairs, and then through corridors until they emerged on Belvedere Rd. Kip moved Stelter under the Waterloo Bridge road where he leaned him against the wall and studied his eyes. "I'm an idiot," Stelter said. "There were always the rumors about that book. I thought it was pure bull. It didn't dawn on me. I don't know what I was thinking. I should have realized it when Russell disappeared. Crap," he rested his head on the concrete, his eyes darting.

Kip could easily see the vulnerability. Could see this fool clumsily struggling, getting run down, or perhaps some monster splitting his skull open on unyielding concrete. This would have been the ideal place to abandon him. Just turn and walk away. After all, Kip was a far better man. Not the kind to exact revenge. Even though he felt certain, this was the man or better said, the monster responsible for killing Dana, Kallie, Kami, and Katie. The most important thing for Kip right now was to see deep into the heart of the man. Needed to see the dark soul, so callous and evil. For a long time, he stared. For a long time searching. How pathetic. How miserable. The only thing in there that Kip could detect—greed. Kip stepped to walk away. Stelter's face suddenly changed. A tremor roiled from chin to brow. He looked at Kip with unalterable pleading, trying to say something, but couldn't. Kip expected sobs. Instead, Stelter lunged and clung on as the distance suddenly seemed too far. Kip stopped and merely gave him a pitiful look.

"Look, uh…" Stelter faltered. "I'm uh… please don't leave me alone. I'm terrified. They kill people who look for that book, don't you know?"

"I know. The price people are willing to pay is ample evidence."

"Help me."

Kip sighed and looked away. He took but a few seconds debating. "You can't go back to your hotel. They'll know. Whoever it is, they'll know."

"You don't know who it is?"

"Could be any one of a dozen countries. Whoever most doesn't want that book revealed. I don't know who it is."

"Laghari? Would it be Laghari?"

"It's not Laghari. Trust me on that one."

"Where's your hotel room? Take me there."

"I don't have one yet."

"I don't care. I'd sleep here if I had to. Just don't leave me alone. Please."

Again Kip sighed. He looked down and to the side. "You'll have to walk. One to two miles."

"I don't care. I'd walk from hell and back if I had too." Kip exhaled and began walking away. Stelter caught up and stayed a step behind. "By the way," Stelter said lowly and guardedly, "you wouldn't happen to have a cigarette, would you?"

CHAPTER THIRTY-SIX

STAGES

Within the hour Ward Stelter stood at a twelfth story window, seemingly mesmerized by the prime London view. There the London Eye still turned, Parliament felt the anchor and Big Ben draped in scaffolding still an annoying reminder that no one could stop time. All of that was periphery. A River Thames dinner cruise boat held his stare as he grappled with his emotions. Embarrassment over his lack of manliness felt the tip of the self-flagellation whip and the spur that brought words the moment Kip re-entered the room. Stelter looked over his shoulder.

"You talked to security?"

"I talked to security. They're pretty vigilant here. I doubt you have to worry."

"You probably think I'm a sniveling mess."

"Have you ever been in the crosshairs before now?"

"Hah… are you kidding? I've lived a privileged life. I've never had to worry about a thing. This has rattled me terribly."

"Why did you venture in then?" Kip asked, finally removing his jacket and loosening his tie. "You'd heard the rumors. You knew the dangers of that book, didn't you?"

Stelter shook his head and almost laughed. "I didn't believe it. I figured a rumor was just as good as a bullet."

"Lesson learned, I suppose," Kip said, while removing a shoe. He lay stretched out and had his hands behind his head when Stelter stepped to the minibar and chose Scotch Whiskey. He then watched as Stelter added a few cubes of ice and simply swirled the warm-amber liquid.

"I should call the wife," Stelter said. "Or maybe not. No reason she should know. Kids probably wouldn't care if I ended up dead anyway."

"How many kids?"

"Two teenagers. Rebels. Can't keep their noses clean. Giving Gloria an ulcer. You?"

"Three daughters. About the same age. I know your heartache. Probably worse."

"Hm…" Stelter scowled, shaking his head again. "You think it's supposed to make you happy, right? Find a pleasant woman… at least half good looking and then pop out a few brats. I can hardly wait to get away from it and then the anxiety when you've got to go back." He then glanced at Kip as if hoping for a commiserating stare, but received nothing but hard, piercing eyes. "Where you from, Wilson? You don't strike me as a big-city attorney."

"How's a big-city attorney supposed to look?"

"Arrogant, suave, street smart, mean as hell. You know what I mean."

"And how do I strike you?"

"Too smart to be an attorney. That's how you strike me. I can see you running a business or two. You're fit too. What did you do, play football? Midwest maybe. Ohio State."

"Hah-hah," Kip laughed. "No. I messed around with all the sports in high school. Then it was time to put the games aside."

"I see. I'm right about the Midwest, aren't I? I'm pretty perceptive about people."

"Bullseye."

"The family lives in Paris then?"

"I call it heaven. How about you?"

"DC. Alexandria, to be exact. We consider that DC. But I guess you knew that about me. What did Dr. Russell divulge?"

"Not that much. I knew he was meeting with a man named Ward Stelter who does something in the US government. That was it. I figured if you knew about the book, you have some rather significant influence, however. Or key ties."

"I get key-tied up the ying-yang is what it is. At least when it really comes down to it. I guess I could consider you a colleague. Appalachian School of Law graduate. Never took the bar, but who cares about that when you can earn top dollar doing something else. Why waste your time? Besides, its people like me that truly rule the world."

"Mid-level bureaucracy job, right?"

"DOD. Now, think about that. Do I look the part? Anyway at all? I look like a marshmallow, prepped for the fire, don't I?" he said in a condescending tone.

Kip laughed. "You could use some sun. Aside from that, I wouldn't be so sure. I hear they're lowering standards all the time anyway. You could be a top recruit."

Stelter now laughed. He finally took a shot of whiskey. He sighed. "I feel much better. I don't recall ever feeling as terrified as I did down there on the street. I just…" he gave Kip a sullen eye. "I froze up, didn't I? The whole world kind of went away. I don't know what you did to me, but you brought me back somehow. How did you know to do that?"

"Intuitive I guess. I don't know. Saw it in a movie maybe."

"Would you do me a favor? I'll pay."

"It wouldn't be a favor then, would it?"

"Guess not."

"What did you want?"

"I'll pay you. You obviously know how to handle yourself. You're clear-headed. Very calm. Just stay with me for a while. Until I know I'm not going to walk out there and take a bullet or something. Is that what they did to Dr. Russell? Could you tell what they did to Russell?"

"I don't know what they did, but it was obvious he was dead. Could have used a bullet. Might have used an axe or something. His head looked split open. That's the best I can tell you."

"Didn't that make you sick? I would have heaved all over the sidewalk."

"No big deal."

Stelter gave him a parasitic stare before taking another swig. "What are your obligations? Is your employer going to fire you if you don't report in or something?"

"I've already been in contact with my employer. Besides, I'm an attorney. I have many employers."

"Of course. I'm not thinking very clearly. Call it oxidized mentality. I know I can't afford what he probably pays, but I'll pay. Two, three hundred an hour. That's a decent rate, isn't it?"

"I'll tell you what. I'm not going anywhere overnight. Let's wait and see how you feel about things in the morning. Would that make you feel better?"

Stelter stared at his drink. "If I could make every day feel as safe as I feel right now, just knowing that, I'd sell my soul."

About the same time, in the Allen residence, the mood was dire and the angst like needles. Edward sat glued a few feet from the TV. Nuts paced behind him and Lisa stood in the far corner where she, Erica and Judge Bailey seemed to find comfort, not fully hearing the news broadcast. On the TV screen the image came from a news helicopter circling the Waterloo Bridge where flashing lights dominated. Nuts stopped pacing and watched over Edwards shoulder just as a reporter came on camera. Lisa noticed Nuts and her sudden outburst echoed her denial stage of grief. "Just turn it off! How can you be that morbid? Do you have to relive it again and again and again?"

246

Edward excoriated her with a bitter look. Nuts crossed over and lowered his voice. "Nobody said it was Kip. They haven't said a word."

"It has to be him. Who else would it be?"

"It's London. Murder isn't exactly a rarity."

"What do they say? What did they last say?" Judge Bailey asked calmly.

"Nothing more. A body dumped from a fleeing van. They haven't identified who it is?"

"Edward!" Lisa exclaimed. "Call Arthur again. Call Willard. Call Nathan. Call someone who has some influence."

"Call your brother, James!" he barked back. "You'll get as much out of him. Let them do their job. Arthur said he would make some calls. He'll call when he knows. You just settle down and chill."

"I can't take this anymore," Lisa moaned. "I've got to get out of here." With pleading eyes she searched Erica and Jacklyn's faces. Jacklyn rose to her toes so she could see the TV. Erica shook her head stoically.

"It's not like you're turning your back on him," Lisa seemed to beg.

"You're like my Mother when Dad's got the game on TV," Erica said. "He can sit through anything, she comes out of her skin. Not that she has any interest in the game, but she gets a sense of the tension. I never get affected. And I don't think it's Kip. It doesn't feel right. I just don't see any point in getting upset."

A few miserable seconds later Edward's phone rang. Lisa covered her mouth and grabbed hold of Jacklyn's arm.

"Yes. Right. Right. Right. Really? Okay. No kidding," his one-sided conversation. "Bloody shame," his last words before hanging up and giving Lisa a heedlessly indifferent glare.

"What?" Lisa barked, getting a hold of both Erica and Jacklyn.

"The Fool Dr. Stephen Russell."

"Dr. Russell?" Jacklyn uttered. "Are you sure? Dr. Russell? That's who is dead?"

"Sure as I'm sitting here."

"O my God," Erica said and hurried over in front of the TV. "You don't think... He wouldn't, would he?"

Nuts seemed to read her mind. "Not on your life. Kip would never..."

"How do you know? Maybe he found... I don't know what he found. But if he got in the right frame of mind in the right circumstance. O my God... I hope he didn't do it. Did they say anything about Kip? What did they say?"

"Arthur found out all he could. Biggest question was whether Kip was dead, right? Well, he's not. They have CCTV all over London. They're going to have to scour a million different images before they know everything for sure. That is if it happened in front of a camera. And..." Edward gave Nuts a caustic look, "murder IS rare in London. Maybe one hundred a year amongst nine million. I call that rare."

"That's enough," Jacklyn calmly said, stepping forward and turning the TV off. "It seems our emotions are out of control. It wasn't Kip. We can all relax and be grateful for that. We're taking it out on one another and there's no need for that."

She got a morose look out of everyone. Edward's chin hit his chest. "She's right." With sad eyes he looked up at Lisa. "Sorry, Luv. I didn't mean to be curt."

"O..." Lisa moaned. She stepped up and embraced his head to her breast. "I get so emotional. Me too."

"That's settled," Jacklyn said. "We don't know what's fully happened. I say we drive into London tomorrow and look for him."

"Where?" Erica asked. "The place is huge."

"Hot spots for rare books," Edward said openly. "Or start near Waterloo and work our way out. He's got to be there somewhere. Besides, we'll go crazy, tearing each other's heads off if we just sit around here waiting for news."

Dinner time at Denny's in Ocala, Florida felt as harangued as the busy interchange where it sat. Agent Eddie Reed sat at a table, watching

Agent Duggan finalize his pacing outside the door and then take a deep breath before returning. "Tech boys say Gerhardt's computer was most likely operated remotely."

"How do they know that?"

"Did you see that keyboard?"

"It looked like a mechanic with greasy fingers manhandled it daily."

"They don't think anyone has touched it in at least a year. And that grease… it has a unique fingerprint. Any old civilian can't get their hands on that."

"Military."

"Right."

"Gerhardt might have that ability."

"True… but someone was operating his computer from who knows where."

"I've been thinking about that. Was there something Gerhardt said that stood out to you?"

"Not particularly."

"Hallucinations. Remember that?"

Duggan covered his mouth, thinking. "I think I know where you're going here. You seriously think that would happen?"

"Why not? AI is everywhere nowadays. It's a possibility. Anyone with common sense accepts the hallucination problem with AI. It learns facts, but tells lies. I can see that. Especially considering these amorphous facts we're dealing with. Easier to consider that than those twelve apostles we're trying to track down."

Unlike Ward Stelter, whose brain seemed ossified with rust, these agent's minds suddenly felt oiled and lubricated, shooting them down a baluster of glossy mahogany. A baluster that would quickly turn razor blade. Beyond that, a wide black abyss. Especially considering the artificial intelligence possibility.

CHAPTER THIRTY-SEVEN

WARD STELTER'S DREAM DATE

There was a curtain of quiet which cloaked the hotel room when Ward Stelter awoke. A mind full of fog made no sense of it, nor did an eye spot Kip McKinney, who stood off to the side, when he peered under an arm. He could tell he'd slept far into the morning. Broken clouds reflected a sun fairly high in the sky and building facades shown bright with the warmth. He lifted his head, trying to get oriented. He now saw Kip who stood there surveying the world. Kip's mind was in a million different places but his eyes rested on the first site Edward insisted he see when they were getting acquainted. The Royal Air Force memorial with its tapering Portland stone pylon topped by a zodiacal globe, bearing a gilded eagle. Not that it meant that much to Kip, but it did to Edward. And Edward wanted Kip to understand the symbols that framed his character.

"What time is it?" Stelter huskily groaned. "Why'd you let me sleep this late? I'll have a headache."

"It's ten-thirty," Kip said and then stepped over and donned his jacket.

Stelter swept the sheets over his lap and sat up. "You're not leaving. Don't leave here without consulting with me or saying something."

"I have things I want to do. I have people I'd like to talk to."

"Are you crazy? You're going out there, knowing what you know."

"What do I know?"

"Don't act coy with me. You know what I'm talking about. Get yourself killed. Hell… what's wrong with you?"

"I'm not worried. Sure, there was an attempt, but it's pretty obvious… the only time the absurd occurs is when someone has contacted the wrong people at the wrong time. I'm pretty careful about who I talk to and when. I think Dr. Russell made contacts he shouldn't have made. He opened the gates. I feel reasonably safe going out."

"Shit!" Stelter said, butt-hopping to the foot of the bed.

Kip turned and stepped for the door.

"Stop! You're not leaving me here like this. You can't."

"I'm not going to sit here."

"Well, at least wait until I get some clothes on."

Kip locked eyes with Stelter for a moment. He then crossed back to the window. This time he eyed the Ministry of Defense Building before looking off to the north. It was somewhere out there where he needed to go. He generally knew the place because of Google Earth, he simply didn't know the exact spot.

Some minutes later, Kip led Stelter to a rental car parked outside the front entry—a compact VW Polo, charcoal in color, a disabled badge, and not a speck of dust. Stelter had grabbed what he could while passing the complimentary brunch offering—a cup of black tea and then whatever he could stuff inside a second cup. Creamed cod with mushrooms and oysters, plus a large spoon full of Indian-inspired kedgeree made with smoked haddock and rice. Atop that he carried a large slice of sweet ginger bread laced with cranberries. Kip was pure business, Stelter the perforated grump. Once inside the car, Stelter sat there glaring. "Mind telling me what you're thinking?"

A glance over his shoulder before calmly replying. "I'm trying to make you and my employer incredibly wealthy men. Any complaints about that?"

Stelter rode for some time before grumbling, "A lot of good that does you if you're dead. Am I going to be dead before this day is over?"

"Beats me." He morosely looked at him. "Hard to say, right. But this much I can guarantee, it won't be because of anything I do. Now, if you decide to play some idiot game, I can't guarantee anything."

Oddly that appeased Stelter quite pleasantly. He nodded, and began working on his breakfast. Moments later, they were on the same route as the night before. No reaction out of Stelter when they swept onto Waterloo Bridge. "You know what you're doing?" Stelter asked when Kip steered down into the Strand underpass. The curving tunnel burped them out moments later onto Kingsway, which brought a contented grin to Stelter's face. "I guess you do. I know I'd be lost by now." Stelter sipped on his tea. "You're not talkative today. Problem?"

"No. Just trying to stay focused." He glanced in the side mirror, an obvious act that turned Stelter's contented grin wary. Stelter now stayed quiet. Kip checked his phone twice. First when they turned onto Camden High Street and second when, forty minutes later, they pulled to a stop in a disabled parking spot across from the Highgate Cemetery ticket office. Kip returned to his phone, Stelter quickly jumped out. A second later, he seemed elated when he poked his head back in.

"Cemetery. This is a cemetery."

"That's right." Kip kept studying, Stelter glanced around and poked his head back in.

"Karl Marx is buried here. Did you know Karl Marx is buried here?"

"Nope."

"Holy shiiz... You may not believe this. Especially after the way I acted last night, but I love cemeteries. Don't know what it is, but I love cemeteries. How did you know to come here?"

"I'm working on instructions my employer provided."

"Treasure hunt. We're on a treasure hunt?"

"You might say that. We'll have to wait and see, won't we?"

"I want to see Marx's grave."

Kip stepped out and looked around. "Fine. I've got other things to do. You go buy a ticket and visit Karl, I'll meet you back here in... I'm not sure how long it will take. I'll meet you back here."

"No. Wait a minute. This has to do with the book, doesn't it?"

"I hope so. I'm not sure yet. Depends what I find. First I have to find a specific grave."

Stelter clearly debated a moment. He got a resolved look. "Karl can wait. He wouldn't like the fact that this is all about money. But then if I get rich, I'll come back and spit in his face." He laughed. "All my bureaucratic devotion and see how easy I turn on them. If you only knew how loathsome some of us were. But then Marx wasn't exactly the most upright of characters, was he? If he's our standard, no wonder we're doomed. Where are we going?"

Kip fished in his pocket and produced a fifty quid note. He passed it over to Stelter. "Go buy us two tickets. I need to find out where Claude Tremblay is buried."

Kip stood there amazed at how school-boy excited Stelter acted, trotting to buy tickets. He wasted little time watching. Back to studying his phone, which included the same code Dana Bailey had scribbled below Banda's name. In mere seconds, he felt fairly comfortable where to go. Through the west gate and soon they were climbing a wide set of stone stairs totally shrouded in overgrown forest and shrub. The world of tombs, tarnished, crooked markers and little sunlight brought Stelter's eyes to bulging. "I would have been a good zombie," he muttered. "This is my kind of place. Do you like cemeteries?" he asked Kip. Kip kept his eyes to his phone. "You've got a GPS marker pinned in here, don't you?"

"That's right."

"Fantastic. Bloody fantastic." The excitement now shut Stelter up. Didn't cull his curiosity, but it did shut him up. As Kip thoughtfully looked for the proper path to navigate toward the proper coordinates Stelter hurried from one curiosity to the next. Kip walked casually, winding, leading them deeper and deeper in. Low markers, tall markers. Carved angels, crosses, emblems and symbols. Family plots covered in ivy and a path of stiff, not quite mucky mud, and Stelter overran the mark when Kip finally came to a stop. He returned to find Kip staring off into thick, overgrown brush where several large tree limbs stretched over and down. Stelter nearly pulled the phone out of his hand. "These are the coordinates?"

"Partly. 506... that means fifth of six graves. 513494 is the north coordinate 0085353 west. It's somewhere in there."

"Fine," Stelter said and bound over a marker before high stepping as if wary of snakes. Through a dark fold in the foliage and between two black tree trunks where he disappeared. Silence.

Kip looked side to side. "You find anything?"

"Good Lord. This is creepy."

"Any headstones?"

"A ton of them. Can't make any sense of it."

"Tremblay? How about Claude?"

"Hell if I know. I can't decipher anything."

Kip was nowhere near as aggressive. He was more concerned about bloodying a shin with the way he gingerly tiptoed before disappearing. Vines grew in every direction, climbing over slumped and tilted markers tarnished to near black. Turning his phone flashlight on Kip crouched and brushed a hand over etched letters that did little. Stelter climbed further in as Kip wet his fingers and tried to wash the name into view. "Geary. This is Geary."

"I think I've got it," Stelter called out. "Back here."

Kip pushed around a tree trunk to find Stelter standing over a tall fallen marker with a cross. "Doesn't that say Tremblay? That says Tremblay. On the base. What are we looking at? Do we have to dig or something?"

Kip scanned around. "No... but we go over there where it's pointing."

A set of six headstones were hard to spot over a low wall of stone. Stelter bolted, leaping almost in one bound. Kip checked over his shoulder before following. Stelter stood there, "Mo-mo... mo key... I can't read that. Can you read that?"

Kip merely rounded the row of headstones and crouched again. He wet his fingers and scrubbed. "Um..." he purred. "This makes sense."

A breath later Stelter stood at his side. "Marks! Those are just like the characters on my paper. They're newer. I mean... not as old as the stone. Still... that doesn't help."

"Yes it does," Kip said, taking a photo. "It's instructions."

"What do you mean?"

"Give me a minute. I have to compare it to another document in my phone. I think I have a translation."

Stelter moved down the row of markers, scrubbing the back of each as Kip compared these characters to what Banda had provided. It took but a moment before he stood. He got a wry grin, looking at Stelter.

"What, what?"

"We move on. You might like it. This is merely instructions, sending us to another cemetery."

"Another? Where?"

"Not too far. Half an hour maybe. Abney Park Cemetery."

Stelter got very bright eyed as he quickly searched his phone. He blinked rapidly. "Not far. Just west of here."

The only delay before leaving Highgate was when Kip positioned Stelter in view of a CCTV camera. He took him by the shoulders. "Don't get so revved up. You lose your head and you might lose your head. Understand?"

"Ha-ha-ha," Stelter laughed and crawled into the car.

Abney Park Cemetery

Stelter rode, hands under his thighs, pushing himself into his seat as they snaked their way through the north London neighborhoods. He wore a contented grin when he turned to look at Kip. "We make a great team, don't we?"

Kip gave him a stiff look.

"Maybe your employer could use a man like me. What are the chances?"

Kip's expression turned derisive before merely shaking his head.

"Yeah, I know. I could offer you a job, but you probably couldn't handle the cut in pay. I could use a man like you. I can tell. You have talents. I wouldn't need to go through those countless interviews. I'd hire you on the spot."

"To do what? Drive you around? Don't waste your breath."

"Hah-hah… of course. Think your employer could use a man like me?"

Kip teased a grin as he shook his head. "First of all, which employer and second of all, what are your skills? Why would my employer hire you?"

"For the teamwork. For the synergy. That's a good reason."

Again Kip dubiously smirked. Stelter repeatedly and playfully raised his eyebrows.

Minutes shy of thirty, they rolled by the cemetery, searching for a place to park. Minutes later, they crawled into a gravel parking lot where Kip took on an aloof air before stepping out. It was a six minute walk back to the cemetery. All the way Stelter scrolled through his phone.

"Listen to this... Abney Cemetery... the resting place for the rebels. If that's the case, this is where I should be buried. It's the leading burial ground for dissenters. I've always been a non-conformist. Plus, Amy Winehouse filmed a music video scene here. I like that. They've got a bush that's over one-hundred and seventy years old and never go mushrooming, they say. Might get arsenic or lead poisoning." He looked up at Kip, expecting an inquiry. Kip had purpose in his brow, nothing more. A quick glance over his shoulder before trotting across a bustling street and Kip didn't slow until he was inside the gate. Stelter didn't catch up until walking in what felt an overrun, lush forest, in which headstones had no order. "What's the matter," Stelter said, "don't like my witty repartee? Am I annoying you?"

"No. I just don't want to dawdle. Who knows if someone isn't watching?"

Stelter took a quick look around. "You're just trying to scare me. Probably isn't another soul who knows we're in here."

Kip winked and remained firm. A moment later, a tall weathered chapel seemed to appear out of nowhere as if it had grown like a mushroom in shady moist soil and protected by thick forest on every side. Gray brick, slate roof, a tall steeple standing over a proud lancet arch. A wrought iron gate protected the drive-through portico with its stout rounded arches and was the draw for Stelter. He hurried his pace, grabbed the bars, pressed his cheeks and looked in, thinking whatever they were looking for had to be inside the chapel. The space was dark and had a green mossy tint. Fully expecting Kip to sidle up, he didn't move until realizing the only sound was his panting. Stelter stepped away and rounded the left side of the chapel. "Not funny. Wherever you went, it's not funny. Wilson? Where did you go, Wilson?"

Now, he stood there cryptically debating, an uneasy feeling washing over him. A wide path led deeper in. It was hard to tell if the dark mouths into the foliage were gates into the underworld, or animal paths, or something very similar to Highgate. "Wilson? Where did you go, Wilson? This is not funny!" Stelter fully rounded the chapel before cautiously sidestepping down the path that led deeper in. Strange shadowy shapes brought a chill. The disgusting meaning of any given headstone seemed more like glue than revulsion. A moment later, Stelter stood in front of a headstone depicting a young girl on her knees, clawing her way up a cross, the anguish in her angelic face tormented. This held his gaze for several minutes.

No sound of shoe's crunching. No sound of wind whispering. No sounds at all. And that's why Stelter nearly jumped out of his skin when Kip leaned and whispered, "Let's get out of here. I have what I need."

"Holy..." Stelter jumped and spiraled, throwing an arm up in defense. "You asshole! Where did you go? Hell..." he slapped his hand against his chest, "I think you just blew a gasket in my heart."

Kip merely looked to the side and nodded. "Sorry."

Stelter puffed. "What? Dead end? You sure? Where did you go?"

"Back in there," Kip nodded over his right shoulder.

"No clue? Let's go look again."

"No. There was a clue," he said, as he began to walk. "Another cemetery. On to the next cemetery."

Stelter stood there watching, a sly grin growing in the way Kip confidently walked away. "Damn," he said. "Damn, I like this man. He does business the way I like business done."

Nunhead and West Norwood Cemeteries

There was a bubble bath of anticipation, as if flowing over the high, rounded edges of a soaking tub in the fifty minute drive from north London to south. Traveling over Tower Bridge, Stelter inhaled as if drinking a can of Pepsi and needing to belch because his stomach acids churned so chaotically. Though the least famous of London's magnificent seven cemeteries there was an orderliness and presentable trimmed nature to the Nunhead Cemetery's entry. As if residence there were astute and highly respected. Spiky iron rails lined the stone wall where a man of seventy-eight or –nine in faded gray work coveralls, rivers of wrinkles flowing down his face and in between a forest of white whiskers, leaned—as if he'd just spent the day searching for his going out date. Or he was the exhausted one responsible for how trimmed and maintained the graves sitting along the central avenue leading to a stately edifice appeared.

"Now, this is much better," Stelter said as they began the walk. "My kind of cemetery. Look… pristinely trimmed, graves and stones well maintained. I like it."

Nothing could stop Stelter from tagging, almost on top of Kip's heels. Listening is a rare skill and playing follow the leader, most of the time, is just as rare. Not so now. Not with Stelter. There was no way he was going to let Wilson lose him again. And thus the reason when a few short steps later, when Kip abruptly stopped, Stelter walked right up his back nearly knocking them both down. Kip ignored him and didn't see the man's apologetic mope when he removed his phone and brought up an image. He compared it to what he saw before him. "This is the wrong place," Kip said, spinning on a heel and reversing course.

"But we haven't done anything. We didn't see anything. How do you know?"

Stelter stood there one moment watching Kip walk away, the other rather entreated with the spires of what could have been a chapel, a memorial, or some kind of tomb. "But I like this place. At least let's look around. What harm is that going to do?" He exhaled with frustration. "Crap!" he surrendered and soon tagged along.

After a twelve-minute drive, they pulled through an iron gate and into a small gravel lot. West Norwood Cemetery & Crematorium, South Metropolitan Cemetery the welcoming signage. Kip pulled nearly a U-turn before stopping and turning off the engine. He looked dead ahead without exiting. Stelter looked on, noticing something very different in the way Wilson sat there. "What? What is it?"

"It seems too easy."

"What do you mean? You mean this is the wrong place? Is someone waiting for us? Let's go. Don't sit here, let's go."

"Not that. This is the right place. I guess it's not that easy. You get the right clues, right? Oh, well," Wilson said and climbed out. What seemed to disturb Stelter was that Wilson didn't walk with the same purpose as before. This seemed a casual stroll as they walked through a second stone gate and soon entered the realm of misfortune. Off to their right, a rather stately cemetery office stood. Several CCTV cameras seemed legion's eyes as they walked on and soon crossed by what were younger graves than they had crossed all day.

"Now, this is better," Stelter said. "This is the best cemetery yet. Well-cared for. Not so overgrown. Granted, I like a forest, but those other ones were ridiculous. What do you think of this cemetery?"

"This is where we're supposed to be."

"You mean this is where the clues were leading?" Stelter grinned broadly. "I like it. I like it like buttered lobster." He clapped his hands and then violently rubbed them together. "Perfect. This is perfect. You know… you may think this is crazy, but this has been one of the best days I've had in years and years."

That brought Kip to a stop. He stared vacantly and caringly.

"I'm serious. You think that's weird?"

"I think that's sad. You found today the highlight of your life… so to speak."

"In a way… yeah. Sometimes you think you have intuition. You think you know how to live and make the right decisions. Think what you're doing makes it worthwhile. But then you get brainwashed. Or twisted thinking invades. Next thing you know that unconquerable monster you thought you were ends up no better than anybody else here."

"What do you mean?"

"I mean look around. Have you ever seen a more subsistence level of living? Doesn't get any lower than this. Subsistence at its base level. Maybe it's because I live most of my life, governed by devil's doctrine, but whatever today was, it wasn't that. I've enjoyed it. I think we're going to be great friends. I see that. I can see that in our future."

"Days not over yet. I'd hold that thought in reserve if I were you."

Stelter stood there staring as Wilson strolled away. He soon caught up to what became a rather pedestrian amble. Hands in his pockets, Wilson seemed the mourner, and this was his realm of reflection and solitude. They turned onto a path and walked into a section far less kept where grass grew tall and headstones seemed to vanish. It was near a weeping willow tree where Wilson stopped and unzipped his pants. "Give me a minute," he motioned with his brows.

Stelter chuckled, looking around. "What's the point? There isn't a soul around." He lowered his chin. "What a prude. I wouldn't care. Whiz where you want," came out in a blue note sound.

He waited and watched for Wilson to reappear. One-two-three minutes passed. "What the hell? He can't have prostate issues. He's not that old. Unless… geez… what a place to take a dump."

Now, he couldn't watch. He turned his back and looked around, wondering just exactly what they were looking for. Another one-two-three-four minutes. He turned back. "Hey, Wilson? You still in there? What gives?"

It was then that he noticed it. Small wafts of bluish-white smoke seeping out between the limbs. "Wilson!?" Stelter blurted before bounding over and then ducking his head just before cutting through the curtain of sad limbs. Instantly, thick smoke blinded him. A breath later, the burning choke not only stung his eyes but caused him to forestall. He madly waved a hand, holding his breath and trying not only to see Wilson but to clear the air in front of his face. He couldn't see Wilson, but could soon see bluish, yellow flames flickering. Right over there close to the trunk and around a tall marker. He stomped his way over and stomped a foot, an explosion of embers shooting up, down, and in every direction. This time he had to exhale and quickly inhale. A big gulp of noxious smoke filled his lungs and produced a violent hack before he doubled over in a painful fit of coughing. Suddenly, in survivor mode, Stelter ducked his head and ramrodded his way out the far side of the limbs. There he found something far worse than what he had under the limbs. A much bigger fire burned. Next to a toppled marker where what looked as if a lead box in the ground, wide open and empty. This he didn't stomp on. Instead, he saw Wilson suddenly emerge from behind a small pine tree. He gruffly looked at Stelter and then walked off as if the Devil himself. Stunned, Stelter didn't debate, he couldn't think. Couldn't form a thought at all. If what burned had been a book, it was no longer. Mere ashes smoke and residual flame. It was now some deep-rooted raging instinct that triggered Stelter. When he realized he saw his newfound fortune already burned up in front of his eyes, he stumbled off, the demand for answers like a maniacal monster, turning his neck and face crimson red.

Wilson walked as he had before. Stelter quickly caught him by the arm, jerked him around, and looked ready to tear his head off. "What the hell is wrong with you? What are you doing here? That's the book, isn't it? Have you lost your mind? Answer me! What are you doing?"

Wilson looked where Stelter had a hold on him. He locked eyes. "Let go or you're a dead man right here."

The power and terror in Wilson's voice caused Stelter to jump. He thought for sure he'd intimidated Wilson to the point of answers. Instead, it backfired, causing Stelter to partly cower. He let go. Wilson pushed around and, as Stelter watched, saw not only his sudden wealth wisp away but a man unaffected by his actions.

CHAPTER THIRTY-EIGHT

WARD STELTER CHECKMATES THE DEVIL

Stelter had returned to see a pile of ash and merely took long enough to calculate Wilson had used an accelerator to cause paper, or parchment, or skins, or whatever it was to burn so quickly. And in his watching, he rationalized to the point of losing the sudden anger. He wasn't shocked, but he was amused to find the man parked, sitting behind the wheel, and waiting, however. He gave him an acidulous smirk when he crawled in. "You know," he said as Wilson pulled away, "I know I ought to be fuming here. But somehow, the trick I feel you pulled isn't on me. There's another book out there, isn't there? Has to be. You said you're going to make me and your employer wealthy. The only way to do that is if there are more copies of that book. You're making it rarer, right?"

Kip gave him a cockeyed nod and stayed quiet. Stelter would have responded except for a sudden incoming message. He checked his phone.

Leatherback spending an inordinate amount of time with new contact. Wanted you to be aware.

Good work, Stelter responded. Keep me informed.

He then gave Wilson a benign look and grinned. "I thought I had you figured out. I don't. I'm feeling a little beguiled. Not manipulated or deceived mind you. I know when someone is deceiving me. This is more like Jud and Ernie Francis."

"Who are Jud and Ernie Francis?" Kip asked coolly.

Stelter chuckled. "Brothers. Acquaintances of Granddaddy Stelter. Jud owned a Gulf Station out in the boondocks. State Route 48. Ernie owned a Mobil down the road a bit. Grand-mamma and Granddaddy lived right in between. He worked for the highway Department, you see. I spent a summer out there as a kid and went to work for Ernie. They were old-fashioned in one way, making me limp out to the pumps where I'd fill gas tanks, and check oil levels and tire pressure. The worst was wiping windshields. Hated it. That's not the point. There was genius to their full-service madness, however. Folks would pull into Jud's place first and he had a clever way of checking tires. He had a razor blade welded to this big gaudy ring he wore. He'd slice a nice ugly gouge and then show them the nightmare. You can't drive on a tire like that, he'd grunt at them. Some would buy new tires from him. Some would bend out of shape and drive down to Ernie's place. Ernie would rant and rave about that monster of a man back there and still tell them they needed new tires. They'd share in the profits. That is if they ever told each other when they made a sell. I can see you doing that. That's what you're doing, isn't it? Making us both a little richer."

Wilson knowingly shook his head and smiled. "Can't fool you, can we."

"So what happens next?"

"Go back to the hotel and wait for my employer to contact me. He knows what I've done."

Stelter relaxed contentedly. A sly grin and easy breathing back to the hotel. He chose to shower first thing. Some thirty minutes later he emerged to find Wilson Graham sitting at the table just then diving into an all-day breakfast offering. Poached eggs and avocado on sourdough toast. Field mushrooms, cream cheese, and a serving of shakshuka. Seconds prior, he had been reviewing the twenty-nine missed calls during the day, seven from Edward, the rest from Lisa. Stelter had a towel over his head, scrubbing his bald pate. He paused, staring at Wilson with utilitarian eyes and hairy armpits. "You know… you should have waited. I would have taken you out to dinner. What is that? That doesn't look very good."

"Who cares? I was starving."

"So, what do we have planned for tonight?"

"We? We don't have anything planned. It's time for us to part company. I've paid for your room and changed the registration to your name. I'm moving on."

"What? What about our deal? I was going to pay you. You were going to stay with me."

"You mean prostitute myself? Please. I've kept you safe all day. I think that's enough. I have other business to conduct."

"You're not forgetting my deal, are you? What about my deal? Where's that million pounds?"

"Is that all you want? A million pounds... huh. If that's all you want, that's all you'll get. Don't come complaining to me afterward. You'll wonder why I don't recognize who you are."

"Wait a minute. What business are you going to conduct? I'll be coming with you."

"I doubt it," Kip said. He dropped his fork, stood, and abruptly walked out.

Stelter stood there speechless. He watched the door clack shut and then tried to wrap a towel too small around his waist. A few seconds later, he stumbled out into the hallway with a sheet draped over him. The elevator doors just then closed. He rushed and watched until the lights counted down to the ground level. He then chose the stairs. A mad dash, a stubbed toe, and sweat dripping when he cracked the door just in time to see Wilson Graham thanking the clerk. Straight back to the elevator and a count back up to level three.

"Fool," Stelter uttered. A reverse scramble. He didn't see Wilson enter the room on the third floor, but Stelter did hear a door clack shut down around the corner. He intended to simply confirm the door and then ran head-on with an elderly couple leaving for dinner.

"Good Lord," the silver-haired woman hooted. "John... do something."

"I didn't think this a bohemian establishment," the white-haired fellow in an ascot grumbled. "Come, Martha, we'll make a complaint."

"No. I'm sorry," Stelter pleaded. "You don't understand. There was an emergency."

"Fire?" the woman crowed.

"No. Did you see a man? Just came off the elevator. I must find him. I'm a doctor. I need to inform him. His angina is more than he thinks it is."

The man shooed with his fingers. "It was the one right there. Just a few steps away. Come, Martha… I'm getting you out of here."

Stelter watched the couple disappear before stepping in and checking the room number. "Three-ten," he chortled. "He's not getting away that easy. Three-ten… we'll see about that."

Stelter returned to the twelfth floor by way of the stairwell. No other discourteous encounters and the first thing he did once back in the room was call down to the front desk. At the clerk's pleasant answer, he tried to mimic her tone. "Yes. I have a business associate who just checked in. Wilson Graham. I need to confirm his room… well… I guess you won't do that. I need to confirm he checked in. Does Wilson Graham have a room?"

"I'm sorry, sir. We have no Wilson Graham on the registry."

"What? Are you certain? I think he just checked in. Wait! Try… oh, what was his law firm? Something, something, and Raja. I remember Raja."

"That would be Baker, Simpson, and Raja?"

"That's it. He is registered?"

"Yes, sir, he is. Shall I ring his room?"

"That won't be necessary. I'll contact him later. Thank you, Ma'am."

Stelter hung up and puffed his chest, thinking himself tenfold cleverer than the astute Wilson Graham.

Considering the way Wilson Graham behaved, Stelter found it prudent to set up shop in the elegant, lustrous, and calm realm of the hotel lobby. He found a high-backed cream leather chair in which concealment was an easy feat and sat low. For a time he watched as LED lights around the bottom of prominent pillars changed the mood. Fusion to shades of blue, shades of green... all the calmer colors. Highly polished marble floors led to his closing his eyes. He blamed the Shakshuka for the unintended dreams. Which, if he had the supposed insight claimed, he would have known the dreams were exactly what Kip hoped for by ordering and leaving the spicy temptation where he had. Short dreams. Fitful thirty-minute periods where Stelter lived in an unwelcome demesne and from which he was glad to escape. Something that would leave Stelter not only foggy-headed but susceptible prey the next day.

The first dream found him floating on a glacial-blue-colored lake, in a thick fog and with three companions in two sea kayaks. Almost immediately one fell from his boat and began to sink. His partner dove in. Stelter felt his heart pounding, stretching over and watching the two go deeper and deeper and deeper until they vanished. A shared panicked look with his surviving mate and suddenly a current began pulling them backward. Blue waters narrowed and morphed as they soon tumbled down wild brown rapids. The sudden recognition of giant tree trunks blocking the river ahead and certain to capsize them ended the dream by coughing them up and over a rocky bank where mud and high cliffs knocked him alert. Their first impulse was to check his watch. 12:33 A.M. remained as digital demons when he closed his eyes. On the shallow, he was glad, truth be told, 6:33 the apt desire. Regardless, he held on for about an hour. Then this...

Small vacation town. Something perhaps on the edge of Lake Louise. Mud lined the gutters as evidence of recently flooded streets and for some bizarre reason, he walked into an old service station with four empty bays. Inside, he found two attendants he identified as Goober and Gomer, greasy, cold, and stupid. 'Sorry,' Goober said. Stelter took it to mean someone had broken in and stolen his box truck. But I need the box truck. To haul my... he didn't know what he had to haul. He simply knew he needed that box truck. He went searching out in the street but instead found a long line of cars backed up at the dry cleaners. A short search left him empty-handed and his stomach churning with pain. It was the sudden pain that woke him. He smacked his lips, groaned, changed positions, and cussed under his breath seeing the 2:16 on his watch. No sense of the time that passed before the next two dreams that felt as if one.

He rode on a train full of hillbillies. Old military hospital cars are void of beds, seating, and handholds. He carried a sack of rice to his chest. He panicked looking at it. Nudging a man who reminded him more of Jethro than Jed he frantically asked, my baby, where's my baby? This isn't my baby. Where's my baby? He crossed into the next car, looking. There he found a giant woman surrounded by her filthy little flock of kiddies. She lay on her side on a bench, heavily pregnant, and with giant zits protruding from her belly. He stood there dumbfounded as she groaned, rolling around in pain. He looked to escape and when he looked back, she'd delivered. Her skinny little daughter sat there beaming, her mother's head now resting on her lap and her showing off what she had and he didn't. Stelter fled to the next car where old-fashioned women in flowery bonnets sat on church pews. Somehow he found a seat right in the middle of them. They began to whisper. 'It's your house. It's on fire. You thought they put the fire out. It's still smoldering. You'd better not sit here. You won't have a house left. The next image was of him scrambling on his belly amongst low, itchy rafters. He knew there was smoke, but nothing he did helped find the flames. This miserable reality struck like a Babe Ruth 54-ounce hickory bat ramrodding him straight in the gut. 4:45 on his watch brought a feeling of relief. No more sleep. No more dreams.

Finally, after the light of day and nearing the 8:30 hour Wilson Graham appeared. A brief stop at the front desk and Stelter knew the exchange was pleasant, hearty and brief. The girl stood there as if carried off into bliss as the two exchanged a quick glance and smile when Stelter rushed by. But there was no humor nor civility in his. He paused inside the doors, expecting to see Graham boarding an awaiting taxi. No taxis, no Graham, nothing. Stelter rushed out into a melancholy morning full of city din. No sign of Graham until he rushed to his right and to where he got his first glimpse of shrouded Big Ben and the Westminster Bridge. There he now saw Graham with his customary purposeful stride, approaching the bridge and not looking back. Stelter gave the skies a quick look before hurrying back inside, nicking a complimentary umbrella and then returning.

How much ground do you dare give a man like that? Stelter gave him what he estimated at thirty seconds and then did his best imitation at incognito by hugging the right side. Over the Westminster Bridge and then a right at the Boudiccan Rebellion Statue. Stelter didn't pick Graham up again until turning the corner and spotting him now approaching the Royal Air Force Memorial. Then it was down to Northumberland Ave., left, and straight into Trafalgar Square.

Stelter agreed with all the tourist guides. One of the most popular attractions and a center hub of activity, even at this early hour, was Trafalgar Square. A handful of tourists lingered at the foot of Nelson's Column. Even more crisscrossed the square and a handful meandered near the closest fountain. The National Gallery held his eye but a moment. A line of limply hanging Canadian flags across the front of Canada House a breath longer and then he began to panic. No sign of Graham. He couldn't see Graham anywhere. A quick dash before he climbed atop the wall next to the large bulbous light nearest the plinth and bronze statue of Henry Havelock. And then he searched. All across the square and then ducking up and back down the sidewalk. It was on his return to the square when it happened. When, like after Raskolnikov's restless night, judgement seems to come to his door. He knows Erica Dennis the instant he sees her also spotting him. She stands with the small group meandering near the fountain. She points at Stelter. The man next to her now suddenly turns. Stelter rolls off the wall and swings behind the light's broad plinth. Boom, boom, boom, his heart explodes inside his chest. He crouches as if in a Raskolnikov search for blood. Synapsis' wildly firing make thoughts difficult to trap. Did she see me? No! She couldn't have seen me. That-that-that-that… that wouldn't be… Leatherback with her, would it? It couldn't be. O my God… it has to be.

Fearful, despairing cries seem to shrilly rise from the street and square as Stelter swings back to peer. The two are arguing. She's pointing, he's dubious. Clearly dubious. Thoughts that had been difficult to catch, let alone run with, abruptly come all at once as he turns away. How many? How many have died. I didn't kill them. It wasn't me! Plausible deniability, all in a flash. Again he peers. They're coming. Here they come. "O my God," he whispers in despair. "What is wrong with me? Don't just sit here. Get yourself the hell out of here."

A quick glance to his left and it felt as if God himself had reached out and cooled his burning soul. He spotted Graham, way up the street and just then pausing to glance at a newspaper he'd just purchased. In a low crouch, Stelter scampered to where some kind of container or trash bin stood on the inside of the wall. He rose high enough to quicken his pace and once at the far end of the square barely paused to check traffic before gritting his teeth and frantically lifting his already burning thighs. At the moment, he lost sight of Graham. It was at the next short corner, where he slid to a stop to look back, that he caught a glimpse of Graham, weaving between pedestrians and headed for Leicester Square. Instead of focusing on him, he looked back for Erica. Again his heart seemed atomic. It felt like it exploded as he spotted her and Leatherback just then pausing for traffic. Stelter spotted a coffee shop up the way and towards Leicester Square. Ten agonizing seconds later, he cut his way in, ducked into a booth and nearly lay his body flat out as he retrieved his phone. He instantly sent a message to what he called the action committee.

Urgent. Need to know the location of Leatherback. Is Leatherback with new target?

There was a brief delay. That violates protocol, came back.

Forget protocol. I must know. Are the two together and where are they? Are you currently tracking them?

Who's authorizing this?

I'm authorizing this. I'm currently in a threatened position. Break protocol. Where are they?

A delay. Last spotted Trafalgar Square in London.

And they're together?

Close.

Is there an asset available?

Three minutes away.

Terminate them. Don't lose them. Send the asset and terminate them. If you can't get both, focus on the target. Target is priority. Repeat, target is priority.

Stelter clutched his phone as if a dagger and rose high enough to look out the window. He spotted Erica and Nuts standing back on the corner and looking indecisive. They moved as if to cross Charing Cross Road and soon walked out of view. Stelter sat up, scooted off the bench, and stood at the door briefly. Now he looked for Graham. Now he sensed perhaps the safety of Leicester Square where he'd once seen Gypsies causing a disturbance. The idea appealed to him. The moment he stepped out, he spotted Graham. The man stood at the corner of Theatreland's Very Own Ticket Booth. "He's meeting someone. He's arranged to meet someone at the theater," shivered out of him. "He'd better not be double-crossing me. We'll see about this."

That's what it took and that was how easily Stelter's fear screwed back into disgust. He looked over his shoulder twice as he beelined the sixty-four meters from the coffee shop to the ticket office. Wilson Graham stood perusing the newspaper and didn't notice Stelter until he stomped a foot at his side. Graham casually looked. "Well, good morning. Where did you come from?"

"What the hell are you doing?"

"Enjoying a morning walk. Reading up on rumors about the royals. What brings you out?"

"Shut up! Are you trying to back out on our deal? We had a deal. Do you have another contact? You're meeting someone, aren't you?"

"I don't recall putting anything in writing. My employer is still willing to pay handsomely for what you have. You realize that, don't you?"

"So, we have a deal?"

"I'll make a deal. I'll give you a hundred dollars for your transcript. You can walk away that much better off."

Stelter sneered. "Don't play that game. I'm not an idiot."

"You wanted a deal, I offered a deal."

"How long do I have to hold out?" Stelter said and looked over his shoulder. "Look... can we get off the street? What's that over there? Is that a restaurant?"

Graham looked at their reflection in a wall of windows. "Yes and no. It's a hotel. Nice restaurant. I've stayed there before."

Stelter grabbed him by the arm and tugged. "Then that's where we're going. I don't want anyone seeing me with you. Not out here on the street. You saw what happened to Dr. Russell. I don't know who to trust. It's safer in there."

They crossed over and just as they approached the hotel/restaurant's entry, a latticework of decorative iron and where several Union Jacks hung limp, the assassin took up his position atop a crane on the next block. Skilled, professional, no need to waste a breath he locked onto Stelter just as he took the door from Graham and paused. The problem for the assassin—a flash of light reflected precisely at that

269

moment and altered his aim but a fraction. No report and no resonating echo, a silenced full-metal jacket bullet stealthily pierced the morning air and struck Stelter millimeters away from a sure kill shot.

"Ugh!" he groaned at the sensation of fire-hot metal ripping into the flesh of his trapezius, cutting straight through his windpipe and exiting between the second and third left-side ribs. "Ugh," another agonizing groan as his legs seemed to instantly lose all control. He helplessly collapsed into the back of Graham's legs.

Kip spun and instantly went down. No delay to scan the street, Kip grabbed Stelter by the collar and quickly pulled him in and didn't stop until positioned safely behind a concierge counter. There was a delayed response inside the hotel. A guest spotted a trail of smeared blood and instantly screamed. Then all hell seemed to break loose. Before Kip and Stelter got anyone's full attention, Kip applied pressure, partly inserting a finger into the entry wound. He then leaned in, nearly touching noses. "How does that feel?" he whispered. "How does it feel, ordering your own murder? Huh? Think about that for a while."

Complete and utter bewilderment washed Stelter's ashen face long. True, on one level there was hostility. Hopelessness too. But with no doubt the inscrutable face of perplexity had his eyes searching Graham's for suddenly begged-for answers.

CHAPTER THIRTY-NINE

McKinney's Justice

Ward Stelter uttered a sharp little cry when they lifted him onto a stretcher. Other than that, not another sound. But then sounds were not wanted nor granted in a world suddenly locked into a spiraling toilet bowl of abject horror and despair. He was desperately trying to put it together, but for a man who conveniently put the devil inside everyone else it was difficult to see through the fog. One thing was certain, things really are not right here in Stelterville. Things in Stelterville have never been right and he knew it. And despite the painful concentration, navel gazing seemed the deepest he could search his own soul. He tried and tried and tried to put the pieces together. It felt eons and yet no answers. But then they must have mixed something into the gases. Because when they put an oxygen mask over his nose and mouth he felt as if forced into sudden drowsiness and delirium. Before unconsciousness came the stark horror of losing control of all his faculties, even memory, began a process of excruciating torture. In his mind's eye the last image and conscious thought was of his hand reaching for an overhead abyss and then the sudden empty void completely enveloping him.

For those who have gone under the knife, they know. So do those who have escaped horror in a fit of fainting surrender. The blind-sided know it as well. Complete oblivion and peace where no one measures time and no one cares. Floating in a world of such seepage, it's not alarming to first hear subtle, gentle voices. Nor does the rhythmic chorus of a heart monitor beeping disturb you. The real annoyance is realizing, especially for someone with wounds such as Ward Stelter's that this sudden horrid pain down your throat is getting worse the more conscious you become. It felt like a fraying steel cable rasping his windpipe to a much wider gauge. Stelter blinked, but didn't fully come around. He contorted, wondering where he was and what was going on. He tried to reach for his mouth, but his arms wouldn't move. When he tried to wet his lips, his tongue wouldn't work either. He surrendered momentarily, completely willing death upon himself. It took mere seconds before he knew even that wanted no part of him. Thoughts still wouldn't come. Nausea did. Again he decided his life was coming to an end; life's great miserable glories as well. Willing everything to settle to an end only frustrated him. He couldn't recall anything ever being so uncooperative.

He finally fully opened his eyes. First confusing image was of the endotracheal tube protruding out of his mouth. He thought aliens had abducted him into a world of sterile white. A breath later and a blue figure appeared on his right. Light blue scrubs, light blue mask, blonde hair pulled into a bun. "I see our patient is waking up," a kind voice uttered softly. "Don't try to speak. It will only make it worse." She placed a hand on his pillow and leaned over him. He then realized he had a tube sticking out between his ribs which held her attention briefly. Turning away, she hummed some kind of sweet tune. A moment later, she stood there with her hands in her pockets. "My name is Kristen. I'll be with you all night long. If you're wondering why you can't move your arms, we've restrained you so you wouldn't pull your tubes out. If you're going to stay awake, I can remove them, if not, it's not because we hate you." She giggled. "Understand?"

He closed his eyes and sighed. He then abruptly opened them, fearing she'd leave him. Struggling, he motioned with his fingers.

"Yes. I know what you mean. I have a note pad and pencil here. Do you want to ask or say something?"

He nodded his head. A moment later, his hands were free. He scribbled a simple line. What happened to me?

"Gun shot. Can't give you the details as to why. You're a very lucky man. A few millimeters forward and it would have severed your carotid and jugular." Her eyes kindly narrowed, smiling. "Is your name Ward? Ward Stelter?"

He closed his eyes, nodding.

"Are you thirsty? I can't let you drink with a straw or anything. That's a nasty wound in your esophagus. That's why we have the nasogastric tube inserted."

Stelter wasn't aware. He strained, looking before touching his nose. He then waved her off, motioning with his hand.

"We normally wouldn't allow this but you have a guest who would like to see you. Your associate who saved your life. Are you up to letting him give you well wishes?"

Instantly, Stelter felt vacant. Frantically, he tried to blink no. His feet felt cold, his heart on a war path to hell. Somehow, perhaps the bias of a seed planted by a conniving Roger "Kip" McKinney, Kristen interpreted those wide eyes as a welcoming emphatic, yes!

"Okay," she held a finger up, "but you only get a minute with him. I'll let you have a private moment and then I'm shooing him out."

She passed through a drawn curtain and disappeared. Stelter had not reckoned on this. Had not considered this heinous crime. Hiding motives took no effort. Hiding trinkets or money stolen a mere hindrance. Hiding your exposed soul under these circumstances impossible. Especially, considering... no, he couldn't know. There is no way he would know that. No chance in hell.

A breath later, the curtain parted and remained parted, exposing activity out in the hallway. Wilson Graham didn't appear until Stelter had had a moment to experience the fiery darts flailed by what felt a thousand accusatory eyes. He wanted to, but couldn't look away. Erica Dennis stepped forward a moment before Wilson Graham rounded into view, the most cruel look of kindness on his face. Kip stepped up, pressed down on Stelter's free hand and leaned close, whispering. "I suppose you've figured it out by now," he uttered. "In case you haven't, I'm the man they've appointed as demon. It's my family you killed. And the way I understand how this works, you don't have the slightest idea of who I am, other than Leatherback. They call me Kip. It was my call sign. Roger McKinney in case you're curious. I also know how this works. I suppose I could attempt to go up the chain, but the chain is rigged and I suppose you're soundly protected. I could kill you here and now. I could have killed you any time in the last few days. That's not who I am. Now, I want you to consider those people out in the hallway. I know it's through them that you try to torment me. I don't know why and I don't care. But now you understand… you're part of my circle and you're just as likely to die as any of them. So, I'd step back and think for a moment about your next move. Think about this… they know. I know. How many people has he told, you have to ask yourself. Will he keep sharing and identifying. I'm not all that clever, nor am I as bright as some of my friends seem to believe. But there are others that are and they may bring this to your doorstep in a way that makes my experience seem like Eden. Do you understand what I'm saying? Back off and stay off. You can't even begin to imagine the hurt coming your way if you don't. Now, I'm going to turn around and walk out of here. I never want to hear or see anything of you and your people ever again. Understand?"

Stelter blankly stared. Kip didn't give him a chance at any sort of response. He turned, closed the curtain and was gone. What no man could describe had already began, but now it began in earnest. Hope deserted him. Peace fled. Agonizing consciousness the purring kitten that now sat, curled into his lap. Torture would have seemed the Eden. Death the blessed release. Tears welled and burned distraught traces down the sides of his head and even brought a sense of deafness, trickling into his ears. Voices exploded in his head. Shrill, despairing, fearful, accusatory voices that knew no limits, nor silence, nor words. He tried to swallow the pain away, but couldn't. All at once, a distant roar seemed to wake the echoes of destroying angels marshaled just for him. They were horse's hooves, pounding the ground, smashing God's glory and mercy. His brain bulldozed incoherent vagaries before word seeds could birth. And if one ever did, those words would fall like empty shells when he tried to describe the sudden torment, misery, and hell. Thus was the state of Ward Stelter's mind at that very moment. The only question lingering in Stelter's mind as Kip greeted his friends before ushering them out, how long will this eternal damnation and torment last?

CHAPTER FORTY

THE WALK OF THE LIVING DEAD

A feeling of Thanksgiving came with the early morning snow. It wasn't heavy. Light flakes swirled with gusts of wind and did their best, stripping hold-out yellow leafs from limbs nearly bare. Wind rushing through rubbing limbs was enough to chase everyone behind doors. But only so far for Kip, Nuts and Jorge. They had installed an inner corral inside the horse barn and it was Jorge, who now stood on a second rail, a can of Coke in his hand, chuckling at Nuts' foolish words and antics. Kip sat on a top rail, polishing the rail where he held a tight grip.

"Bouge toi idiote [move you silly woman]," Nuts grunted at the shiny two-year old perlino mare and stomped his foot. The horse stood as if pinned against the rails, head erect and hind quarters facing Nuts.

"Use your flag," Kip said calmly. "Look at her posture. She doesn't respect you at all."

"I have been using my flag. She doesn't like it. She doesn't respond." Nuts tapped the flexible stick with an orange flag attached to the ground and stomped again.

"She will. Step. Take a step to your left then raise the flag to a higher level. You're acting scared to death of her. Let her know you're not afraid. Get her moving and she'll keep moving. She needs to expend a lot more energy before she's ready."

"Aller à cheval," Nuts grunted and finally had enough courage to step. The horse spun away and trotted, following the rails right.

"Now follow, turning with her. Keep working that flag," Kip said and chuckled mildly.

"Finally," Nuts howled. "Finally she gets the idea. Why did it take her this long?"

"Because you were letting her take charge. That's why."

Nuts continued working the horse. Jorge took a sip of Coke and chortled, "El Nuez no sabe hablar caballo. Y ella no sabe Francés. He tinks it talk French. Jorse don't talk French." He laughed.

"So, Kip," Nuts then said. "Have you made a decision?"

"You're bringing that up again. I don't know."

"What's so hard? Make a decision. You can't lose."

"Hah. Don't be so certain."

"What?" Jorge snorted. "What you talk about?"

Nuts grinned wide. "He didn't tell you? He's got a bucketful of Thanksgiving invitations. I'll fully understand if he doesn't accept mine. Now, as far as Dr. Parker, Judge Bailey and that sweetie Erica Dennis... holy... he's got his hands full."

Again Jorge laughed. Laughed heartily. A breath later, his laughter abruptly ended. He dropped off the railing and stared. Nuts suddenly stood still and Kip merely glanced over his shoulder. Instantly, he knew why and what caught their attention, but still gave it little deference. There, a very recessed, dark-eyed, gaunt and pale Ward Stelter stood, draped in a coat that looked three sizes too large, a look of misery nailed to his face. Instead of paying him attention Kip watched the mare come to a stop. Jumping off the rail Kip stepped in and took the flag from Nuts and got the mare moving the opposite direction.

"You saw that, didn't you?" Nuts muttered. "You know who that is?"

"I saw. I know who it is."

"What are you going to do?"

"Nothing."

"I'll kill him if you just stand here."

Kip forced the flag into Nuts' hand and paused a moment. "Keep working her. I'll get rid of him." A moment later, the mare trotted by just after Kip crawled through the rails. He fronted Stelter. "What are you doing here? What do you want? If you've come here to beg my forgiveness, I've long let go. You're forgiven. You can go. I refuse to live with a grudge anyway."

Stelter said nothing, standing there watching the horse.

"Are you okay? You look terrible."

Stelter now made eye contact. A deep-rooted, painful brush against a troubled mind. "Look," his voice was extremely raspy and slow. "Can I talk with you? I'm not here to ask forgiveness. I don't deserve it."

"I'm not stopping you. Talk."

"No. Can we walk?"

"Depends. Do you have a weapon hidden in there? You've got enough room in that coat to carry a cannon."

Stelter gave him a chagrined look, spreading his arms. "I hardly eat. I almost never sleep. I probably wouldn't have the strength."

Kip studied the man's eyes. Never had he seen such dejected gloom. He shrugged and walked by. Stelter slowly caught up.

"If you're not here to beg forgiveness, what do you want?"

"Help."

"Help?" Kip stopped and stared. "I'm not a doctor. I'd rather not serve as your mortician either."

"I may need that sooner than you think."

"What then? What help do you need out of me?"

"I think I can give you another head."

"Why me? Go to someone who matters. I'm not the law."

"I doubt anyone else can or would do anything about it. Look, I'm not capable. Look what you did to me. You've turned me into a vegetable."

"I didn't do that. You did that. You and those who you choose to listen too. What? You didn't have a backbone before now?"

Stelter sighed, looked down and to the side. "Haven't you read Ordinary Men? Don't you understand the excuses people make when authority figures grant them allowances? I know it's not an excuse, but it has an effect."

"I've read Ordinary Men. Life isn't always a binary choice. You don't offer sympathy to a pathogen either."

"You offered it to me once. Please offer it again. Please."

Kip stood pensively for a moment. "What are you suggesting?"

"Just a visit. Confront him. Make him realize the life he affects."

"Who?"

"His name is Clark Hoffman. He lives in the exclusive area of Woodley Park. Works for the DOJ. I've learned my orders came through him. Everything I was doing I stopped doing. I can't guarantee he won't start it up again. You don't have to identify yourself. Just figure out who he is and bring him the hell he deserves if you have to."

"I don't see that as my responsibility. Besides, Thanksgiving is just over a week away. I'd like to focus on that. That means a lot more to me than that."

"One day. Just give me one day. With your resources, you could go and come back before lunch. Besides... there's something you should know."

"What?"

"I didn't put in the order to kill your parents. Someone else did that. It had to be him."

Kip sighed heavily, shaking his head. "I should have known. Good hell. You people are low. I never even considered that. God, you're evil."

"Get in your plane. Come help me."

"It doesn't work like that. Look at the weather."

"I've checked the weather. It's supposed to clear up soon. I've even arranged for a rental. I also contacted Dulles."

"You're determined about this, aren't you?"

"Very. It feels like the last spark of waning hope. I have to do something. I can't die like this. I am dying. Can't you see death in my eyes?"

Kip rubbed his chin for a moment. "Stay here. I'm going to consult with my friends. It's a more weighty matter for them in the long run."

Stelter stood there as Kip returned to the corral and briefly met with Nuts and Jorge. Nuts followed when Kip returned. Nuts refused to even acknowledge Stelter. "This is it," Kip said. "We'll do this and that's it. Nothing more."

Stelter nearly collapsed in relief. Emotion surged. His face contorted, fighting back the tears. With a hand to his mouth, he simply turned and trudged away. Kip stepped to follow and Nuts grabbed his arm. "I didn't realize," he said. "He is really in bad shape, isn't he?"

Kip glanced at Stelter and then studied Nuts' eyes briefly. "I'd give him two weeks at the most. I think he's starving himself to death."

"Probably doesn't dare wrap his lips around a barrel."

"Maybe we do this and he can find his appetite again. I want you with me. Let's go."

Nuts hesitated but a moment, watching. He'd always had incredibly deep respect for the man. But he knew this was nobility he'd most likely never witness again. With a newly formed current of contrition Nuts lowered his jaw and followed.

At eight minutes before ten Kip sat the Pilatus down with a gentle rock at Dulles. At 10:40 A.M. they pulled to a stop in front of a red-brick colonial-style house with tall white pillars. The neighborhood was more like a Sherwood Forest setting, deafly quiet and clearly exclusive. A few burnt-orange leaves held on, but for the most part, Sherwood was naked. Stelter reached from the back seat and straightened himself up. "I'll try to do the talking. He should be here. I think he always works out of his home. I had a hard time collecting information. I'm partly going on hope."

Kip and Nuts exchanged a look and stepped out. About ninety seconds later a sixty-something, blonde-headed woman with her hair in a ponytail and a bleak, long look on her face came to the door. She stood snugging a white cashmere sweater.

"Ma'am," Stelter sounded like gravel going down a garbage disposal. "My name is Ward Stelter. I work at the Department of Defense. These are my associates. Perchance, is Clark Hoffman in?"

Instantly, she was suspicious. Stelter could have passed, but Kip and Nuts, in their Levi jackets and cowboy boots betrayed the game. "Excuse me," she eyed Kip and Nuts briefly, "Why would you want to see Clark?"

"Is he in?"

Kip interjected, "His name came up during a guarded discussion on a very sensitive matter. We felt a personal contact was more appropriate. We'd just like a brief word with him. Won't take long."

She hesitated, contorted her face with confusion, and then touched her fingers to her lips before looking over her shoulder. "Uh… would you come in a moment?" She led them through a plush living room and into a dining area where she invited them to sit. She folded her arms, remained standing, and studied them for a moment. "I don't understand," she said.

"Ma'am?" Stelter said.

"I thought… I mean… if you are who you say you are," she raised her brows, "which doesn't seem likely, you should know."

"Know what?" Kip asked.

"Clark is dead. He died close to six years ago now."

Stelter got a very troubling and alarmed look on his face. With a pleading sulk, he stared at Kip.

"Ma'am," Kip said. "My name is Roger McKinney. This is Tony Ford. We're associates, but not with the DOD. We're former military; however. What's your name?"

She seemed to smile in relief. "Samantha. I go by Sam."

"Sam, I'm very sorry to hear that about your husband. We were unaware. We were merely part of a guarded discussion. We didn't have any reason to assume… I'm sorry if we've brought up bad memories or ignited feelings."

"Oh, no. You're all right," she waved her hand. "It's not like I'm still grieving. It was very mysterious and difficult at the time. Very confusing."

"Suicide?" Kip asked.

"You knew?"

"I'm perceptive. I deal with these kind of matters."

"He owns a funeral home," Tony said proudly.

Those words caused Sam to nod slightly. "You probably understand the emotions then."

"I've had my own grieving to deal with. Plus, whenever someone suffers a loss, it's like I suffer it too."

"I wanted to kill him for what he did. I was so angry. So hurt. Something was bothering him. He wouldn't talk about it. He became so distraught and disconnected. I didn't know what was wrong and I couldn't get it out of him." She paused and gave Kip a sympathetic look. "I can't believe I'm talking about this. I haven't even talked to the kids about this. All these years. I hope I'm not bothering you."

"Not at all. Do you have any idea of what Clark was working on at the time? Was he overworked? Any new influences?"

"He always overworked. I couldn't tell that anything significant had changed. But he changed. Far less talkative. That's what made it so frustrating. We could always talk. And then nothing."

"I hope we haven't opened any wounds. Is there anything we can do? Would you like us to leave? We're not here to press anything out of you."

"No. You're okay. In fact, it feels good to let it out. It's not that I had to suddenly let the dams burst. It does make me feel better to at least air it with someone. I'm not really suffering."

"You have a nice home. Thank you for inviting us in. It's been a pleasure to meet you."

"Can I ask one question?"

"Please."

"Why would my husband's name come up in a guarded discussion involving the DOD? Was it classified?"

"Yes!" Stelter said. "We can't discuss it. Sorry."

Kip read the change in her face. Nuts assumed the discussion was over and stood. Kip grabbed his arm and kept his focus on Sam.

"I trust you," she said directly to Kip. "I don't know what it is about you, but I trust you. Can I share something? I haven't even dared…"

"What is it?"

"Our safety deposit box. We agreed to keep secrets there. That if anything ever happened… you understand? I haven't dared even go near the bank, let alone... I'm wondering… Clark never left a note. Nothing. Would you go with me to the bank? If there are answers there, I'd like someone there with me when I discover them. I'd like you there with me. Could you do that?"

"He most certainly will," Tony said. "Chère Madame."

She squinted biliously at Tony and cleared her throat. "If you don't mind, I'll drive. I saw that tiny… I have a much more comfortable car. Is that okay?"

"Oui, Oui," Tony said and patted Kip on the shoulder.

Sam Hoffman delivered them to the bank in a pearl white Lexus ES. The bank sat in a neighborhood where you got a clear sense of the nearby Smithsonian National Zoological Park. Inside a secluded booth the tension felt palpable after Sam placed the box on a table and scooted it towards Kip. He paused briefly before opening the lid. He didn't take the liberty, but removed and passed each discovery to Sam. First document was the home insurance policy. Mortgage documents sat stuffed down the side. A DOJ contact list revealed nothing and it wasn't until Kip removed a stack of fifty gold coins before the strange emerged. The words written on a lined, legal-sized sheet of yellow paper caused Sam to pause, touch her lips and remain still. Kip expected words out of Tony, instead, Stelter rasped his words out.

"That's it. What does it say?"

"O, my God. I had no idea." She gulped. "I don't dare share."

"Won't be a surprise," Stelter said. "Go ahead."

"He couldn't. He wouldn't. It's a confessional. He couldn't live with himself. He couldn't believe he was involved in something like this." She gave Kip the emptiest forlorn look. "I can't say this. I can't say what he was doing. I simply can't believe it."

"I think we know what it says," Stelter said. "You can say it."

"No, I can't. I don't believe it. I won't believe it." She threw the paper on the table and pulled her hands back. She frantically shook them as if that would rid the soiled disgust. Kip took the page and studied it. When his face turned despondent, Tony reached for it. Kip pulled back.

"He was trying to expose this plot. And I know this man," Kip said. "I've met him. Tony knows who I'm talking about."

"Who?" Stelter asked.

"A journalist. He tried to interview me once. Wanted to do a story. I didn't trust him. I didn't feel right about it. I think he was trying to do a hit piece on the Navy. Apparently, Clark contacted him, wanting to expose the work he was involved in. A whistle blower's contact."

"I don't recall any whistle-blower stories," Stelter said. "If anyone would have known, I would have known. Who's the journalist?"

"Vincent Wampler," he knowingly glanced at Nuts. "He's not well known. Well… he is if you read the right stuff."

"He still writes. He does blogs, and vlogs and stuff like that," Stelter said. "I saw a recent article of his in *The Atlantic*."

"We need to pay a visit. We need to find out why he didn't follow through. Maybe somebody got to him. I'd like to know why," Kip said. He moved to stand then didn't. He reached for Sam's hand. She was teary when she took his. "One thing you can find comfort in, whatever he was involved in, happened after he was gone. He was trying to stop it before it happened."

"How do you know that?"

"Because I'm the man they targeted. My parents, wife, daughters and a friend are dead, but it wasn't at his hand. I hope you find comfort in that."

"Well, then whose hand was it, if it wasn't his? I don't understand."

"It was mine," Stelter stood and said flatly. "I took orders from your husband. It's my fault and I'm trying to fix this before I'm dead. Look at me. Can't you see I'm dying?"

"You won't have to go far. Should I drive you there?" Sam said. "I know where Vincent lives. Clark would drive by and make a point about it. I thought it was so strange. Suddenly, it's making sense."

They took the Duke Ellington Bridge to cross over and find the nearby Brightwood Neighborhood. A dreadful chill brought gooseflesh to Stelter's arms, to the point of mild shivering as they rode. His teeth slightly chattered, his hands shaking, but not his limbs. Doughy emotions dovetailed into the stark reality of mismatched numbers, which he wasn't quite ready to reconcile nor did he fully know how. But then a career built on dowdy, narcissistic morals and stitched together as fabled fabric, easily frayed, and he was unraveling even more than it had. That, despite feeling as if the period of gestation had come full term. Stelter sat slumped against the door when Sam wheeled past a Safeway Grocery Store and steered down the block. She eased off the gas in time with a mild uncertain sigh. "Oh, no," she said. "What is this?

Stelter sat up to see a Brightwood Police Department cruiser parked up ahead and on this side of the intersection. "Just pull over here," Kip said. "Is that his street?"

"That's his street."

"Now, that's weird timing," Nuts said. "Étrange indeed. Why would there be cops here?"   Sam pulled to the curb opposite of where the cruiser sat parked. A fairly beefy officer guarded the way. Several other emergency vehicles sat parked midway down the tree-lined street, emergency lights all excited. Sam guardedly folded an arm around the one touching her lips as Nuts followed on Kips heels, piling out. The officer held a hand up as they trotted over. "Roads closed, gentlemen."

"We can see that," Kip said. "Are we allowed to ask who?"

"Sorry. I can't give out any information."

"That's him," Nuts declared. "That's got to be Vincent Wampler's place. Just got to be. If it wasn't, something would be really wrong. Now, what's going on?"

"Excuse me," the officer said. "Did you say, Wampler?"

"We were coming to visit him," Kip said.

"You're acquainted with the man?"

"I've met him. We have a bone to pick with him."

283

The officer held a finger up. "Wait right there, please. Just wait right there." He stepped to his cruiser and called ahead on the radio. Less than a minute later a sedan whipped out from behind a command vehicle, came racing up the street, its engine growling in a strain and sounded just as strained coming to a quick stop alongside the cruiser. A familiar face appeared over the top of the cruiser along with the expected tone. Agent Shaun Duggan rose up and gave them a bit of an incredible Hulk sort of sneer. "Holy crap!" he howled. "Why am I not surprised. What in the hell could you possibly have to do with this?" Agent Eddie Reed appeared and circled the cruiser.

"What are you doing here?" he asked. "There is no way you could have known. Who tipped you off? Unless you were involved."

Kip lifted a finger. "I think we need Mrs. Hoffman over here. Give me just a minute."

Agent Reed followed on Kip's heels as he trotted back to the car. Sam had the window cracked. "I think you'd better come over here and meet these agents. Bring the note."

Ward Stelter was like a gruesome creature following in the shadows as they crossed back. Kip took the note and handed it to Agent Duggan. Duggan read maybe three lines. "Hoffman? Who the hell is Clark Hoffman?"

"My husband," Sam exhaled. "He's dead. Going on six years now."

Duggan paused and scoured her briefly. He then went on reading. Before he was finished, he stood leaning against the cruiser, confounded and scratching his head. He exchanged several intense glares with each given individual. "Well... talk about bizarre. It's taken us months to tract this guy down. How did you know to show up?"

Kip felt obligated to protect Stelter on a certain level. He nodded. "We received a tip about Hoffman. We just happened to travel here this morning. We found that note in his safety deposit box. His guilty conscience was more than he could handle. We came here, hoping to find out why Wampler didn't follow through and publish a story about that plot you just read about."

"What's going on here?" Stelter asked. "Does this involve this Vincent fellow?"

"He's got a six-inch knife sticking out of the side of his neck," Agent Reed said.

"I don't get it," Nuts said. "What's going on?"

"If it were anyone else I wouldn't say," Duggan said. "I don't know why yet, but he apparently had a grudge. He set up an artificial intelligence app. From what we've discovered his little AI scheme has been receiving and directing this whole operation. From Mr. Gerhardt in Florida to Lowe in Ithaca. Who knows how far it goes. If this Hoffman fellow was the key cog and now this. Holy crap. This is frightening."

"Wait a minute," Stelter frantically said. "Are you telling me I've been giving and receiving instructions from a computer? This whole thing... This whole... O, God..." Stelter moaned, his eyes rolling back into his sockets. A second later, his knees buckled, dropping him straight to the ground.

"What's with him?" Agent Duggan said derisively.

The police officer responded immediately. Down onto a knee with a hand to Stelter's chest. He then lowered, listening for breathing. "This man isn't breathing. I think his heart has stopped. Call in an 11-41." He then instantly started heart compressions, the force too powerful for Stelter's emaciated body. You could hear his sternum crack. Agent Reed made the call. Kip went down on his knees to assist. A bewildered Samantha Hoffman took a few steps back while the growing look of masked justice caused Nuts to tighten a straight caustic line with his lips.

It took five minutes before the ambulance arrived. In the few minutes of stupor after watching the ambulance pull away, Agents Duggan and Reed privately consulted, supposing the party responsible for Vincent Wampler's death was an action committee who moved rapidly to stay ahead of an FBI operation narrowing down on them. For Roger "Kip" McKinney it was another matter. He still stood there scanning the street and neighborhood, wondering if an adroit Antione Banda wasn't concealed somewhere nearby.

CHAPTER FORTY-ONE

FREEDOM FLIGHT

Roger "Kip" McKinney sat alone, pensively lost in thought while engines on his Pilatus warmed. There was no judgment in his thought. No bitterness. There was sorrow; however. Along with a growing gnaw of distrust and cynicism. Nuts crawled in, plopped down in his seat, and gave Kip a dull look. "Talked to Agent Duggan. Stelter is dead. Dropped dead right there in front of us." Nuts sat there as if expecting some kind of finality statement. Kip didn't react. "Talked to Judge Bailey too. She said she'd get hold of Erica and meet us at Philly International."

"Did you fill her in?"

"Nope. Well… I told her we had some good news. I don't know if I'd call it good news though. What a nightmare world we suddenly have on our hands. Right?"

"It's always had its share of nightmares. This is nothing new. Different, not new."

"Ick was right."

"What do you mean?"

"He lectures me every time I see him lately. About deep fakes. About artificial intelligence. I would have never guessed this whole sorted mess would lead back to that. How much do you trust Agent Duggan? He doesn't seem that tech-savvy. He was miffed with you for not telling him about Stelter a lot sooner."

"Duggan was frustrated. He directed all his aggression at me. No big deal. Besides, they finally figured it out."

"Binary monsters."

"Who?"

"That's what Ick called it. Binary monsters, hiding behind masks and capable of taking on any chosen character. Or snakes in the grass, hidden and ready to strike at any moment. Even Stelter was duped. I don't know why you let him off the hook the way you did."

"Justice came calling. Granted, I didn't see the point in trying to pursue it. Stelter appeared to have protection, right? I couldn't rationalize climbing the ladder, informing someone who might be far more aggressive. Know what I mean?"

"So, now what?"

"Somebody else's problem, not mine."

"Until someone decides to make you a target again. No guarantees against that. Would you have ever guessed this Vincent fellow, doing what he did? Some kid in a basement decides to turn the dogs loose—just as a joke or because of insecurities or teenage rejection and we're in deep doo-doo. It doesn't even have to be personal. Right? Was it personal with Wampler? It wasn't, was it?"

"Who knows? Maybe it was. That rankles. Or an app made it personal. That's freaky. This much I know, I haven't felt this relaxed and relieved at the same time. At least not in the last three or four years. I hate to admit it, but I sensed something was wrong. I just didn't know why nor how."

"Ick says the big worry is an artificial app choosing to run some malevolent operation on its own. No one tells it. It just learns the way of things and likes the idea."

Kip studied Nuts for a moment. "It probably has the worst of human tendencies, depending on who wrote the code. Throw it down and it bounces off the pavement and takes its head off. Maybe that's what happened. Maybe it felt threatened and turned the action committee back on itself. Think that's who killed Wampler?"

"Hope so. Or it was like your sister-in-law. Perhaps a computer app can fill up with hate and jealousy too."

Kip looked away and sighed. "I guess you contacted Philly. You ready to go?"

"I'm ready." Nuts got a sly grin. "You ready too?"

"What do you mean?"

"You might be flying into a hornet's nest."

"You mean Jacklyn and Erica? I don't see them scratching each other's eyes out over me."

287

"What are you going to do? One might press you on Thanksgiving... right there in front of the other."

"I could tell them I already have a dinner date with April Parker. How would that work? Or with you."

"Hah! You know Dr. Parker isn't interested. Everything she does is out of sympathy for what she sees as a lonely old man. You go up there to her brother's place and you don't fit in."

"I don't mind it. They're intelligent, enjoyable people. It does hurt to be with those kids though, knowing what I've lost."

"Then I'll spoil everything. As soon as we see Jacklyn and Erica I'll invite them to my place. That way it takes you off the hook." He chuckled slightly. "If you had to pick, which one would you pick?"

"You've got to be kidding. First of all, you're not going to invite them like that. I'm going to be honest with them. I'll take the first invite and apologize to the other."

"No. I think you should make a choice. The one you want the most."

"Like what? Clarify."

"For compassion's sake, you'd choose Jacklyn. Now," he shrugged his brows, "if you were going on looks alone and maybe the hopes of havin' a new kid or two racin' around the house... you couldn't do much better."

Kip laughed. He didn't say a thing until after they took off. At 25,000 feet he turned and grinned at Nuts. "I don't want to talk about the women in my life, but then when I consider what Duggan and Reed were talking about, it might just be better to fuss about that than the ramifications of AI. I don't worry like a lot do, but sometimes you wonder."

"I don't trust it. What if an app suddenly decides things on its own, like you suggested?"

"Highly unlikely."

"Yeah, right. I can see it slithering around the net, following algorithms of miscreants, selecting one vile trait before the next. We are doomed."

"Hm-hm," Kip mused. "I have some hefty investments in AI. It will be a boon for the medical field."

Nuts gave him a derisive look. "You don't see the irony? It most likely killed your family. It has problems. Perhaps it follows random false references. It has to mirror human frailties."

"It didn't, people did. People who couldn't tell good from bad. People who merely responded to what they thought was an authority figure. I guess they felt justified."

"I can't believe you. You ought to be outraged."

"It still hurts. I'm not outraged."

"It's going to get worse."

"How do you figure?"

"Haven't you ever selected a song online and then let it go? You start with a pretty nice song. It then goes downhill, the music getting worse and worse until you want to blow your brains out the stuff is so vile."

"Someone's algorithm. You can change the songs if you don't like where it's going."

"Yeah. But look at what they do."

"That is a flaw. I guess it all depends on who's doing the pre-training. Plus, if the neural network architecture is flawed, it transforms the output into something, possibly meaningful for one person, possibly deadly for someone else."

"See. Just what I was saying."

"Perhaps. But then not all of us believe what we're seeing. Some of us have a sense about when someone is lying to us."

"Yeah. Coming from a man who has a gift. We don't all have that kind of gift. If I understand what you're saying, AI interprets and forms its responses based on the data that trained it. Right? It can only do what someone trained it to do, right? Sounds exactly like Vincent Wampler."

"Perhaps. But I'll take human intuition every time. I can't help it if people are gullible. The thing is, AI can be incredibly smart and stunningly stupid at the same time. They talk about hallucinations.

289

Where it spits out lies or misinformation. I'd say that's pretty stupid. So, it has flaws. They should focus on narrow AI. That's where they train it to do tasks based on facts learned. Such as in the medical field. I would push the brakes on artificial general intelligence. Where it learns on its own. You need guard rails for that... in my opinion."

"That's just as terrifying as a world of cyborgs. I don't like that. I'd rather be dumb as dirt and decide things on my own. Then you've got to consider how it tracks people. I know some would gladly surrender to Big Brother, thinking that some utopian Disneyland. Not me. Think about this. Hoffman killed himself six years ago. The attack on you essentially started four years ago. Somewhere in between there, who knows what the zeros and ones were doing. Motivation means nothing to zeros and ones. Have you ever noticed how science tends to tear things down, trying to get to the bottom of it? Ick says zeros and ones tell you what to do, not what you ought to do. He says it has no moral backbone. It never grovels. It's never anemic. It has no ethics. Sure, it watches everything you do. It knows your face. It can learn your limp. It can add up your social credit score. But then along comes this hallucinogenic malfeasance where it can't find the target, but still needs a target. It can't find who it wants to condemn and so it condemns someone else. I guess it's fine unless it crosses into incompetence. AI has no choice when its creator has all the worst traits. I've listened to the music. Suddenly, you're following the artificial crowd down a hole where the worst of traits dwell. It's not for me. No, sir. Not for me. Not yet anyway."

"Of course not. Consider this. Like I was saying, what if AI hacked into the creator? What if it figured out the manipulation? Maybe it ordered the hit on its creator. Have you considered that? These could be ancillary issues."

"Or the bantam edition of the creator becoming colossal."

The two went silent. It was obvious how conflicted Nuts felt by the way he stirred and kept looking out the side window. He'd start and stop and then started again, but never spit anything out until Kip nudged him. "I guess it comes down to this," Nuts finally mulled. "They need a way to know if what they are seeing or hearing is AI-generated or not. There has to be some way to know for certain. I won't trust it until then... or until I possess the kind of gift you have. If you can know when people are dead somewhere, you're more likely to know when someone is lying to you, right? Well… that may be our only hope. And as far as that goes for me… I may never get there."

"Well…" Kip smiled and winked. "A lot of good that did me. I didn't hone in on that premonition. I might do better the next time. But… I guess, in one way, that guarantees me a job as your friend, doesn't it."

CHAPTER FORTY-TWO

SELF–INFLICTED CURE

A warm southern breeze lightly brushed Erica Dennis' hair aside as she stood watching, the electricity in the air causing her to bob with excitement. They stood in the unofficial Philadelphia observation area, which was alongside Fort Mifflin Rd.—near a wide-open grassy field and a short walk from the Sunoco fuel storage tanks.

On the flip side, on the vinyl side of life, Judge Bailey stood there filled with angst. This felt like a terrifying moment for her. Deep-rooted anxieties stirred her in such a way that she couldn't fully identify the single culprit emotion. Always a skeptic, and even now scoffing at her skepticism.

While Erica's cheeks were a vivid rosy color, Meghan's felt pale and tarnished with the stains of ageless tears. Their eyes met after Erica stomped her feet as if to warm them. She folded her arms tightly and smiled. "There's another set of lights. Do you think that's them?"

Judge Bailey glanced to the sky before checking her watch. "If Nuts was right, I think we have ten more minutes. And I'm not sure which runway they'll land on. Nuts didn't say."

"What do you think they'll tell us? Are you scared? Your face is so full of melancholy. I'm hoping it is good news. You don't seem so sure."

"Um…" Meghan purred and didn't know what else to say. She stayed quiet. And it was odd. All the noise of jets coming and going and yet she felt so keenly tuned in to every one of Erica's mannerisms. Like she could hear even the most gossamer change in every emotion. The sweet kiss of a cue ball on a delicate corner shot would have echoed resoundingly.

"I've been thinking," Judge Bailey said.

"About what?"

"Dana. I've been replaying so many things I've forgotten. I never did mention Toby Heath, did I?"

"You've never said anything about Dana. You know that."

"Right."

"What about, Toby Heath?"

"Another one of Dana's friends. He was special though."

"How so?"

"He was like Kip in many ways. You know… quiet confidence—good looking. Smart. Kind. I had a terrible crush on him. I was so deeply jealous of Dana. He had blonde hair and the most intriguing color of eyes. Kind of a greenish brown. He could turn my knees into water with a simple gaze. There was a grassy field in our neighborhood where we'd watch him play football. He could have been a star, but he didn't care. Some days he'd play with guys who were big and talented and he fit right in. Even dominated. On other days he'd play with the awkward ducks who struggled to fit in. He always found a way to build their confidence. He was something."

"He'd let them win?"

"Yeah. Always. I don't know how Dana knew, but I guess she wasn't that interested. She found a way to turn the tables and out of nowhere, Toby was paying attention to me. I couldn't handle it. I don't know what was wrong with me. Whether it's an innate cynicism or flat-out fear, I don't know. I was just fifteen years old. Still—I have had and still have a hard time letting people get close to me."

"That's sad. I'm sorry. I feel close to you. You're friends with all of us, aren't you?"

"This is different."

Erica went quiet, a sad look pulling her eyes down. Meghan nudged her a second later and pointed. "I think that's them. We need to hurry. They want to meet us just outside the Executive Terminal."

Erica delayed long enough to see the sleek little blue and white number turn at the end of Runway 35 and then begin its taxi. Several minutes later a growling Nuts pounded his chest and rubbed his belly the minute he walked out of the terminal. "Domes! Nourriture!" [Ladies! Food!] He grinned.

Erica hugged them both. Judge Bailey evaded, pretending preoccupation with Nuts' culinary needs by pulling her phone out and exacting a search.

An agreeing nod from Kip drew them all straight to Meghan's car.

By the rush and mood, little was said until they sat at a table inside a Ruby's Tuesday. And it was Nuts who couldn't contain himself. He blurted the whole story. From Stelter showing up, to meeting with Samantha Hoffman. He seemed sincerely saddened about Clark Hoffman's suicide and blown away by the discovery of Agents Reed and Duggan at Vincent Wampler's home. That Wampler was dead brought no satisfaction. With so little contact it was hard to fathom that he was ultimately responsible for a trail of sorrow and death. Blaming AI felt vacuous. And through it all, while Erica and Judge Bailey sat on the edge of their seats, Kip sat back, listening calmly.

"One thing he left out," Kip said sadly. "Ward Stelter died. His conscience got to him, I guess. He simply dropped dead when he learned a computer was behind their operation. And it bugs me how we were all oblivious to who was actually behind all of this. It may not bode well for our future."

Erica gasped at the news, Judge Bailey showed no emotion. "That bothers you more than just bugging you, doesn't it?" Meghan said.

Kip shrugged. "Yes, it does. It's sad. I got to know Ward. There was a part of him I liked. He was a useful idiot when it came down to it. Used and abused. People don't deserve that."

"So, does that tie it up?" Erica asked.

"Who knows?" Tony grunted. "Until somebody else begins looking for a random target, simply to feed a hunger—and hatred."

"No," Kip said confidently. "That will be the end of it."

"You sure?" Erica asked.

"Yes."

293

His bold proclamation brought silence.

A few seconds passed before Judge Bailey touched his hand and nodded. The two stepped aside while Erica and Nuts began discussing food options.

"Listen," Judge Bailey folded her arms and said softly, "I wanted to thank you in private. What you did for me... what you did for Dana. I judged you horribly and you didn't deserve that."

"I never took offense. Don't worry about it."

She paused briefly and swallowed. "I've been thinking."

"Yes. About what?"

"You."

"What about me?"

"I'm pretty observant. As a judge, they pay me to assess things from a neutral position. Granted it is hard to do that sometimes, but I think my assessment now is spot on."

"Meaning?"

Judge Bailey nodded toward Nuts and Erica. "She likes you. Very much. I think you would make a good couple. I know her well. At least consider it."

"I've got a lot of deep wounds. I'm wary."

"I understand. Think about it. And don't waste a lot of time."

"Hah," Kip laughed. "You sound just like Lisa. Did she talk to you?"

"No. I'm an independent woman."

"I know."

"So, will you?"

"Don't worry about me. I'm well aware of Erica. She's kind and thoughtful. And I'm not blind."

A brief pause.

"Listen, I'm going to leave. I'll pay for a taxi if you'll get Erica home. I'm just... I don't know. I've heard enough and I want to be alone. I just... I just want to leave. Understand?"

"No problem... and I'll take care of the taxi." He sighed. "And if you ever need anything, let me know. We all made a good team once we earned the trust."

"And stopped framing you as a killer," she laughed.

They both laughed.

"Thanks, Kip," Meghan said, touching his arm. "Have a nice flight home," almost felt like an act of desperation as she turned and hurried out.

Kip stood there watching until her Volvo was out of sight. A wonderful glow seemed to completely envelop Judge Meghan Jacklyn Bailey as she drove away. No man indeed has greater love than he who lays down his life for his friends. She loved him. She knew she loved him. Deep inside, however, she knew her kind of love would tip the scales both peevishly and corpulently wrong.

Passing judgment had never brought this kind of feeling. To gladly sacrifice and give him to one she felt more deserving began healing a jealous wound that had existed, regretfully, for as long as she could remember.

Made in the USA
Las Vegas, NV
05 February 2024

85335517R00173